PRAISE FOR THE THEIRS NOT TO REASON WHY NOVELS

"Both highly entertaining and extremely involving in equal measure." —*The Founding Fields*

"Fast-paced with terrific battle scenes and deep characterizations." —*Genre Go Round Reviews*

"An engrossing military SF series." —*SF Signal*

"Reminiscent of both *Starship Troopers* and *Dune*." —*Publishers Weekly*

"Full of suspense, danger, and intrigue . . . Fans of military science fiction will definitely want to check out this surprising and exciting novel." —*SciFiChick.com*

MORE PRAISE FOR JEAN JOHNSON

"Jean Johnson's writing is fabulously fresh, thoroughly romantic, and wildly entertaining. Terrific—fast, sexy, charming, and utterly engaging. I love [ ] —Jayne Ann Krentz, *[ ]es* bestselling author of *Trust No One*

"Johnson spins an in[ ]y and magic." —Robin D[ ]d-winning author of *Ghost Killer*

"A must-read fo[ ]tasy and romance." —*The Best Reviews*

"[It] has ever[ ]danger, excitement, trickery, hope, and ev[ ]ex." —*Errant Dreams Reviews*

"Delightful entertainment. —*Romance Junkies*

FIRST SALIK WAR

THE TERRANS

JEAN JOHNSON

ACE BOOKS, NEW YORK

ACE

An imprint of Penguin Random House LLC
375 Hudson Street, New York, New York 10014

THE TERRANS

An Ace Book / published by arrangement with the author

ACE and the "A" design are trademarks of Penguin Random House LLC.
For more information, visit penguin.com.

ISBN: 978-0-425-27691-4

PUBLISHING HISTORY
Ace mass-market edition / August 2015

PRINTED IN THE UNITED STATES OF AMERICA

10   9   8   7   6   5   4   3   2

Cover illustration by Gene Mollica.
Interior text design by Laura K. Corless.

Penguin
Random
House

AUTHOR'S NOTE

For those of you expecting more heavy military science fiction as in my previous series Theirs Not to Reason Why . . . this story is not the same as that five-book series. Instead, the overall story of the First Salik War, particularly the first two books, is mostly about First Contact. There should be a fair bit of military action in the third and final book since there is a war going on in this story . . . but in general, this is a First Contact series. As a result, please think of this book as Act I of this series, which is a story being told in three parts.

The characters are not the same, the situations are not the same—okay, the big bad enemy *is* the same—and yes, it is set in an era two hundred years or so earlier than Theirs Not took place. This story, the tale of the First Salik War, has also been one that I've wanted to tell for many years now. It's just a different type of story from Theirs Not to Reason Why.

Which brings up the question of why we are going backwards in time two hundred or so years from the previous story. The best way I can explain it is that Ia's tale is like a keystone in an arch. It supports and strengthens and locks everything together. You have to understand what the keystone is and how it works before you can understand how the rest of the arch can function so well as a whole. Since Ia, a postcognitive and a precognitive, could and did influence things that take place in Time itself, her story had to come first—I know it's technically a bit backwards for an analogy, installing the keystone first, then building the rest of the arch around it, but you can do that a lot easier when the arch is actually just a series of interconnected stories.

If you have read the Theirs Not to Reason Why series, I hope you'll be able to pick out the influences that Ia's tale has had throughout this science fiction universe, both directly and indirectly. I've been working on several interconnected story arcs for a couple decades now, so . . . well . . . things are going to be subtly complex and multilayered.

And if you are new to this universe (Hello!), do not worry about having to buy the previous five-book series. You should be able to understand and hopefully enjoy this one on its own merits just fine.

Here's hoping you all enjoy Act I of the First Salik War,
Jean

CHAPTER 1

Her uniform still fit. Mostly.

Jackie could see a blurred version of herself in the semi-polished steel doors of the elevator car. Gray military uniform, black and blue stripes on the sleeves and pant legs. Black for the Space Force, blue for the Navy, gray for the Special Forces, the actual branch she had belonged to, once upon a time. A slight hint of red to her tanned face, proof of a few hours too many soaking up the sun on the local beaches over the holidays. Long brown curls coiled and pinned at the back of her head, below her officer's cap. Shiny twin silver bars on her lapels, shoulder boards, and shirt collar proclaiming her old rank of Lieutenant Commander. Medals decorating her chest . . . and the buttons of her jacket straining to keep the coat properly closed.

Of course, it had been a decade since Jacaranda MacKenzie had been a Lieutenant Commander in the United Planets Space Force. For half of that decade, her job had been to sit in a chair and translate speeches for politicians . . . and for the other half, it had been to sit in a chair as a politician, except for when she was standing and making speeches.

Exercise was therefore an imperative in her off-hours: mixed martial arts lessons three times a week, jogging every few days whenever she had free time and flat roads or good beaches, and, of course, swimming and surfing whenever possible, though that felt more like playing around than a proper workout. But it had been ten years since she *had* to stay in top shape, and the inevitable encroaching of middle age plus a decade of desk work had added a bit of padding to her frame.

So, if she didn't breathe too deeply, her jacket still fit.

It didn't help that she'd been given just four days' notice of her reactivation, from New Year's Eve to now. That had barely been enough time to shut down her newly opened apartment on O'ahu, repacking the few boxes she had unpacked. Just days before, she had moved out of her Councilor quarters on Kaho'olawe, only to have to repack everything. All but her most immediate needs were now tucked into a storage unit in Honolulu.

Four days was barely enough time to repack and store things. It was not enough time to order and receive a new uniform. If she really was being reactivated for duty, she would have those new uniforms soon, but not right now. Right now, she had to remember to breathe lightly, and find an excuse to unbutton her jacket if she had to sit down.

The elevator stopped.

Taking a shallow breath to brace herself, Jackie stepped out of the lift and into a lobby-like space on the eighteenth floor. The sun didn't fall directly into the room through the greenish-tinted windows, but it did illuminate enough that the overhead lights weren't really needed. The waiting area held several potted plants, a dozen chairs and padded benches, a watercooler, flatpics of tropical flowers on the walls, a single, wood-paneled door aside from the metal ones for the lift . . . and three people, besides herself.

Two of those were occupying a couple of the chairs, seated with a pair of empty seats between them in the way that said they were either polite strangers or mild acquaintances. The nearest one was a tallish, pale-skinned fellow with long, light blond hair pulled back in a ponytail and hazel eyes who sat with his elbows on his knees, clad in a neat, cream-colored suit with a pale yellow shirt decorated in white flowers with little green leaves.

The other seated figure was a woman with a complexion more olive than pale. She, too, sat there in a civilian suit, though hers was a dark, rich brown with a knee-length skirt and a plain pink shirt under the jacket. Her hair brushed her shoulders in big, dark, wavy curls, her features more Hispanic than Caucasian. Both of them looked around Jackie's age, midthirties.

A somewhat-younger-looking woman, the kind with classic African features, stood by the green-tinted windows. She was dressed in the blues of a well-fitted Space Force Navy uniform.

Like Jackie's, her hair had been pinned up off her collar, but hers were neat columnar dreadlocks pulled back into a thick bun at the back of her head. Unlike Jackie, her overall figure was tall and slender.

The waiting room was high enough in the Tower that the view looked out over the edge of the caldera toward the northwestern side of the island. That was the side where everything had been left natural, an island desert made of reddish soil, scrubby sage-green bushes, and very few palm trees. Kaho'olawe was in the rain shadow of the other islands, and under normal circumstances could not support a lot of life. Not on its untouched side.

As a native Hawai'ian, Jackie thought it was beautiful. The eastern sides of the isles were lush and green, the most commonly seen version in all the tourism brochures, but not the rain-shadowed sides. Personally, she loved both views, and moved to stand by the windows so she could look out at the stark, colorful landscape, too.

"Whoever thought *this* was a tropical paradise?" the other woman murmured, gesturing at it briefly before refolding her arms. "Look at it. Dry as dust, most of it."

"The island's fine," Jackie murmured back. "It just needs a little more water and some tender care to make it thrive. Like everything else in life."

"In other words, giving it a little *aloha*?" the other lieutenant commander observed dryly.

"That's why it's called Aloha City," Jackie agreed. Everyone knew the story of how the capital had been picked.

Back in the year 2113, when the various governments of the world had argued, even nearly fought, for the honor of hosting the capital of the then newly formed United Planets government, the natives of the Hawai'ian Islands had worked together to put an end to the arguing. The concept was *aloha*, which meant more than just *hello*, or *good-bye*, or even *I love you*. It also meant bringing people together in compassion and cooperation. To share, rather than divide. To welcome, rather than to spurn.

Her mother's ancestors had pointed out that the nearly barren, mostly unused island of Kaho'olawe was about as far away from any large landmass—and thus any big political influence—as any location could possibly get, while still being reasonably close to major metropolitan conveniences on the other islands, such as nearby Maui, O'ahu, and the Big Isle. The land, they said, would be leased at generously low rates, and the architecture would be built to blend into the southern side's augmented landscape from the ridgeline down to the shoreline, providing a relaxing setting for weary civil servants to enjoy at the end of each stressful day.

According to Jackie's late grandfather, a Councilor who had served for many years, the real selling point had been reminding everyone that it was a *tropical paradise*, and thus an ideal location for dignitaries to visit. That, he swore, had finally convinced the major political powers to agree to place the capital there. The idea of getting to spend time there during the Fellowship Lottery had convinced the general populations of the world as well. All-expenses-paid visits to a tropical paradise certainly did not hurt . . . but those buildings were on the other side of the caldera from the waiting room's current northward view of desert-dry hills and tufts of bushes.

While irrigation ruled the southern half, the locals had encouraged the new government to take over *only* half of the island, leaving the other half untouched for their continuing cultural use. They had even footed the bill for the desalination plants that had turned the lower half of the island into the irrigated tropical paradise her paternal grandfather had so admired during his years as Councilor for Scotland back in his own day. All that, in return for a very modest set of rental fees and very strict regulations on what could be built, where it could be built, and from what materials. Southern Kaho'olawe looked like a lush, green, tropical paradise, a flower-filled, greenery-cloaked delight to the senses of its many visitors. The barren northern side of the isle . . . was its true face.

"I'd almost rather be looking at star charts." The other woman sighed. She had a faint accent, one that Jackie couldn't yet place.

The angle was wrong to read the other woman's nameplate. Jackie gave up trying to peek discreetly at it and just used the title that went with that blue uniform and the twin silver bars on those collar points. "I'd rather look at all of this, Lieutenant Commander. I spent nearly five years touring the outer edges of the system, back when I last served. This is a lot more colorful than staring at black space broken only by the tiny pinpricks of distant stars."

"I just like the view of the capital side better," the lieutenant commander demurred. "Even if it's tiny, compared to my home town of Yaounde—Yaounde Prefecture, inside Cameroon Province," she clarified.

"I'm local-born, so, I guess I'm biased toward the dry as well as the green sides of the isles around here," Jackie said, shrugging. *Yaounde, Cameroon. That means her accent is Ewondo mixed with French, which was what was throwing me off,* she decided.

She couldn't blame the woman for calling Aloha City small. Compared to a landlocked metropolis like Yaounde, Aloha City had nowhere to sprawl once it had covered the southern shoreline, and there were prohibitions about building too high. All they could do was build down, hiding a lot of the city's infrastructure that way.

There were a few exceptions on not building too high; the Tower was one, the tallest structure on the isle, though it was quite short compared to other buildings elsewhere on Earth. The heart of the Space Force had been designed to look like olivine, the green crystal that made certain nearby beaches famous for their green sand. The Lotus was another; more formally known as the Council Hall, it had been sculpted from white metal and golden glass as a giant sphere with a petal motif. There were a few other spectacular buildings, but most of the rest of the main buildings and support infrastructures were either designed to blend into the palm trees on the south side, or were built into and beneath the caldera here at the eastern end of the island but built to remain low in profile.

Subtly tugging at her Dress Grays to try to make the jacket front look straight and neat like the other woman's deep blue version, Jackie wondered just what sort of place she'd be sleeping in by the end of tonight. Her orders had been to prepare for a long absence from her current home and to show up ready to travel at the Tower's eighteenth-floor lobby. So here she was, luggage in her rental car in the garage down belowground, ready to . . . wait for more orders, apparently.

"View or no view, *I* do not like to be kept waiting." The seated woman in the brown outfit sighed, echoing Jackie's thoughts at least somewhat. Her accent held a Spanish lilt to it. "There are far more useful things I could be doing right now."

The blond, long-haired male seated near her spoke up as well. "When *I* have to wai—"

The elevator dinged, cutting him off. All four of them turned to look at the metal doors. The man who emerged wore the same Navy-blue uniform that the woman did, if with only one bar for his insignia. A lieutenant.

He was fair, if somewhat tanned, his blond hair cropped in a buzz cut under his Dress cap. The newcomer's strong stride spoke of constantly exercised strength, too; this was no desk jockey of a junior officer. Jackie would have bet from his tightly contained energy that he didn't just go on long runs to stay in shape; he probably went on them to have fun, like she went surfing to have fun. Only much more frequently.

Her gaze moved to his upper chest. The name patch said *Colvers*. A glance at the woman showed her wearing two silver bars, a Lieutenant Commander, just like Jackie. The woman, whose name tag was now visible, was Mbani. The woman lifted her chin at the newcomer, greeting him with some familiarity.

"Happy New Year, Brad. I was wondering if it'd be you," the lieutenant commander said.

"Ayinda," he greeted her, then glanced at Jackie, his gaze first going to her naturally tanned, round face, to her reddish-brown curls pulled ruthlessly into a coiled braid, then down to her insignia and scattering of medals from her years of service. "Lieutenant Comman . . ."

Colvers stopped midword, staring at the Psi Division flash-patch affixed to her jacket's right shoulder. The Radiant Eye was a symbol of the Psi League, but the military's psychic corps had commandeered a version of it. There was the horizontal ellipsis outlining an eye shape, and a circle-within-a-circle for the iris and the pupil, plus the eight rays emanating from the center of the pupil. But the curves that outlined the outer edge of the iris were actually made from the curves of a laurel wreath. Eyeing the black-on-silver design of her flashpatch, the lieutenant's lip curled up, and he backed up a step.

Jackie wasn't unfamiliar with that kind of reaction to that particular patch on her sleeve. Mbani, however, arched her brow at that. "You have a problem with courtesy, Lieutenant?"

The youngish man looked like he wanted to say, *Yes, very much so*, at least where it pertained to Jackie in her not-quite-perfect uniform. But after a moment, he swallowed it down, though he remained several meters back. "Sir, no, sir. Greetings, Lieutenant Commander . . . MacKenzie," he stated, his eyes flicking to her nameplate before shifting away again. "I just don't know what a *psi* is doing here, mingling with Navy personnel."

Jackie frowned in puzzlement. It was one thing to be startled by the presence of a psi in the military; there weren't many who were willing to serve, despite the military desperately needing them to help thwart Grey visits. It was another to actively display dislike for someone with psychic abilities.

The other lieutenant commander lowered her brows as well, but it was the tall, pale blond man seated behind the lieutenant who spoke up at his words. His accent hinted at some Scandinavian country, and the polyglot portion of Jackie's mind tried to identify it by that alone, a mental game she liked to play whenever she thought she'd be working with a certain group.

"I thought the Navy carried the psis around the system to scare off the Greys," the seated man stated, his hazel eyes flicking from person to person before returning to the newcomer. "Why would the two groups *not* mingle? I think it would be difficult to carry them around without all the mingling."

Finnish, Jackie pinpointed. Focusing on discerning the correct language kept her from dwelling on just how offensive the lieutenant's attitude was. *At least, I'm pretty sure his native tongue is Finnish, given how he pronounced* around *each time with the full diphthong they use for words like* sauna.

"Because they don't put psis on *my* ship," Lieutenant Colvers stated bluntly. His accent was North American, possibly Canadian.

"Lock-and-Web it, Lieutenant," Mbani ordered. Her accent was still very faint, but lyrical. The taller woman squared her shoulders, staring down the newcomer. "We don't know what the mission is, or why *any* of us are here."

"Yes, ma'am," Colvers muttered under his breath. Turning away from the two on their feet, he eyed the pair in the lobby seats. "So who are you two?"

Before either could speak, the door that was a flat panel of wood, not two polished panes of metal, swung open. The man who stepped through was short, Asiatic, and stocky. He swung his body with the stride of a horseman and greeted them with a grin.

"Well, five warm bodies, six if you count mine. It's nice to see y'all are all here. Extra nice to see you two again," he added, nodding to Mbani and Colvers. The commander's accent was discernibly Texan, as was the slight swagger and the friendly demeanor. "But we'll get to the 'old crew week' stuff later. Gentlemen, ladies, if y'all will follow me?"

The civilian male hesitated, pointing at his chest with raised brows. The newcomer nodded, so the Finn unfolded himself from his seat, showing within seconds that he was easily the tallest in the group. The woman next to him rose as well; she was just a few centimeters taller than Jackie, who stood a few shorter than the other lieutenant commander. Gesturing for the others to go first, since she didn't want to bump into anyone accidentally, Jackie followed at the rear while the blue-uniformed commander led them into the maze of hallways beyond the eighteenth-floor lobby.

Three, four turnings brought them through that maze to a conference room that overlooked the southwestern side of the island. The iridescent cubes of the Department of Departments were visible directly ahead, if only at the bottom edge of the windows. Lush green trees, wind-swayed palm fronds, and faux-thatched rooftops dotted the landscape beyond. Part of the great, glass-and-metal-faceted curve of the Lotus could be seen off to their left, too. But the view, while spectacular, was nothing compared to what was seen inside the room.

Most of the conference room was ordinary enough. The table was long and had the standard embedded display, though it was dark at the moment. A dozen or more padded chairs lined each side. A lieutenant in a black uniform with three stripes decorating the sides of it—gray, brown, and blue—was working the cabinets and cupboards at the far end, where the coffee dispenser sat. He was busy setting out mugs and glasses, should anyone want anything. All of that was to be expected.

What was *not* expected was the sight of the former Premiere of the United Planets Council, Rosa McCrary—former as of just three days ago when the new year had turned over and she had officially stepped down a year early, citing personal reasons—plus the new Premiere, Augustus Callan, who until three days ago had been the Secondaire. The Admiral-General sat with him, clad in a very formal dress uniform with no stripes of color whatsoever, just the five stars of his rank and the dozen or so medals that were his minimum required display.

The four-star officer seated next to them, sleeves striped in blue and gray, was almost an afterthought to Jackie's bemused mind. Gathered in this one, modest-sized room, were the top leaders of the United Planets . . . and she, Jacaranda MacKenzie, had been summoned here in a military capacity, not a civil-service one. That was the odd thing. Last month, it would have been normal. She had served on many committees involving the military, thanks to her years of service as background experience. This month? Not normal.

Rosa rose first, smiling in welcome and offering her hand to most of the newcomers as the group entered. "Come in, come in; please be seated, Commander Graves, Lieutenant Colvers. Lieutenant Yarley will get you whatever you'd like to drink, Dr. de la Santoya, Mr. Thorsson . . . coffee, tea, juice. Good to meet you, Lieutenant Commander Mbani . . . ah! There you are, MacKenzie. We won't be able to do this without you."

The graying blonde didn't offer her hand to Jackie at the end of the line as she had the others, but instead clasped her own together and bowed. Not deeply, but out of warm respect nonetheless. Jackie returned it because she had respected Rosa's leadership . . . but this was the woman who had taken her aside two months ago, requesting that she step down for a term, citing the very minor number of anti-psi dissenters in her constituency as the reason why. It was easy to guess that Rosa didn't want to clasp hands because she didn't want to inflict any personal opinions on Jackie; the woman was thoughtful like that. Thoughtful, and more.

Now that her commission had been reactivated, Jackie wondered what Rosa and her former Secondaire were really up to, invoking her old her commission like this. Turning her attention to the others, she eyed the dark-haired man who now represented the highest level of government. His four-year term as Secondaire had impressed her and everyone else, though it remained to be seen if he would be as good a leader as McCrary had been.

"Honorable McCrary. Premiere Callan," she added, nodding politely to him. They had worked together during her stint as a Councilor. She had also served on committees with the foremost of the three officers in the room. The other two, she had to read their nameplates as she greeted them. "Admiral-General Kurtz, it's good to see you again. Admiral Nayak. Lieutenant Yarley. Happy New Year to all of you."

She received a smattering of Happy New Years in return. Her gaze strayed to the two high-ranked officers in their midst. Kurtz had iron-gray hair that stood straight up in a very short, very flat-topped cut, and skin that was almost as pale as the tall Finnish fellow's. Nayak had jet-black hair, twisted and pinned up in a bun at the back of his head, with skin that was only a little darker than Jackie's natural tan. Both senior officers rose briefly in return, politely murmuring their own seasonal greetings, then reseated themselves.

At a gesture from the Premiere, the six newcomers eyed the chairs and picked out positions; Colvers, Graves, and Mbani took the side of the table where the two Command Staff officers sat. The woman and the Finn picked the side McCrary and Callan occupied. Jackie considered the table, with the Premiere at one end . . . and picked a seat near the other end, on the civilian side, placing an empty chair between herself and the dark-haired doctor.

Not out of a lack of friendliness, just as an act of caution, since she hadn't been fully introduced yet, though the Radiant Eye patch on her sleeve was silent testament as to why. Sitting down also gave her the chance to discreetly unbutton her jacket, easing the strain on the button holes. When the lieutenant stooped near her to get her order, she quietly requested an unsweetened iced tea, if he had it. She was already tense enough that she didn't need coffee to stay alert.

"Let's get this meeting under way," Premiere Callan stated as soon as everyone had settled into place, some with mugs of coffee, the rest with iced tea or water. "First, the introductions. I'm sure you all know who I and my predecessor are. McCrary is included in this meeting as a civilian consultant. Of all of us, she is the one who was kept informed at each step of the way as events and information initially accumulated, and will continue to keep track of the psychic elements, though the burden of ultimate responsibility has now landed firmly in my lap. Admiral-General Vilhelm Kurtz will have final say over all military operations, save only what I myself or Secondaire Pong veto or approve. Admiral Daksha Nayak will be your immediate military liaison."

"Lieutenant Commander Jacaranda MacKenzie is receiving a promotion as well as having her commission reactivated," Admiral-General Kurtz told them next. "She is also being given a lateral transfer to the rank of Major instead of Commander. This is being done to differentiate between her and Commander Robert Graves. She will share joint leadership of this crew with Commander Graves, and full authority of it under special circumstances.

"Until those circumstances kick in, Commander Graves will be in nominal charge of each mission, and in charge of the ship itself," the Admiral-General explained, without explaining much of anything. "That ship will be the *Aloha 9*, which should be quite familiar to at least three of you—before you ask, officers, your former crewmates have been reassigned to other vessels."

Even as he spoke, Lieutenant Yarley came around to Jackie's side again. This time, he set a smallish box in front of her instead of another iced tea. The style of the box was familiar; all newly designated ranks came in one of these boxes, which were filled with rank pins. One set was displayed uppermost on a black-velvet card, the rest were always tucked beneath it. Cracking open the lid, she eyed the silver oak leaf on display with a touch of wariness.

Not for the first time, Jackie wished *she* had been given a touch of precognition among her gifts, so that she could know what was going on. This "specific circumstances" clause—indeed, all of this, being asked to step down from the Council when she had done a good enough job to earn a second term, having her commission reinstated—was confusing. Kurtz continued, forcing her to pay attention.

"When those circumstances kick in, she will be in charge of all missions, and Commander Graves will be second-in-command. Lieutenant Commander Ayinda Mbani will be third, followed by Dr. Maria de la Santoya—you have something to say, Lieutenant Colvers?" the Admiral-General asked when the younger man shifted abruptly at his words, head raising in startlement.

"Admiral-General, yes, sir," Colvers stated, brow furrowing in a confused frown. "If this is a military operation, *I* should be next. The doctor—no disrespect, ma'am—is a civilian, sir. I outrank her in every way as an officer in the Navy."

Rosa McCrary gave him a smile that was half grimace. Her normally cultured Australian accent deepened for a moment. "Actually, we're not completely sure which category this mission falls into, military or civilian. Dr. de la Santoya's authority would only be activated if bad things were to happen to the others . . . and if bad things are happening, then it very well may *not* be a case of military jurisdiction."

"I . . . don't understand, sirs," Colvers said, looking at the leadership at the table. He wasn't the only one confused.

"As with Major MacKenzie," Premiere Callan told him, "de la Santoya has some governing experience. Hers was at the regional level, which may not be at the Council level, but it is more civilian-leadership experience than you as a soldier have had. As for the particulars . . . we would like to get through the introductions first. You will be working together for an unspecified length of time, which could be quite long. Please let the Admiral-General continue."

Chastised—however politely—Colvers sat back.

"*You* would be next in the chain of command after the doctor, Lieutenant," Kurtz continued, tipping his head at Colvers. "Followed by Dr. Thorsson, there. Starting with him and working our way back up, these are your mission positions: Thorsson has a double doctorate in xenogeology and astrophysics. His rank will be considered Specialist, for all he is still very much a civilian consultant. Lieutenant Colvers will be acting as your group's backup pilot, gunner, chief engineer, and so forth.

"Dr. de la Santoya is licensed to practice general medicine in both gravity and zero-gravity conditions. She has also studied what little we know so far of xenobiology, so she is your medical expert for this mission, as well as your backup civilian leader—I am *not* finished, Lieutenant," the Admiral-General added as Colvers drew in a breath. "Lock-and-Web it."

"Sir, yes, sir," Colvers muttered.

Lock-and-Web was a phrase that, before today, Jackie hadn't heard in years, but its repeated use now brought back memories. Floating around on gravity-free spaceships that could take off and move at a bare moment's notice, one had to constantly be clipping, webbing, or storing in drawers and cupboards anything that could possibly turn into a projectile weapon because of a vector change. Drawers and doors had to be latched, spare straps retracted or bundled up and knotted out of the way, and trash managed as much as possible. Even on the great rotating space stations—where the ever-ongoing argument of centripetal versus centrifugal forces provided a facsimile of gravity—everything had to be locked and webbed for safety's sake.

It could also be used as a somewhat more polite alternative to *shut up*, in both the military and civilian spacefaring sectors.

"Lieutenant Commander Mbani is your chief astronavigator, backup engineer, and backup gunner. Commander Robert Graves is your chief pilot, backup gunner, backup engineer, and nominal head of all missions until the special circumstances take place. Your head of all missions after that point will be Major Jacaranda MacKenzie, who will also be your communications specialist as well as your government liaison."

"Admiral-General, sir," Mbani stated carefully when he paused to let that sink in. "I'm afraid I must side with Lieutenant Colvers in expressing my confusion. Why are civilians being inserted into our chain of command?"

"That would be my cue to speak," Rosa stated bluntly. She tapped the table, and the screens came to life. "Eight months ago, the Psi League started collating reports from registered precognitives. Dreams of certain people meeting with *non-*Human races."

"The Greys?" Thorsson asked. He looked at Jackie. "You are in the Psi Division. You are strong enough to thwart them, yes?"

"I can," Jackie admitted, glancing warily at the head of the Space Force to see if Kurtz objected to her admitting that much. When he didn't even blink, she added, "Three times, already. I can do it again if needed."

"Good," Graves said. "I don't like 'em, and I don't want to deal with 'em. So long as you're along . . ."

"These aliens are *not* the Greys," Premiere Callan corrected them.

That snagged everyone's attention. The Grey Ones—for lack of a better name—had proved to be disturbingly real a few hundred years back. They were advanced beyond anything humanity had ever seen, and the only thing that could keep them at bay was strong psychic energies being projected in their faces. Preferably into their minds, but even just levitating things around them was enough to harm the aliens.

The Space Force tried to recruit psis for protecting all the research domes and mining stations in the system. Psis were carried on board to be able to project kinetic inergy at Grey ships at a moment's notice, preferably from a safe distance but not always. The Greys were behind far too many of the "kidnapped and experimented upon" stories that had plagued Earth for centuries.

Jackie herself had been requested as both a very strong telepath and a modestly strong xenopath—a particularly effective form of psi weaponry against them—to go into the military, specifically to serve on the Space Force's patrols. Three of her medals, and the shoulder tattoo hidden by her uniform, were for three different instances where she had single-handedly chased off a Grey ship before it could capture any Humans for experimentation. Earth had too many psis for them to like approaching it these days, but they loved—if the alien race had any such emotional equivalent—to swoop in and pluck people out of research domes and orbital stations.

But the Greys, however dangerous, powerful, and meddlesome, were a known quantity. Semi-known, technically; they weren't the sort of visitors who were willing to sit down and chat for a while. Yet, this mission was *not* about the Greys? That was . . . news.

"New aliens, Premiere?" Jackie asked, voicing her confusion. "Are there any descriptions of this new race?"

"New *races*, plural," he corrected, and nodded at his predecessor.

Rosa tapped her controls, sending text descriptions and sketches to each seat across the table console. "You'll each be given a full set of all the data collated to review in your free time, but to summarize . . . the images reported by the precogs have been of many different types. Lizardlike people, catlike people . . . even giant spiderlike people have all been noted in these precognitive visions."

Jackie shuddered. She had always feared and hated spiders. The possibility of an alien race that looked like . . . ? She pulled her thoughts back to the information being shared as the ex-Premiere continued.

"These visions have not gone away. They have kept growing in strength and number; at first, only the strongest precogs had flashes of visions, a couple of them with only a dozen images between the lot . . . but five months ago, even the weaker precogs started seeing these alien races interacting with Humans, including military members. Two of them have photographic memories—one from the Psi League and one from a pagan branch of the Witan Order. The League helped them both to coordinate with the military to look for familiar faces.

"As the world's second psychic to hold a civilian office above a regional level, nearly everyone in the League who had these visions recognized *you*, Jackie," McCrary told her. "That was the real reason why I decided to request that you step down from your Councilorship, so that you would be available for these missions. I'm sorry I couldn't tell you or anyone else any of this earlier, but we didn't want scraps of information turning into wild speculations."

Jackie nodded, accepting the reason and the apology.

"Your telepathy includes a very strongly ranked xenopathy," Rosa stated next, tapping the tabletop away from her screens. "You have both military and government experience, you have proved you can make good, swift decisions under various circumstances, and you have the ability to talk with the Greys, cetaceans, pachyderms, and the greater apes. You are, in a word, ideal for dealing with these new races in a hopefully positive, peaceful way, should the visions prove to come true, and we suddenly have a lot more versions of sentiency to deal with."

"What if they're not peaceful?" Colvers asked the former Premiere.

"We have taken that side of things into account, and will be prepared to deal with it," the Admiral-General answered. "You worry about your own mission parameters, soldier. Those are to explore new star systems, as the other *Aloha* ships are doing, and to establish hopefully peaceful contact with as many new life-forms as you can manage under MacKenzie's leadership. *If* this isn't just the precogs booting their dreams into the wind."

"I have a question, sir," Jackie said. At his nod, she asked, "If a bunch of alien races are going to be encountering us, shouldn't I stay here in the Sol System?"

"Most of the images suggest you'll all be somewhere else," Admiral Nayak told her. "We have not yet found any truly inhabitable worlds in the systems of our nearest stellar neighbors, but in several of the images, the landscapes seen included patently alien plant life. To be fair, we have only just begun exploring beyond our system with the new other-than-light ships, but at the distances our OTL ships can travel, it is only a matter of time before we encounter those inhabitable worlds."

"More to the point," Rosa continued, "one of the strongest images was of MacKenzie, here, performing Mankiller-style at a big hula festival here on Earth . . . and the precog in question had reason to believe it was *after* First Contact had been made."

Jackie closed her eyes for a brief moment, stifling the urge to groan. "It's called the Merrie Monarch Festival, not 'some big hula festival.' There's a lot more to it than just hula . . . and yes, I did agree to perform holokinetically this year," she added, opening her eyes. "It takes place in the week following Easter . . . which falls on the first weekend in April, this year. It starts three months to the day from now, in fact, and I perform on the sixth of April."

"Then we'll need to get you into the stars as soon as possible," Kurtz stated. "You'll have two weeks to train on your ship's systems, *all* of you—and I expect the three of you who are familiar to step up and help the three who are not. Once you are reasonably trained, you will be expected to launch and start taking your place on the scouting rosters, seeking out new star systems and dropping off surveillance satellites and hyperrelay units as you go."

"Up until the moment of First Contact, Commander Graves will be in charge, and you will all be expected to follow his commands until that point," the Premiere instructed them. "After that point, Major MacKenzie will be in charge. Your official government position at that point, Jackie, will be Ambassador of the United Planets, and you will have full rights on the Council, from proposing legislation all the way through to voting on related issues, with the caveat that your vote is to be confined to those items that affect your constituency on an interstellar basis only—you don't have a vote on what goes on strictly back home, but you do have one if it involves anything from outside this system."

"What would be my constituency, then?" Jackie asked, curious in the face of that unusual restriction. "All of the scouting ships outside the Sol System? Anyplace where we've left a hyperrelay satellite?"

Premiere Callan gave her a sober, level look. "The *entire* United Planets is your constituency, Jacaranda. Within and without the Sol System. Your vote will only register for anything involving territories and peoples outside the United Planets, specifically those things you will be facing in your role as Ambassador. You will also have authority to broker initial treaties to ensure neutrally peaceful interactions with any First Contact races."

Jackie sat back, trying to absorb that. The only Councilors who had jurisdiction that broad were the Premiere and his or her apprentice, the Secondaire. If *she* had that kind of authority . . . that would make her the third most powerful person in the United Planets. She wasn't sure if she was ready for the responsibility, but as Callan continued, Jackie pulled her wits together. She might not be ready at that moment, but she would have to be, soon.

"Once you have hopefully established neutral, peaceful relations, Ambassador, you will then itemize and prioritize various recommendations before turning over each matter to the Council to decide as a whole," he told her. "You are also expected to stay on top of all interstellar matters in order to provide solid counsel, as well as to vote on each related issue."

"Unfortunately, not all of the precognitive visions were of peaceful coexistence," Kurtz warned the six of them. "There were images of the ship you'll be assigned firing its cannons, and of strange vessels engaged in heavy combat. There were images of personal combat as well, including some scenes of rather grisly violence. You may have to make some rather tough decisions as a crew. Not all of these visions may come true, and we would prefer it if you did not declare war on anyone, Ambassador," the Admiral-General added dryly. "But as a soldier and an officer, we know you are aware that there are times when a fight is inevitable. Try to make it *evitable*, if you can."

As an attempt at humor, the joke fell a little flat in the face of the somber news. Thorsson shook his head. "I am not certain I should like to be on this expedition. I know kendo and judo, but I have not fired a gun. I am a scientist, not a soldier."

Rosa McCrary reached over and touched his hand, using some of the same soothing charm that had made her the steady, beloved rock of the last four years. "I know what's in those reports, young man, and I find the worst of the images a bit frightening to contemplate, myself. But you are one of the top scientists available for gauging whether or not a planet has readily available resources. More importantly, you will be able to gauge if a planet or moon is suitable for dome colonization . . . or hopefully even direct colonization.

"If there are other races out there, and they do seem to require similar, oxygen-breathing environments, then it might be possible they know of worlds we could expand to, or perhaps jointly colonize. *If* we can get along," McCrary allowed. "Earth is still very overcrowded. Our torus stations have gravity, but a very limited amount of living space. Mars and the Moon are growing overcrowded despite being strictly for research and resource gathering . . . and the gravity is far too light on those two for safely raising children," she finished. "Someone has to be on hand to discern if there are new worlds we can safely claim."

"You are very much part of our long-term plans for these missions, Thorsson," Premiere Callan stated. "This isn't a short-term deal. If we find new sentients out there, and if we can establish peaceful relations, then we need to be able to convey our needs and wants to these people, whether they have two arms, or four arms, or a dozen legs. You are a part of Ambassador MacKenzie's initial, official embassy."

Again, Jackie shivered, shrinking a little inside. Firmly, she guided her mind away from thinking about multilimbed arachnids.

Rosa lifted her chin at the Finn. "You'll also be helping Mbani double-check your headings and locations. There are a lot of stars within twenty-five light-years of here, and you might end up going out even farther than that. Astronavigation has gotten good, with all the satellites that are being planted in our nearest neighboring systems, but you may end up a hundred light-years from here, or even five hundred. What we know of those star systems is five hundred years old, so your job is to discern the new differences and bring back details and recommendations."

Mbani eyed the tall blond, and shrugged. "I do hope you're very good at astronavigation, Thorsson. The only thing we can be grateful for is that a hyperrift exit won't open near a high-gravity well, so at least we won't smack into a moon or a planet when we emerge in a new system. Very small asteroids are another matter, though."

"Oh, sure, cheer me up with bad news," Thorsson quipped. "Next you'll tell me the ship we're on doesn't have a sauna."

Colvers gave him a bemused look. "Of course it doesn't. OTL ships are too small for such frivolities."

Thorsson sighed heavily, dropped his elbows to the table, and thumped his brow into his palms, the picture of dejection. He smiled shyly in the next moment, letting everyone know he was only teasing. Jackie smiled back, but few of the others did.

"I have a question." Colvers eyed the senior officers and the Premiere. When Callan nodded, he asked it. "Why weren't we told any sooner? Not *her*," he added, poking a thumb in Jackie's direction. "But the commander, the lieutenant commander, or me? Why weren't *we* told weeks or months ago?"

"Because unlike most other psychic abilities, precognition isn't something that the wielder can reliably control, never mind summon up on demand," Jackie explained. That question was one she herself could field. She wasn't a precog, but she had studied that ability alongside all the rest while being trained by the League. "And everything a foreseer sees is only a possibility, one that can be altered even just by knowing it's a possibility, and therefore potentially avoidable."

"We had a few reports coming in from several months ago, but it was only very recently that the psis had several visions all at once. When that happens, that usually means it'll happen soon," Premiere Callan stated. "As MacKenzie has stated, anything can change and prevent those visions from coming true . . . but the closer to an event, the more frequently they'll show up, and the more likely they'll actually happen."

The former Premiere nodded, agreeing with him. She gestured at Callan and herself. "We can only act when we think there is something worth acting upon. Otherwise, we'd end up chasing would-be/could-be shadows, and that's just frustrating. Not to mention it wastes resources. Now that we know it's coming up soon, with reasonably high probability that it will actually happen, it's finally worth acting upon. Even if that means a very short lead time before events actually happen."

Admiral Nayak looked at the others, then tapped the surface of the table. "Time to open up your dossiers and begin reading. Major MacKenzie, you'll need to sign quite a bit of paperwork before Premiere Callan can leave, government authorizations and such, so you'll need to start with that. Colvers . . . whatever personal opinions you may have about your teammates, keep them to yourself. This goes for all of you. Cooperation and courtesy may one day save your lives."

"Yes, sir," Colvers murmured. The others nodded as well and returned their attention to their pads.

"Most of the forms have been slightly modified from the Councilor ones, so at least the content of all that paperwork will be familiar, if tedious," Rosa commented in an aside to Jackie.

"You will also be expected to recite the Oath of Civil Service every single day, MacKenzie," Premiere Callan added, giving Jackie a level, firm look. "Recite *and* log it every day, so the citizens back home know that you're taking that oath to heart. We're handing you a huge chunk of authority. We need even the skeptics to know you can be trusted with it."

Jackie nodded since that was all she could do. She had recited that oath five days a week for the last five years and was quite familiar with the lengthy piece. The situation was serious, so she tried a little bit of humor to leaven it. "Do I at least get weekends off?"

"Only if you're here, at home, and off duty," he told her. "If you're out there, there's no such thing as a weekend holiday in space."

"Or saunas in space," Thorsson mumbled under his breath, face still braced in his hands. He got another sympathy pat out of Rosa, but only a brief one.

"By 'here,' the Premiere means in Earth orbit. You will all be moved to special quarters on Space Force Station *Mac-Arthur* by the end of this week, if not sooner," Admiral-General Kurtz stated. "The Space Force will be footing your relocation, transportation, and other mission-related expenses, in the understanding that what you are allowed to bring up to the *MacArthur* will be examined and regulated— you will have a little more leeway than the average military personnel in terms of quarter sizes and such, but not by much, and certain items will still remain on the prohibited list.

"This and other points of information have been collated and arranged into files for each of you to peruse. The core information and regulations remain the same, but the rest has been tailored to your particular specialties. Lieutenant Yarley will distribute your mission pads now."

Nodding, the youngish man with the single silver bar on his uniform collar points fetched a stack of datapads from a side table, handing them out with a quiet double check of each name. Jackie accepted hers with a sigh, anticipating all the paperwork ahead. Sure enough, the very first section in the files was a thick data packet of forms to be read and signed on the spot.

"Thank you for your cooperation, gentlemen, ladies. Unfortunately, the Admiral-General and I have other work to do," Premiere Callan stated, as each of the six settled in to read. "Admiral Nayak will be taking over and handling things once we have gone, though Honorable McCrary will remain to help answer any questions you may have. I realize this isn't a *typical* mission by any means . . . but while precognition in general is nebulous at best, these *are* certified and tested precogs giving us visions of what might happen. Rosa and I both agree that we would rather have the United Planets prepared and have nothing to do for our trouble, than be caught off guard without any contingency plans at all, should the worst of the visions come true."

Jackie rose out of polite habit when Premiere Callan did. So did the others. Once he and the head of the Space Force had left, they settled back down, eyeing each other with wary curiosity. All except for the Finn. Thorsson glanced at his datapad, turned it so that the lettering was upside down, turned it again, and raised a hand palm upward in confusion. "They want me to . . . to decide on spatial coordinates for explorations based on a bunch of *words*? Jumbled dreams?"

"You're not the only one," Mbani told him. "This isn't my idea of scientifically conducted astronomical observation, either."

"You're a psi, MacKenzie," Colvers stated, slanting Jackie a shuttered look. "Why don't you pluck it out of the air for us, and make things easier?"

"I'm not that kind of psi, Lieutenant," Jackie demurred. "I don't have precognition. The most I could do is ask to meet with the precogs, get their permission to go into their memories of their visions, and try to project a holokinetic image of what they see . . . with no guarantee that what I'd be projecting is in any way accurate. Memories are easily disturbed and altered."

"That could be helpful, though," Thorsson pointed out. "I am a visual person. If I could see what they saw, even if the image was nebulous, it could help—it could be an image of a nebula, yes?" He smiled at his joke, looking around to see if the others had a sense of humor, too.

Jackie returned it wryly, Mbani flashed him a grin, and Graves smiled but shook his head. "You might wanna work on your jokes a little more there, Thorsson."

"Call me Lars, please," the geophysicist returned politely. "We will be working together."

"If you could return your attention back to the reading and the signing, it would help speed this along," Admiral Nayak stated, interrupting them. "We won't be done until I've scheduled movers to get each of you packed and up to *MacArthur* within the week."

"I'm already packed and ready to go," Jackie stated. At a snort from Colvers, she addressed his unspoken skepticism. "All my things were packed up so they could be moved out of the Councilor apartments here on Kaho'olawe and into a place on O'ahu. I'd only opened up . . . five, six boxes? I have a kit bag ready to go in my car, but if I'm allowed the time to visit my storage unit, it'd only take me a couple of hours to sort out what I'd need for living in space. Presuming the military issues me new uniforms and such," she added, glancing at the admiral.

Nayak nodded. "You'll get that, but you'll also be expected to pack a few changes of nonmilitary formalwear as well as Dress uniforms. You'll have a week to go shopping, so start thinking of something flattering yet conservative; we don't know if bare skin is an insult or an invitation in the eyes of some alien species, nor what sort of an invitation that might be, in their eyes."

"Actually, Jackie, if you're already mostly packed and ready," Rosa said, "and I know you have formalwear you can use, then we can have you go on a fast tour of the various provinces this week. We were thinking it would be nice if you could use your Mankiller abilities to be able to put on a little 'show' of what Earth and its colonies look like, when introducing us to foreign nationals. Nothing that would give away our location in space, of course, but something to show them what we're like, holokinetically."

She sighed. "I was hoping to spend my downtime practicing for the Merrie Monarch Festival, ma'am."

"I'm sure you can incorporate the projections into the Festival, or vice versa," Rosa dismissed.

Jackie frowned at her, but the older woman had turned to the doctor, who was puzzling over something in her datapad notes, muttering in Spanish under her breath. As much as humanity had managed to finally gather itself together into a single, united government, there were still regional differences, provincial prides, and district-based cultural observations that just didn't blend all that well. Hula was enjoyed in many regions, not just Oceania, but it was not exactly universal as a form of dance.

Sighing, she turned her attention back to the forms awaiting thumbprint signatures on her pad. This mission was already beyond odd, and not just by its parameters. Thorsson had a weird sense of humor, Colvers seemed to have something against psis, and she had no idea what quirks Mbani, Graves, and de la Santoya would manifest. Precognition was indeed nebulous, rarely found in any great strength, and easily misinterpreted . . . and it was forcing the six of them to work together in the hopes of navigating their people toward some sort of success instead of a disaster.

Ambassador of the United Planets. To unknown alien races. Joy. I wonder if they've modified the Lochaber Speech to incorporate whatever that *entails?*

CHAPTER 2

JANUARY 11, 2287 C.E.
MACARTHUR STATION
EARTH ORBIT

"On your left! Move and lose it, *sir*," she heard coming up from behind.

The only thing the owner of that voice didn't do was brush rudely against her. He carefully did not touch her, but Lieutenant Colvers didn't hesitate to make subtle digs at her "unfitness" for command each time he passed her on the track. The new uniforms she had been issued did fit, but they were two sizes larger, and it was clear she'd still need at least a size larger for some time while she got back into better shape.

Gritting her teeth, Jackie resisted the urge to increase the pace of her jogging. Colvers was used to jogging along the running path spanning the length of the outer torus. Used to the different-than-Earth gravity, since he, Ayinda Mbani, and Robert Graves had gone *down* to Earth for their initial meeting. It had been ten years since Jackie had lived and worked in gravity-free environments and torus space stations. She knew how to run safely when the station constantly made her feel like she was being pulled ever so slightly off dead vertical, but it had still been ten years, and ten years of *not* jogging every single day, at that.

At least TUPSF Space Station *MacArthur* was capable of hosting Earth-like gravity along its outermost torus. And at least Jackie was in reasonably good shape. Lars—the geologist had asked everyone to call him by his first name, not just the chief pilot—had already given up running when Jackie had passed him a quarter kilometer back. He had joined just two laps ago, and was now walking with his hands on his hips, breathing through a grimace.

Dr. de la Santoya had insisted that they all endure a regimen of exercise to combat bone-density loss and other problems inherent when working in space. She, of course, had been jogging in tandem with Ayinda, another case of first-name familiarity being granted. Both ladies were ahead of Jackie, probably by a third of the torus by now.

The jogging path came up on the section seal right before the alpha quarantine sector. The quarantine section only occupied half the circumference of the tube forming the ring beyond that seal, but it did make the path bend. The section had been built with long-term foresight; it had its own power system, its own life support, hydroponics, medical center, and living quarters capable of hosting up to fifteen people with ease, or thirty with crowding. It could even be decoupled and towed away from the station, though a similar quarantine pod, beta, would have to be decoupled from the far side of the torus as well to ensure the great wheel remained stable.

On the bright side, it was very nicely appointed inside, since there was no telling how long anyone would have to remain in quarantine after encountering alien life. Of course, aside from the Greys in their invasive ships and some vaguely prokaryotic sludge they had found on two proto M-class-style worlds, they had yet to encounter anything worthwhile. The main jogging route had an excellent view of the exercise deck inside, with its own, much smaller jogging path, a weight room, a little garden with plants that were as innocuous as centuries of recorded allergies could be cleared from those lists, and so on and so forth.

Of course, the greater portion of the station was superior. Multiple gardens, though most were designated for growing food, both in the main part and in the quarantine areas. The gardens had bugs as a part of the pollination needs, though there were repeller fields and microshock bands keeping insects out of the scoutships.

And, of course, there were spiders in the gardens. Jackie could only thank anything that was listening that Lieutenant Colvers hadn't been around when she had found *that* out first-hand and shrieked like an arachnophobic idiot, summoning two security team members to see what was wrong. Thankfully, the team members had been discreet about not mentioning it to anyone.

On the bright side, there was even a swimming pool for doing laps in the main torus. The water served as an emergency backup reservoir in case a huge disaster happened and the regular shipments of cometary ice didn't make it to the station on time for purifying into hydrofuel. But that was a worst-case backup.

The pool was on the other side of the beta quarantine unit. It took her, at her current jogging pace, a good five minutes to reach it. Mainly because she wasn't sprinting but also because the track had not been laid straight. Its planners had wanted to give its users things to see along the way, goals to reach at shorter intervals . . . and to avoid the psychologically disturbing view of constantly running uphill everywhere. The design was similar to most other stations in the system, whether they were busy sharing Earth's orbit, or the Moon, Jupiter, Saturn, or even the beginnings of a habitat for Neptune, though that station was still slowly making its way outbound through the system. Stations did not move fast and were not designed to be moved fast.

This particular space station was not the largest—that was space station *Freedom II*—but neither was it small; the outermost torus on the lowest floor, where the jogging track lay, was a good kilometer and a half in circumference, maybe a little more. Jackie hadn't paid enough attention to the orientation lecture to remember it to the last centimeter since that wasn't necessary. Its size kept the spin slow enough, less than two revolutions per minute, to make docking easier at the core; that reduced the Coriolis effect nausea to virtually nothing and ensured plenty of space. Living quarters, exercising facilities, entertainment areas, and the life-support aquaculture bays were all on the outermost ring. Labs, manufactory bays, and storage spaces occupied the median torus, and, of course, the docking bays filled the spindle, the axle of the great spinning station.

Smaller counterweight tori spun in the opposite direction on either end. They contained the fuel storage and main engines that powered the station, along with various weapon turrets for defense of the station. Between the spokes supporting each torus lay broad sheets of solar cells, augmenting the station's power needs. And to ward off harmful radiation, all of the main structure was wrapped in ceristeel, the miracle child of modern space hulls. Crafted from a mix of ceramics and metals, the stuff could be polished and repolished to reflect cosmic and stellar radiation. It was incredibly tough, it was heat- and cold-resistant, and it made the station blend into the night sky, save where the glow of Earth's dayside—and the mass of city-strewn stars of its nightside—gleamed off the hull.

She knew it did because she passed one of the viewing ports once she got past the pool to the next section of interest, a lounge area lined with fragrant plants and gaming tables. The pool was empty at this hour, but the gaming area had at least three tables occupied. One was a spirited game of ping-pong, one looked to be a bridge game, and one had three people doing what looked like homework, save that they were fully grown adults. Reports, most likely. Beyond them, she could see out the currently open viewing window to the port-side counterbalance, which gleamed in streaks reflecting the planet below; she knew it was the port one because the torus had little red blinking lights on it at regularly spaced intervals instead of green.

Jogging past, she remembered the last time she had seen a counterbalance ring through the station's own windows. *On the* Margaret Bower, *with my quarters a tiny closet of a space on the quarterdeck level of the outer torus. I had half the room of an officer, technically less space than a private— though I, at least, didn't have to share—and the blessing of not having to worry about bumping into a roommate. Literally bumping. I kept hitting the walls with my arms whenever I had to dress.*

Privilege or not, sharing quarters was not a good idea for someone of her strength. Most telepaths *weren't* into reading others' minds; in fact, most were a bit obsessed about mental privacy, wanting to keep other people's thoughts *out* of their heads. Jackie was one of them. At her rank of ability, unless the other person had practiced mental shielding for a full year, a simple touch of skin on skin was enough to hear surface thoughts. Without physical contact boosting her abilities, she was able to wall out the sounds of a thousand minds all within range, muting it to a dull mental rush like the sound of the seashore heard from beyond the edge of the dunes. Ignorable, for the most part.

Colvers had slyly suggested putting her into alpha or beta quarantine quarters, since it was surely a strain on the station to give her an unshared cabin otherwise. The Admiral had given him a look, then stated that the quarantine space had to be kept free in case anyone came back with any diseases. De la Santoya had muttered something under her breath. It had taken Jackie a moment to translate it from Spanish-accented Brazilian, which was actually a lot more similar to Portuguese but not quite like it. Her comment had been, *"Like prejudice, you bigot?"*

She'd had to bite her lip to keep from laughing, warmed at the otherwise-acerbic woman's quip. Prejudice wasn't a disease in the sense that touching one made it contagious. Circumstances could make it so, such as how one was raised, the environment in which one worked, the flow of open information being throttled down and controlled, but not physically.

Jackie didn't know what Colvers' problem was, other than that he hated psis and disdained working with her. She did know he was annoying her with his little "fat" quips. She was not fat. She was stocky in the way that many who were either Scottish or Polynesian were stocky. Big-boned . . . and a bit curvy. But she could dead-lift more than her own body weight without breaking a sweat, she could flip a full-grown man who was bigger and taller than her with her martial arts training, and when she performed a *haka*, a war dance, she was considered downright intimidating.

She couldn't help it if most of the time she preferred smiling pleasantly and making herself seem harmless and helpful instead. Those were more important skills in the world of diplomacy, public service, and being a Councilor, a representative of the people. But no, it wasn't her demeanor that had Colvers' running shorts in a snit . . . and here he came again, running up behind her.

"Shake a leg, not an ass, ma'am—on your left!"

Fat jokes. Inappropriate behavior for an officer in the Space Force. Particularly toward a superior . . . but he always raced on too fast for her to call out a reprimand. Deliberately, no doubt. Sighing roughly, Jackie continued onward at her own pace. She had another half torus to go before she could quit and hit the shower in her quarters, have a meal in the nearest galleyspace, and get ready for the morning's training lesson on ship systems and communications equipment.

If he catches up with me again, I am going to remind him that those comments are utterly inappropriate . . . and if he tries to brush it off with, "Well, you didn't say anything before, so why say it now?" I am going to tell him flat to his face that it is not my job to rein in his poor judgment when he is an adult who supposedly can think for himself in advance of opening his damn mouth. Only without the swearing, of course.

He didn't pass her again, though, not by the time she reached her exit point. Sighing, Jackie jogged through one of the many section seals that partitioned off the torus into quickly sealable compartments in case of an emergency and detoured off the path to the galleyspace on the torus that served coffee and snacks to station personnel. Her quarters were above it, a short jaunt down a side corridor and tucked behind a storage room. Ordering a breakfast sandwich and a cup of tea, she paid for it by extending her identity bracelet to be scanned, then munched on the food as she headed for the narrow stairwell to the next level, tucked between section seal and coffee shop.

The café manager had kindly given it up for her, moving in with one of his fellow sergeants elsewhere. Twice the size of her last cabin on that other station, not nearly as luxurious as her apartment back down on O'ahu—smaller than her bedroom would have been, in that apartment—but at least it was neat and private and a couple bulkheads away from any other personnel quarters. The previous owner had left his bookshelves for her use, too; Jackie didn't know the man other than in passing, but at least they both shared a liking for physical books, not just electronic ones.

She had only brought a few up with her, though, not wanting

to clutter hopefully temporary quarters. Either she'd be living out of various locations while they figured out First Contact with whoever or whatever might be out there—four-armed aliens, giant sentient spiders, lizardmen, catmen, things that were either frogs or octopi or worse; the precog reports varied that wildly— or she'd be assigned a specific post somewhere and could move more of her things into that place.

Presuming those aliens weren't out to eat her. She had read those reports, too. Unpleasant. Unbraiding her hair and showering quickly, she dried off, re-bound her thick curls into a multi-pinned bun to keep it from flopping in zero gravity in weird, annoying ways, and dressed in her uniform for the day. Army wore green, Marines wore brown, Navy—space navy, that was—wore blue, and Special Forces—chaplains, psis, medics, and true special forces, the kind trained to kill with a pinky finger or infiltrate enemy intelligence networks—wore gray.

All casual, solid-colored uniforms had a black stripe down pant legs and shirt and jacket sleeves alike, unless their owners were in camouflage fatigues. She dressed in solid colors, since there was no point in wearing camouflage on a space station in her mind-set. Hers had an additional blue stripe next to the black, indicating she was on loan to the Navy; her Dress Blacks, her most formal uniform, had been reissued with both a gray and a blue stripe. All of it two sizes bigger, though if she kept exercising daily, she'd eventually need to go back down at least one size.

Jackie didn't bother with her Dress clothes. Today was just another training day, which meant practical clothes. She was supposed to learn advanced signaling and code translation today, along with a drill on emergency procedures, and a refresher lesson in free-floating comestible containment procedures. In other words, lunch in zero G, to practice not getting tiny droplets or crumbs drifting into anything sensitive.

Part of her wished someone would invent artificial gravity. Wave a magic wand, say the magic word, hack the right code, slip and fall and come up with the perfect thingy along with a bruised, aching skull while doing something in the bathtub. She'd happily trade an ache in her head for a day or two. Unfortunately, the only pain in her life was a certain copilot.

Her work console beeped as she headed for the door. Detouring, Jackie checked the incoming identity, recognizing it quickly. Her sister Hyacinth was calling. Not an emergency, just her sister wanting to chat. She'd have to let it go to messaging and call her back later since there was no time right now to learn how her niece and nephew were doing, or anything else. Leaving her quarters, she locked the door and headed left along the main hall to the nearest elevator shaft.

The ride up to the docking spindle always felt a little weird to her. Acceleration made her feel like there was a persistent illusion of gravity tugging at her body, but the fact that the car was moving toward the spindle meant that she was experiencing less and less of that tug. She wasn't the only one who looked a little discomfited by the ambivalent sensations, either; there were five others who had stepped into the lift with her, each with varying levels of discomfort and unease in their downturned mouths and hunched shoulders.

Oh, and there was that annoying voice on every single ride, pleasant, neutral, masculine: *"Please hold on to the handrails and keep your feet in the toe loops until the car comes to a complete stop. Mind your step. Please hold on to the handrails and keep your feet in the toe loops until the car comes to a complete stop. Next stop, Docking Bays 7 and 8."* When the car stopped, and the doors slid open, it changed to, *"You are now in a microgravity environment. Please be careful when exiting the car."*

Jackie gestured for the others to exit ahead of her. Two were servicemen who had ridden at the same time as her the last few days; both gave her a brief smile before pulling themselves out smoothly, efficiently. A third was a female tech who eyed her Radiant Eye shoulderpatch, nodded, and released the toe loops, tugging herself forward and out the hatch with equal experience. The last two glanced at her, shrugged, and pulled themselves out carefully, but with control. Today, everyone aboard was experienced at moving in a zero-G environment—technically, if you were near the outermost edge of the spindle, there was a slight tug outward, but that was it; the station's high orbit wasn't close enough to Earth to feel more than the tiniest tug planetward.

Mostly, it was helpful for finding drifting objects since they'd inevitably drift to the outer wall, but not so much of a tug that a person couldn't still be considered floating. Since no one seemed to be struggling to maneuver gracefully, Jackie let go of the handrails, pulled her feet out of the toe loops, and soared into the corridor and around the corner. It was hard not to "swim" against the air with arms and legs; in order to handle null gravity, she had to think of herself as if she were diving, and that meant having the urge to kick and stroke.

It was hard not to do it with a superhero pose with her arms, either. Every telekinetic strong enough to lift themselves and fly inevitably tried it that way, but both the Witan Order and the Psi League, the two largest training organizations, discouraged such things on anything other than the most playful of moments. The ability to lift things with mental rather than physical effort was a rare privilege, and wasn't to be rubbed in others' faces . . . and doing any superhero-style or masked-vigilante-type activities required a license. Most rarely bothered. Telekinetics could earn a lot more money holding down a job that paid them to exercise their minds and usually chose working in the private sector.

Of course, no one knew where psychic abilities came from, only that they started appearing in increasing strength within the last century and a half. The Greys were suspected. They were kidnapping Humans for some sort of biological hybrid experimentation, and sometimes returned them; that much, the United Planets knew about. The best xenotelepaths in the military had tried to figure out why, but the gray-skinned, black-eyed, hairless beings' thoughts were too weird to fully grasp at a distance, and they never kidnapped psis, so doing it with the helpful boost of physical touch just hadn't happened yet.

Jackie wasn't so sure the Greys were involved in creating psychic Humans since they loathed and avoided her kind, but she didn't know who or what else was involved—certainly not the government, whatever conspiracy nuts tried to claim. Science knew how to identify psychic abilities as genuine or not, thanks to the invention of KI meters that could detect the peculiar energy fields that were being used, but they couldn't find it, let alone generate it, outside of a living sentient being.

As for programming it genetically? Despite many advances in biology, nobody could figure out what made someone like Jackie different from someone who couldn't fly or read minds.

Despite having exceptionally good gene maps in the late twenty-third century for DNA, RNA, microRNA interactions, and more, no one knew how psychic abilities worked.

Passing a clutch of workers steadying what looked like a greenish, nauseated newcomer, Jackie slowed, caught a hand loop, and pressed her palm to the scanner for the docking area for her ship while her body drifted past, orienting her the other way. Up and down made little difference up here; spindleward and rimward, port and starboard, those were the directions that mattered. For the convenience of speaking about it, *down* was toward the outermost torus, of course, but where she was going, it was all microgravity.

"Hoo!" someone muttered, awe coloring his tone. "She just zipped and . . . and flew!" Looking up in relation to her body, Jackie eyed the newcomer. He still looked a bit pale and green, but at least he seemed distracted from his nausea by her. "Hey, how can you do that?"

"Telekinetic, Rank 12." Why wasn't the airlock panel opening? Oh, right; her thumb wasn't positioned right. She tugged herself a little closer and rolled her thumb awkwardly to get more of the print visible.

"Z'at strong?" the new crew member asked. "Uh, sir?" he added, catching sight of her silver oak leaves on her collar points and shoulder boards. "That sounds really strong."

"Strong enough to fly on Earth." The light turned green, and the panel hissed open.

"Hoo," she heard behind her. "Wish I could do that . . . uhhh, if it came without nausea . . ."

"*I* certainly wish you could handle zero G without threatening to puke on us all," one of his companions quipped. Laughter followed his words, but it was good-natured teasing.

Sealing the door behind her, she floated in relative quiet to the next one. Palm prints to get in and out, each ship assigned its own dock, personnel restricted . . . Nobody wanted these new ships stolen and taken for a joyride. Or damaged. Jackie knew from her time spent studying the Space Force's budget as a Councilor just how much each modest, shuttle-sized craft cost. But it was just the thought of the idiocy of someone taking it without knowing what they were doing that had made such precautions necessary.

Opening a hyperrift on a remote corner of Mars to test how the things would react in an atmosphere had proved to be a bad idea, and on Earth, it would be that much worse. The tiny pinpricks that swirled into ship-swallowing straws, sucking them along spatial shortcut paths, did *not* like being touched by matter. More than a relative handful of cosmic dust, and the tunnel would collapse, crushing whatever it caught in its maw. The resulting explosion had been a mix of fusion and fission, had kicked up a medium-sized dust storm that had altered the Martian weather patterns for a week, and had left charred carbon on the ground two kilometers below.

It had even vaporized the ceristeel plating on the remote-piloted ship. No one wanted to contemplate what would have happened to an actual pilot on board. As a Councilor who had actually served in the military, Jackie had been picked multiple times to serve on military oversight committees, hence knowing the budgets and the testing reports and more. She never would have pegged herself to be picked for actually serving on one of these OTL vessels, though.

The airlock into the shuttle was an airlock. Boring, predictable, paneled in white to show how clean it was. Beyond, the access corridor wasn't much better. There were four entrances to the shuttle, the one she currently used near the rear on the starboard, two amidships on top and bottom, and one to port, near the bow and its cockpit. Loops of metal stuck out on all four walls, and latches hid cupboards both shallow and deep. There was a "dorsal" for top and a "ventral" for bottom in relation to how the ship would function when perched on a gravi-tied surface, plus starboard and port, bow and stern, but no real gravity.

The engines for powering the insystem thrusters lay in the rear, along with the reoxygenators that mechanically scrubbed carbon dioxide out of the air, using catalysts to turn it back into breathable oxygen. OTL shuttles were too small to carry enough plants for that, let alone the aquaculture necessary for scrubbing water clean, too. Most of starboard was taken up in crew quarters—spaces for sleeping bags to be clipped into place, toilet and showering cupboards, that sort of thing—and interior storage space.

Portside lay the scanners and the launch bays for sending

scanner-equipped hyperrelay units into a star system to collect data and report back at intervals to the Space Force. And, of course, the front of the ship held the cockpit, with enough seating for all six to ride in acceleration-cushioned comfort. Entering the cockpit, she found Robert Graves already there.

"Hey, there, Major," he greeted her, lifting his tanned chin a little. He had to brace his hands so that the movement didn't put a spin on his efforts from momentum.

"Good morning, Commander," she said, pulling herself by her arms toward her station. Comm systems, translation programs, backup scanners, even a backup gunnery position. It was all hers to manage, though she was still at the hunt-and-peck stage with the instruction manual floating at her side while working.

Remote-controlled gun pods sat on both wings, dorsal and ventral turrets that could swivel and fire in near full hemispheres, save only that they would not fire on the ship they were attached to, of course. Those silvery wings held the water tanks that provided the fuel for the ship, with a reserve tank beneath the corridor she had floated through. There were also two missile-launching tubes, and two laser cannons, each placed bow and stern. As much as humanity wanted to believe that any aliens encountered would be friendly, pure pragmatism said that some simply would not be. That meant the military ran the space exploration program, and that meant going armed.

Colvers would be the main person to fire any such weapons if they were needed. *A task well suited to his nature,* a snide corner of her mind quipped. Adjusting the headset, she flicked a switch—and both she and Robert flinched at the feedback squeal. Thankfully, the automatics shut it off before it could do more than make them grind their teeth in pain. Unfortunately, it took her five squealing tries to figure out what had been done to make that happen, and get it undone and locked down.

"Sorry, sorry. I'm wondering, though. If I looked through the logs of who accessed this shift between now and the time I went off duty yesterday, if a certain *someone* would show as having accessed these systems," Jackie muttered.

"Aw, he's a good guy normally," Robert told her, pausing from his efforts at adjusting something under his piloting console. "I don't know what bug he's got in his ears about you, but he normally gets along with most everybody. Very gung ho for the military side of things, but that shouldn't be a problem, since you're military, too . . ."

"Well, he should remember that I am now his superior and can slam his butt off this team if he doesn't get that bug *out* of his ears," she retorted. "Barely a few days on the job with him, and he keeps digging at me disrespectfully."

"Maybe he's the type that needs t' go a few rounds with you before you'll earn his respect?" Robert asked, grunting a little. "There . . . fuses replaced. Maybe *now* I can adjust the leg rests on this new seat . . ."

"This is disrespect for *me*, not my abilities, Robert. If I thought a couple rounds of . . . of kickboxing or judo or whatever style he knows would do it, I'd do that."

"Maybe he's jealous you got a tour of Earth?" Robert offered next, playing devil's advocate.

"I'm pretty sure it started the moment he realized I was a psi," she countered flatly. "I don't get the prejudice against that. It's not like I'm a psychopath or a danger to society. Psis are fellow Humans. We're just as likely to be good, law-abiding citizens as the next guy. And it's not like I *chose* to be born this way. It's like being jealous of someone because their eyes are gray, or because they can throw a fastball better, or because they can play the cello like a virtuoso at the age of five or whatever. Everyone can do something better than someone else, and is worse at something else. I don't understand why he's so . . . so booted that I have psychic abilities."

Pulling himself out from the hole where his legs went during flight, he opened his mouth, closed it with a thoughtful frown, then spoke. "I was going to say, maybe he's jealous of your abilities, but he doesn't seem jealous. More like just plain upset." He thought a moment, then shrugged and twisted himself, curling his legs around and into the footwell. "Maybe someone who was a psi offended him, and he's just taking it out on you?"

"That would make sense, but he needs to grow up, realize that I had nothing to do with it, that I shouldn't be punished for someone else's problems—his included—and act with mature civility instead of immature rudeness and disdain."

The cabin hatch opened, and the blond devil himself floated inside. He smirked her way, but his blue eyes were cold, not warm. "Haven't gotten started yet, have you?"

"Already started . . . and now I'm busy tracking down just who had access to this panel after I shut it down yesterday. Oh, look, it *is* you, Lieutenant," Jackie said, shifting her eyes from her screen to his face. "Tampering with my workstation should have been beneath you, Lieutenant Colvers. It was immature and unprofessional. It is the sort of behavior that is usually abandoned in Basic Training under the discipline required by the Space Force. It is most assuredly *not* behavior expected and required of an officer of said Space Force, Lieutenant.

"Coupled with all the inappropriate and unprofessional 'fat' jokes you've been throwing my way, all of these actions which you have chosen to undertake are aiming you and your career toward a disciplinary hearing, *Lieutenant*."

Using his rank over and over was an attempt to get him to realize just how poorly he was behaving. Officers were supposed to set good examples, not bad ones. Officers were held to a higher standard of conduct. And officers were supposed to show respect toward their superiors in rank, the exact same as enlisted and noncommissioned or warranted members of the military.

She didn't want a disciplinary hearing invoked because there were too many visions of Colvers being involved in the missions ahead, most of them listed among the "friendly alien encounter" ones the precogs had seen. It wasn't exactly superstition, wanting to avoid negating those friendly encounters by not having the right personnel on hand. She knew that the registered precogs were seeing real glimpses of possible futures. Jackie was just glad *she* wasn't a precog; that kind of power seemed like a nebulous, annoying headache to hold instead of something concrete and reliable like telekinesis.

Eyeing the quiet, almost sullen man, she continued. "If you can set aside whatever problem you only think you have with me—a problem I suspect is actually the fault of someone else, so please stop applying it to me—if you can do that, then you can and will make an exemplary member of this team. Your skills and abilities as pilot, gunner, and so forth are not being questioned, Lieutenant Colvers, but your professionalism *is*. That professionalism needs to exist *outside* of working hours as well as within them. Once we go into space, there are no nonworking hours. So get out of the habit of sniping at me even when you're off duty, and stay that way. You can hold your opinion, but you need to hold your tongue. It is unprofessional, and the Space Force both expects and demands better conduct from you. Have I made this clear, Lieutenant?"

"Sir. Yes, sir," he replied, his tone clipped, his gaze dark and displeased, but at least his words seemed to be obedient.

She had carefully phrased things so that the Space Force was the party with all the expectations of his better behavior. *Let's hope a little smear of diplomacy on top helps the message taste better.* Of course, he knew he was being verbally disciplined by a higher-ranked officer. The use of *sir* was not an insult, either; it was exactly what he should be saying to her.

When the various military forces had been combined into one organization, the Space Force had decided to consider *sir* gender-neutral and thus appropriate for addressing all officers. The Space Force did not care about one's gender, whether it was the one a person was born with, or the one they identified with, save only for what actual physiological requirements needed to be met for certain activities. Modern military life contained too many force multipliers via its hardware, its equipment, vehicles, and so forth, to make differences between the genders important. Stamina, hand-eye coordination, and general fitness were requirements, but not gender. However, the Space Force *did* care about discipline within its ranks.

The Peace Force units spread around the United Planets had already instituted a tradition of caning as punishment for major crimes committed by its members—bribery, treason, theft, rape, all the good things. The Space Force, she knew, was wavering on whether or not to apply that high of a corporal punishment to infractions against its own highest rules and regulations; in fact, she had served on some of the Council committees discussing that very topic.

Nothing Brad Colvers had done so far would have merited a caning, but if he didn't clean up his act and resume treating her with the respect she was due, he *could* do something wrong, and at the wrong moment in time. A potential First

Contact situation had no room for such problems, particularly any tangible displays of disrespect or derision.

Movement at the back of the cockpit distracted Jackie from her thoughts and her efforts to ensure every last scrap of her controls were back to their original settings. Ayinda was the next to pull herself into the cockpit, with Lars at her heels. Literally, for she almost kicked him with a stray swing of one leg. He caught her boot and grinned.

"Should I call you Achilles, for having caught you by your heel? Toss you aside like a fisherman who caught a boot instead of a bass? Or sing that classic song 'Boot to the Head'?" the Finn asked, displaying his odd sense of humor with a grin.

The astronavigator chuckled and hauled herself into her seat behind Brad, a position she had flown in several times before with the lieutenant and the commander both. "None of the above, Lars. None of the above, today."

"Then there is hope for tomorrow." Lars took his place behind her at the rearmost starboard station, activating his various screens and scanner consoles. His seat was parallel to Jackie's at the back of the cabin.

Robert's pilot seat was to the left of Brad's, with the doctor's station behind the chief pilot, and in front of the communication station. Maria didn't really have much to do other than monitor the crew's health and the ship's general life-support conditions, but it had been deemed easier to upgrade the rearmost port seat in the extended cockpit with translation matrices and broad-spectrum broadcast equipment than try to fit it all into the middle seat, portside. A seat that was currently still empty.

Robert *tsked* as he brought himself into alignment with his seat, warming up his own dashboard. "I see Maria is late this morning."

"She had a late-night call with her family. Relatively speaking—pun included," the Finn geophysicist joked. "I understand it was daytime for them, late night for her. I passed her still getting breakfast on my way here, and she told me why she was running late. Though no pun this time; she was standing and walking, but not running. She told me there were twins born to one of her cousins, and she was willing to give up sleep and be a little late to celebrate that."

"Well, she'd better get here fast," Colvers muttered, "Or a certain officer will throw the rulebook at her."

Jackie didn't pretend ignorance about who he meant. She didn't address it directly, though she did speak up. "Considering the birth of twins is a joyous thing, and not a case of insubordination . . . I'm sure Commander Graves will let it slide."

"I don't know. Do I get a slice of birthday cake?" Robert joked, just as the cockpit door slid open.

"Birthday? Whose birthday is it?" the doctor asked, pulling herself into the now-somewhat-crowded space.

"Your cousin's twins, so maybe we could have twice as many slices?" Lars joked, smiling at their medical specialist.

"You wish," she snorted. The Spaniard pulled herself past Jackie's spot with a little wave. "Nobody hurt themselves on today's simulation runs. I want to be able to nap through everything. Oh, and if anyone asks, two very healthy baby girls, 3.550 kilograms and 3.727 kilograms. Both of them within a hair of 40 centimeters, one under, one over."

"Two little girls, nice. First birth, or second?" Robert asked.

"First. They've petitioned for a second birth, and got it. About half who have twins first birth get a second. Triplets, not so much," Maria added. She tipped her head and shrugged—and hastily grabbed at her console as the act made her start to drift away from her seat. None of them were strapped in yet. "Then again, I don't know many women who, as first-time mothers of triplets or more, would want to go through that again. Not if it's the first round."

"Have you had any children yet, Maria?" Robert asked her, looking up and back over his shoulder.

"*Dos, gracias.* A boy and a girl, Suzie and Michael, fourteen and thirteen respectively. Rolo wanted one of each, and I obliged him. Now they are being cared for by their father and his new wife. Which is fine by me," the doctor added, holding up a hand to forestall any comments. "It was a good divorce. We fought too much, and in all the wrong ways. *They* rarely fight, and she gives our children lots of love. They also get to have at least one more, since Paula hasn't had any yet. 'An heir for everybody,' and all that," de la Santoya quoted the motto of Population Control. "Whereas *I* get to come back to a career I

love, without being told in so many words I'm stupid every day
for working up in space when planetside pay is better."

"Do you miss them?" Jackie asked, curious.

"I usually get them on the weekends, which gives Rolo and
Paula time for themselves. Well, when I'm not stuck in space, I
can babysit," Maria amended, reaching up over her head to turn
on the life-support sensors. "Anyone else have *bambinos*?"

"Two," Robert admitted. "Boys. Dale and Evan, sixteen and
fourteen. Roger's got 'em bunking with his sister's kids on their
ranch. The husband and I wanted 'em to grow up knowing
where food actually comes from, so it's up at dawn, muckin'
stalls, feedin' cattle, fixin' the electrofence, and layin' plans for
the vegetable greenhouses come spring. Anyone else?"

Lars spoke up. "Just one. But he is not really *my* boy. My best
friend in college wanted a child, and asked me to be the donor.
The clinic had some very interesting magazines for the donors
to get in the proper mood. One of them had this—"

"*Thank* you for sharing," Brad interrupted him. "We don't
need the details."

"Any children for you, Brad?" the doctor asked him.

Jackie had her mental shields up, but something beyond
the walls enfolding her mind made her look sharply at the
lieutenant. His face was tight, his expression shuttered. "We
need to focus on our jobs."

Something about the topic of children, or something related to it, had upset him. Jackie found herself concurring
out of sympathy. "Yes, let's focus on our work, please. They
want us launching outsystem by the end of the week, and
Lars and I are still in need of practice on our training."

"Well, we'd be launching a lot sooner if *someone* hadn't
taken the first week off," Colvers said, his tone laced with a
pointed reprimand.

"I didn't take the week off. I was *working*," Jackie countered just as acerbically.

"Oh, sure, working on what? Handshakes and smiles all
around? Visiting every corner of the planet so your face
would be all the more well-known?" he prodded.

"I was working on an introductory presentation for any
peaceful, friendly aliens we encounter," she stated, struggling to keep at least half her attention on her console tests.

She still had a few subsystems to check, to make sure his tampering had been cleared out of the system.

"What, a song-and-dance routine? You think flashing your fat thighs will—"

Jaw clenched, Jackie unleashed her psi. The whole cockpit vanished around them, leaving them floating in space. Colvers swore, Ayinda yelped, and the doctor started muttering a prayer in Spanish, crossing herself. Robert twisted in his seat, looking all around at the star-strewn night enveloping them; he bumped into the holokinetically cloaked console and clung to it, hands clasped on apparently nothing, though something was obviously there.

". . . I like this," Lars murmured, his voice warm and his head nodding in appreciation as he peered around. "Can you do auroras, too? I love watching the aurora borealis, back home."

A whoosh of sound—she had an aptitude for sonokinesis, too, tied to her holokinetic ability—and the stars swirled, twisted, dove . . . and they appeared to arrow down toward a blue-white-green-brown marble that rushed toward them, swelling faster and faster.

"Okay . . . Okay, that's *enough*! Thank you!" Robert called out, clinging to his unseen console. "*Thank* you, Major."

Jackie halted the image and dissolved it with a faint tinkle of crystalline chimes. She rubbed at her forehead. It wasn't easy, blanketing the whole cockpit from their sight; so many angles of viewpoint to work with in such a confined space was far more difficult than it seemed. She had rushed the image of stars-to-planet because she hadn't wanted the flaws to be noticed by anyone.

Brad pulled himself around in his seat, glaring at Jackie. "Don't you *ever* do that again!"

"Behave professionally, *Lieutenant*," she countered, holding his gaze, glad she wasn't much of an empath. Just the look on his face was not pleasant; being hammered by his actual emotions would have been worse. "You keep pulling fat jokes out of the air, I am going to *alter* that air until you change your attitude. You will now take a twenty-minute break, Lieutenant Colvers. Do come back sooner, should you regain your composure and your professionalism."

He snarled under his breath as he exited, displeased at being ordered to leave. But he left, letting the hatch hiss shut behind him. If he had left without asking or receiving permission first, it would be seen as Dereliction of Duty, a serious accusation under Space Force law. If he had attacked her, which he looked like he was a handful of heartbeats from doing, that was an even worse offense. Brad would never thank her for it, but as a superior in his chain of command, by ordering him to take that break, she had saved his boots from being court-martialed.

Finished with her prayers, Maria crossed herself one more time, then said in a shaky voice, "It has just occurred to me that . . . that you could kill someone with that gift. Make them think a cliff is bigger than it is, make them walk into an open elevator shaft . . ."

"I am well aware of the difference between what I *can* do, Doctor, and what I *should* do. I pass each of my ethics exams with flying colors twice a year, like clockwork. Because I *am* ethical and moral," Jackie stated flatly. "And I recite every day, in the Oath of Service, that I will not use my powers, responsibilities, privileges, skills, or abilities to break the law. That would be breaking the law."

"But you are also a soldier, *mente bruja*," the doctor returned quietly. "And soldiers sometimes have to kill."

Jackie sucked in a breath. The nickname, *mind witch*, wasn't an insult, and wasn't meant as an insult. It was the rest of Maria's statement that disturbed her. Jackie punched at commands on her console, trying not to think too hard. She let out a hard breath a few moments later. ". . . I know. And the precogs are showing things where we may have to get in a fight. Myself included. Let's get back to work, shall we? Colvers messed with my consoles, so I want to do a sound-check test to make sure I've fixed everything. Doctor, would you be willing to go aft and check the rooms for the intercom system with me?"

"*Sí.*" Maria pulled herself free of her station.

"*Gracias,*" Jackie murmured.

CHAPTER 3

This was it. This was the moment prophesied. Heart pounding in terror, brow dripping sweat into his eyes, for a moment Li'eth seriously contemplated telling the priests to stuff their tomes and portents out an airlock. Mentally, not personally, since they were not here to yell at. For a moment, the weight of the laser in his hand was a tempting weight. The kind one applied to one's head.

The *T'un Tunn G'Deth* was not quiet in the last throes of its death. Claxons blared, sirens wailed, and through the ship's intercoms, his fellow soldiers could be heard screaming, either in defiance as they fought or in pain as they retreated, or in begging for someone to shoot them. Some of the monitors on the bridge still worked, most turned inward, showing the backwards-kneed, tentacle-armed monsters sweeping the other decks, shooting to maim and incapacitate rather than kill. Of the three that showed exterior shots, one showed a close-up of the enemy vessel latched onto their hull, and two showed debris drifting away from the far side of the ship. The last of the three also held a sliver of a view of the urine-yellow methane planet whose mining stations they had been trying to protect, and a view of more ships fighting in the distance.

Gravity fluctuated, making his stomach lurch with the unexpected loss-and-tug downward. The scanner tech, Ensign Gi'ol Chasa-nuq'ara, looked up and back at Li'eth, her blue eyes wide, her face pale and sickly beneath her gray spots. "Captain . . . the rest of the local fleet is . . . We're trapped. The Salik shot out the mail courier. Their homeworld fleet . . . they won't know we need . . . *needed* help for another three hours . . . half an hour to speed up, use faster-than-light, then . . . then slow down again . . ."

The Gatsugi home fleet would not be able to save them in time. Their enemy was almost to the bridge. The blast doors would slow them down for a little while, but not nearly long enough to hope for a rescue.

Li'eth swallowed. This was it. He opened his mouth to give the seemingly suicidal order to surrender—prophecy said that *some* of them would survive—but a *zzzap* and the smell of scorched flesh jerked every head of the crew toward the sound, and the sight, of a male body slumping sideways in his restraint harness.

"This is it, then," Leftenant Superior Dai'a Vres-yat muttered, eyes wide with horror at what the portside scan tech had done. She swallowed and looked down at the gun holstered on her thigh. "I . . . I guess . . . we only have . . . one choice left . . ."

Something *thumped* on the blast door sealing the bridge. Everyone froze. The console with the dead tech had a monitor showing the corridor leading to it, and the armored aliens contemplating how to get inside. The Salik were clever; they would figure out a way.

". . . *I* will surrender." That caused heads to whip around. Of the twelve remaining members of the crew on the bridge, eleven of them looked at their commanding officer. "I suggest you do, too."

"You're insane!" Leftenant Superior Shi'ol Nanu'oc hissed. "Do you *want* to be eaten alive?"

"No. But . . ." Drawing in a deep breath, he spoke firmly. "I have been holding a secret, passed to me from the highest levels of the Empire. I was informed that this ship, particularly its officers . . . will be involved in a prophecy."

"Oh, not that *damned* Sh'nai nonsense again!" V'kol dismissed, scowling at his friend and Captain. The leftenant superior turned away from his useless console, most of the gun emplacements on the ship long since damaged beyond any help.

"While there is life, there is *hope*," Li'eth asserted, holding his friend's gaze.

"*What* hope?" Shi'ol demanded. The image on the monitor for the corridor outside showed a large bulky weapon being brought forward. "I'm going to *die* on this ship, and one of my stupid cousins will get the title . . ."

"This ship's officers, *some* of its officers," Li'eth stressed, "will not only survive, but be rescued from the enemy's grasp by beings from the prophesied Motherworld. If they find us in that grasp, they will join with us and help us *defeat*—"

"*Taka taka taka,*" V'kol mocked bitterly, fingers and thumb flapping like a beak as he interrupted his commanding officer. "I am not inclined to throw my life away, but *neither* am I inclined to risk the high likelihood that I'll be *eaten alive*. Do you even know who *will* survive?"

Li'eth bit his lip. He couldn't say that *he* was destined to survive without the others demanding why. That was a secret he did not dare let out, lest he be hauled all the way to the Salik motherworld to be eaten, a fate that would more than likely throw off the prophecy of being rescued while still in space. At least he had applied a fresh layer of concealer to his cheek just this morning. With luck, the tough covering would not wear or peel off before he was rescued. If he was. "The legends say that five will survive. We know the Salik eat the officers last, saving them . . . us . . . for 'special' meals."

"You don't even know if this *is* that ship," the gunnery officer scoffed.

"If it is . . . then doesn't the *Book of Sh'nai* speak of the Motherworld having everything we need to defeat our enemies?" Ba'oul Des'n-yi asked. "If this is that ship—if *any* of our ships are that ship—then doesn't the hope of *one* of our ships being the one whose crew greets the beings of the Motherworld mean it's worth risking death by . . . by being eaten alive? If it means setting up everything so that the Salik *do* get stopped . . . then . . . then *I* will surrender, too. If the Captain will, I will. I'll take that risk."

Gi'ol swallowed, but nodded. "I will, too."

Shi'ol, seated on the far side of the room from the scanner tech, rolled her eyes. "Oh, why not . . . I'd hate to let the title fall into a collateral line if there's a chance I might survive . . . and if I tell them I'm a Countess as well as an officer, they might save *me* for last—if only so we can be in accordance with prophecy," the blonde added as the brown-haired weapons officer gave her a suspicious look. "I'll even kiss the feet of whoever gives us whatever it is we need to defeat the Salik."

Considering their logistics officer was rather proud of being the 373rd Countess S'Arrocan, and did not hesitate to wield her title in off-duty superiority over the mostly common-born crew, the idea of the arrogant woman kissing *anyone's* feet was a high concession on her part.

"I don't know if I can risk it," one of the other ensigns down at the front of the bridge said, her eyes wide, her voice tight with fear. "I'm not one of you . . . a-and my *jungen* isn't fancy, or . . . or special . . . They'll eat me alive."

It pained him to do it . . . but Li'eth unstrapped from his seat. The blast door *pinged* and cracked; the actual view of the door wasn't on camera, but it seemed they were using some sort of laser to burn their way through. Stepping down through the tiers to the ensign's station, he unholstered his laser and offered it to her. "Do what you feel you must, Ensign Kar-tal. As I will do what *I* must. This ship and her officers are involved. Some of us will die . . . but some will survive."

She took the weapon with trembling fingers, gaze locked on the weapon.

"If you are still alive when they cut through . . . drop your weapons and place your hands on your heads in surrender. Comply with everything they'll tell us to do . . . unless and until they come to eat you. *Then* you give them every last scrap of hell you can."

He paced back to his station, hoping he looked confident. Hoping he sounded calm. He didn't feel that way inside. Thirty-two years was not nearly a long enough life span. He did not want to die just because the Sh'nai prophecies might have been misinterpreted.

"Most likely . . . they'll just stick one of their stunner weapons inside, once they've bored a hole, and knock us all unconscious. A mercy, for not *having* to say, 'I surrender,'" he added grimly. "But while there is life, there is hope—too many of the Sh'nai prophecies *are* coming true, Leftenant Superior Kos'q," he added to V'kol, hearing the officer draw in a breath to protest. "Dislike the religion all you like, the words of the Immortal *have* guided us with palpable accuracy through the millennia. Misinterpreted, sometimes, but accurate when viewed in retrospect. The time of the return of the Motherworld *is* very near, and this is the ship that starts it.

"We just have to hold on to the hope that *some* of us will survive to see it all unfold." Reseating himself, he didn't bother to strap back into the restraints. The gravity weaves lurched again, their power source faltering. Giving up, Li'eth relatched the buckles, not wanting to injure himself before capture. The Salik tended to eat the injured ones first, along with the weakest, least-ranked, and least-interesting sentients.

JANUARY 14, 2287 C.E.
BARNARD'S STAR SYSTEM

The rushing, swaying, nauseating whirl of hyperspace whooshed silently back into normality. Clinging to the armrests of her chair, Jackie could not convince her fingers to let go. It was all she could do to keep her breakfast down, though from the way her body was screaming with hunger, the half sandwich she had eaten was long since gone from her stomach. Except it was still in her stomach, threatening to come back up. Hypersickness. She hadn't experienced it before, though she and Lars had been given a lengthy class lecture on what to expect of its effects and side effects. Jackie had additionally received advice on how to handle the psychic side effects.

Breathing hard, she focused her gaze firmly on the back of Maria's head, then on the back of Robert's head as he quickly checked off their arrival location with the help of his copilot and their navigator. Hands trembling, she pulled the nutrient pack from its clip on her console, brought the straw up to her lips, and pulled the valve open with her teeth, sucking at the sugary-salty-meaty stuff inside. At any other time, it would have tasted nasty, but her body craved it so much, the flavor seemed fantastic right now.

While the various proteins, electrolytes, and carbohydrates soothed her shaking hunger, Jackie focused on the numbers in her head. Facts and figures, ones she had memorized for this flight, as something solid to concentrate on instead of her stomach and her nerves and her trembling limbs.

Barnard's Star was considered an excellent test case for navigation calibration since it had a very concise movement pattern among the various stars surrounding the Sol System. Astrophysicists called it "proper motion." It moved at an apparent 142km per second, making it important to get the exit point aimed right when firing the "spark," the packet of strangely entangled energy that opened the hyperrift. It wasn't the fastest in near-Sol space; that honor went to Wolf 424, moving at 555km/s in relation to their home system, a measurable fraction of the speed of light, but Barnard's Star moved fast enough to make it a solid, accurate navigation test.

More urgent than that, however, was the need to brake quickly. Entering and exiting a hyperrift tunnel required moving at half Cee. Half the speed of light—150,000km/s. Fast enough to kill themselves on anything larger than a basketball, which was the limit the smallish ship's insystem thrusters could swerve out of its path as makeshift shields. It was important to slow down and ping the nearest hyperrelay unit . . . which was technically her job now, but which Robert had promised to handle for her while she recovered from her first taste of hypersickness. That ping would hand them the latest scans of the system's known objects.

"And . . . we are coming to a stop forty-six thousand klicks from the hyperrelay," Robert finally announced with satisfaction. "Delightfully close without any real risk to the probe."

"That's 46,143 klicks, give or take a kilometer in relative positioning," Ayinda corrected. "Lightspeed delay on both signal and pingback is negligible."

"Oh, so precise," the pilot mocked lightly. "But excellent piloting, yes? I always come out within a few planetary diameters of my goal."

"Yes, Robert, you win the bet," Ayinda singsonged. "I have to buy you a drink, next time we're on Leave."

"Shouldn't our *comm tech* be handling the navigation ping?" Colvers asked.

"It's her first trip through hyperspace, Brad. Lay off," Ayinda told him.

"Is that an order, sir?"

"Do you want me to inform the major, here, just how many trips it took you before you stopped heaving your boots up?" Robert countered. He didn't mention that Jackie technically had not heaved yet. They'd all know if she had.

Brad kept his mouth shut.

"Ignore them, you two. How are you doing, back there?" Maria asked, craning her neck to look behind her. "Lars? Jackie?"

"I'm surprised you're not feeling ill," Jackie muttered, grateful her nausea was fading.

"I've been through hyperspace five times now, but just to Alpha Centauri and back. A, to be precise. Didn't get close to Proxima B, but the view was nice," Maria confessed.

"My stomach is okay, but . . . I am having troubles with my . . . other end," Lars confessed, sounding miserable. "Is it safe to move about the ship?"

"I am not cleaning up *that* mess," Ayinda muttered. "Commander?"

"It is indeed safe to move about the cabin," their chief pilot stated. "We'll be here for an hour, taking measurements and calibrating for the return trip. Hey, Jackie? How are you feeling?"

"This sludge is still tasting good, but it's calming my nausea," she confessed, grimacing between swallows. "How much of the bag does one have to suck down before it starts to taste bad?"

"Usually about half," Maria told her. "The first time, you'll want to drink a little more, and when you string several jumps, the whole bag after the first two, no matter what it tastes like. Brad, you should be sucking, too. And *you*, Roberto. I am not treating you for hypersickness. You are adults, not children. I do not heal stupid, so start drinking."

"Yes, ma'am," Robert agreed

"Aye aye, Doctor," Brad added.

"And *don't* sass me," Maria warned them.

"No, ma'am," both men said in unison.

Jackie and Ayinda both slurped on their straws, exchanging brief looks and silent shrugs. Her bedside manner was not the absolute best, but at least Dr. de la Santoya was conscientious about her work.

"Jackie, how are you feeling psychically?" Maria asked next.

Swallowing her current mouthful—the nutrient juice was starting to taste a bit odd—Jackie tested her mental walls. "I'm centered and grounded just fine. I was warned not to 'anchor' myself when entering a hyperrift, so I didn't get super-nauseated or a reaction headache from that."

"Anchor?" Robert asked over his shoulder.

"It's some mumbo jumbo about sinking mental claws into the world around you," Colvers dismissed, sounding bitter. "Do we *have* to listen to this? Can't you go back to the crew quarters?"

"My *job* is to monitor the automatic chatter between the ship and the local hyperrelay hub," Jackie said. "Which I am doing, now that I'm used to my first OTL trip. The connection is holding steady, if a bit on the low side for signal strength, and the latency is minimal, with no signal delay, not even all the way back to Earth. There are also twenty-one ships on assignment at the moment, linking with forty-one hubs. The TUPSF *Aloha 9*," she added, meaning their own ship, since there were currently thirty-five active in the fleet of this particular type, with more being added each week as they came off the assembly lines back home, "is currently linked into the network with . . . twelve channels out of twenty.

"Current scanner data from the Barnard System are transmitting on five more, with three in the clear. Stress testing in . . . ten seconds." She sipped at the pouch, grimaced at the taste, and clipped it back to her console. Tapping in a couple of commands, she sent a pulse of data packets through the system, and waited for the various ships and *MacArthur* Station scattered through the network to receive and send it back. ". . . Ping . . . and pingback, round trip to the farthest was 4.31 seconds."

"Good, now how about giving us a telepathic pingback?" Maria asked.

Jackie stilled, her eyes flicking to the copilot. Colvers looked rather stiff and unmoving. She returned her gaze to the woman seated at the station in front of hers. "That would depend on what you mean. Do you mean contacting one of you specifically? With permission, of course . . . Or did you mean lowering my mental walls to try to get a general sense of the minds currently within range?"

"You are *not* touching my mind, you modofrodo!" Colvers snapped, his shout overwhelming the modest confines of the cockpit. "You touch my mind, and I will *kill* you!"

"Lieutenant Colvers, *stand down*!" Robert shouted back, while the others gaped, stunned at his outburst. "Stand. Down! You do *not* threaten an officer of the Space Force—and you *certainly* do not use language like that. I will overlook this incident *once*, but *not* a second time. Do you hear me, soldier?"

Brad muttered something.

"I didn't hear *you*, Lieutenant. Did *you* hear *me*?" the Texan demanded.

"Message received, Commander," Colvers growled. Audibly this time.

"*. . . And?*" When his copilot said nothing, Commander Graves stared hard at the junior officer. "You owe Major MacKenzie an apology for threatening her life. Not a fake one, nor an insincere one. A *real* one."

He didn't face her, but Jackie could see just enough of his face to notice the way his muscles flexed in his jaw, clenching his teeth for a moment. A deep breath allowed him to speak. "I apologize for threatening you, Major MacKenzie."

She didn't verbally accept it. "Whatever your problem with me may appear to be, Lieutenant Colvers, you are going to have to air it politely very soon, and find a way to get past it. I would like to say that I would never touch your mind, particularly with said attitude problem running rampant through your thoughts . . . but the truth of the matter is, *if* the precognitives are correct, and *if* we do contact friendly, sentient, alien lifeforms . . . then at some point, I am going to have to learn their language, and transfer that language to the rest of this crew.

"That will require prolonged mental contact between you and me, should you wish to remain a member of this crew. Think *carefully*, Lieutenant," Jackie added. "Think about *why* you want to be on this ship, engaged in these missions. Precognitive placement or no, if you continue down this path of resentment, anger, bitterness, and blindly judging me for perceived crimes I personally have never committed against you, I will remove your presence from these missions. I may even have to involve the legal division of the Space Force. Believe me or not, but I would rather not have to do any of that.

"Now . . . *why* do you have to be on board this ship, Lieutenant? Convince me of that, and remind *yourself* of why it's important for you to get along with everyone on board. Including me," Jackie said, watching the back of his head, the set of his shoulders, the tension in his arm. The rest of him was too hard to see at her current angle. "Feel free to speak honestly. Just do it politely."

"This is *my* ship. I crewed it for *months* before you came along!" Brad snapped, resentment laced throughout his dark tone. "We might not be the first crew, but we are among the first, and should be honored and respected and treated properly by everyone around us. But in *you* come, with your mind tricks and your fake dreams of what's supposed to be, reading our thoughts behind our back, *lying* to us, snickering and plotting and—"

"Whoa!" Ayinda asserted, holding up her hand. She reached around his seat and poked him in the shoulder. "She has *not once* lied to us. I think *you* are mistaking her for someone else, soldier. So you are going to sit there and tell us who *really* pissed you off—and it *isn't* Major MacKenzie."

"I will not!"

"That's an order, Brad," Robert told him. "From me. An order from your commanding officer."

"One moment . . . before you answer that . . ." Jackie felt bad that he was being forced to confess . . . but the issue did need to be discussed. She checked her console, pressed several commands into the system, then nodded. "Okay. Everything but the black box has now been shut off. This is officially off the record. Go ahead, Lieutenant. Get it out into the open. *All* of it, if you please."

He sat silently for so long, Lars came back. The Finn drew in a breath to ask a question. Quickly holding up her hand, she whispered in Finnish, *"Keep quiet and let the copilot speak."*

Colvers seemed irritated by the geophysicist's return . . . but after another thirty or forty seconds, once Lars had settled in place, he finally spoke. "I was engaged. To a psi. Alicia Fawkes. She was a civilian consultant to the Space Force Navy. And the bitch booted me out the door because *I* wasn't one. She married some mental freak she worked with, named Wyzer Beekins—who the frag names their kid *Wyzer Beekins*? Wyzer, with a

W Y Z, as if there's something oh-so-special about weird name spellings . . ."

"It's not a usual name, I'll admit," Robert offered lightly. "But as far as points go, a lot of people have relationships that e—"

Brad interrupted him. "My *point* is, telepaths are deceitful modos! If she starts working with any aliens, she'll turn on us and betray us to them, peaceful or otherwise," he asserted, slashing his hand through the air, before clenching it in a fist. "They'll have something she wants, and she'll want it so bad, she'll turn on us and cast us out of the ship, out of the fame, out of the spotlight, out of everything *we* worked hard for, while dragging *her* deadweight boots in our wake."

Gesturing in the weightless depths of space made him shift in his harness in counterpoint. Brad grabbed at his straps to steady himself, then looked away, out at the stars beyond the cockpit windows. If one ignored the panel-screen projections forming the heads-up displays for piloting and targeting, and the shimmering effects of the insystem-thruster field, sheltering their vessel from impacts with tiny objects, it was a pleasant enough view. He wasn't the only one who looked out the viewports, but Jackie doubted he was actually *seeing* anything out there.

Their tactical displays were still projecting things like relative speed in relation to the local star, which itself was traveling fast through the night. Near-space objects within a few hundred thousand kilometers were ringed with color-coded outlines, and approximate locations for objects farther out were circles and boxes and triangles on the screens with lines pointing between them and their text-based labels. The displays of those distant celestial bodies flickered and jumped from time to time as the incoming lightwave readings allowed the navicomp to update its projections more accurately.

But beyond all of that . . . the night sky was stark, spangled with pinpricks of light that neither shifted color nor twinkled, thanks to the lack of an atmosphere outside. They shimmered a little, the pinpricks turning briefly fuzzy as the fields brushed aside stellar dust. Jackie found it soothing, even if the lack of minds beyond this one small cabin was frighteningly blank to her inner senses. From the way Colvers seemed to be calming down, the one hand in view no longer fisted, it was a tiny point of similarity between the two of them . . . so maybe he was seeing the view rather than whatever uncomfortable memories were trapped in his head.

"You do realize that Jacaranda MacKenzie is not this Alicia Fawkes, right?" Robert finally asked his copilot.

"I *know* that. But she's still one of *them*," he added fiercely. "She'll ditch us for someone . . . some *thing* shiny and new, and we'll be left in her dust, and off the team, and our lives in ruins!"

"The only way any of us could get kicked off this team, *Brad*," Maria stated bluntly, "is for one of us to do exactly what you are doing. Acting *loco* and causing problems. Like you *already are*."

"You are a good pilot, Brad, and a good mechanic. But I have to agree; you are indeed acting *loco* in how you're handling all of this," Ayinda asserted.

He twisted in his seat to peer at the navigator, then narrowed his eyes, looking beyond her dark features to the pallid face of the geophysicist. "I suppose *you* have something to add to this?"

"Me? No . . . I'm too lazy to dig holes that don't need digging," Lars added lightly.

The lieutenant blushed, then twisted the other way, peering at Jackie. "And *you*? Do *you* have something to say to me?"

"Yes. I will reassure you right here and now that I will never boot you out of a relationship with me, Brad Colvers," Jackie stated calmly. "Because I will never *be* in a relationship with you."

"Why, because I'm an anti-psychic *bigot*?" he challenged her. At least he had the grace to admit it.

"Considering that when I merely *touch* someone, I am so strong a telepath, I have to actively block out whatever they're thinking . . . yes, that *is* one reason. But it isn't the biggest reason," Jackie told him. "Even if you weren't a psi-hating bigot, I simply have no interest in being romantic with anyone at this point in my life."

"So, what, you're an asexual freak?" Brad asked, tossing the hateful words over his shoulder like verbal garbage. Ayinda reached over the back of his seat cushioning to smack him in a glancing blow along his buzz-cut scalp, muttering something about sticking to only one source of bigotry at a time.

"No, I enjoy sex," Jackie defended herself, ignoring their byplay. She skipped over the information where lovemaking could get derailed very quickly for her if her partner started thinking about the proverbial grocery list, or cracks in the ceiling, or whatever nonpassionate things might cross their minds mid love play. Even cuddling came with risks of reading a stray, disturbing thought. Most people just weren't practiced at watching their thoughts and shielding them from being picked up while touching someone else. "I'm just not interested in dating anyone at this point."

"How can you not be interested in dating anyone?" Lars asked her. "I am Finnish, and the Finnish people are almost the worst when it comes to asking people on dates, but even we manage it. Sometimes."

"Between five years in the military—where you don't sleep with anyone you work with," she added pointedly, "unless you want to get slapped with a Fraternization charge and thrown in the stockade—and five years of hopping from island to island as a government translator, more at home in hotel room after hotel room than an actual apartment or home, plus five years on top of *that* of pouring all of my energy and attention into being a good representative for Oceania . . . *when* would I have had the time or energy to date anyone? Everyone I was meeting was a coworker, a client, or a constituent, and I saw no point in ever trying to date one of those.

"As for the nonmilitary, nongovernment side of things . . . My eldest sister Hyacinth has already had her and her husband's allotted two children, so she is able to successfully distract our mother from demanding grandchildren from our brother and me. So all of that is covered," she stated firmly, sweeping her hand. Like Brad, the weightlessness of the ship made her body shift slightly to the left when her hand slashed to the right. She compensated with old, remembered skill, bracing herself by shifting shoulders and flexing thighs against the harness straps and the chair cushions. "Of course this doesn't deny the fact that I would *like* to date someone . . . but trust me, Lieutenant, it will never be *you*. Thus you can rest easy knowing that I will never dump you for someone named Wyzer Beeker."

"Wyzer *Beekins*," he corrected, rubbing at the bridge of his nose.

"Well, on that one point, you and I do agree; it's a *very* odd name," Jackie said. "I'm sorry your fiancée booted you, but as the Commander was no doubt going to say, a *lot* of people get booted out of relationships around the world. It isn't something new, it isn't going to stop happening, and it doesn't happen simply and solely because of psychic abilities, *or* a lack thereof. She could have just as easily dumped you because she loves cats and you hate them."

"I don't hate cats."

"It was merely an example, Colvers." Jackie checked her boards, then glanced his way again. It was far easier for her to look at him than the reverse, and he was still rubbing the spot where his brow met his nose, as far as she could tell. "For the record, I don't hate you. I don't even hate you for hating me so stupidly and needlessly. But neither do I care about you, save as a member of this team. A *functioning* member, which means no more fat jokes, no more kicking your boots at my abilities, and no more comparing me unfavorably to someone I am not and will never be.

"I am *offended* that you suggested I would ever betray the United Planets, but I do not hate you. Now. Take in a deep breath, let it out, and think of me as a fellow Human being. As a fellow functional member of this team. Or at the very least, a walking, talking communications antenna if you must dehumanize me in any way. Work with me, not against me, Lieutenant Colvers. Can you do that much? Because I really do not want to *have* to remind you that there are over one hundred active pilots in the OTL program besides yourself, with no doubt five hundred more sitting on a standby list . . . but only *one* major xenopath suitable for First Contact situations on both the civilian and military fronts."

Brad mumbled something. Seated to his left, Robert cupped his hand behind his ear, float-leaning closer. Or trying to; their chief pilot shifted oddly in his seat from the action-reaction of their weightless environment. His copilot muttered again, this time loud enough to be heard.

"Fine. I'll *try* to treat you like a functional member of the team."

"Thank you, Lieutenant. I'll return you the same courtesy. As for working with any alien races, that *will* be my job, literally finding ways to work peacefully with them, not against them . . . but I will never betray my fellow Humans. I am Human, they are not, and that is that. Now, if we're all settled, I'm bringing the cockpit recorder back online," Jackie added in warning. "I'll have to file an explanation why I turned it off, but I do believe fervently in mental privacy. Including protecting yours."

Maria twisted in her seat to look back at Jackie. "Okay, now that everything *is* settled? Can you please follow through on your required psychic tests so that I can check them off of my list? It's a small list of things to do, but I *am* taking my job seriously."

"She is *not*—"

"Lieutenant," Jackie interrupted him. "I am simply going to do a general sweep. I have a twenty-two-year record of spotless ethics versus efficiency, the last fifteen of which has been spent under close military and government scrutiny. As the Psi League says, what was yours will *remain* yours." Hearing a mutter under his breath, Jackie rolled her eyes. "Seriously, Brad, if you'd stop to *think* about it, you'd realize any sane person—and I do qualify—would be extremely reluctant to touch the thoughts of someone as heavily bigoted as you. And I *am* reluctant. So this will just be a passive general scan for sentient thoughts within my mental range."

"Fine. But if you read my thoughts . . ."

"If you would calm yourself and stop thinking so *loudly*, so impassioned and forceful with your hatred and pain amplifying everything, then the details will not register in my telepathic sweep. Mind your own thoughts, Colvers, and I'll attend to mine. I also suggest you sign up for a course in general psychic meditation, of grounding, centering, and *shielding* when we get back. *Any* Human can do that much with practice, and thus block out general scans and accidental eavesdropping—after all, if you don't learn to talk *quietly*, of course someone is going to overhear you shouting every single word. Even if we *don't* want to overhear it. Now, be quiet, calm your thoughts, and let me do my job. Professionally."

He subsided. His fingers were fisted again, save for the last two, which gripped his armrest to keep his arm from floating randomly in its half-tensed state, but Lieutenant Colvers said nothing more.

"Right, then. Everyone, just calm your minds, and ... think about vegetables. Like what is a rutabaga, or rhubarb, or the differences between zucchini versus summer squash. Carrots versus yams. Anything boring and food-based, so I can sort out your thoughts from any others that might be near."

That got a snort out of the lieutenant. "Any others that might be *near*?"

"I'm a Rank 15, Colvers. The last time I was in the military, I could trance while sitting in a station in orbit around Jupiter, and while focusing in a particular direction, I could hear the cargo-ship crews as they flew in from the Kuiper belt as soon as they crossed Uranus' orbit. Be very glad I have very tight mental shields, and a strong aversion to touching anyone's mind accidentally outside of the needs of a moment like this. Learn to control your own thoughts, to shield them with discipline, and you'll be that much more safe.

"Think firmly about food for the next few minutes, to ensure I don't overhear anything else," she finished.

Quiet filled the cockpit. Not silence; the thrum of the engines powering the insystem-thruster fields and the subtle whoosh of the air recyclers prevented absolute silence. But quiet followed her words. Satisfied after half a minute that they were complying, Jackie drew in a deep breath, pictured clenching her irritation at Colvers in her hands, pictured herself opening those hands and releasing all such negativity, and exhaled as she did so.

In with the good air, out with the bad air, as the ancient saying goes. Draw in the positive energies—or neutral, at the very least—and expel all the harmful ones. Third breath ... center my scattered bits of psyche ... blend and accept ... blend and rinse clean ... blend and make smooth and whole ... A fifth round usually wasn't necessary, but Jackie didn't feel centered until the sixth inhale-exhale round of visualizations.

When she did feel that inner *bump* that ended with a sense of smooth inner calm filling her whole body, she realized just how off-center Brad had thrown her with his shouting and his hatred and his spurious death threat. Setting all of that carefully aside, she unfurled her layers of mental shielding. Each mind came into reach slowly as she allowed her shields to open up first in this direction but only so far, then in that direction a little bit more, like uncurling first her right arm partway, then her left. Each time she found and identified someone else, she unfurled a bit more.

Lars was thinking about rye crisps, rather than the vegetables suggested, and picturing which cheeses to pair them with. Ayinda was longing for a sandwich loaded with slices of crisp vegetables and alfalfa sprouts. Maria was thinking firmly about the dry, unleavened taste of a communion wafer paired with the bitter tannins and rich flavonoids of red communion wine. Of course, they were all stuck with thick gloppy things in pouches until they got back to a gravity-style environment where crumbs wouldn't be a free-floating threat to control consoles and more, but they could think about such things.

Robert's food thoughts were filled with spicy corn chips smothered in equally spiced meat, salsa, guacamole . . . she moved on from his thoughts, ignoring the way her stomach rumbled with hunger. There was a food pack in the galley storage cupboards which approximated the meat and vegetables found in a nacho dish, but it just wasn't the same without any fresh-made chips to dip. And Colvers . . . was thinking about bread. White bread, its bubbles, its softness, turning it over and over in his mind—the bread collapsed, smashed into a lump in his mental fist. A deep breath, and he started again. A loaf of bread. A slice of bread . . .

Blocking out that, too, now that each of their minds were identified, Jackie cast her thoughts outward. First in a general sphere that swelled silently, invisibly around them. It took very little inner energy, but it did take a great deal of concentration. At around a total radius of twenty kilometers, forty klicks in diameter, she could barely sense the others, but she had every centimeter of that span covered. Far enough to have brushed another space station had they been in orbit, or another ship traveling in relatively close formation.

But that was a full sensing, not a patrol-style sweep. Twenty klicks was her limit. Jackie had to bring her mind back, retracting slowly, not wanting to strain her mental muscles as it were. If there had been more than the six of them, or if anyone had been out there at the fifteen-klick mark, she might not have been able to reach even to the eighteen mark without extra effort, particularly if that spurious extra mind was noisy with loud, strong, unpredictable thoughts.

Instead, she switched to a cone-like arc of mental focus, expanding her range considerably. Dead ahead in stellar navigation terms was always zero by zero. She swept to her right, going around the compass, mind stretching out for hundreds of kilometers, coming around back to 359 by 359 and then to her starting point, then she swept up, back, down, and around. Nothing. An angular sweep down to her right, up around to her left and back to center was also clean. Sweeping down and left, up around to the right—she snagged on something.

Eyes snapping open, she stared sightlessly at the back of the doctor's chair while she sorted out the . . . half dozen Human minds. Two pilots, two navigators, a medic, and a planetary scientist—military, not civilian, but still a scientist.

"Ullupi Hadrismattar," she murmured.

"What?" Ayinda asked her.

"Captain . . . Ullupi Hadrismattar, Space Force Army," Jackie repeated, latching onto that name and that rank. She could almost see the silver bars and the name tag on the other woman's green-hued uniform, her clairvoyancy riding bootstrapped to her telepathy. "Which ship are they on?"

"Uhh . . . the *Aloha 25?*" Lars offered. "She is a good geophysicist, and a good colleague. Why do you ask that?"

Shaking off her focus, Jackie called up the data on the *Aloha 25*. Nothing. Trying one number higher, she discovered it was the *Aloha 26* that had that particular captain on board. "Pinging the *Aloha 26* . . ."

Pingback came very quickly, traversing hyperrelay channels.

"This is the TUPSF Aloha 26. What is your query, Aloha 9?" a smooth male voice asked. That would be the copilot, Lieutenant First Class Kiril Leonidovich.

"No query, Aloha 26, just a 'hello and welcome to Barnard's Star' from the 9," she replied. *"You're estimated to be roughly off our starboard bow at the . . . 337 by 39, by about three*

*thousand klicks. Let me know when your navicomp has our po-
sition and speed pinged, please, and what the results are."*

A pause, and the reply came back, *"Navicomp has you
pegged at . . . 3,447 kilometers as of a quarter second ago,
on our 243 by 237; we are free of your heading by 252 kilometers and rapidly widening . . . Commander Jjorge wants
to know, how did you know we were here?"*

*"I was scanning your direction—Major Jackie MacKen-
zie, Psi Division. What was yours is still yours,"* she added
politely, formally. *"We're just doing a shakedown cruise of
the new crew configuration, which includes giving me a
taste of non–Sol System aethers."*

*"Well then, welcome to Barnard's Star, Major. We'll just
be arcing around your position to point us home; we're inbound with a glitch in our refrigeration system, of all things.
Half the food packs are frozen."*

*"Sorry to hear that. Have fun chatting with the repair
squads, 26,"* Jackie told him. *"We'll be home in . . . 7 hours
28 minutes, if all goes well. Aloha 9 out."*

"Hopefully it will. Aloha 26 out."

"You actually picked up their thoughts at nearly three and a
half thousand kilometers away?" Colvers asked her, skeptical.

"A name and a vision of a name tag on a dull green uniform shirt, with captain's tracks on the collar point above it,"
Jackie confirmed. "The more minds there are in an area, the
more my distance gets foreshortened. It's like trying to hear
someone speaking at the far end of an athletic field. The
more people that are talking between you and them, the less
clearly you can hear them. When you're buried in a whole
crowd at your end, you cannot hear them at all, just the
people immediately around you."

Ayinda looked over her shoulder, her expression sympathetic. "You must hate really big cities, then."

"On Earth, I have to limit my range very severely to avoid
being overwhelmed. In deep space, I can reach pretty far,
though there does come a point in the territory covered where
I lose track of my own body, and I tend to have to consider
that my limit."

"Ugh, do we have to hear the lectures on how it all works?"
she heard the lieutenant mutter.

"You did ask. Plus, knowing what I can or cannot do may one day save our lives," Jackie said. "But just to reassure you, I am done 'lecturing' for now. Everyone and everything appears normal, including me."

"Good," Maria stated. "Any headaches, dizziness, or pains from overextending yourself?"

"None."

"Then let's get under way to our next destination. Roberto?"

Their chief pilot nodded and started murmuring directions to his copilot and their astronavigator.

Breathing deeply, Jackie finished her sweep and extended her focus in the general direction of the other ship, whose flight path was being tracked on one of her secondary screens. She aimed ahead by a few degrees, to compensate for the lightwave lag between what her ship's sensors saw and what the other ship was actually doing, and picked up a sense of the crew's reluctance to cease their mission mixed with anticipation of being able to relax while the repairs were being made. Plus a bit of speculation on whether or not they'd be assigned to one of the spare ships . . .

Playing with relativistic speeds was fun. Playing telepathically at relativistic speeds was a subject not quite as fun, for the Psi League and Witan Orders both agreed that it was better to hedge on how telepathy and such seemed to be slightly faster than light itself—for which, the reasons were still unknown—than to reveal to the nongifted that they could detect things which science's many instruments could not.

After all, it had taken the psychic community centuries to develop machines which *could* sense genuine psychic energy, dubbed kinetic inergy for how it didn't obey the usual electromagnetic rules, or even occupy the same frequencies and amplitudes. Science finally could verify genuine psi powers, separating the actual psis from the deluded or the conniving, but there were still far too many mysteries to say they completely understood it.

And people like Brad Colvers often chose to hate the things they did not have and could not understand.

CHAPTER 4

Naked. Constantly on display for their captors like a meat animal waiting to be selected and butchered. Exactly like a meat animal waiting to be selected and butchered. Li'eth knew he was going to have nightmares about this for years to come if he survived.

If.

They had come for Ensign Gi'ol Chasa-nuq'ara, today. She had given Li'eth a stricken look as they stopped at her cage, just across the aisle and down two spots from his own. Seconds later, Gi'ol had slumped to the bare metal floor when stunned with the flash-*pzzzt* of the enemy's nonlethal weaponry. She would wake up before the end, however. They would make sure she was awake long before the end.

The Enemy had two goals in life, after all: galactic conquest, and lunch . . . preferably still kicking, screaming, and begging for mercy.

Coming for one of the officers, though . . . that meant there were no more enlisted prisoners on board. As he'd thought they might, the laser-wielding Salik had drilled a hole through the bridge blast doors, shoved through a couple of their nefarious stunner grenades, and plugged the hole quickly, letting the grenades knock everyone out. The Captain of the *T'un Tunn G'Deth* and his bridge officers had awakened an unknown while later, trapped in the prey cages of their enemies.

They woke stripped of all weapons, clothes, and tools, of course. Nothing that could be used for either an escape attempt or an easy suicide. No recessed or glazed lights inside the cage, just the orange glow of the lamps built into the walls over each cell, so there was no way to break the covers and use a sharp shard to slash one's wrists. In fact, the cages themselves held little more than the hard floor for a bed, with a matching flat ceiling and side walls, the latter enclosed to ensure no prisoner could reach through the bars and throttle a fellow captive in a much more merciful death than what actually awaited them.

On the one wall with bars, a dispenser had been bolted to them with a soft straw for drinking water—too soft and floppy to impale oneself upon, too short to wrap around the neck for strangulation—and a shallow metal dish with a very rounded rim next to it for holding their food. The last item, a flush basin for biological waste, sat at the far end of the rectangular cage from it. There was enough room in the cages to stretch out with a little bit more to spare, if one didn't mind putting either head or feet beneath the basin, and very little headroom. Li'eth's hair just brushed the roof of his cage when he fluffed it up; V'kol, at a thumbwidth taller, would have to be careful when pacing to avoid hitting his head with each subtle bounce in his stride.

The low ceiling, Li'eth knew, was designed to intimidate the Salik themselves. Roughly the same height as a V'Dan, their eyes sat on bulgy, short, thick stalks that aimed a little more upward than most sentient races, allowing them to swivel and look around in a rather wide field of view. Their backwards-jointed legs and flipper-feet meant that their stride was very bouncy on the ground. Salik prisoners—they ate their own kind, not just other races like the V'Dan— would be faced with smashing their eyes on that ceiling if they weren't careful, a bit of psychological and mild physical torture piled on top of all the rest.

A bit of amusement for the enemy, tormenting their sentient prey. Mind games. Predinner show, because there were visual sensors all down the long row of cages in this particular cargo hold.

The central aisle didn't have a low ceiling; the space over their heads contained storage cabinets. Sometimes, crew members would come down the aisle, smacking their broad, flat lips in *pwok-pwok* noises meant to remind their sentient cargo that they were going to be eaten soon, and grab whatever it was they needed or put something back. Sometimes they slapped the bars with their tentacle hands, their peculiar bouncy gait bounding a little higher with each step while they strutted past, whenever they moved unburdened.

Sitting there with his back against the rear wall, arms wrapped around his knees, Li'eth hated the waiting and waiting while the remnants of his crew were whittled down, bit by bit. He studied his naked, lightning-striped limbs, and contemplated the most unique difference of the amphibious enemy.

Salik arms were unique among sentientkind. They had an upper arm bone, but it was thicker than usual to support their unusual musculature. At the elbow joint, rather than starting a new bone, evolution had given them tentacles. There were two points where each arm split; the one at the elbow was called the macrojunction. Halfway down from that, each tentacle split in half again at the microjuncture, leaving them with four tapered, curling limbs.

Instead of fingers, they had suckers . . . and they used that uniqueness to guard their various controls. Some needed to be pushed, but most of those found on a military ship required suction to lift them up, a safety feature that no other race could get past without mechanical aid. Certainly, every last prisoner cell was operated by suction-touch, not by pressing any buttons. Same with the doors, same with the lifts . . .

Escape without help was near impossible. A rescue even with prophesied aid would be very difficult. And while he chose to believe the Sh'nai writings that spoke prophetically of this time, this place . . . Li'eth was finding it harder and harder to believe he *would* be rescued.

It did not help that he had no way to protect himself from the residual fears and despairs of the previous inhabitants of his cell. Object-reading was not common among the Sh'nai faithful, but it wasn't entirely unique either, for those who had holy gifts. His ability to sense the previous occupants' thoughts, emotions, even their physical actions—mostly pacing or trying to concuss themselves on the bars—wasn't a pleasant experience. The least tainted place was this back edge, but not the corners. Too many frightened, forsaken souls had huddled and wept in the corners. The middle of the wall was safer.

As for his other abilities, his very minor, erratic fire-calling ability was of no use; despite trying and trying, he couldn't even summon up a tiny spark. He could make the warm, heavily humid air seem a little cooler, but that only made his body feel clammier when the moisture in the air condensed on his skin . . . and it, too, was sporadic. His ability to heal with a simple touch was of no use, either; it was as difficult to control as his fire-calling under the best conditions, and he doubted it could handle something as horrifically damaging as being bitten and chewed to death by the sharp teeth of his captors.

He couldn't even read their minds. *That* would have been useful because he could have gained tactical knowledge that could be analyzed once rescued. If rescued. But the Saints had not gifted him with that particular power. Li'eth had never been able to glimpse the thoughts of the other Alliance races, just his fellow V'Dan.

Of course, if he could have read others' thoughts, he would have been assigned to a diplomatic career long ago, not a military one. Reading the auras of those around him . . . that one had almost sent him into a diplomatic career. It should have if the war hadn't happened, hadn't extended his military career. He could do it fairly well, but it was useless right now. His fellow captives were muddy and dull with fear and despair, and their captors were exuberantly bright with sadistic joy and smug superiority. Any two-credit xenopsychologist could have guessed as much.

Noises echoed down the corridor, the measured slap-slap of booted flipper-feet.

V'Dan toes were short and pointed forward, extending as individual digits with no webbing to speak of. Salik toes were long, pointed backwards, and came with stiff but still flexible webbing, since as a species, Saliks were designed to spend the first five years or so of their lives in water, learning how to hunt. Backwards-pointing feet were meant to ensure they could also travel easily on land to hunt dry prey, with powerful leg muscles that could leap up and slam down onto an opponent. They were at a disadvantage on ships designed for V'Dan and Solaricans and more, and preferred open combat. Unfortunately, Li'eth and the others were already captured and caged.

It was too soon for another victim to be selected. Too

soon for the guards to come by with the porridge-glop that they served as prison food. Grain-based, thank the High One. Nothing meat-based, and nothing too stiff to choke on. He supposed it might be possible to drown in the stuff, but he was not yet despondent enou—

"By the Saints!"

Startled, Li'eth rose to his feet, approaching the bars warily. Others in this wing of the prey cargo hold either rushed to their cage fronts to look or shrank back as far as they could get, covering their eyes. One of the men who was looking screamed, stumbling back. It sounded like one of the leftenants superior from the engineering section of the ship. Another cursed, while a third officer heaved up the contents of her stomach. Underneath it, he heard the thump, thump, thump of flesh striking bars . . . but it was a little stiffer than a tentacle should sound. Nor did it have any of the faint sounds of suckers smashed against the bars, pulling and popping as they released.

As the Salik came into view, Li'eth noted the marks on the alien's uniform. It was the captain of the ship. He came down every so often to psychologically torment his captives, and Li'eth supposed this visit was perhaps a little overdue. So when he looked at the object striking the bars of his own cage as it, too, came into view . . . he flinched. He didn't scream, didn't cry out, and didn't vomit, though it was a close thing for all three, but Li'eth did flinch.

Two of the alien's microjuncture tendrils were wrapped around Gi'ol's bloodless right arm. It had to be hers; Li'eth recognized the gray *jungen* spots, particularly the one on the base knuckle of her thumb—*Its thumb,* he quickly corrected himself. *Its thumb. The thumb, the arm, it, thing, no gender, nonliving object, just a* thing, *nothing to focus on, no sense of identity, Saints dammit . . .*

The captain bared his teeth in a predator's smirk, his wide, fleshy lips bending with rubbery grace, his nostril flaps whistling slightly with each inhale. "Tassty bridge crew, Captainn," the Salik offered. He lifted the arm, eyed the fingers, and bit one off in front of Li'eth. "A bit dead now, but . . . no matter. We'll eat another one sssoon."

"Choke on it and die."

"I thought you *liked* our visssits. Our . . . chats," the alien offered, still grinning. Li'eth focused firmly on those stubby eyestalks, and not on the bits of flesh caught in those teeth. "Would you like to be eaten next?"

"Tell me something *interesting*, plant-hunter," Li'eth countered, dredging up his courage with the insult. His faith. "I know you only *think* you're going to eat me."

"You thhhink you will esscape?" the captain countered, swiveling both eyes to look at him. The Salik tore off another finger and chewed thoughtfully, powerful hind molars cracking through the bones before swallowing it all. "Will you?"

Don't think. Don't think. He stared down the Salik's nearest eye. "I'd slow down on eating us, if I were you. That is, if you want to live a few extra days."

"*Shh-nakh'whsh,*" the officer snorted, nostril-flaps working. Like the K'Katta, they spoke a language type that no one else could duplicate among the known races. Unlike the K'Katta, they could still master Imperial V'Dan, the trade tongue of the Alliance. In fact, they were quite good at the glottal stops compared to the others, though as a species, they lingered a bit on certain consonant sounds. "You know nothing."

"I know prophecy," Li'eth muttered, trying not to think about how much poor Ensign Gi'ol must have suffered, being eaten alive one and two and five bites at a time, depending on how many were given the honor of devouring live, sentient meat. "You will die. All of you will die, in due time."

The captain snorted again, ate another bite . . . then slapped the ragged remains of the hand against the bars of Li'eth's cell as he turned and walked away. There wasn't much left in the way of liquid blood in the . . . thing, but a few brownish clots broke free, spattering on the bars and staining the floor.

Li'eth closed his eyes and resolved not to stretch out anytime soon. *This is for the good of the future . . . Sacrifices are being made, but the war will turn around, and in the end, we will prevail . . . We* will *gain new, powerful allies . . . and together, we will drive the Salik straight to hell, Saints willing . . . If the High One was right.*

Saints, let Her be right!

JANUARY 28, 2287 C.E.
GAMMA DRACONIS SYSTEM

The *Aloha 9* swept smoothly back into realspace under the control of its now-fully-experienced crew. Robert, Brad, and Ayinda were long since accustomed to the effects of living too fast for the rushing seconds it took to transit hyperspace, and so was Maria. It had taken Jackie and Lars a good five missions apiece to get over the strongest feelings of nausea—and so forth—but now they were accustomed, even inured. It was amazing what a body could get used to with constant exposure.

Prepared by two weeks' worth of multiple jumps per day, Jackie reached immediately for the readied nutrient pack with her left hand and sucked on the straw as soon as her teeth had the valve open. With her right hand, she called up the onboard hyperrelay to ping *MacArthur* Station, informing them that they had arrived, then accessed the scanners so that she, too, could see what this new system looked like.

At least they hadn't hit anything yet. That was a very real danger when entering a new system. Weeks were spent analyzing the lightwave readings of possible visitation candidates, with astrophysicists back home discerning what the rotational plane was and carefully selecting entry points that were either above or below that plane, in the hopes of limiting the chance of a crew running into something small and hard to see in that new system. There were stars with celestial bodies that orbited wildly off the stellar equator, but those were rare, thankfully.

"How far off are we?" Robert asked Ayinda.

"Just a moment, just a moment . . . seven light-seconds. We overshot our mark," the astronavigator told him. "Not by too much, though. Tolerance is any arrival within twenty light-seconds of mark, so don't you dare pout, Commander."

"It is a new star system," Lars agreed, his tone absentminded. He peered at his screens. "The angular-momentum measurement isn't going to be precise until the probes have had a good week's worth sent home for analysis. It will be good for the navigation programming to get insystem readings. This star is so big and inflated—it is not quite twice the size of our sun in its mass, but it is very bloated by comparison. I wonder what that has done to the orbits of the planets around it . . ."

He sounded lost in his work. Jackie had to attend to her own as she received pingback from their headquarters, along with an invitation for an open-channel chat. The lag time was almost a full second turnaround, not quite half a second one way, so it wouldn't interfere with communications too much. *"This is the Aloha 9 to MacArthur Station. We have achieved safe entry into the Gamma Draconis System, and will be skimming the system and launching our three surveillance relay drones over the next eight hours. Do we have any other instructions at this time?"*

"Roger, Aloha 9; the astrophysicists are eager for any and all information you can give them on that system. As per usual, try to get enough lightwave information on all the nearest systems around it to pick the next good one. Otherwise, there's nothing out of the ordinary on this end. Try to get some interesting pictures of the system while you're there."

"Roger that, MacArthur. We'll turn our attention to getting the first of the surveillance probes sent out. Next system data stream will be sent in five minutes; next audio contact in thirty minutes, unless we do find something interesting. Aloha 9 out," Jackie added.

"MacArthur out."

"How does our current flight path look, Robert, Ayinda?" she asked her crewmates. "Clear and smooth? If so, I'd like to go get the first of the relays ready."

"First of all, wait until we're at a relative dead stop," Robert told her. "*Then* you can move. If we have clearance."

"Not yet," Ayinda stated. "We need a solid half hour of lightwave readings. New system, remember?"

"Ah, right. Don't be in such a hurry to pull up your bootstraps, Jackie," Robert amended over his shoulder. "You'll get them launched in due time."

"At least she's pulling her weight," Brad muttered.

"Colvers!" Ayinda snapped.

"It was *not* a fat joke!" he defended himself sharply.

"At Ease, both of you," Jackie told them. She kept her tone soft, since he *was* trying to behave. "Now, since I have some time before I have to go prep for launch, I might as well make a telepathic sweep of our nearspace. So try to think about fruit or something."

Colvers, when she lightly swept her unfurling gift past him, was strongly thinking about nuts. And of her being one. Jackie let it pass.

———————

Four hours later, Robert, Ayinda, and Lars were sleeping in the crew quarters, their arms drifting lightly in front of them as they floated in their sleeping sacks. This mission had taken them quite a ways from the Sol System, and each jump required a bit of rest between. They could string up to four jumps in a row before having to rest for several hours, but as each system jumped to was still a fairly new entity, mission protocols demanded taking a few hours between each hop.

That added up after a while. They had drawn straws—figuratively, using a random number generator programmed into the ship's computers—to see who got to sleep first. One of the pilots had to remain on duty at all times, and someone had to monitor the scanners to provide a second set of eyes, particularly if the pilot had to use the facilities. At the moment, Maria was busy somewhere in the back, while Jackie and Brad sat watch in the cockpit while they drifted toward their next drop-off point for the last of their allotted three probes.

Silence reigned in the cockpit . . . if one didn't count the soft tap of controls, and the thrum of engines and thruster fields, and the faint beeps of various machinery functioning around them. Finally, Brad lifted his chin. "Everything looks safe. You can prep for probe launch when ready. Sir."

"I'll have to call Maria up here to take my place at the scanners," she reminded him. A quick check of the interior cameras showed the doctor working in the kitchen area. Opening the intercom, she spoke quietly, since it looked like the door between kitchen and the cabin with the three lightly tethered sleepers was open. *"Jackie to Maria, can you come take my place at the scanners?"*

The dark-haired physician looked up and over at the camera, nodded, and held up a couple of packets wrapped in thermal cloth. A few moments later, she pulled a third one from the oven, closed the door, and kicked off one of the cabinets, twisting midair to plant her feet and soar in nearly the opposite direction. A few moments later, the cockpit door opened, allowing her entry.

"Time to eat, *amigos*. Food first, probe launch after," the doctor asserted. "But you can take this back with you. Just pack away the garbage before you slip into your p-suit," Maria added, handing a packet to their comm tech. "You like the cheese tortellini, yes?"

"Not when I'm about to drag on a pressure-suit," Jackie demurred, reaching for her breather mask. It was hard to enjoy food with a perpetually semi-stuffed-up nose. Zero gravity didn't allow the body to clear the nasal passages effectively. "I get like Lars does about half an hour later."

"*Sí, sí,* I forgot. Well, I'll have it, then. Gravy meat-loaf hash?" Maria asked.

"I'll take that one," Brad told her, pulling his own mask away to speak clearly before reapplying it, sniffing deep to try to clear his own sinuses. Jackie gestured for him to take the offered meal. Maria pulled herself that way, handed over the packet.

"That leaves the pork meal," Maria stated. "It's the barbecue one."

"The one that tastes utterly unlike a properly pit-barbecued pig." Jackie sighed. It had pineapple and seasonings, and . . . Unfortunately, no matter how much the Space Force's chefs tried, the microgravity environment itself dulled one's taste buds and sense of smell. Even if they had packaged up a real *lu'au* meal, slow-baked barbecued pork, ten kinds of fish, and plenty of fresh fruit . . . it would not taste right in space. Not until they got back into a gravitied environment, even a simulated one like the *MacArthur*, would the food be able to smell—and thus taste—right. Jackie held out her hand toward the pork packet. "I'll take it anyway. I'm not going to waste one of my tubes of poi paste, though. Better a disappointed tongue than a disturbed digestive tract, however tastier it'll make the stuff."

Shrugging, Maria handed it over. Brad snorted . . . and coughed, quickly covering his mouth to prevent droplets from spreading. He grimaced at his shirtsleeve afterward. "Ugh. Dammit. I can't even change my shirt for another three and a half hours—don't make me laugh again, dammit. I still can't get the image out of my head of Robert trying to brush his teeth with your poi stuff, last week."

"That's what he gets for forgetting to replenish his own, then trying to root through *my* locker for more toothpaste. But I can be nice and fetch you a shirt before I put on my p-suit. After I eat," Jackie offered, smothering a yawn. She carefully opened the resealable packet, mindful of the faint steam that streamed out and curled around, hovering in an odd way before it dispersed and faded. Pork and pineapple scent clung to the mouth of the packet, which meant she had to all but stick her nose in it for a sniff to be sure it smelled alright. It did. Sort of; it was hard to smell much, still. "It won't delay the probe's launch by that much more since we're already delaying it for a midnight meal."

Clipping her own pack to her station, still wrapped in the thermal cloth to keep it hot, Maria unzipped her coveralls and pulled out the other packets, also wrapped to keep their contents hot but easily handled. "Tonight's selection of side dishes are peas and pasta in a thick crème sauce . . . brown and wild rice with *molé* sauce—that one is mine—and clam chowder."

"You actually *like* the space *molé*?" Brad asked, skeptical. "And I want—"

"Chowder!" Jackie quickly interjected. "Dibs!"

"Dammit!" he swore, aiming a glare in her direction.

"You did claim the meat loaf for lunch," Maria pointed out, juggling the unheated food packets she had brought along with the heated ones. "Each of us gets one dibs at a time. But if you like, you can have first crack at the dessert packet. Jackie, for cheeses, we have gouda . . . and two others, brie and . . . Colby-Jack."

"Gouda." She held out her hand, accepting the packet.

"Why should I even bother asking . . . Brie for you?" Marie asked Brad, adding a packet of mouth-sized crackers and a spoon for each of them to eat with. The solution to making crackers crumbless in space was to make them easily fit into a mouth whole. No outside-the-mouth bite, no problem in zero G.

"Please," he agreed.

"Colby-Jack for myself . . . and now for dessert. Chocolate mousse, apple-pie innards, or fruit cocktail. Brad?"

"Fruit cocktail," he said.

"Chocolate, Jackie?" Maria asked.

She shook her head, mouthful of pork in the way. Chewing quickly, she swallowed. "Not with this stuff. Apple, please."

"*Gracias*, the mousse will go very well with my *molé*."

Brad shook his head, muttering, ". . . Bootless."

"Be nice to her," Jackie countered mildly. As far as insults went, calling someone *bootless* wasn't much. But still . . . "No calling her weird or cowardly. She's our doctor, and can hide all the painkillers if something goes wrong."

"Oh, and I thought you actually liked me," Maria teased back. "See if I'll dispense you any aspirin, for that."

"Hey, even I know there's no aspirin on board," Brad countered. "It's all non-blood-thinning stuff, to limit problems with cuts in space."

"Eat your packets before they grow cold, *amigos*," Maria ordered. "Leave the medical talk to me."

Complying, Jackie chewed and swallowed. The barbecue pork was bland but chewable, the peas and pasta peppery but otherwise mushy. The chowder was rich and creamy, thick enough that it clung to the spoon and could almost be chewed, and the apple-pie innards—crust meant crumbs, and thus was not allowed—were actually good. She had plenty of water to drink at her station to wash it all down, but didn't drink any since she was expected to climb into a pressure-suit for a good hour-plus. She wasn't thirsty, so it was wise not to tempt her bladder.

Flattening the plexi packets when all three were through, Jackie took them with her back to the kitchen cabinets, where she placed them in the compactor. They would be extracted when the ship returned, boiled and pressure-washed to clean them—the sterilized, food-scrap-laden water would be cooled and shunted to the station's aquaculture bays—and then the plexi would be treated with a special solvent that would collapse its polymer chains and allow them to be re-formed into new products in a near-endless loop of recyclability. Eventually, the polymer chains would break down, losing their molecular bonds, but even that could be reconstituted chemically into other things.

For now, packaging had to be as light and flat as possible. Spoons were reusable titanium, wiped clean with sanitation towelettes that went into a different compactor, and the spoons were tucked back into their carrying drawers, where they fit under elastic bands to hold them in place. As for personal cleanup . . . that meant using the bathroom facilities. The suction-cup thing hadn't changed much in over two hundred years, but that was the trial and the trouble of weightlessness. At least cleanup was easy, and being vacuum, it eliminated the end result of drinking very easily. The other side of things . . . it worked awkwardly, but it worked. Thankfully, that wasn't a problem this time.

But that did remind her of her duty to replace the fluids she had eliminated. The air of the ship was low in humidity, as was their base space station. Rehydration was an imperative. Drinks . . . well, the other two had drunk water at their stations. So had she, and so would she, when she was done with the hyperrelay launch. After wiping her hands clean and compacting those sanitation cloths, Jackie picked up a couple extra packets to replace the ones they had been using and ducked into the main crew cabin since she had one more thing to get before she could return.

Lars snorted and woke a little. He blinked at her in the dim lighting, mumbled a greeting, and relaxed back into sleep again. Robert and Ayinda kept sleeping, her thin dreadlocks and both sets of their arms drifting outward from head and shoulders.

Using her telekinetic abilities to dodge around them without brushing against either, Jackie found Brad's locker and opened it, fetching out a clean bundle from the shirts compartment. She knew he wouldn't particularly *like* her touching his things, but since everyone was packing their cabinets to military specifications, she didn't have to rummage all over the place to find exactly what was needed. Every single locker was arranged the exact same way; only the sizes of garments and the rare few personal items, such as hairpins and ties, varied . . . but they were all kept in the same bins, position-wise.

Juggling his shirt and the collapsible water packs, she "dove" back the way she had come. Entering the cockpit, she passed the water bags and the shirt to Maria to distribute—knowing

Colvers would feel more psychologically comfortable accepting it secondhand from the doctor—and received Brad's used shirt in return from her fellow female. Garment in hand, she reversed course, this time to the side opposite the kitchen cabinets at the back of the crew quarters. As she left, she realized she hadn't given Brad's bared chest a second thought. Their conversation from that first trip to Barnard's Star drifted through her mind.

Half-naked men—unless they had hang-ups or were only interested in other men—were often curious to know if a female thought they looked good. Particularly if they exercised enough to have good musculature. It was only Human nature; females liked to know the same thing. However, she had no interest in any part of Brad Colvers' hide. He had nice muscles from an aesthetic point of view, but . . . like so many other males in Jackie's life, he just wasn't interesting beyond an aesthetic view.

Same with women. It wasn't their fault; Jackie did find many males and even a few females attractive-looking. Aesthetically pleasing. Even arousing to look at. It was touching their *thoughts* that distracted and dismayed her . . . particularly that one idiot—she couldn't even remember his name anymore—when she was a teenager, the one who had been thinking about making out with another girl while busy kissing and fondling *her*. Not exactly something she cared to repeat. Stuffing the shirt into a duffel meant for their dirty clothes, she started stripping out of her own garments, not entirely the easiest of tasks without gravity, oddly enough.

Emptying her pockets first, she put the pens and pocket tools into a mesh bag, along with her watch, trying not to move too much because it just felt too weird. Zero G did weird things to naked breasts, weirder even than floating weightless in a lagoon without a swimsuit, but she didn't have a choice. The modern Space-Force-issued space suit was a pressure-suit. Not the kind with compressed air, bulky and awkward to move in, but rather, the moment it was exposed to vacuum, the thick, stretchy material swelled up and put pressure on every inch of one's skin.

The trick was to ensure it was skin, not clothing; in true vacuum, pores and hair follicles tried to invert themselves, leaving an astronaut with an awkward, growing, uncomfortable prickling sensation. The highly advanced, foam-like material of the suit's innermost layer filled in all those dimples first, as soon as the pressure dropped to one-quarter sea level on Earth. It then started firming in place in those pores at one-eighth. That meant being naked was the most comfortable way to go. It also meant, in the event of a pressure drop, one had to hurry to get into the things or suffer that prickly pore inversion until enough atmosphere could be regained to soften the foam.

Once her clothes were added to the laundry bag, Jackie opened the locker with the p-suits and pulled out one that was approximately her size. It came with an inverted-T-shaped piece that fitted around her breasts, filling in the space between and underneath for a more secure fit—if a man wanted to use the suit, he simply pulled the piece out, but hers had been custom-fitted for her. As the official communications officer for the crew, she was the one who had to be in a pressureless bay a couple times each system, to ensure the probes were activated and launched properly.

There were plans for larger, longer ships that could launch the probes via machinery yet still fit through a hyperrift tunnel, but for now, the Space Force had chosen the cheaper method of launching each one by hand. They were still trying to figure out how to get a better seal on the suits than they currently had, one that wouldn't require quite so much huffing and puffing, tugging and grunting. Jackie kept thinking she was going to tear the semistretchy material if she pulled too hard, but a solid, long tug was needed to get her feet into the leggings and the leggings up into place.

By the time that was done, she had somersaulted twice and bumped off bulkheads and cabinet handles three times, until she gave up and used telekinesis to stabilize herself. Wiggling her hips into place, she pulled up the peach-lined, silvery-coated fabric. Jackie worked it up over her shoulders, first the right one, then the left, the one with her tattoo. The center of it was of the Psi League's symbol of the Radiant Eye, surrounded by a trio of jacaranda blossoms, the flowers rendered in violet blue and the rest tattooed in black around her deltoid, including the three rows of outward-facing shark's teeth surrounding the flower-draped Eye. Tattoos weren't usually found on civil servants, but she was proud of the three Grey-thwarting missions each row represented. Covering it up was a necessity, however.

To do so, she had to tug her arms into the sleeves with yet more grunting, then adjusted the T-pad, and worked on pulling the edges together. Not because the suit didn't fit—it did, unlike her uniform back at the beginning of the month—but because it was simply that tight a fit. The exterior was coated in a less-than-stretchy emulsion of powdered ceristeel, the same ferro-ceramic compound that coated the exterior of their ship.

It would protect her from overly hot starlight, zipping gas particles, and even allow her to retain body heat in the frigid depths of space for two-plus hours before endangering her vitals. It wouldn't fare as well against a solar flare or an ion storm—a confluence of ejected stellar matter meeting up with an agitated planetary magnetic field—but beggars couldn't be choosers. If she ever found herself in such dire straits, she might survive if she found shelter behind something, like a cargo-bay door . . . though ideally she wouldn't take a spacewalk at all while a flare was passing through.

That gray layer was the final layer in a good six different materials, each of which had to be overlapped just so, and the belly-button nodule fitted into place just right. All of it fitted to cover her like a second skin, if a padded second skin. The research scientists kept promising improvements in the p-suit materials, things that would make it faster and easier to don, but Jackie wasn't going to hold her breath—gravity would actually help in donning the awkward things, but nobody had yet figured out how to make it artificially, outside of giant spinning wheels.

Pressing hard to seal each layer of the seams, she sealed the suit to the O-ring section at the top of the garment, made sure all the connections were tight, then pulled out the rebreather pack and connected its hoses to her helm. One-way valves delivered oxygen-laden air to the bubble, and accepted carbon-dioxide-soaked air for scrubbing and recycling.

There was only a small pack of water with a thin sipping straw in the helm, just enough to wet the mouth once in a while, because this wasn't a suit designed for long-term use. For those, they had the more bulky air-pressurized suits, which came with water, emergency food, cooling units, and so forth. Frankly, Jackie had been told over and over during her first round in the military that the p-suits were for light labor use and emergencies that could be fixed within minutes. Hard labor was handled either by drones or hardsuit repair pods that could be lived in for hours, even a day or two. Anything in between could be handled by spacing out the repairs . . . and anything that needed longer than that, they were as good as dead.

Not a cheerful thing to hear, but that was the Space Force, bluntly honest about the risks. *After* one got in. Shrugging into the rebreather pack, she buckled it between her legs, over her shoulders, and around her waist. A careful adjustment of the helm socketed it in place, and a firm twist aligned the faceplate with her front-looking view, sealing helm to suit. The back was covered in ceristeel to help reduce unseen impacts and stellar radiation, and the front had a tinted shield that could be kept down for more protection, or raised if face-to-face communication or nontinted inspection was needed.

The helmet contained not only the water pack, visor, and air hoses, it also contained a miniature computer that inflated the helmet, then tested it for leaks. Seeing her heads-up display blinking green, Jackie nodded. With the pickups that monitored her face, she blink-coded the comm system on. *"Jackie to the cockpit, can you hear me?"*

"We can hear you," Maria responded. *"Suit telemetry is online, all systems looking green."*

"Confirmed," Jackie agreed. She closed the door to the p-suit locker—and yelped as the ship jerked, struck by something. *"What the . . . ?"*

The three sleeping in the next cabin down the passage snorted awake. The ship jolted again, and Jackie found herself tugged portward. Her fingers didn't have a good grip on the handle, and she tumbled free. Instinct tightened her telekinesis around her in a bubble, bouncing her off the far cabinets twice before she could extend invisible braces. The others were still caught up in their sleeping bags, dangling sideways by momentum but otherwise unharmed thanks to the positional bungees.

"All hands on deck!" Brad snapped. *"All hands on deck! I have no idea how this happened, but there's another ship out there, and it's huge! It's grappled us with cables and is reeling us in!"*

"Get me a visual!" Jackie ordered. *"Brad, get me a visual!"*

"Dammit!" he swore over the intercom. *"I can't fire the*

thrusters; one of the grapples latched onto the nose cone! We try to pull out of it, it'll damage the OTL, and we won't be able to get anywhere."

"What's the configuration on that ship?" Robert called out, crawling out of his sleeping bag faster than the other two. Clad in undershorts, a tee shirt, and socks, he should have looked ridiculous floating through the cabin, but somehow he didn't. Palming the intercom, he repeated himself. *"Lieutenant, report—what is the configuration of that ship? Is it the Greys?"*

"Negative, it's no ship I've ever seen before. Five lobes, orange running lights, odd beige hull . . ."

"Could I please *get a visual on my heads-up display?"* Jackie asserted, aggravated. Robert bumped into one of her force lines, blinked in shock, and gripped the solidified air for a moment, using it to push himself toward the cockpit. Belatedly, she released the field with a flex of her mind and pushed off the port wall. They still had relative zero gravity, but the ship was being hauled sideways around them, which meant navigating by floating had suddenly turned a bit tricky.

"I have it!" she heard Maria reply. Her HUD flashed, projecting a field of stars and a very strange ship, very non-Grey in its architecture. Five lobes was right, but they poked in different directions like a caltrop, rather than like a flat star, with no hint of aerodynamic aesthetics.

"That's definitely *not Grey,"* Jackie asserted over the link.

Blink-coding her helmet to release its locks, she reached up and twisted it free, shutting off the rebreather pack to conserve power and oxygen. Since her helmet was now powered off, she rolled onto her side, oriented herself, and pushed off into the main crew cabin to look for a spare over-the-ear headset. Lars had two in his hands and passed her one as soon as she slowed to a stop in front of him. Nodding in thanks, she twisted hers on and waved Lars past her.

With the helmet dangling off her back, she was not the most graceful of crew members right now, even counting Robert in his socks. *"Confirmed, that is* not *a Grey ship."*

"Are you sure?" Brad challenged her over the earpiece.

"I've faced down three of them and chased them off, two of them from a very close and personal distance. That's why I have the three rings of shark's teeth guarding my Radiant

Eye and its jacaranda flowers," she explained. *"Three times, I've defended the Sol System from those buggers, and that's definitely not them."*

"I thought that was just a tribal tattoo," Ayinda called back over the intercom from the cockpit, where she had vanished, pulling herself in Robert's wake.

With Lars out of her way, she was free to move toward the cockpit finally. Her p-suit was an awkward choice of outfit but no worse than the current sleepwear of half the crew. *"It is, but I'm also half-Polynesian, so there's no such thing as 'just' a tribal tattoo."*

"You can talk about your skin-based fashion choices later," Brad asserted. *"It looks like we're being pulled into a hangar bay of some sort."*

"Ay, ay, ay!" Maria muttered over her headset. *"Look at the size of that thing . . . That has to be at least forty decks deep, if it can swallow us like a shark eating a guppy!"*

"There's no way with a configuration like that, that it can go through a hyperspace rift," Robert agreed. He glanced back as Jackie opened the cockpit door and passed through, letting it close behind her. Palming off his headset, he spoke normally. Or as normally as a wobble of fear and worry in a man's voice could sound. "So, Major . . . we're about to make First Contact. This means I have to officially hand over this mission to you. So . . . what do we do now, sir?"

"Well . . . don't damage the nose cone," Jackie asserted, pulling herself into her seat and strapping in . . . after battling with her loose-floating helmet to wedge it in next to her along the port bulkhead. "Brad's right about that part. But . . . I need to fire up the hyperrelay hub before we're drawn in. At the rate we're being moved, I should be able to make at least one report before we get into an atmosphere-laden environment . . . using the relay would be very *bad* after that point . . ."

"What do we do about the grapples?" Lars asked the others. He rubbed the sleep sand from his eyes as he did so and batted the stuff away in annoyance. The normally affable, laid-back Finn frowned unhappily at the approaching maw on the side of the ship. "They are the things drawing us in."

"We can't do anything just yet," Brad said, shaking his

head. "Even if she's already suited, Jackie can't get out there and get them unhooked on her own. They're too big and too secure. I can't get a good viewing angle on the jaws, but it looks like they're giant springs. We can only hope the hook will let go of the nose cone at some point without damaging it."

"Either that, or someone will have to go out there with Jackie to help remove it," Robert agreed. Both men paused, then looked back over their shoulders at Jackie, who had fired up the hyperrelays and was awaiting pingback. She looked up at them, looked at the hangar bay they were being pulled into, and shrugged.

"They *might* be friendly, if overly grabby in their curiosity," she pointed out. "Lars, the moment we're inside, I want you to start taking scans of their materials. Metals, organics, atmosphere if they close the doors and flood the bay—anything you can get. Maria, see if you can do the same. Brad . . . stand by on the guns, just in case. I'd *like* to think these aliens, whoever they are, are friendly . . . but we know from the foresight dreams that some of the xenotypes we'll meet will *not* be. If nothing else, I will go outside and free the ship so we can leave—I don't *have* to have help pulling those claw-jaws open, remember."

"It wouldn't be wise to send you alone," Maria warned her while Jackie worked on getting the comm system warmed up and pinging.

"I'm already suited, as it is—*Aloha 9 to MacArthur Station, we have made First Contact with an unknown species; I repeat, we have made First Contact with an unknown species,*" she asserted, not waiting for an actual reply once she got pingback. *"We are being hauled into some sort of large ship's hangar bay, estimated size around forty decks. The hangar bay looks big enough for three shuttles, and . . . whoa . . . aliens with tentacles, that is* not *a good sign."*

Her console buzzed as they started to cross the opening. Jackie swore, hand slapping the console to shut off the hyperrelay, though the fail-safes had already tripped. "Atmosphere! They have some sort of . . . of force field that's keeping the air inside! Dammit, even if it's just a pinhole hyperrift . . . !"

"Thank you for *not* blowing us up, *señorita*," Maria praised

Jackie, crossing herself. "I'd rather not die on a First Contact date."

"*De nada*, and neither would I," Jackie muttered back.

She eyed the space-suited figures, with their curling arm-limbs, bulky bodies, and wrong-pointing knees, and tried not to think too closely on the memories she had pulled from five of the precognitives who'd had those recent, predictive visions of aliens and other things. Tentacle-armed aliens were pretty much the bad guys, according to multiple precog consensus. Mind racing, she tried to figure out what to do.

"I think we should stay in the ship until we see what *they* intend to do. But . . . I'll go stay in the portside airlock and try to read their minds from there. If they try to open up the ship one way or another, I'll go out and make First Contact in person rather than from a careful distance."

"Major, that is *very* dangerous," Robert warned her, using her rank to remind everyone that she was officially now in charge. She could feel him pushing that message at the edge of her mental walls, wanting Brad at the very least to grasp the change in power.

"I know it is, but this *is* why I am here. I'll power up my helm but not seal it until I have to go out," she added, adjusting in her seat as the cushions started pressing into her thighs and buttocks. "I . . . wait, is that . . . *gravity*?"

The others looked at her, looked down, then looked around. Lars spotted it first, pointing at Ayinda's hair. "Ayinda, your dreadlocks are not floating anymore. They're starting to hang *down*."

"Boot me," Robert breathed, looking out the front windows. "They have *artificial* gravity . . ."

CHAPTER 5

The pull of gravity increased perceptibly, and Lars quickly bent over his console controls. "Let us hope it is not much higher than Earth-normal."

"Do we put down the landing gear?" Brad asked, as the cables, being manipulated by robotic arms, started to shift and lower them.

"I'd rather not," Robert returned, twisting in his seat to look Jackie's way. "Putting down the gear opens up part of the ship, sir, exposing the wheel wells. Ceristeel's pretty tough, but it's thin in the wells, and there are a few exposed sections that aren't armored at all in there. I'd rather let the ship rest on its belly than give these aliens access to our innards. The hull can take it, so long as their version of gravity won't kill us."

"Agreed," Jackie returned quickly. She pulled her gaze away from the bay, working to unbuckle herself from her chair with one gloved hand while the other poked at the controls. Thankfully, modern p-suit gloves were vastly superior for working in than the air-inflated ones in the old-fashioned kind, or the secondhand waldo gloves of a true hardsuit.

"Ow . . . something's underneath me . . ." Ayinda muttered, adjusting herself in her seat. She squirmed again, and finally dug out a pen from under her rump. Clipping it to her station, she shook her head. "Artificial gravity. Great. Technologically advanced First Contact with a most likely hostile species, and I'm sitting here in my underwear, on a pen I didn't realize was floating underneath me until now. *This* is going to look great on the history vids. Presuming we all survive."

"We'll survive," Jackie muttered back, fixing her station so that it would provide several different camera hookups and an audio feed to her p-suit's helmet, and a second audio feed to the headset hooked around her ear. "I don't know how just yet, but we'll survive. There . . . everything's set up for remote control on my end. I'm headed to the airlock—at least I can *walk* there, now."

"At least they're pulling us in with the right orientation toward the floor—ha!" Brad exclaimed, as the cable attached to the front of their ship, visible through the front viewports, detached. "It's no longer messing with our nose cone!"

"Let's run a diagnostic to make sure it's still aligned for proper use," Robert ordered him. "Major, permission to orient the ship toward that opening? We don't have to worry about twisting damage nearly as much with the nose cone now free."

"Granted," Jackie allowed, unbuckling the last of her straps, freeing herself from her seat.

"Gravity has stabilized," Lars told everyone while Jackie worked her way out of her seat into the aisle. "It seems to have settled at 0.87Gs." For a moment, he managed a smile despite the serious situation they were in. "That should be just enough to put a spring in your step."

"I'm just happy it's not twice Earth's gravity, or some other ridiculously hard-to-manage number," Maria replied. "High gravity stresses the body in ways that . . ."

Jackie palmed open the cockpit door and let it slide shut behind her, cutting off Maria's next words. Her helmet dangled awkwardly down her back, bumping into the top of her buttocks with the sway of the ship as Robert gently fired the thrusters, twisting it on its hull with a scrape that rattled briefly through the ship. She had other things to think about.

These aliens were the ones the precognitive visions had warned about. They were quite distinctive, too. Heads like frogs, legs like ostriches, arms like an octopus split in half and stuck on each limb. The others in the visions looked like cats, or lizards, or spiders, or weird four-armed beings with fluffy hair-stuff and big black eyes. Only the ones that were repeatedly foreseen committing acts of harm toward the others looked like frog-octopus things. Frogtopi. Frogtopusses. Evil, horrible, bloodthirsty things. She could feel herself starting to sweat and shook her head to clear it.

Calm yourself . . . A wayward curl escaped the pins holding her hair in place. Scooping it up, she felt for a pin, wound the lock in among the others bunned on top of her head, and pinned it back in place. She headed toward the side airlock, positioned over one wing. *Calm and center, ground . . . dammit, can't ground in space; make a bigger bag for your negative energies, cleanse it, and use it to power your shields . . . That's better.*

"What is the atmosphere like out there, Lars?" Jackie asked through her headset mic, once she felt calm again.

"Close to ours," he reported. *"It's 76 percent nitrogen, 19 percent oxygen, carbon dioxide is a little high at 0.52 percent, but the atmospheric pressure is low, just under eight hundred kilopascals."*

"That is a little low, but not enough to endanger anyone— start worrying if it reaches five hundred, or the carbon dioxide reaches 4 percent," Maria interjected. *"At 5 percent, your co-ordination starts to suffer noticeably, and five hundred kilopas-cals is where you start having trouble exercising in half-sea-level air pressure. Anything else, Lars? Any trace gases to worry about?"*

Lars finished his report. *"The rest . . . lesser gases, typ-ical stuff for an M-class world, plus some hydrocarbon-like particles—I think they're using some sort of fancy biodiesel fuel, high powered but old-fashioned. Trace amounts, but nothing near toxic levels, correct, Doctor?"*

"Correct. But that doesn't account for any possible pathogens, that's just the molecules detectable in the air."

"If I have to go out there, I promise I'll keep my helmet on for as long as possible," Jackie reassured them.

"It is also very humid," Lars added. *"Ambient tempera-ture is . . . thirty-one Celsius . . . and humidity is 93 percent. Over 4 percent of the air out there is water vapor."*

"Bootstrap me," Brad breathed into his headset pickup. *"That's some pretty thick sweating weather out there. At least it's not in the upper thirties."*

"It's over forty Celsius up at the hangar ceiling," Lars pointed out. *"The bay height is just short of thirty meters."*

"That's good to know, but are they moving toward this ship?" Jackie asked. She reached behind her back to try to get ahold of her helmet. It was awkward. Batting at the thing three times, she gave up and brought it up and around via telekinesis. *"What are the* aliens *doing?"*

"From the looks of things, they have what appear to be scanner machines in their . . . tentacles?" Robert told her. *"Looks like they're trying to get a reading, first. And there are some hovering things."*

"Probably cameras," Brad offered. *"They're too small to be weapons systems, from the looks of things. At least, I hope they're not flying grenades."*

"Accessing my heads-up," Jackie stated, adjusting the helmet so that it sat offset from the O-ring, allowing her to breathe the *Aloha*'s air. *"I am going to pick some of the aliens and attempt to scan their mind. Maria, use the two-tone signal I set up to get my attention."*

"Ready," the doctor relayed.

Several miniature viewpoints appeared on the inner curve of her helmet, each one a different camera angle of the world beyond their ship. She studied each one, blink-coded off the ones that had nothing useful, and studied the remaining six that had the most aliens in view. Each one within the hangar bay appeared to be in a pressure-suit of some sort.

There was also a large viewport behind them, up one floor from the looks of it, and those aliens were not in pressure-suits. The glass, or whatever it was, bore a bit of a tint that made it hard to see through, but the skin colors looked beigeish. More on the greenish side of beige, though, rather than the brownish beige of a Human.

First, one of the nearest ones. Those do look like scanner equipment . . . Orienting herself in the airlock so that she faced the same way as the camera, Jackie unfurled her mind. She had sensed by now enough of the thoughts of the other five Humans on board the *Aloha 9* to quickly identify and set their presences aside; once that was done, she became aware of just how many aliens were nearby. Hundreds. Thousands, maybe.

She couldn't sense any form of shielding, which meant all of those minds were open to her, unsuspecting. Cold, slimy—was that her subconscious projecting that mental imagery? Amphibians and cephalopods were water-based creatures, but an octopus was actually rather intelligent, comparatively . . . Her xenotelepathy latched lightly onto a random thought; one of them was remembering its—his?—childhood. Images, not words. Feelings, not words. Impulses, not words. That was fine, though. Most people didn't stop to think in actual words unless they actually stopped to think, in her experience.

. . . Swimming and breathing underwater, but the mental images were harsh and hungry. Fierce with the need to hunt, cowed by the even more ferocious mother figure who swam nearby. His instincts still screamed that he would obey Her or be eaten, the Mother Huntress . . . but for now, he had to obey his commanding officers only because they were in power. If he found an opportunity to advance within the rules . . . say an "accident" . . .

Jackie pulled back, blinking, eyes seeing but not registering the white walls of the airlock. *Oh, those are unpleasantly vicious thoughts . . . but at least I can make mental contact, and easier than with a primate or a cetacean, the nine-tenths sentients back home. Easier than a Grey, too . . .*

I need to learn their language—basic commands, comprehension of signs, that sort of thing first, she decided. There'd be no point in learning how to greet each other just yet. If First Contact was to be made, it would have to be made face-to-face, and she could do that then. Right now, she needed to know how to get her ship in and out of *this* ship, how to manipulate doors and lifts and such.

Leaning forward, she sent her mind outward again. She narrowed it down quite a bit, though; too many of those cold, cruel thoughts were out there, so she didn't cast as broad a net as before. Still cognizant of her own location, her own senses, what she did wasn't true OOB, out-of-body travel. Just as well; those psis who could go OOB had reported extreme disorientation without a planet to ground them. Skimming a mind here, a thought there, she searched for aliens manipulating controls, for their associated thoughts.

Or rather, for the image-thoughts that would allow her to process nouns and verbs. For those glancing at signs or reading symbols on monitor screens, they looked up, rather than looked level or even down, which was the preferred method for Humans and their version of eye sockets. These aliens' eyes were built differently, too, seeing a skewed version of colors. Extra colors her brain could not process, and some which looked dull and muted to her, while others were emphasized, almost garish in their own way.

Odd ocular input or not, it still gave her a rapidly growing list of command words. Up, down, left, right, stairwell, lift, numbers for deck designations, sanitation supplies, armory locker, do not use lift in event of an emergency, prey pens . . . prey pens? She followed that particular alien's thoughts, his body unseen because of the bulkheads between them. His, because females were usually mother-hunters? A pursuit for another time. Prey pens, that was important. Not because she was curious to know what these ate, but because of the horror of learning at the same time two things: what those squiggles on the wall meant linguistically, and what these aliens ate literally.

Confirming the worst of her people's precognitive visions.

He smacked his microtentacles along the bars of the cages, most of which were now empty. Only five left. That alien ship was alien, strange, unseen before now. No one knew what it was, so the Highest Officer had commanded that one of the prisoners be dragged out to try to identify it. With that series of thought-images came a bit of hunger, a sensation of drooling. A smacking of those broad, frog-like lips. *Maybe he would get to beat the prisoner. Maybe even bite a little . . . he wasn't high-ranked enough to actually chew whole chunks of the prisoner, their Highest Officer, but maybe just a little bite, to help convince the prey to speak . . .*

Jackie almost withdrew in disgust, but just then, the cages with prisoners came into range, along with the mental presences of those prisoners . . . and shocked her into losing her grip on that alien's mind. *Humans! Humans! Boot me out an airlock door—that was a* Human *mind!*

Panting in shock, she forced herself to recenter her thoughts, then leaped forward, up, and to the side, to the deck with the cages. To the . . . five? Five! Five Human minds, most sunk into despair, anger, hopelessness—fear! Fear that . . . *Wait, one is . . . one of them is a psi?* Eyes wide, she stared at the airlock wall, then tried again. *Fear, despair, hope, anger . . . and really horrible shielding skills,* she realized. *Maybe someone who was latent but who made a breakthrough under the stress of being captured?*

She surged forward, projecting an image of herself knocking politely on the door of a home. (*Hello, there. Who are you?*) (*???*)

For a moment, all she got was a return blast of startled, almost stunned confusion—then a mental garble of images interspersed with words in a language she did not know. A language she *did not know.*

Like her father, Jean-Jacques MacKenzie, Jackie had been a natural polyglot from infancy onward. She had been able to converse fluently in eight different languages before her powers had manifested with puberty at the age of twelve . . . and now as an adult of thirty-five years, spoke over ten *times* that, once her telepathy had been trained to interface with that part of her mind. A perfect match for serving in Oceania, in the subprovinces of Polynesia, Micronesia, and Melanesia, where a large number of Earth's languages—many of them low-population tribal dialects—were spoken. It had made her an outstanding Councilor because she hadn't needed a translator to discuss in person the problems of her constituents, or anyone else, for that matter.

But this was a language she did not know, that was not related to any language she *did* know . . . *Except maybe Euskarrian? The Basque peoples? A few of the root sounds, maybe . . . ? Or coincidence? There's a bit of ancient Egyptian consonant patterns associated with his words, some Aramaic, old Han dialect, some Sanskrit and Urdu perhaps . . . ?*

(*!!!*) The other Human's mind, adult, male, and desperate, grabbed onto hers and tried to shake her mentally. He flung images at her, of a half-eaten arm in the alien's grip, of piles of bleeding bodies, of being naked and caged like a herd beast locked up for transport. Images of him and her, hand in hand, running away, running through the stars with the other four prisoners, leaving their alien captors far behind. Far behind, and preferably dead.

It was all crude telepathy, half-trained at best, fading in and out as he stumbled along physically, arm wrapped in the grip of those horrid tentacles. The minds of the others burst with shock, fear, even pleading as he was led away. They were not actually telepathic like him, but their mental images and even their emotions were strong in their despair and their belief he was being led to his death.

Jackie did her best to project soothing, calming thought-images at the male. Once she got him somewhat calm, she pulled back. Or tried to pull away; he clung to her thoughts, surprisingly strong in his resurging fear spike. Shaping her thought-images carefully, she projected the need to consult with others, and that she would return. His grip loosened somewhat, but he didn't completely let go. Not that she could blame him—whoever he was—but she needed to be more aware of her own body than of his, right now.

Her timing was good; two seconds after she came back to herself, breathing deeply to settle her nerves, Maria sent the two-tone chime through her headset and the speakers in her helmet. *"I'm here. I'm good. What's happening?"*

"A couple of them look like they might be trying to shoot gun-like things, out there," Maria told her. *"We're registering—there, did you hear that? Electricity and some sort of sonic pulse in one."*

The hull did buzz a little. *"Is it getting through the hull?"*

"We're well grounded," Brad told her. She could almost see his eyes rolling, given his tone. *"This ship is capable of flying through an electrical storm. Remember the* Councilor One*?"*

"Considering my grandfather died on it, yes, I remember the Councilor One *incident,"* Jackie retorted. *"These are an alien race with alien technology. There are no guarantees until we've seen and examined what they can actually do. Besides, we have a bigger concern."*

"What would that be?" Ayinda asked.

"They have Humans on board. Five captives . . . and just like the precogs' visions suggested, they are slated to be eaten by these frog-octopus things out there."

"Some other crew was captured?" Robert asked, his tone startled.

"They're not from Earth. They speak no language I've ever heard of—and I've heard many more tongues than I can speak fluently." Chaos erupted in her ears, each of the other five trying to have his or her say. "Silence! *That's an* order," Jackie added sternly. *"One voice at a time. At the moment, that voice is mine. Organize your thoughts . . . and keep an eye on what they're doing to the hull.*

"As far as I can tell, the frog-aliens are bringing one of their prisoners down to try to get him to tell them if his people

have seen one of our ships before. I'm going to try to contact the Human again. Learning his language at a distance is very tricky, so only interrupt me if they're making any sort of headway on our hull, or they look like they're going to pull up something big enough to smash their way in."

Thankfully, that got her comm silence. Or at least enough quiet that she could ignore the mutterings still coming over their pickups. Closing her eyes, Jackie concentrated on the tenuous connection she had been maintaining to that mind. Below the level of communication but still keeping herself aware of his movements through the ship . . .

(!!!) An image blasted at her, of himself and four other Humans, all spotted or striped in nonnormal colors, nonnormal ways, desperately needing to get out of there. A jumble of thoughts of weapons, of the current alien ship ripping open with them safely on another ship—her ship, presumably, but it came with a sense of artificial gravity in his mental assumptions and a configuration that wasn't anything like either the five-lobed frog-people's ship or the delta-winged OTL-to-atmospheric design of the *Aloha* series—and so on and so forth.

She projected a firm sense of calm upon him until his whirling thoughts slowed, then constructed an image of the frog-tentacled aliens gripping a weapon-like object, it shooting something, that something blasting a bulkhead into chunks of wall, of changing the object in the alien's hands several times, with it sometimes setting things on fire, sometimes making things break up . . . and then sent him a pulse of inquiry. Asking him in images and feelings what sort of weapons his captors wielded.

A sense of a deep breath, and a shaky but determined projection in return of several carefully paced images. A weapon like some of the ones she had seen. Of its being fired at a fellow Human—with blue spots on their tanned face— and of that Human's eyes rolling up and their body slumping down. They still breathed, but were clearly unconscious for some time, as the enemy came up, slung the Human over its shoulder—an impression that most of these aliens were indeed male—and carried it off to be stripped and chained up.

Some sort of stunning or tranquilizing weapon, then. One with an impression of electrical energy mixed with sonic energy. Like the thing they used on the *Aloha*'s hull. She sent a pulse of understanding, and a query. Another image, of a laser rifle shooting orange beams, burning things in lines. The Humans returned it . . . but again, the enemy shot well, the Human female collapsed in agony—still alive—and the alien came up, stunned the Human, and carried her off. A jumbled impression of the Humans being . . . eaten alive. Unpleasant.

A third image—an enemy killing a Human, coming up . . . poking and prodding and lifting and dropping the dead Human . . . and the alien pushing it away and walking off. So the aliens preferred live prisoners to dead kills, just so they could eat their prey alive. She sent another pulse of confirmation, of understanding. Then sent him an image of the cells he had been in, the other four Humans, and a pulse-question, followed by the bars vanishing. She constructed a backwards-kneed, flippered lump of an alien stepping up with weapons, with similar weapons dropping out of ceiling compartments, in the style of questioning pulses asking what sort of security measures stood in the way of their freedom.

Stunner rifles, bulky security doors, and smooth panels marked with circles in different colors. It took both of them several tries of back and forth before he sent her a simple, drawing-style projection of a suction cup lifting up on a line. The security measures were physiologically based. She—according to him—would need suction cups of all sorts and sizes to get the bars open without blasting them down and burning the captives in the attempt, or risking lasering the occupants.

"Boot me," she heard Robert say over the earpiece and the speakers. *"They* do *have a Human on board!"*

"A very naked *Human,"* Ayinda added. *"He's up there in that observation window overlooking the bay, port side."*

Jackie cleared her mind, slipping out of the male's clutching mental fingers. Not dropping the link between them, but slimming it down to a nondistracting level. *"Okay. There are a total of five Humans on board, not including ourselves. The true aliens, the ones looking like crosses between a frog and an octopus, I have managed to discern their intentions . . . and they confirm the precognitive visions. These aliens eat living sentient prey, which is what they will do to us as soon as they figure out we're the same general biology as their current prisoners."*

"So what do we do, Ambassador?" Lars asked her, all trace of his usual oddball sense of humor gone. *"If we attack, that would be starting a war. If we do not attack, we could end up being dinner. I do not wish in any way to be dinner."*

"I need to do one more sweep of the ship to be absolutely sure . . . and then I am going to go out there and I am going to rescue all five of them. Even if they are not our Humans, they are Humans. Any of their captors protest or get in my way, I'll . . . just knock them down. Stun them, hopefully. I don't know how durable their physiology is compared to ours, but it should be comparable if they have similar gravity, atmosphere, and so forth . . . so hopefully I won't kill any. But I will not leave those five Humans in their grasp. We know from the precogs that the aliens are hostile. We haven't seen much of that from our fellow Humans out there. This is my judgment as mission commander . . . and I accept full responsibility for any consequences that arise from it."

"You?" Brad asked her. *"Alone? On a ship big enough to hold thousands of these aliens?"*

"Yes. I need the rest of you to ready the ship for departure. Since most everyone in the hangar bay is in a pressure-suit, it won't be too much of a slaughter if we blast that . . . force-field thing out of our way, venting the hangar when it's time to go. But only once myself and the others are on board.

"Maria, I realize this is going to put us into an automatic quarantine situation. We don't know what pathogens they're carrying, and they don't know which we're carrying. It could be like encountering one of those isolated Amazon tribes, so you're going to need to break out the health-monitor bracelets," Jackie said. She reached under her helmet to adjust her headset on her ear, then readjusted the helm, socketing it and giving it a firm twist to seal it in place. That activated the rebreather pack, and her heads-up display started greenlighting again for all of its functions. *"I'm going out there sealed in the p-suit with the visor down, confuse the aliens a little bit longer.*

"I may be Human-shaped in general, but if they can't see that I don't look exactly like the ones they have—no visible stripes or spots—it might slow them down, make them hesitate. After all, we know from the Greys that there are biometrically symmetrical aliens with two legs, two arms, a torso, and

*a head out there that aren't actually Human. I'm going to
keep my pickups wide open, video and audio both, so start
recording as much of this as you can . . . but a lot of what I'm
going to be doing is psychic, so don't expect me to talk my
head off."*

"You're both brave and bootless, Major," Brad told her. She
didn't know if he saluted or not, though his voice for the first
time did have a slight edge of respect in its tone.

"Thank you. Cycling the airlock now." She closed the inner
door with a touch of the controls, then waited for the small
chamber to suction its atmosphere out. No point in exposing
the aliens to an excess of Human-based pathogens . . . or
rather, not Human, but Terran, Jackie decided. She didn't know
yet what these other Humans called themselves, but her group
came from Earth, and that meant they were Terrans. The
Council had long ago decided that *Terran* was much more dignified as a label than *Earthling*, after all, even if it wasn't officially implemented in their name for themselves. One could
say they were from Earth, Mars, the Moon, a space station . . .
but they were all Terrans in the end, as in originating from the
same planet.

Which meant these new Humans came from Earth, too,
and would surely be Terrans somehow. *Escapees from a
Grey experimentation project, maybe? That would be the
most logical, and might account for the weird body paint
and hair dye that isn't actually paint or dye . . .*

As soon as the lights switched from orange to red, then to
green, Jackie tapped the button for the outer-airlock door. It
hissed open, alien air whooshing in around her. They would
definitely have to use the quarantine sectors now, either alpha
or beta. Someone would have to pilot a ship to dock simultaneously with the far side to keep the torus counterbalanced . . .
and she was getting ahead of herself in her thoughts.

*First get the non-Terran Humans out of their suckered
clutches, Jacaranda,* she ordered herself, easing up to the
doorway for a peek. *And to do that, you have to catch every
single one of those stunner guns and make sure they don't go
off while pointed at you. So . . . xenopathic awareness
sphere . . . The impression I got was a short-range capacity
on those stun guns, thankfully. Two aliens near the cockpit—I*

*can sense Robert already activated the blast shields, prevent-
ing them from looking in, leaving them with camera scans.
One alien at each wing . . . two more at the rear . . . half a
dozen more just beyond them . . . wrap your mind around
each weapon and get ready to shove any of them upward if
their owner seeks to fire it . . .*

The door's hissing open had caught their attention, but
they moved warily into view, using bits of equipment for
cover. There were two other ships in here, vaguely shuttle-
sized, a little smaller than the *Aloha* and very much more
like bricks than the delta-winged Terran vessel. Bits of repair
equipment, fueling pipes, that sort of thing. Stepping out
onto the glossy, mirror-polished portside wing, Jackie looked
around, quickly finding and identifying aliens with anything
remotely like the weapons her panicked fellow psi had projected . . . and caught sight of him in the big viewing window
up and slightly to her left, in the side wall of the hangar.

Naked indeed, with a golden tan, messy blond hair streaked
in darkish red from the stripes that branched across his hide
from scalp to toes, a somewhat short, reddish blond beard with
a hint of red along one upper edge, on his left—no, his right
cheek, her left.

(*!! . . . You?*) came the thought-image as he leaned forward, pressing one hand to the transparent material between
them.

(*Me,*) she replied, and lifted a gloved hand, spreading her
five fingers slightly, very much like he was doing but in mirror image. With every exchange of images, she was getting
a grasp of his underlying language, cognitives, nouns, verbs,
descriptors . . .

(*They shoot you! Think you me!*) The underlying image-
pulse meant *weak*, *prey*, *food*.

(*I know.*) Pulling back mentally, she reached instead into
the mind of one of the aliens by an airlock door not far from
the window, on an upper level. The stairs they used were
broader-stepped than Humans tended to build, but the alien
was busy climbing them quickly, some sort of device in his
tentacles, his mind filled with images of cold, precise scientific observations. The units of measurement meant nothing,
but he had taken a scan of her body. The readings were fuzzy,

but definitely one of *them*—and he placed his tentacle on the airlock, manipulating the suit's suckers with his own inside, in a specific pattern, intending to make his report to the officer standing next to the striped Human.

Jackie thrust off the wing, jumping into the air and soaring straight for that opening airlock. She bubbled, drawing in her arms and knees in reflex, mentally cushioning the blow of crashing into the technician. He sprawled across the floor with a muffled sound from inside his suit, and she landed inside the airlift, ship boots clunking on the metal floor. The alien rolled, trying to get himself into a position where he could stand; Jackie pressed him into the corner, squishing him lightly. A lift-press of telekinesis on the controls on the open side got the outer doors shut, a lift-press in a similar pattern on the inner controls got those ones open.

A force bubble slammed outward from the doorway the moment it cracked open, knocking over the ten or so aliens within twenty meters of her position. Darting out and to the left, toward the long alcove with the windows, Jackie firmed that telekinetic wall behind her and expanded the wall in front of her, parting it right around the Human even as she slammed the rest of her mental force into the true aliens, bowling them over. With telekinesis for her shield, she didn't have to run as fast as Brad Colvers. She just had to be able to run, to stay ahead of the enemy.

Unfortunately, she had to run several decks and back, which would exhaust her, though not as much as if she kept flying the whole time. The striped male gaped at her, one eye burgundy-hued, the other a more normal gray, both wide enough that she could see the whites all around—then *he* whirled and pounced on the tangled, tumbled aliens next to him, yanked up a weapon, and quickly fired on the nearest aliens still struggling to right themselves on the floor. The weapon flashed in light and buzzed through the air, washing over the non-Humans struggling to rise with little snaps of static. They collapsed. He whirled once she reached him, one arm sweeping out to shove her past him, and shot the others.

Just in time, too. Four of them had been about to return fire. Whirling to face her, he said, *"Sha-lou sha'ala fassou oua na'vikko chula f'sess. Fa-lou sou'kem?"*

Definitely no language Jackie knew. Alarms started blaring and lights flashed around them, pulsing orange-red. She shoved at him an image of their location, an image of those barred cells, a dotted line that meandered, and a pulse of query. He blinked, narrowed his eyes as he mulled over her meaning, then nodded and pointed back the way she had come. Picking up a few more objects from the aliens, he thrust one of the stun rifles at her, clearly expecting her to take it.

Jackie had no clue how to fire it. At least it operated on squeeze commands, not suction—though she had the impression from his mind that the controls to change the settings were suction-based—but she almost refused to take it. Then realized the others would probably want weapons . . . and that the Space Force would most definitely want samples of these hostile, sentient-eating aliens' weapons.

Picking it up, she grabbed three more like it, bundled them together, and slung them over her shoulder as if on an invisible carry-strap. The Psi League had developed several different training programs. Telekinetics who could do more than just move a penny a few inches were given exercises on how to carry and hold something in a particular way, even through other distractions. She had learned to carry equipment in the psi version of Basic Training, and even carry injured comrades. Slung over her shoulder, those guns would stay put unless she shifted them herself, someone much stronger than her mental muscles wrested them away, or she lost consciousness.

The lattermost would require vigilance; these weapons were no laughing matter. Being knocked unconscious would put Jackie in a very bad situation. Hyperaware of the danger, she kept scanning all around as she ran beside the naked, red-striped man.

Naked feet and p-suit boots slapped along the metal floor, barely audible over the ongoing wailing of the alarms. They reached an area where she had the impression from his mind that it was a lift, but he took the stairwell next to it instead. Aliens up above, armed and coming for them. She rushed another wall of force that toppled them—broke some flippered feet from the sharp cries and sharper spikes of mental agony—and her guide zapped them with his weapon as they reached that level. Two floors up, the door he picked didn't want to open.

The mental image she got from her frustrated, naked companion was that it was code-locked. She sent him an image of a frogtopus alien haloed in important shimmering lights, everyone else facing and bowing, with a uniform of the sort lifted from his fellows' minds. A query of where their commander might be located. She got back an image of *down*, that these aliens thought of *down* as more important than his—their—kind thought of important things being located *up*.

She stabbed downward, seeking the bridge. Found it after a few moments of skipping from mind to mind. Raced from mind to mind within the bridge until she hit on a smug technician who was gloating over the sequence he had played. She prodded his mind—these aliens had *no* mental shielding whatsoever—into thinking of how to undo it. The moment he did so, she flexed and pulled on the pattern of the door's control panel in front of her, getting it open.

Another blast of force knocked over yet more aliens. This time, she swept them off their flippered feet, sending even the ones that had braced themselves flailing and tumbling down the corridors in three separate directions.

She let Red Stripes shoot at them as they passed, then it was time to dig out the codes for the prey-brig. That took a full minute, and required three more blasts to keep the corridor clear, plus concentration to ignore the hissed babble of her erstwhile partner. The shock from the mind of the security officer was worth it, however, when the security door hissed open . . . and every last cage lock inside snicked free in a massive *k-chunk* that echoed up the length of the hall.

Red Stripes barked an order through the doorway while Jackie took a precious moment to expand her mind in a great sphere, sweeping the ship for any other Humans. She did not want to leave anyone behind to a horrid fate of being eaten alive . . . but there were only the five—six including herself—at the prison bay, and the five of her crew in the shuttle bay. No other ships in immediate range, for that matter.

"Robert to Jackie . . . they're bringing up what look like laser guns," she heard in her ear.

"One moment . . ." Bare feet slapped their way. Her companion hurried the coming prisoners with hissed words and a swoop of his arm. Jackie barely heard, barely saw. Her mind

focused on an old exercise, one developed by the Psi Division of the Space Force for powerful holokinetics like herself. There were a couple others who could pull it off on the scales that she could, but most could only do it in relatively smaller doses. Still, when coupled with telekinesis, it could be very effective at unnerving an enemy.

Mind floating halfway out of her body, attention turned back toward her ship, she watched, readying the illusion. The aliens in the hangar back pulled back from the ship, making room for the big cannon being brought in. A *clunk* echoed through the bay—sonokinesis—and the ship rocked . . . and collapsed.

Chunks of itself broke apart, and the *Aloha 9* reared up, forming a giant humanoid robot that just barely fit under the ceiling. The aliens gaped, then scrambled to get out of the way of the mecha robot. The mecha turned and knelt, swiping fists down toward the cannon being brought in. The aliens guiding it scrambled out of the way, tentacle arms flailing, and the cannon itself was flung aside—another force smack from her telekinesis gave it extra oomph. It smashed into one of the shuttles, spat smoke and sparks, tumbling down to the floor, and died.

With its objective complete, the robot turned, hunkered down, and re-formed itself into the ship. None of it was reality, all of it just a telekinetic blow coupled with a projection of light and sound that had made the ship look like it wasn't there, that the robot had indeed reared up and attacked. Even the Greys fell for illusions like that, despite their vastly advanced technology; they tread warily around Terran ships because some could "transform" and bash like that. The projection cost her, though. That big an illusion, remotely projected, one she couldn't see and guide directly . . . she staggered a little, exhausted, and leaned her shoulder against the wall the moment she came fully back to herself.

The other four reached their position. Gesturing with a hand, Jackie brought around the four weapons, separating them and holding them—levitating them—out to each of the others. They gaped at the weapons, gaped at her . . . and Red Stripes babbled something with mental tones of *holy* and *powerful* and *I told you so*.

That last one was a bit weird . . . but it spiked hope in all five of them, particularly the four who had just been freed. Red Stripes gestured back down the hall, started trotting that way . . . and slowed when he realized Jackie wasn't yet following. Nodding her helmed, visored head, she pushed away from the wall, staggered for a few steps, then breathed deep the recycled air in her helmet and hurried after the quintet.

She had to tumble a few more packs of aliens off their flippered feet, but by the time they got down to the airlock door, the tangled wake of tumbled and stunned bodies piled behind them at various cross-corridors and in the stairwell had discouraged anyone from approaching again. The aliens inside the hangar bay started to surge their way when the door opened, but the *Aloha* clunked and lifted its robotic head with an audible creak . . . and they quickly scattered, leaping over objects with frightening grace, alarming height, and unsettling speed just so they could land and huddle behind them for cover.

That was the true advantage of the mecha illusion: Pure light and sound was easy compared to wielding enough telekinesis to bowl over a bunch of heavyset beings. It was a bluff, but a very effective bluff.

Jackie's companions shot at them anyway. Some dropped, insensate. The rest hid. Breathing hard, Jackie extended a ramp from the wing, composed partly of holokinesis, partly of telekinesis—hovering planks of a plain matte gray, since she was starting to get rather winded. Red Striped eyed her, eyed the steps, eyed the airlock door, which slid open—or rather, revealed itself to be open—and quickly mounted, leading the others.

Jackie came last, dissolving the steps in her wake. All six of them crowded into the airlock, and she thumped the buttons for closing it while Red gave an order that had all the weapons being passed to the tall, brown-haired, brown-and-pink-bearded fellow with the vivid spiral stripes several shades brighter than Red Stripes' hues. Pink Spirals touched a few buttons on each weapon, and their power lights, orange-yellow, dimmed and vanished. Which was good, in her mind. It meant they knew they were in safe territory and that they were going to be good, peaceful guests.

(. . . ?) Red sent to her.

Jackie held up her hand in a *wait* gesture, catching her

breath. Robert was trying to talk to her at the same moment, and his query was more important.

"*Okay, so we have some, ah, alien Humans on board, sir. What do we do now, Major?*"

"*I have . . . one more trick up my sleeve,*" she panted, still trying to get her wind back. She rested her hands on her knees, turned sideways to the others in the airlock so that her helmet didn't thump into anyone. That forced her to avert her eyes from the genitalia of the dark-skinned male with the blue crescent marks dotting his brown hide. "*Lars, Maria, get down here and . . . use gestures to get them strapped into acceleration seats in the crew cabin. Feel free to raid the lockers for clothing for 'em. We're all going to be stuck in quarantine together anyway.*"

"*What's the trick?*" Ayinda asked.

There, she had some wind back. "*I'm going to read the alien commander's mind, find the command codes to lock out their weaponry, and shut them down by yet more telekinetic manipulation of their control boards. Then I will hopefully also unlock that force field, and if I can, shut down their whole ship. I don't know how fast they can get everything back up and running, but the moment I do it, we all have to be strapped in, because I want you three to get this ship the heck outta here.*"

"*Any particular heading, Major MacKenzie?*" Robert asked. "*Diagnostics claims the projection dish is still viable, thank God.*"

"*I suggest we take the fastest route to hyperspace that won't crush or kill us,*" Jackie said. "*Make a jump of one second, two at most, then execute a vector change by five degrees—any length and direction Ayinda says is clear, up, down, left, right—and let us drift, but keep up the insystem fields, and keep an eye rearward for pursuit. If we're pursued, hit another rift for two seconds, and another vector change, but make it ten degrees in the direction of home. If not, then just continue on that original bent heading while we figure out what we're going to do with these people, beyond the obvious of rescuing and clothing them.*"

"*Got it.*"

She could barely hear the others; the five Humans crowded

into the airlock with her were babbling in a round of questions and arguments with their red-striped leader.

"That'll put us either in interstitial space or in the Oort cloud for this system, as its heliopause is bigger than our own," Ayinda warned her. *"I cannot guarantee we won't hit a rock. Space is vast, but we're dealing with probability odds nonetheless."*

"The exact distance is flexible; adjust it as you see fit to get us clear of any rocks. The important thing is to get clear long enough that I can learn these people's language, and finally make real contact with them."

"What about the 'contact' you made with those octo-frog aliens?" Brad asked.

"The only contact they were interested in was in knocking us unconscious so that they could throw Mr. Red Stripes back into his cage, strip and lock me up as well, take apart this ship, and have each one of us for lunch, preferably still alive so we can kick and scream in their version of dinner and a show. I got that directly from their minds and from Red Stripe's mind, not just hinted at in the precog visions. Those frog-octopus-ostrich things are not friendly to Human life-forms."

Red Stripe said something curt and sharp, slashing his hand. The others fell quiet, and he started to make his way to her. The door behind them opened, rushing a little bit of air into the cabin to equalize the pressure. Maria eyed the quintet, then smiled and held up bundles of clothing. They all looked at each other, looked at her, looked back at the helmed Jackie, minds filled with a babble of images of *children* of all odd things to be thinking about in that moment.

Red Stripes gave an order, nodding in permission, distracting them from their thoughts. That was a thankfully Human-interpretable gesture. One at a time, they filed out of the airlock, accepting underpants, shorts and tee shirts. Waiting her turn, Jackie learned what the words for *thank you* were. So did Maria, she suspected, even without the advantage of "overhearing" the underlying meaning pulsed behind it.

The central corridor was a little awkward with its foot loops on the "floor" of the hallway, but the colorfully marked strangers only tripped a couple times as they spread out. No bras for the two ladies, but that could not be helped; they did manage to puzzle out which ones were the undershorts and that they were meant to be put on first, then the knee-length shorts.

Maria then pulled out the first of the health-monitor bracelets. She tucked it around the arm of the short woman with the most vivid skin coloring—medium brown tan for the majority of her skin, but with lightning-forked stripes like Red Stripes that came in two shades, moss green and soft cream on tanned skin. The non-Terran woman jerked when the doctor touched her, and flinched back at the *snick* of the bracelet's clasp catching.

Babbling something, she stared at it in fright and pawed at it, trying to get it off. Jackie, trying to get her helmet off, quickly intervened, projecting directly into the two-striped woman's mind an image of the bracelet being connected to a viewscreen of a heartbeat line pulsing away, and of her striped self smiling happily. It also helped that Maria held up her arm, showing off an identical monitor bracelet on her own wrist. Jackie quickly showed an image of Maria's smiling face next to a similar heartbeat monitor. That soothed the short woman's fears, but the others were now babbling. Returning her attention to the link she had with Red Stripes, she shared the same image with him.

He nodded after a moment, and explained that the bracelets were for monitoring health, nothing more. Glancing her way, he caught sight of her face as she lifted the helmet free of her head . . . and blinked at what he saw. (*Child!*)

The exclamation was so strong, so startled, Jackie actually turned to look behind her at the closed airlock door. Which, of course, was closed, and had nothing there. She looked back at him. (*No child. Adult. Me, adult.*)

He blinked, his thoughts a confused whirl for a long moment, then he shook it off and frowned in concentration, sending an image of them leaving the alien ship, of it blowing up, and the however-many-of-them sailing off with happy smiles. She winced a little, since blowing up the alien ship was not on her list of things to do.

So far, they hadn't killed anyone. Broken a few limbs, yes. Knocked many unconscious one way or another, yes. But killed, no. There was a peculiar feel to the aether when someone or something died. Jackie was no ectomantic psi, capable of communicating with the deceased, or rather, communing with echoes of residual psychic energy, but she did know when someone or something sparrow-sized or bigger died.

Instead, she sent back an image of the alien ship shutting down, all of its lights going away, the bay opening up, and the Humans getting away with happy smiles. With it, she sent a mental image of the five of them following Maria and now Lars into the starboard cabin and letting themselves be strapped into the fold-out acceleration seats set in the cabin floor, preparing for said escape.

He eyed her, then slowly nodded. Gave out more commands in their language. Jackie left them to it, grateful Red Stripes was able to get the others to cooperate.

Closing her mind, she sorted through and set aside the babble of ten Humans in close proximity, and worked her way through the alien minds outside. Orders were being blared, and the lights were still flashing, but the beings inside the hangar were forming an orderly retreat. *They* were technicians far more than heavy-duty soldiers . . . and no one wanted to risk Robot Ship waking up again; two of their cohorts with badly damaged skeletons were being carried out on stretchers.

If they hadn't been highly skilled technicians, they might, Jackie realized, have been placed on the dinner list. The threat of being eaten alive was a good tool for crew discipline, it seemed . . . but no one had expected a robot ship, and so the crew members carrying the injured ones weren't sure if that was to be considered stupidity—and thus reason for being eaten—or a purely uncontrollable accident. For now, they were being treated as accident victims.

She shuddered and moved on. The bridge was down a few more decks, deep in the heart of the awkwardly lobed vessel. Finding the commanding officer, she delved awkwardly into his brain. Long seconds stretched, turning into a minute as she tried to find the right commands.

He only had some of them, she realized. The other belonged in the microtentacles of the chief engineer in an upper position. Splitting her mind, she sought out and sank into his mind as well. Found the right commands. Found the right consoles. Practiced silently—wasting another minute—and then held herself carefully together so that she could open her eyes and move to the cockpit.

That was something she could not do just yet. Lars stood at her elbow, waiting patiently to catch her attention. At some point he, and presumably the other two, had gotten dressed, though like Maria, he wore the Grays of the Special Forces as a specialist consultant. Striped with the black of the Space Force, as all casual uniforms were, and striped with the blue of the Navy to indicate he was working primarily with the latter, but still plain gray.

"Are you back from soaring through mind and space? Yes? Good," he said. "Maria and I are agreed, one of us should stay with them, to provide noises that are soothing if nothing else, and to provide eyes and ears in case they get into anything. We saw the red-striped male seemed to be in charge, through your helmet cameras. So. Maria has gone to disable my station. He will sit there, and I will take his place with these others. Maria needs to monitor their health from her station, and the rest of you are all needed in the cockpit. I am the one free to sit with them.

"So. Do you know the words for 'please stay' and 'please be patient' so I can keep them in their seats?" he asked her politely.

Jackie shook her head . . . then nodded, reaching out to Red Stripes. A couple of pulsed thoughts, and his voice floated out of the crew quarters. He stated two phrases, somewhat similar to each other. Lars nodded and left to join them, practicing the words under his breath. Grateful the geophysicist was willing to help herd their unexpected guests, Jackie picked her way to the cockpit. Then had to reach out and urge the now tee-shirt-and-shorts-clad Red Stripes, mentally and physically, to rise. That let Lars take his place, allowing Jackie to guide Red Stripes mentally through the kitchen and corridor cabins to join her at the cockpit door.

Another awkwardly projected set of commands got him to help her in stripping off the rebreather pack, and with it her helm. Now that she no longer had her helmet on, with the vents circulating air in the cabin, she could smell how much he needed a bath, but she had to set that aside. Jackie stuffed it into the storage locker by the airlock and guided him into the cockpit.

Helping him strap into Lars' seat was necessary, since the man kept blinking and staring at the faces of the others, then at the consoles. His mind couldn't settle on any one subject. *Children* was one, though she couldn't for the life of her have said why. *Handles* was another, with an impression of disbelief coupled with disappointment, a hint of *primitive technology*? But she got him strapped in, and got herself strapped in across the aisle.

"Commander Graves," Jackie managed aloud. "Are you prepared for a swift departure?"

"Say the word, and I'll bring the thruster fields online," Robert promised her. "It'll knock over a bunch of things in here, though we shouldn't end up hitting the ceiling."

Reaching for those distant consoles, picturing them firmly in her mind—she had a touch of clairvoyancy, which was attached to her holokinesis, which was attached to her telekinesis—Jackie danced phantom sucker cups over the consoles down on the bridge, and up in the engineering bay. First things first: Gravity dropped abruptly, leaving them all in zero G, aliens included. *That* was to ensure that there would hopefully be fewer aliens near control panels that could counteract her work. Ayinda's dreadlocks started drifting upward again, as did Red's matted blond locks.

Gravity off, check. More alarms blared outside; the bridge crew were strapped in their seats, looking up at their monitors as they reacted—but she shut off the ship's main generators, darkening a lot of those screens. And after that . . . the command codes for the ship's weaponry. Not only did she shut them down, she *changed* the commands for accessing the guns. Just by a few pushes and pulls, a few different circle-key points, but enough to hopefully slow down these aliens so the *Aloha* could get away.

The moment the hangar bay went dark, Robert warmed up the thruster engines, scraping the hull off the ground. Brad shook his head. "You didn't cut the doorway field. We're still stuck in here!"

Whoops . . . I'm getting tired. One more mind-read, this time from a technician nearby, and Jackie found a console near his limbs. The field shut off—and air rushed out of the bay, dragging forward the hovering ship and anything else not bolted down. The decompression wasn't dramatic like in entertainment shows, but things did lurch doorward, and kept drifting that way under the lack of any artificial gravity to give them firm friction against the floor.

Power monitors spiked, the *Aloha* kicked forward under thruster power, and they sailed free. Past a couple startled, limb-flailing, pressure-suited alien techs who had been swept outside by the lack of gravity and the exiting atmosphere. A surge from the ship pressed the Humans into their seats, leaving tumbling aliens, floating toolboxes, and enemy vessel all behind, but not so hard that they couldn't breathe or speak.

"We should be . . . clear," Jackie managed. "Free to flee. I changed the codes on their weapons. I think. 'M exhausted, though. Going to need rest and food, then I can tackle our guests."

"Lurching through hyperspace isn't going to do anything good for you, either," Maria warned her. "Not on top of exerting yourself so much. But that *was* rather impressive, *señorita*. Flinging aside aliens, and that robot you created!"

Jackie shut her eyes, gripping the armrests. "I'd rather have been practicing schools of . . . of tropical fish, for the Merrie Monarch Festival."

"You'll have time to practice while we're in quarantine," Maria told her. "But first, we have to get out of here."

"Already on it," Robert grunted, accelerating a little faster. They still had a couple more minutes to go to reach half Cee, the requisite speed for navigating a hyperrift successfully. If it weren't for the invention of insystem thruster-field technology, not only would it be impossible to do anything other than communicate through pinprick hyperrifts, they wouldn't have been able to reach out to the other planets in their home system, never mind travel to distant stars like this one. But it still took time to get up to speed, and there was no telling how fast the tentacled frog-people would get their systems back up and running.

CHAPTER 6

Li'eth was so wrapped up in the aftermath of shock after shock from their rescue that he barely felt their acceleration easing. He did notice the spark-bubble that flashed out from the nose of the rapidly traveling vessel; it was bright, abrupt, and unexpected. He noticed it when it turned toroidal, collapsed, then exploded, expanding into a great, gaping, golden-white maw. *That* caught his attention, but only for an eyeblink, because he noticed that they dove *into* it, whatever it was.

The next thing he knew, they were shaking through a tunnel streaked in odd shades of multigray chaos, before being spat out the far side. Reeling in his seat, Li'eth clutched at the armrests, heart pounding, stomach roiling, and head spinning. His mouth was dry, and his tongue had a slightly metallic taste on it.

"Gloin vabhen!" the female in front of him ordered, sitting in the middle seat of the three arrayed on the port side of the cabin. Or at least that was what it sounded like to him. *"Fheer shantu gshelguh."*

The gibberish she spoke probably wasn't that, but with his head throbbing and the whole cabin feeling like it was spinning and sliding off to one side, he couldn't be sure *what* she had said. *No, that's our vector changing,* he realized, feeling his body tugging down and back to the right, which meant they were flying up and to the left. The acceleration eased, leaving them still speeding rapidly through empty, dark, star-strewn space. Not that he had much of a view, but at least he could see a little bit out the silvered cockpit windows.

Li'eth didn't know what to make of this ship, that tunnel, or the child-faced people who had rescued him and his few remaining crew. It was obvious from her closely formed space suit that the first woman, the Great One with the powerful mind, was a fully formed adult. Curves for hips, breasts, waist, even her legs and arms were shapely, fully mature. But her face, her scalp . . . Tanned, smiling in a friendly, re-assuring way, but devoid of proper marks.

All of them lacked marks, from the tanned woman with the dark curly hair to his left, to the dark-skinned woman in front of him, the pale woman to her left, the tanned and not-tanned men in front of both of them, and that pale blond fellow who had looked to be as tall as V'kol. It was discon-certing. None of them looked like an actual child.

Instead, they looked like unfinished adults. Their auras looked mature . . . well, most of them. The one two seats in front of him flared a little. The woman in the portside middle seat was quite calm by comparison, though the male in front of her, with the black hair and tanned skin, was calmer than anyone, save maybe the blond with the long hair seated some-where aftward.

The blond male up front . . . his very short, almost fur-like hair reminded Li'eth of a juniormost crew member on one of his earliest ships, back when he was still an ensign fresh out of the academy. Li'eth couldn't remember the man's name, but the private had been given the worst jobs, the scutwork, never trusted with any task requiring authority or care . . . and all because the man had been markless. Li'eth had felt nothing but pity for him, until one day the ship's computers developed a set of glitches no one knew how to fix, glitches that were throwing off their interstellar navigation ability.

The crewman had knocked on Li'eth's cabin during his sleep cycle, his aura calm and steady, and had handed a data-crystal to the very sleepy ensign. Li'eth had secured the crystal in a drawer and gone back to sleep, having been up for a good thirty hours trying to help fix the problem since he'd come on board assigned to work with the navigation department. It wasn't until a full day later that he had gone back to his quar-ters after helping install a crude patch in place that allowed them to fly, but forced them to stop every light-hour traveled to double-check their heading. Only then had he remembered the crystal and slotted it into a datapad to see what was on it.

The code that scutwork private had written was pure genius.

It was a mathematical program that worked *around* the glitch, compensating to the ten-billionth place for the problems in the processors, allowing them to fly straight. More than that, the realization of what he had in his hands had shamed Li'eth. The crudely patched problem that his fellow bridge officers had come up with over the last four hours, but which still left them drifting off course by five-thousandths of a percent . . . had been solved near perfectly by the juniormost crew member.

Li'eth had gone to the man, had offered to personally set him up with the Royal Astrophysics Computing Corps, or perhaps the Royal University of Mathematics . . . but the man had only shaken his head and replied that he'd still never get anywhere even if Li'eth could get him a job there—a job not involving scutwork and floor sweeping and brute gun-toting, that was. Li'eth had then offered to pay for inked marks, but again had been met with a sad shake of that blond, short-haired head.

I'd not be myself if I got all marked up, Ensign, sir, was the reply. *If you can't accept me for who I am,* as *I am . . . how much else of my life would have to turn into a lie?*

These people were *not* V'Dan. He knew that. Habit kept his eyes and the brain behind them trying to *view* them as V'Dan, as strange, half-formed, incomplete adult-children, but the Sh'nai writings spoke of them as a separate race, for all they were supposed to be from the fabled Motherworld of the Before Time. Knowing that *he* had a part to play in all of this—not the details, but the general gist of it—Li'eth started repeating in his mind over and over, *They are adults, and I shall see them as such. They are adults, and I shall treat them as such. They are adults, and I shall respect them as such . . .*

Conversation flowed between the other five while he sat there and thought. The Great One was speaking into a headset, shaking her head, nodding, shaking her head. The dark-haired woman in front of her turned and eyed Li'eth a few times, then finally reached over, tugged at a silver packet, and flipped her hand at him with a pointed look. Li'eth, not sure what she meant by it, reached out to her with his mind.

And got mentally slapped. His hands felt a phantom sting, as if he had been a child reaching for a sweet at the wrong time of day, though it had been delivered to his mind, not to his body. The Great One spoke aloud, staring hard at him.

"Please wait," she asserted in Imperial Common V'Dan, her pronunciation rather good, considering she had only heard him say it a couple of times in her head. She emphasized it with a mental image of him resting, composed, in his chair. And followed it with a picture of him taking the silver bag from its clip, twisting the straw-end thing, and tugging on it to . . . break the seal, he realized so that he could drink whatever was inside.

He was thirsty, and it would fill the time while he waited. Unclipping the bag, he twisted the straw, and cautiously sipped. Some sort of *citri*-flavor, he realized. It tasted really good, too, sweet and something else, something his taste buds were craving. Salt, that was it. A touch of meatiness, too?

As he waited, Li'eth watched the frustrated-sounding Great One, and reviewed his memories of seeing Salik after Salik—pound for pound as heavy as a V'Dan, if not a little heavier—being flipped up into the air and dashed against walls and floors with nothing more than a thought from her. A strong thought, but still, nothing more than a mere flex of her mind, repeated many times.

If she can do that, then . . . maybe she knows the secret of how to make our abilities work when we want them to, instead of sporadically? Just from that demonstration alone, she is clearly more powerful than most of the Holy One Saints in our entire pantheon . . . if you discount most of the legends as sheer hyperbole. Perhaps close to their equal with the hyperbole . . .

Finally, the woman said something in a very assertive tone, then a more polite one, and ended whatever communications system these people used. She rubbed at the bridge of her broad, tanned, unmarked nose, sighed, then sent him an image. One of both of them drinking from the silvery packs, of her eating out of a different packet, and then her . . . sharing something with him? No—teaching him! Teaching him a language? Her mental projection had her pointing at objects and saying words, then picking up an object—a bowl—and carrying it to a table in the vision, along with a simple string of words that probably meant *I carry the bowl to the table*.

She then pictured *him* telling *her* how to say it in his own language . . . and then pulled back the viewpoint of her projection, showing him that this elaborate pantomime of the two of them cooperating was merely a vision *within* a vision, for the two of them sat cross-legged on a surface, with her hands interlaced with his, both of their heads bowed, and little bubble-clouds merging overhead to form that vision of each teaching the other their words.

Oh! She means to teach it to me mind-to-mind! I . . . did not know that was possible, he acknowledged to himself, blinking a little. Not that he should be surprised; she was clearly the best-trained Great One he had ever heard of, let alone encountered. There were holy priests back home who would flush and pale for hours, perhaps even days in envy of her abilities, he was sure.

Part of him was very leery of letting her farther into his mind, however. He had too many secrets, too many things that had to be kept secret or they could become a very personal danger to his existence and freedom. These people might have rescued him and the other survivors—and how he wished they had come earlier, when there were still dozens of crew members alive!—but he didn't know their motives. Other than somehow it would all work out well enough to end the war the Salik were slowly but steadily winning.

On the other hand, they were essentially trapped with strangers, with no way to communicate anything beyond the most basic, gesture-driven needs. The prophecies had never said this Motherworld would somehow magically know how to transport them to the right home system. Without real communication, without real language knowledge . . . He would have to trust in the future the holy writings had predicted, and hope that this Great One had a sense of discretion, should she learn anything about his past.

(*Yes,*) he projected at her, agreeing to the language learning. She smiled a little in relief and said something to the others. Three of the four in the cockpit relaxed and said things in what sounded like slightly joking tones. The fourth, the short-haired blond man, tensed and muttered under his breath. The Great One replied to his mutterings in a tone both dry yet soothing. Assuming their emotions were as V'Dan as they looked—minus the lack of marks—it was a subtle display of diplomatic maneuvering. Over what, he didn't know, but Li'eth had heard that kind of tone before, slightly exasperated, somewhat amused, and a hint of dismissive, all coated over with a conciliatory reassurance.

The liquid in his drink pack was finally starting to taste odd. Salty and unpleasant. Li'eth realized it was an electrolyte restorer; those always tasted good whenever a body desperately needed rehydrating until the body received enough. As there were only a few sips left, Li'eth finished drinking anyway, then carefully reclipped the used packet under its tension spring.

She touched his mind again—or rather, widened that ongoing perception link between them—and projected an image of the two of them moving . . . elsewhere. Of strapping themselves into place so that they didn't float randomly while they worked. He nodded, adding a pulse of *yes*. Then fumbled his way through the odd restraint clasp, until he was free and could follow her through the cockpit door. Then through a side door, more of a hatch, where they had to maneuver around the markless blond male with the long hair and the long limbs.

Or rather, they stopped there so that she and the male could have a conversation. He finally nodded, and she soared gracefully into the next section. Li'eth had to pull himself after her, but there were plenty of handles. He'd seen the size of this ship from outside. It should have been just big enough for generators that could power gravity weaves in the deck, but there weren't any. That didn't bode well for how advanced their technology should be.

"Captain!" Ba'oul called out, spotting him first. "What's going on? Who are these . . . people?" he asked.

"And *why* did someone give a starship into the command of children?" Shi'ol added, her tone tart with dismay and disgust. Li'eth couldn't see her face since the Great One was in his way, but he could hear just fine.

"When are we going home, sir?" Dai'a asked, her tone plaintive, her gaze clouded with the lingering horrors of their recent captivity.

He opened his mouth to speak, but found it subsumed by another projection from the Great One. From the wide-eyed blinks of the others, they were receiving it, too. A vision of them unbuckling from their seats, drinking and eating from packets, came to them. They were invited to stay in this cabin, with images of them going to the doorways but turning back rather than crossing into the next rooms. A rather . . . odd . . . image of the biowaste facilities followed, projected first in reality of what the closet-like chamber looked like and which door it was, then she used a *drawing* to demonstrate the elimination of waste. But the message got through, at least.

The next set of images were a little confusing. It showed her and Li'eth sitting strapped into seats in a different section, of her touching his head . . . of the others—even her own people—coming close, but being blocked from touching them. Wire mesh, cages, a clear-dome force field, repeatedly they were blocked. And when one of them was allowed to touch them, the image of the Great One snapped to her feet, anger on her face, finger pointing far away, and her abilities flinging the person—the blond, markless man with the long hair—far away, but without harm.

"What . . . ?" V'kol asked. "Mind-speaking . . . she's a *Great One*?"

Ba'oul rolled her eyes. "If you hadn't noticed her knocking over the Salik who tried to attack us, then yes, she's a Great One. A *child*, but a Great One."

"Everyone, please. We have been rescued. We will be going home soon. *But*," Li'eth cautioned, "we need to learn each other's language before we can exchange star-chart information and help them to help us *find* our home. This woman is going to teach it to me, and she's adamant about our not being touched while we do so. I have no idea what sort of . . . of holy ritual or power this is, but it's clear she's very powerful, so if this woman says, or projects an image, that she can teach me her language, or learn ours, or whatever it takes . . . we will be *patient* and give her the time to do so. We will follow her rules while doing so, too. Do not touch us, and . . . relax, stay in here, and drink the pouches of electrolyte water they gave you."

Shi'ol snorted. The Great One who had rescued them had grabbed a bundle of clothes and pulled herself back to the previous chamber, where it was clear she was peeling her way out of her current suit. "That's not a woman. That's a child with breasts."

"They are the same species as us, but they are *not* V'Dan, Leftenant Superior Nanu'oc," Li'eth chided her. "Get that through your heads, all of you. They are our hosts, and we will act with as much courtesy, civility, restraint, and common sense as we can muster. And we will *not* take offense at anything they do or say—*or* appear like—because we are not them, they are not us, and we are very much dependent upon their goodwill to get back home. They are willing to help us, but we must be patient and polite if we are to find out whatever it is they will bring to our war that will help us to win it. We will treat them as we treat all non-V'Dan, as members of the Third Tier or higher."

"They don't even have artificial gravity," Ba'oul stated, gesturing at their surroundings with the hand not gripping a handle to keep him floating in one place. "And their flight capacity was very rough and nauseating at one point. These are not exactly inspiring predictors of what they can do."

"That's because we . . . I don't know, jumped into some sort of space-tunnel thing during the rough moment. Something they did with this ship has made them feel relaxed enough to not worry about pursuit," Li'eth explained. "I don't know what they did, because I *don't* know their language, so I am going to help her learn to communicate with us."

Dai'a eyed him. "Sir, you *are* a Captain, our highest-ranked officer. Is it *wise* for a . . . a member of a foreign nation to read your thoughts?"

"I have given that a lot of thought, just now," he told her, feeling a little grim. "I don't think we have much of a choice. It may be that however this works, it will require both of us being able to sense each other's thoughts, mutually. Of the five of us, only I have that ability."

"Oh. I forgot you were a Great One. Sorry, sir," she apologized, her voice dipping so low, it was almost a mumble.

"It's alright. You haven't remembered because it hasn't been nearly as useful as I'd like," he admitted. "Maybe if I'd been the one in the family picked to go into the diplomatic forces instead of the military, or gifted with an ability to read *alien* minds, not just our own kind . . ."

Voices in the next section drew their attention. The woman with the black hair conferred with the woman with the deep reddish-brown back and forth for a bit, then did something in one of the cupboards. Sighing heavily, the

Great One projected another round of thoughts. This time the images were a set of progressions.

In the first series, Dai'a and Ba'oul were selected, while V'kol and Shi'ol waited impatiently. The two were fed packets of food while the dark-haired woman watched carefully, intently. Dai'a and Ba'oul—in the image—started looking unhappy, clutching at their stomachs, rubbing at their arms, and the other woman quickly touched each with an implement, some sort of delivery system for medicine, then watched them with a concerned look until they both looked better after a few moments.

The image repeated, two others were selected—Shi'ol and V'kol—they ate different food-objects, and this time both were happy, and the doctor looked relieved. Then and only then did she offer the same sort of food from the second part to the other two, and carefully watched them with concern, medical device ready in her hand for the slightest show of stomach upset or whatever.

Li'eth blinked. "I . . . think they're going to make sure their food is compatible with our bodies, and that the two of you will be first, Dai'a, Ba'oul."

"That would make the girl with the pale skin and black hair their medic," V'kol said. "Though I guessed as much from these monitor things."

"Woman," Li'eth corrected, catching it a few seconds late. "She is a woman, not a child."

He sent an agreement to their hostess, who had changed into gray trousers and a gray shirt, each very plain-looking but striped down the sleeves and legs with a black and a blue line. She, the black-haired woman, and the long-haired blond man all wore gray clothes with black and blue stripes down the sleeve. The other three, he realized belatedly, were clad in blue with black stripes down their sleeves. *Does that mean these three are higher-ranked than the other three?*

He didn't have time to find out. The Great One darted out the forward door, space suit in hand, and vanished for a few minutes. She poked her head through the aft hatch and sent him an invitation-image requesting he join her. Pulling himself by the handles, Li'eth maneuvered into the central corridor. At the far end of the corridor from the cockpit, she had attached restraint straps to opposing walls and gestured for him to join her in working his way into one of the harnesses.

It took a bit of squirming, but once secured, he was able to float comfortably without fear of bumping into anything. That was when she reached for his hands and started to sink her way into his mind. He flinched a little, overwhelmed by her presence, and she jerked in reaction, wincing. She tried again, slowly and carefully. He tried to reach out for her, but this time his gifts lurched, spiking. She jerked her hands free, wincing, then breathed deep herself. Three slow breaths, and she looked calm.

Once again, she reached for him. Her aura was calm, a softly shimmering cascade of calm creams with a hint of soothing, cheerful peach. He didn't always see in the same colormood hues like what the Gatsugi used, but pastels were gentle and calm, saturated hues were intense and healthy, dull hues were affected unpleasantly by inner emotions or physical ailments. Blue was the normal colormood for happy in Gatsugi terms, calmly pleased in Human ones—close enough to count—but he suspected this light peach was that calm sort of happiness that happened on a really good, easy-going day . . . and he suspected she was projecting it deliberately.

By comparison, his own aura flared and shifted awkwardly. He tried to help. Each time he did, they only got so far before his holy powers surged like a bucking animal. Finally, she pulled her hands free, blew out a slightly irritated breath, and studied him a long moment. He tried to send her a pulse-thought of apology, realizing her aura was now spiking a little, colors changing quickly, though not with any uncontrolled flares, unlike his own.

She winced a little at his attempted apology-pulse, but nodded in acceptance, and thought privately some more. Brown eyes studied his face thoughtfully. Finally, she squared her shoulders, straightened her posture as best she could in the lack of gravity, and held out her hands, looking rather formal and formidable. Knowing this effort was important, Li'eth placed his hands in hers, placed his trust in the child-looking woman across from him, and tried to relax, to let *her* do all the work.

That was precisely what she did. She swept into him like a gale-force wind, swirling up, in, around, and all but forced his eyes shut. Li'eth felt like he had to steady himself against the dizziness being evoked. Li'eth abruptly felt like a puppet in her arms, that he was a bodysuit. That she was going to wear him while she worked. No longer able to see the predominantly white-paneled corridor, with its excellent lighting, he found himself in a great, dark, empty place, like a warehouse so vast, he only knew there were walls and a roof because the air was calm, not windblown, and the ground was hard, polished stone.

A cone of light shone down from overhead, its source distant and indistinct despite its strength. All around him—both of them—were scattered bits of clothes. She walked around from behind him, circled him with an intense, studying expression in her brown eyes, then snapped her fingers. A drawer opened in his stomach, tilting out like some sort of built-in bin. It was a little alarming, until Li'eth remembered that this was a metaphor place, not anything representing reality. That, and she had a drawer-bin thing of her own, tilted out from her own lower torso at a touch of her fingers to her upper stomach.

A sweep of her hand sorted the clothes. Some were in her people's style. Some were in his. They soared around, then dove into each owner's bin. It felt weird, but Li'eth had no power to resist; she was circling him from the outside, but still controlling him from the inside in a display of multitasking that left him feeling a bit in awe. There were other garments, too, he realized. Ones that felt like *Other* to him. To her as well, for she flung them out of the pool of light, letting them vanish into the dark.

When the last garment was stowed in place, and he was feeling oddly full . . . she spun rapidly in place, her body jiggling and bouncing. He didn't have time to take note of anything interesting in those wiggles, though, for around her were several monitor-like images hanging in the air. Dark liquid flung outward from a centrifuge's mesh basket. Pale solids remained. The darkness felt ill and wrong, the pale felt healthy and right. Sieves appeared, with water that rinsed through the clothes, clean from above, dirty where it went through the sieve. As she spun, the darkness flung out of her body, sucking itself off in a conduit that went into a giant jar. When the "water" ran clear, there was no more darkness, and the images of sorting and sieving and cleansing changed.

Now there were rectangular bricks of hole-scattered objects, absorbent sponges in a mild cream shade. The clothing turned into a sort of blue liquid while the sponge compressed, then the sponge soaked up the liquid, turning more and more blue, the holes filling in with each indrawn breath. After five or six breaths, the sponge was now a solid, smooth brick of homogenized translucent blue, no sign of the coarse sponge texture. The floating images showed her gripping the brick, parting it to show that the interior was smooth and whole, then she pressed it seamlessly back together, whole and strong and stable.

The same thing, Li'eth realized, was happening inside him, under her puppet-master touch. It was imperfect, but when she finished absorbing his clothes into his body, turning them mostly homogenous within the rest of himself . . . he felt better. That was when he realized each piece of clothing was itself a deeper metaphor.

Pants for determination, socks for merriment, military uniform for obedience to duty, formal vestcoat for pride in his lineage . . . they were facets of his personality, he realized. Not literal clothing, but parts of himself, his own inner body as it were. With three deep breaths, he tried to blend and accept the last bits, letting go his last wisps of inner resistance, until his own sponge-brick turned gelatinous smooth.

That earned him a smile and a pulse of approval. She reached out, scooped up his brick-self, and reshaped it into a sphere, with a flattish spot to stand upon. Put it inside of him . . . and then pricked it so that it seeped into every cell of his body, filling him with a great sense of balance, calm, and relief, of a stable strength he had not felt in years. Or perhaps never; the strain and stress that vanished almost made him as dizzy as her initial assault, for as that selfness filled him, when he breathed deep, accepting and blending it into body and soul, he almost wept with how good it felt.

No . . . not good. *Centered.* All around them were images of giant whirling storms with an eye in the center, and of a Li'eth-shaped dot moving into the center of the storm. A point of calm untouched by the raging winds of existence. A state of being that was vastly preferable to having the bits and pieces of himself scattered all over the place, trampled upon and kicked about by anyone and everyone passing through.

(Centered. Yes. You are now centered. Remember this feeling, this method,) she told him, pulling back her puppet-self. Two deep breaths, and her aura was calm, once again peach-soft.

Looking down at his limbs, Li'eth realized that for the first time in his life since he had started seeing the things, *his* aura was calm. Calm, steady, and perhaps not spike-bright when it pulsed, but neither pastel-low nor dulled in its intensity. Sensing more was coming, he looked into her eyes again.

She had one more lesson for him. Her own inner bubble, as transparent as glass, peeled away from her physical center, swelling up to encompass her whole self, as if a personal force field were being erected.

It acted like one, too, in metaphor-space. Things came flying her way, bits of foreign clothing, even an old battered boot, but they just bounced off that bubble. It flexed, but it held. It shifted and spun, never breaking under the various blows, for it held, protecting and defending her. She breathed deep and exhaled strong, showing him that it was not so solid that it would suffocate her . . . and layered three more behind it, letting the next incoming boot "pop" the first, only to bounce off the middle one, while the inner became the middle as a fourth moved up behind them. She turned the shield-bubbles as hard and opaque as stone, as fragile but impressionable as paper, as strong as spaceship glass, and as flexible as an elastomer. Showing without words that these shields could have different abilities, different functions, all at a thought.

Cautiously, experimentally, he focused on pushing a bubble of his own outward . . . and felt it giving him relief from the pressure of the others' minds even as it traveled outward through his body, bumping and molding against hers . . . and then melding and merging with her shield-bubble, until the two were in a great oval. She blinked in surprise and gently extricated herself. Mostly. The shields parted with difficulty . . . and the moment they bumped together, once again, they merged into a single, larger bubble.

She frowned for a moment, then shook her head, visibly choosing to move on. A pair of chairs appeared next to them, facing each other. Gesturing, she urged him to sit across from her, then held out her hands. Li'eth complied. This time, his aura twitched once or twice but did not buck, did not kick, and did not knock her back. And this time, when she took his hands . . . she guided him into closing his eyes, breathing deeply, physically, until he opened his real eyes and stared at her.

In the visions, her hair had been loose and flowing, hanging halfway down her back. In reality, it was coiled and pinned firmly in place on her scalp. Realizing this was reality helped center himself in his own body, to the point where he could feel a little bit of dizziness. It was nothing, however, compared to how *calm* he felt, how stable inside. Not a tangled mess of locks but a neatly coiled bun. Tidy, like her hair.

(*Ready?*) she thought at him, pulling his attention away from her curls. At his nod, she tightened her grip on his fingers slightly, then loosened it back to a comfortable level. (*We begin.*)

He had just enough time to take in a breath, before his mind and hers fell into a sea of images choked with vocabulary, starting with numbers. Binary for ones and zeros, yeses and nos, then progressing to trinary for no-yes-maybe, then a leap to base ten mathematics, the counting games each had learned as a child to learn all those numbers, and from there all the other games each had played as a child, counting games, naming games, learning games, cultural-context games. And with each scene drawn up, every single item within each image was identified and labeled.

Blue or black or greenish brown, large versus small, curve, line, corner, *grass* was this kind of plant-based ground cover, and it was green and thin-bladed, while *vesh* was that kind of ground cover, soft, fuzzy, broad leaves in a fairly similar shade of green, with words like *dirt* and *soil* and *sand* and *clay* underneath, with *bushes* as a broad category that narrowed down part by part, bit by bit, until branches gave way to twigs gave way to leaves gave way to veins and stoma and chlorophyll, only to spool into *moss* and *shuwv* upon which *bugs* crawled and *gluks* crept, with *chiton* and *antennae* and *thorax*, *abdomen*, *compound eyes* . . .

Every so often, she would pause the images and remind both of them to breathe deeply once, twice, thrice, before diving in on the fourth inhale. Early-childhood memories mixed with teen years—and yes, she was learning things about him, but she sent him pulse-thoughts of *It will be fine* and *These things are yours, and will remain yours to speak about* along with *I am trusting you to keep what you learn of* me *to yourself as well* . . .

Those mental reassurances were pulsed over and over, gentle, repetitive, solid and sincere, a background tempo that was slow and soothing despite the vast speed at which he—they—were learning. The feeling brought up a memory in him, of watching a series of pictures taken of a woman's face once each and every single day for years upon years, from the very first day when she had gained her first *jungen* marks, visible on her face and shoulders and throughout her sleek black hair in spotted aquamarine blue, to the day when there was far more gray and white than black among those strands, save for those steady blue marks. Faded a little, perhaps, but still *jungen* blue.

Each picture, both then and now, lasted for barely a swift blink of time before being replaced by the next. But though it was said that a picture could convey a hundred sentences of information, this was more like ten hundred, or twenty hundred. And they overlapped in many ways, like how so many of that woman's early images had been taken standing in front of the same set of windows, often seen at night, sometimes seen during the day, but sometimes the window covers changed, the *curtains*, that was her people's word-sound for the hangings. Later ones were taken in front of other windows, some for many years, some for short periods of time, but *window* was frequently there, and always there was *woman*, and *eyes*, and *nose*, and *hair*.

This was very much like that. Peripheral words that weren't used as often would take time to recall, but the basic set that everyone used, those returned time and again, wearing grooves in his thoughts like feet gradually wearing grooves in a carpeted floor . . . and it kept going on and on . . .

Jackie was used to the overly full feeling in her head. Red Stripes . . . or rather, Li'eth, which she had learned among his many other names meant *Year of Joy* . . . was not. He had no practice in sorting through languages delivered in rapid-fire training, though he did know more than one language, some of which she had learned along the way in passing. So when the session came to an end, and she realized through his shared thoughts that he couldn't open his eyes . . . she swept into his mind and tipped him into sleep with a careful, smooth underthought.

Withdrawing her fingers from his as they grew lax with slumber, she stared at him, once again able to see her physical surroundings. Thankfully, no one had touched them during the entire process. That would have been bad. As it was, she had been forced to take over his mind in order to control, subdue, and train the very basics into his virtually untrained gifts.

His understandable caution and reluctance, more subconscious than under conscious control, had bucked her out of the link like an untrained horse trying to get rid of rider and saddle, and maybe because of a burr under that saddle blanket, too. But now, he understood what she'd been trying to do. Now, he had the barest rudiments of true control. She would have to continue to help him work on that.

Somewhere in the jumble of V'Dan vocabulary in her head—they were an odd people, the name for themselves, their language, and their main world were all *V'Dan*, though that was not the oddest she had ever met, linguistically—there were images of him trying to *pray* his gifts under his control. Religious mumbo jumbo. Jackie was not overly religious. Spiritual, yes; she enjoyed participating in the ritual dances and storytelling of her mother's Polynesian-bred background, and some of the cultural observances of her father's dual inheritance, French from her paternal grandmother's side and Scottish from her late grandfather's side. But religious? Not really.

Certainly not for something as important as training psychic abilities. Most certainly not for someone of his strength. About the only *good* thing in his lack of self-control and training was that he had natural shields *restraining* his abilities. That meant it was difficult for him to reach out and invade another's thoughts. Like he nearly had with Maria's. Luckily, she had sensed it in time and stopped him.

There were rules about how telepaths were to behave. Not laws—and this had been argued most fiercely in courtrooms years ago—because every budding telepath would have been repeatedly arrested and imprisoned for breaking those laws purely inadvertently, accidentally, uncontrollably . . . but rules, oh yes. Rules enforced by other psis, even by clusters of psis. She wasn't *the* most powerful telepath out there, but a group of five or more who were at least Rank 8 in strength could group together and slap *her* down quite firmly, for all that she was a Rank 15.

Li'eth felt like a Rank 8 right now, but with the potential to grow maybe close to her own strength. As the only other psi within range, it was up to Jackie to ensure he was trained, and up to her to teach him how to behave before they encountered any others. On top of everything else, though . . . *she* had to be very careful in how she behaved.

She knew things now, things about him, who he was, who he pretended to be. She did not have all of his memories by any stretch, but she knew more than enough that there were not only military secrets she had learned in at least some small part, but government secrets, too. Major secrets, ones he feared getting out. At some point, her own military, her own government, could try to demand that she give up those secrets, or demand that she use those secrets. The problem was, the Psi League motto stood in their way. The very strict code of ethics of a League member stood in their way.

Her own Oath of Civil Service stood in their way. She swore to its ethics each and every morning—recorded, no less—not only to ensure that her actions served the people she interacted with but the people *they* interacted with as well, even the ones outside her own "constituency" of the United Planets.

That was another point, a side note but an important one to consider. They weren't just the United Planets anymore, alone save for rare visits from an occasional enemy they called the Grey Ones, because they didn't know the name the Greys used for themselves. These V'Dan were part of an Alliance. Just a handful of sentient species, but they were out there, a Collective, two Empires, more . . .

Maybe I was right to start thinking of ourselves as Terrans, and them as, well, V'Dan. They are not Terrans, but we are . . . and for the sake of diplomacy and the giant gulf of thousands of years of completely separate history, we

*must approach them as neighbors-across-that-gulf for now.
Even I cannot assimilate every nuance of a culture from just
one person, despite being able to assimilate tens of thousands of words in a matter of hours.*

Drawing in a deep breath, she unbuckled her harness and
used a touch of telekinesis to ease away from the sleeping male.
Li'eth. *Year of Joy.* Among other names, some of which—the
most important ones—his own crew did not know. Ethically
speaking, she couldn't let *them* know what she knew, either. Not
without his permission in advance.

What was yours is still yours wasn't just a catchphrase for
telepaths; it had to be a bone-deep philosophy. Not only to keep
themselves separate from the memories of others, or risk losing
all sense of self and descending into either schizophrenic or
multiple-personality-disorder madness, but to protect a person's right to mental privacy. The only crimes she *had* to report
when sensing another's thoughts were actual murder, rape,
pedophilia, aggravated assault, major property damage, or
major theft—any of the major felonies. Even then, it was not
admissible as evidence. The Peácekeepers still had to wade
through the process of finding actual evidence, though they
could use whatever was reported to help point them in the right
direction.

The only legal use of abilities like hers in a court of law were
the hiring of a Truthsayer, who could only answer one of three
things while scanning the mind of a person undergoing interrogation. The legal counsel could ask her, "Is that statement
true?" and she could only answer "Yes," "No," or "Unclear." It
was up to the lawyers to ask the right questions, to dig out the
kernels of truth. One had to be at least a Rank 9 to be a Truthsayer, but Jackie had been far more interested in following her
father's line of work. She had served a few times on practice
trials in the law school of Honolulu University, just as she had
tried out other psi-based careers during her training, but that
was it.

All of the weight of her years of ethical training, her daily
Oath, her duty to those her people interacted with as well as
to her own people, all of that weighed heavily on her in the
zero-G environment of the *Aloha 9.* So when she floated into
the main compartment of the crew cabin, she *knew* that

Leftenant Superior Shi'ol Nanu'oc was the next-in-command of the survivors, with their captain asleep.

She knew the woman's name, and had glimpsed memories of her sometimes arrogant personality. But she had to pretend she did not yet know. There was a very real set of reasons why most telepaths avoided learning more than they had to about other people. It just made following the rules so much easier.

Her entry was quiet, but it still turned a couple of heads. The first two to notice their entrance were Dai'a, the deeply tanned woman with the two shades of *jungen*, and Lars, who was playing a game of magnetic checkers with her at the back of the cabin. Dai'a looked up abruptly—up being relative—and that made the Finn curious. The geophysicist lit up with a smile when he saw her, while the life-support officer cast her an anxious, hopeful look.

In Terranglo, Jackie addressed Lars first. "I've learned their language as well as given him ours. The one I transferred languages with is their captain, so I need to find whoever's next in charge. I'll spend several minutes talking with the others, reassuring them, then I'll give a translation to everyone else. Your patience is appreciated, Lars."

"I will let the others know," Lars assured her, and touched the headset over his ear, murmuring to the others—the other Terrans. The other V'Dan, who were floating behind him, had turned at the sound of her voice. The blonde woman with the grass-green rosette-clustered spots dotting her golden pale skin, narrowed her eyes.

"About time they stopped holding hands!"

Jackie could feel the angry pulse of thought of the other woman, that it was disgraceful for an unmarked *child* to hold hands with a grown man. She had a better grasp now of what the reasoning was behind that *child* label these V'Dan used, but that wasn't a good enough excuse in her own mind. Counseling patience, reminding herself firmly that neither side knew much about the other, still, she switched to V'Dan, speaking with Imperial High V'Dan fluency so that she would sound like a social equal to the other woman. She didn't quite understand their Tier system but knew that she had to establish at least some level of self-rank.

"We were not holding hands in any romantic manner,

meioa," Jackie said carefully. The last word she used was actually Solarican in origins—some sort of feline-like race of sentients—and it meant *honored one* when used without a suffix indicating one's familiarity with the other person's gender. Using the genderless version was considered more polite, so she didn't bother to tack an *-e* onto the end of the word. Her words not only made Shi'ol gape, but made the other two males twist and turn themselves so they could stare at her, and made the life-support officer blink in surprise. *"Physical touch amplifies my 'holy' abilities, as you call them. Physically touching those whom I exchange a language with makes the process happen a lot faster and a lot easier.*

"As you can hear for yourselves, I have learned Imperial High V'Dan, and am capable of answering some of your questions, and of posing some of our own," she added. Shi'ol drew in a breath to speak. Jackie quickly lifted her hand between them, with the palm facing herself instead of Terran style toward the other woman. The gesture in V'Dan culture meant *please wait, I am not finished.* *"I will need to eat and rest soon, to finish assimilating and memorizing what I have learned, but that is only because I am* very *experienced in transferring languages. Captain Ma'an-uq'en is not, and will need to sleep for a few more hours to set our people's language,* Terranglo, *firmly in his head. As will each of you in turn, when I go through the transfer process with you as well.*

"In the meantime, allow me to make introductions. I am Ambassador Jackie MacKenzie. *I also function as a soldier, in specific a* Major, *which is a midranked officer of our people's Space Force,"* she stated, phrasing it in a way that the V'Dan would be able to pronounce. They had a lot of glottal stops, some subtle and some strong, along with other quirks of speaking. Thankfully, one of her first languages alongside Terranglo had been Hawai'ian, which meant she was no stranger to pronouncing those glottals. *"These title and rank were given to me by our government, the United Planets. Our group identity name, I will call* Terran. *We are* Terrans, *we are of the Terran United Planets, I am a Terran. It comes from one of our oldest known languages, and means 'Earth-like.'*

"You are on board one of our exploration vessels, which we call Aloha 9. *The word* aloha *has several meanings, most*

of which involve kinship, compassion, greeting, and other pleasantries, and the other word means the number nine— one thumb shy of both hands," she added, lifting both hands with the fingers splayed but her left thumb tucked in. *"There are over thirty such vessels currently in use."*

Robert, Ayinda, and Brad floated into view. Adding in the three of them to the others crowded the main crew cabin a bit, but Brad tucked himself into the opening to the kitchen area so it wasn't too crowded.

The commander and chief pilot eyed her and her upraised fingers and smiled. "Telling 'em what our ship number is?"

Jackie smiled back. "Yes—the language transfer was a success, and Captain Li'eth Ma'an-uq'en is sleeping it off, so please let him rest."

Lars, floating off to one side, nodded. "I have had a language transfer. It is very important to sleep immediately afterward. Our brains retain new information best when we are allowed to sleep on it."

Shi'ol frowned at the others and spoke sharply. *"I demand to know why this ship is crewed by* children.*"*

Jackie felt her smile stiffen a little and counseled patience. *"Meioa, in our culture, your statement—that we are children—is considered to be very rude. Not to mention highly inaccurate. Each and every one of us is well above the legal age of adulthood. To continue to refer to us, or to act toward us, as if we were children would be insulting. I realize you know nothing about our culture yet, however, so I choose not to take offense. Please refer to us as adults from now on."*

The other woman stiffened and spoke firmly. *"I am Leftenant Superior Shi'ol A-kai'a Nanu'oc d'Vzhta ul S'Arroc'an, 373rd Countess S'Arroc'an, and I demand to speak to whoever is in charge here."*

"Are you the next-in-charge, when Captain Ma'an-uq'en is asleep?" Jackie asked mildly. *"He informed me that he is the one in charge of all of you."*

Shi'ol smiled tightly and braced her hands on her hips. The gesture made her start to rotate slightly, forcing her to lift a hand to the nearest wall for stability. *"Yes, I am. I demand to speak to whoever is in charge."*

The others did not object, though the man with the bright

hot-pink stripes did roll his eyes a little. Jackie faced her verbal opponent calmly. *"I am in charge of this mission. Moreover, I am at this moment the third-highest-ranked person in our entire government. Only the* Premiere *and his apprentice, the* Secondaire, *are higher in rank, power, and authority."*

"Apprentice?" Shi'ol all but snorted.

"Your captain informed me that your government system is an Empire, a monarchy with a chartered set of laws detailing the rights of the people versus the rights of the Imperial Throne. Our government is a democratic republic, *wherein our people are selected by a series of competency tests followed by votes of confidence from the groups of people each member represents. He mentioned it was similar to the government of the Artisans Valley, save that instead of ruling over hundreds of thousands people in a single region, our government functions to guide and serve tens of billions of people scattered across several locations.*

"Now, please mind your tone and speak with a great deal more of courtesy and respect. You are guests *in our house,"* Jackie emphasized. *"You are now dependent upon our goodwill and our willingness to provide hospitality. Please do not repay it with disrespect and hostility—a countess of* our *people would be much more respectful than you have appeared to be, so far,"* she added, sensing Shi'ol was about to dismiss her. *"Please also keep in mind that I will be dealing with Captain Ma'an-uq'en as your leader, not you, so please do not try to arrange any deals or make any promises. Those are for him to arrange, as your duly appointed leader."*

That earned her a smug smile from the countess. *"Only in matters military. I* outrank *him in all civilian ways, and our government is civilian, not military."*

"Our current situation is purely military, meioa," Jackie countered blandly. *"And will remain so for quite some time. Please behave with a greater level of courtesy and politeness, or at least restraint and tact, or I will have to ignore everything you say, turn to the next-ranked person among your group to speak with, and I may even have to ask your captain to discipline you. Your attitude is* not *giving a good impression of your people's ability to be mature and polite when negotiating for hospitality with strangers."*

"I will stand witness to you being a rude idiot, Shi'ol," V'kol stated. He turned his attention to Jackie. *"Since we do not have a ship, Leftenant Superior Ba'oul Des'n-yi over there is third-in-command and our chief pilot whenever we have a ship. Leftenant Superior Shi'ol is our logistics officer. I am Leftenant Superior V'kol Kos'q, tactical officer. That lady over there is Leftenant Superior Dai'a Vres-yat, our life-support officer. Would you please introduce us to the others, and tell us their names and designations as well? We are all curious about each other, I am sure."*

"Your courtesy and civility are deeply appreciated. I will first tell the others your names," Jackie replied. She wished any of the other three was second-in-command with Li'eth unconscious, but no, she was stuck with the rank-conscious countess. Switching to Terranglo, she introduced everyone. "The male with the red stripes sleeping in the back of the central corridor is Captain Li'eth Ma'an-uq'en—it's not quite pronounced like *mannequin*," she added. "This blonde woman with the green leopard spots is Leftenant Superior Shi'ol Nanu'oc, a very prideful and prickly countess in civilian rank, and their logistics officer in military rank.

"The others are all Leftenants Superior as well," she continued. "The third-ranked is Ba'oul Des'n-yi with the blue crescents; he's a pilot. The hot-pink-striped fellow here is V'kol Kos'q, their tactical officer, and the lady with the irregular green and cream stripes on her brown hide is Dai'a Vres-yat, in charge of their life-support systems. I will now introduce the rest of us to them.

"The darker-skinned male with the short black hair is Commander Robert Graves—*you would say Captain Superior, I think. Robert is our chief pilot, and he holds a military rank equal to my rank of* Major, *save that his is associated with piloting,"* she glossed over. *"The dark-skinned woman is* Lieutenant Commander Ayinda Mbani; *Ayinda is our navigator and her rank would be equal to your rank of Captain. Behind them, the short-haired blond male, is* Lieutenant First Grade Brad Colvers, *copilot to Robert. Brad's rank is the equivalent of a Leftenant Superior.*

"The lady with the black hair is Dr. Maria de la Santoya, *a civilian contracted to work with the Space Force, and the*

long-haired blond fellow here is Specialist Lars Thorsson, *our mission geophysicist and backup navigator. In military terms, I function as the communications officer, and now that we have made First Contact with non-Terrans, in both military and civilian terms, I am in charge of this mission."*

Jackie made sure to speak slowly and carefully, at a measured pace, so that her companions could pick out their titles and names and give a friendly wave to match face and body to name and rank or designation. Everyone looked at each other, giving little nods, then Brad spoke.

"I'm going back to the cockpit. I'll send Maria in to greet everyone."

"Good idea, thank you. She can give us a report on their health," Jackie added. *"Maria will be joining us shortly. I'll introduce you to her, then translate while she discusses your health. We have been presuming that you are somehow fellow* Human *beings like ourselves—that is the name we call our own species—but we are not yet completely sure. She will have more information from her monitoring efforts."*

"Captain Ma'an-uq'en swore that we'd be rescued by a powerful new set of allies," Ba'oul stated while they waited. *"But if you will forgive my initial impressions, you do not seem very advanced, and thus not very powerful.* You *seem powerful, as a Great One, with your holy abilities, but . . . you don't even have artificial gravity."*

"True, but we have only just begun to learn things about each other," Jackie countered as Maria poked her head in through one of the hatches. *"Time and more language transfers are required before we can learn more.* There you are, Doctor." She quickly ran through the introductions of the others, adding, ". . . and I have told them who you are, and that I will translate your health report on each of them."

Maria blinked, drew in a breath, and shrugged, gripping the edge of the doorway to keep herself floating in place. "They all have a little bit of nutrition deficiency, but not by much. That captain of theirs will need to eat when he wakes up, but otherwise they are all quite physically healthy. Psychologically, you would know better than I. No outward signs yet of microbial infection from our germs to theirs, though their immune systems have been stirred. I've been having them swap medbands with the others in the crew so that our own health can be monitored—I can't wait to get back to the station so I can monitor everyone because that's the only place that has enough bracelets, plus better equipment.

"We might suffer some sort of cold or fever in the next week or so. It depends on how quickly and how well our immune systems can recognize the intruders and fight them off—we could be very sick, going into quarantine, or we could be just fine. We had three spare bracelets, but we really needed two more on this mission. Robert, hand your medband to Jackie; she's been in physical contact the longest."

Peeling it off, he sent it tumbling gently along the length of the cabin. Jackie didn't even have to guide it telekinetically, but then their pilot had plenty of experience at maneuvering in zero-G conditions, including sending things to companions across a cabin. Catching the band carefully, Jackie latched it over her left wrist, just in front of her ident bracelet.

Maria nodded in thanks and continued. "My medical opinion is that we need to hurry back to *MacArthur* to get into quarantine, where we can have access to a much greater array of medical aid and be monitored much more thoroughly. The longer we delay, the worse our bodies will suffer from the effects of hyperspace sickness and disease-based sickness. The combination is rarely pleasant."

"Are they Human, though?" Jackie asked.

"The DNA scanner says they are"—the doctor shrugged, flipping up her hands—"though I suspect all of them have a little bit of extra code in their genes. I suspect it's to make them look like they were painting twentieth-century 'modern' art on themselves," Maria added dryly. "That much, I've been able to determine, is not paint. Well, the one with the red stripes has some sort of paint on his face, but the rest of them are all just . . . dirty? They've been caged up without a bath for a while now . . . in case you haven't *smelled* it."

"Be respectful, Doctor," Jackie admonished, watching Maria wrinkle her nose. "They didn't exactly have a choice in facilities. And from what I understand, the *jungen* as they call it is something which everyone is infected with from the womb onward, and which after a weeklong fever, marks them with these colors and patterns. I haven't found out the reason *why* just yet, but there is one, I am sure." Switching languages, she said, *"Our doctor says that you are indeed fellow Humans as far as we can tell. This means that we will be able to render medical aid. For the moment, you appear to be mostly healthy, but each side is now exchanging pathogens, viruses and bacteria. We will each likely be sick for a while, some more so than others.*

"It is important that we get this ship back to a space station with proper quarantine facilities, where we can be monitored by several professionals. Our method of interstellar travel accelerates biological processes, making us hungry, thirsty, nauseated, and so forth. It is a very swift form of flight, but can only be undertaken safely in short hops. We will be able to get under way as soon as your captain has awakened and eaten, and the doctor has checked him to make sure he isn't . . . uh . . ."

Jackie found herself blinking and trying to sift through the thousands upon thousands of words she had learned. After several seconds, she gave up and used different phrasing to work around the fact that the V'Dan didn't seem to have the word for *allergic.*

". . . We will make sure before we jump that he is not suffering from any food-borne illness. It is important for his ability to communicate that he be allowed to sleep at least three hours, so we will have that much longer to wait before making the first of several jumps. It will take us approximately ten jumps, and more than two days—Terran days, we don't know what your time units are, just yet—to get back to our base station," Jackie explained. *"We limit multiple jumps to three or four at a time, with several hours' rest in between because they do strain our biology. Undertaken in moderate, well-spaced amounts, they do* not *pose any significant risk of bodily harm. We do not take any risks with yourselves that we do not undertake ourselves, and those risks have already been minimized.*

"The doctor will want us to take just one jump, then monitor your health for a while, to see how well your biology reacts to a full jump, rather than the tiny one we endured getting ourselves beyond the range of the Salik." Switching languages, she said, "Maria, my apologies, but you were thinking rather loudly that you just want one long jump with a pause

first, to monitor their health, before undertaking three hyperspace jumps in a row. I took the liberty of informing them that this is what we will do."

"De nada," Maria dismissed in Spanish, lifting a hand. "I'm not Colvers, to fuss over someone overhearing my loudest thoughts. It is no different for a telepath in such moments than for a regular person overhearing a conversation in the next room. You cannot help it, not when I'm the one stressing my thoughts . . . perhaps even in the hopes you *would* overhear."

"Gracias," Jackie returned, grateful for her understanding.

"De nada," Maria repeated, and grinned. Then dropped her grin and pointed her finger. "And I need *you* to eat something again. You just expended another large amount of your inner resources, transferring a language. When will it be safe for you to do another round? So far only you and Sleeping Beauty in the next cabin over can interact with these people."

Jackie nodded and held up a finger, switching languages. *"I will need to eat something, then I will have enough energy for one more transfer before we will make the first jump, at which point I must eat again, and sleep. As we will be stuck with each other for several eating-and-sleeping cycles, and as this is not a formal moment, I am going to state that it is socially and culturally acceptable to use our first or given names, not family names and ranks or titles, from this point forward, until we are once again in a formal situation of introduction and formal negotiation. Which will not happen for a while, as I have said.*

"With that in mind, Dai'a, I would like you to be the next person to receive a language transfer. Will you give me permission?" Jackie asked politely.

"I am the next-in-charge. You will give this language to me," Shi'ol stated sharply.

"You are currently being watched very carefully to see just how arrogant and offensive you might act," Jackie returned neutrally. *"Your language transfer will wait until after I have had a chance to consult with your superior officer as to how to deal with you. Please take the intervening time to review how you have chosen to address me, how you have spoken about myself and the other Terrans, and please think carefully on exactly what sort of impression you are giving us*

Terrans on what the V'Dan Empire is like in how it treats the strangers it meets. In the meantime, I thank you for whatever patience, courtesy, and discretion you do display."

"It is you who must impress me, as the current representative of our government," Shi'ol countered, chin lifting a little.

"According to what I learned from your own captain, you have not been granted any legal authority to claim any sort of representational position. Only he, as the military superior in this group, has that right of representation—I did not learn everything of your culture, but he was careful to inform me of that much," Jackie replied levelly. "I wondered at first why he was so careful to insist upon that . . . but now I do not wonder nearly as much."

Spots of pink appeared on the other woman's cheeks, clashing a little with her grass-green spot clusters.

Dai'a spoke up before Shi'ol could, dragging the topic back to Jackie's question. "Will this language transfer thing hurt?"

"You may have a headache, and your dreams will be awkward for a week or so. You must also speak as much as possible in the language once it is learned, using it more often than your own tongue, to make sure it sets itself in your mind," Jackie cautioned her and her fellow V'Dan. "It will be as exhausting as running a long race, the kind that takes hours to travel, for all that it will be mental running. But it will be worth it.

"First, I will teach all of you to speak our main trade language, Terranglo. Then I will teach the members of my crew how to speak V'Dan, along with the observers who will be watching over us in quarantine. Oh—please forgive me, as I almost forgot," Jackie added, wincing a little internally. "Everything you do—which all of us will be doing—from the moment you came into view of my helmet cameras to the moment that quarantine ends will be recorded and observed. This is not meant as an invasion of your privacy but rather as a safety procedure.

"At no point will any of those recordings leave Space Force Special Forces Judge Advocate General jurisdiction—that's the legal and ethics division of our military. There may be requests for publicly accessed interview recordings," Jackie added, "but unless there's an act of lawbreaking involved, if you choose to refuse, our laws will help enforce your decisions *on the right to relative privacy. We would not monitor anything if it weren't for the fact that we need to monitor for cross-contaminating illnesses, health-wise. For everyone's safety, yours and ours, that level of monitoring cannot be refused. Please take reassurance that we six will also be under that exact same level of scrutiny for that same reason as well.*

"Additionally . . . though we do not assume that you are, we do realize you are a new group, with an entirely new culture and attitudes, and the military will want to make sure you don't turn out to be insane, brutal murderers at some point," she finished, injecting a touch of humor into her tone. *"We're hoping that you are not, and we believe these are reasonable precautions that your own military and government would want to take, so it's only fair to our way of thinking. Our ethics, however, require us to mention it up front."*

". . . Right," V'kol stated. *"Well, it's good to know that, as you snoop upon us, you have* some *ethics—this is what we call mild sarcasm,"* he added. *"No true offense is meant."*

Jackie smiled. *"None taken. Irony is endemic among our shared species. Dai'a, have you made up your mind? Would you like to be one of the first interpreters for your people, alongside your captain?"*

"If it doesn't hurt," the green-and-cream-striped woman offered hesitantly. *"Then . . . yes, please?"*

Jackie nodded. *"I'll do it as soon as I have eaten."* Switching languages back to Terranglo, she said, "I'll be getting some food, doing a language transfer on Dai'a, here, and by the time it's done, Li'eth should have awakened, had time to eat, and then we can jump. Dai'a and I will sleep while the doctor monitors everyone for a few hours, then we'll string a few jumps, everyone will rest for a bit, then I'll transfer a few more languages. First the V'Dan—they call themselves, their language, and their planet V'Dan—and then I'll take two volunteers among our own crew to learn their language. By that point, we should be within hopping distance of *MacArthur* Station, whereupon we can all have a nice hot shower, a long nap, and I can begin transferring languages to everyone else."

Robert and Ayinda nodded, and turned to leave the cabin. Maria ducked out of their way, then pulled her head and shoulders back inside the crew compartment. "I've already begun sending biology readings of our guests back to the medical staff on the station. They are all lividly curious to know how these fellow Humans came to be, with their colorful hides, their extraneous genetic markers, and whatever led to them being on that other alien race's ship."

"They're called the Salik, and they are even more nasty than the precognitive visions implied," Jackie stated. She smothered a yawn. ". . . Pardon me. Right now, I really need food, I need to get Dai'a's translation session going, and all the rest can wait until we've caught up well enough that most everyone can actually talk to each other, rather than relying upon just one or two of us to translate."

"Agreed." Maria pointed at the kitchen compartment. "Go. Eat. Don't make me shake my finger at you."

Jackie pulled herself toward the back door, so she didn't have to float through and bump against the others. "Yes, Doctor. Of course, Doctor. On my way, Doctor."

"And no sass!"

"Whatever you say, Doctor."

CHAPTER 7

JANUARY 29, 2287 C.E.
CPP 17BETA SYSTEM

Nauseated groans erupted around her as they bumped back into realspace. Jackie reached for the electrolyte pack clipped next to her acceleration seat, twisted the straw to break the seal, and started sucking on the contents. She heard a couple of the others fumbling for them as instructed, and one who fumbled for a spacesickness bag, though after breathing slow, controlled breaths for a few moments, Ba'oul did not actually retch.

This time, she was seated with all five of their guests, as the one person who could translate V'Dan. On the first leg of their escape, she had been needed up front to use the hyperrelay's emergency channels to contact Premiere Callan, Admiral-General Kurtz, and Admiral Nayak to discuss what to do with this unanticipated First Contact situation. True aliens were one thing, but Human "aliens" were another.

Admiral Nayak and Admiral-General Kurtz had argued against teaching the non-Terran Humans how to speak and understand Terranglo. Callan and Jackie had argued *for* giving them that information, so that they could at the very least be able to read emergency-procedure flyers and be able to communicate with anyone they encountered while guests of the United Planets. She had also explained that it was difficult to transfer only one language at a time and not exchange both languages.

In the end, Jackie had requested the Premiere—Commander-in-Chief of the Space Force—to make a final ruling. He had put his foot down, supporting her decision to teach Terranglo as well as learn V'Dan.

Gently, in V'Dan, she said, *"Keep breathing, slow and steady. Remember to drink the liquid in small sips at first. Keep drinking it so long as it tastes good. The doctor will be here shortly."*

"What was that awful ride?" Shi'ol asked. She sounded far more miserable than arrogant, at least. *"Traveling faster-than-light never feels that awful."*

"Yes, why does the ship have to shake?" Dai'a added. *"I still feel nauseated by it."*

"It's . . . some sort of very strange travel method," Li'eth tried to explain. *"Some sort of tunnel . . ."*

"It is called 'hyperspace' in your tongue, and it's an off-shoot of mathematics, along the lines of cosmic strings and space-folding theory," Jackie explained, removing the straw from her mouth. *"We use a great deal of energy tuned in a very special way to force space to bend and connect two points together in a sort of cosmic tunnel, and we force it wide enough so that a ship of this size can go through. The bigger the ship, the larger the tunnel needed, the shorter distance that can be traveled and the slower the ship has to go, with an upper limit on how fast and how far."*

"How fast and how far is *how fast and how far?"* V'kol

asked. *"Do you know the speed of light in the vacuum of space? Can you use that for a reference?"*

"Oh Tee Ell, which in Terranglo is shorthand for other-than-light," Jackie explained, *"can create a hyperrift—cosmic wormhole—big enough to let a ship of approximately this one's size travel at a distance of roughly two Human resting heartbeats per light-year, with a year being the time it takes for our main world, the one our species evolved upon, to travel a full circle around its parent star. As for how long a Terran year is compared to a V'Dan . . . we don't know that yet, but I can tell you that we normally sleep 365 times in a single year, give or take a day every so many years."*

Ba'oul choked on his drink. Little droplets of electrolyte juice went flying forward. He muttered an apology and slowly waved his arm ahead of him, trying to capture the wayward bits of liquid by trying to get them to adhere to his skin via surface tension before they hit the back of V'kol's acceleration chair. *"Sorry—did you say two* heartbeats *to the light-year? You said, the distance light travels through space in one of your years? Three hundred sixty-five cycles of sleep?"*

"I did. We travel in thirty-second jumps—about thirty-three heartbeats," she explained, since an average heartbeat was around sixty-six beats per minute. Reaching out with her mind, Jackie corralled the wayward drops, bringing them in close to land on Ba'oul's shirt and be absorbed by it. *"Which means we travel about fifteen light-years per hop."*

The intercom clicked on, bringing Robert's voice to all of them. *"We have achieved a stable path in the CPP 17beta System, nice boring red-dwarf system, just some burned chunks of rock several light-minutes away on the system's plane as we traverse the nadir hemisphere, and nowhere near our location or dead-ahead course. You may let our guests know that they are free to move about the cabin."*

"What did he say?" V'kol asked their interpreter.

"He says we're drifting through the edge of a star system with a small red star, along the bottom half of the sphere, and that we should consider ourselves free to unbuckle," she translated. *"Since the doctor will have already transmitted*

our position to our superiors in the military, that means she should be here in just a few more moments."

"Transmitted?" Dai'a asked.

"OTL *requires a great deal of energy to open a hyperrift big enough for a small starship to get through it,"* Jackie explained. *"But to open a tiny pinhole tunnel just big enough to transmit a communications signal means that the signal takes roughly 150 light-years per second."* They all turned and stared at her. Even Shi'ol, wide-eyed with a strange mix of disbelief, hope, and even a touch of awe. Jackie faltered for a moment, then finished her explanation. *"At the distance where we met you, almost that many light-years away, we had only a single second's worth of lag in communicating with the main hub on the station we're headed for."*

Li'eth pulled free of his seat, twisting to grip the back of it so he could face her. *"You have a way to talk with planets* light-years *away? Right now? This very second?"*

"I have no idea what he's saying, but his legs are blocking my way," Maria stated from the hatchway. The captain's bare feet were indeed just centimeters from her face, and she raised her arm to make sure he couldn't accidentally kick her. "Also, I would like to *strongly* recommend that I be the very next person to have a language transfer, on the grounds of medical necessity. If anything goes wrong, I need to be able to understand them instantly, not secondhand. Additionally, I would *love* it if every last one of them took a shower; my nose is rather sensitive to certain smells."

"I will concede your reasoning, Doctor," Jackie allowed. "I'm sorry I hadn't thought of it, or I'd have done you second, not Dai'a . . . but at least I now have their language solidly implanted from two different perspectives. That'll make transferring it to you a lot more accurate."

Li'eth looked between them, then addressed the others in V'Dan. *"I told you the prophets all said the Motherworld would bring powerful new technologies into the Alliance to help us win the war."*

Jackie blinked. That had not come up during their language transfer. In Terranglo, she asked, "Li'eth? *Your* people have had precognitive visions of meeting *us*?"

He nodded, switching to Terranglo as well. "It is written

in the *Book of the Sh'nai* for all to read, and said to have been penned by the Immortal High One herself. The translation is approximate, but the essence of the passage is, 'When the tentacled ones attack, and defeat looms on the horizon, the Motherworld shall arise and guide Her Chosen People and their Allies to victory with powerful new technology and unbreakable will.' No one can communicate instantly between star systems . . . except for you, which would be a powerful technology indeed, if it is true."

Great, more religious who knows whatsit to deal with. Jackie had to set that aside. Not just her disinterest in religious trappings but the entire topic. She switched back to V'Dan. *"We will have to explore that option later. For the rest of you, the doctor will be undergoing the next language transfer, so that she can attend to your medical needs more swiftly. After I have eaten and slept, however . . . so please allow me to translate for her now."*

"I would rather Dai'a did that right now," Li'eth countered. *"Now that I am rested and you are not busy, you and I need to hold a discussion of several matters. I am told you claim to be an Ambassador for your people, yes?"*

"I am not claiming, I am an Ambassador. The only Ambassador we have, as we are a single, united, multiworld government," Jackie explained. *"In terms of military rank, I am a midlevel officer at best, the equivalent of one rank higher than you yourself, a Captain Superior, if I understand how to compare the two systems now. In terms of civilian political power, I am the third-highest in rank in our entire government, as of the moment of First Contact with you and the Salik."*

"And I told her that I should be the one to make all civilian-government decisions, as a Countess of the Empire," Shi'ol asserted. *"There is no one here of higher civilian rank than I."*

(*I hesitate to breach your privacy, Li'eth,*) Jackie sent to him quickly, silently, on the heels of the other woman's assertion. (*But I know that you outrank her—and you and I need to discuss my people's ethics about knowing versus discussing such things, versus the very real need to make sure this First Contact is handled with appropriate care and decorum, rather than arrogance and rank-pulling.*)

(Agreed,) he sent back, holding up his hand to silence his logistics officer.

(I took the liberty of claiming this mission is still a military-based matter at the moment, and thus my government will treat these moments as military-over-civilian authority for the time being,) she added quickly. *(We can continue to use that excuse for a while, if you like, though it will need to be resolved.)*

(Clever.) Out loud, Li'eth stated, *"At the moment, I am still in charge, Leftenant Superior Nanu'oc. I also know more about what the prophets had to say about this moment than any of you—certain information marked for a captain's eyes only, just as I knew our ship in particular was targeted by prophecy. I will therefore remain in charge. Stand down and be silent until you are enlightened, Leftenant Superior. Is that understood?"*

She narrowed her blue eyes for a moment, then bowed her head slightly. *"Understood. Sir. But I will remind you as a Countess must remind a commoner that you are not allowed to make any* civilian *agreements with these people, unless and until* you *can prove you have the Empress' authority to do so."*

"That goes for you, too, Countess," Jackie stated mildly, joining the conversation. *"As we have just met, you do not have that authority yet. The only one that can be said to count right now is military authority—much as a border guard has the right to permit or deny passage to anyone, even to a civilian diplomat."* Her interjection earned her a sharp look. She changed the subject. *"Dai'a, please do as your commanding officer requests, and translate for our doctor. Your Captain and I will hold our conversation in the corridor. Much of it will be done via mind-speaking, what we call telepathy, so that we do not disturb anyone else."*

Taking her drink bag with her, she exited through the back door. Li'eth and Maria maneuvered to get him past her and her inside the crew cabin at the midpoint hatch. Beckoning for him to join her at the aft end of the main corridor, Jackie caught and steadied him as he floated into reach. She touched him deliberately because she wanted to check on his shielding. It was . . . unsteady. Much better than it had been, but he was starting to come uncentered, and that would cause his shields to spike and flare.

(*First things first, Li'eth. You and I need to practice your grounding, centering, and shielding techniques. Normally we "ground" our energies in whatever planet we occupy, but when in space, there is nothing of the sort to ground into, and letting those energies drain into the void can be exhausting. So I will show you how to separate out, bag, and purify negative mental energies,*) Jackie told him. (*We do so by using a similar set of visualization exercises to the first ones, and we will discuss the why as well as how to blend back together the scattered facets of yourself to achieve a very calm and stable, centered psyche.*)

(*We have more important matters to discuss, Great One,*) he stated, shaking his head.

Jackie shook hers in counterpoint. (*This is far more important. My people have several rules on how those with these mental abilities must behave. You tried to read Maria's thoughts earlier without permission. I had to stop you from doing that, as that is against the rules. You can send an inquiry seeking permission or denial, and you must obey whichever one you receive, but that is it. You are also, by the standards of my people, very poorly trained. The only way you will be* well *trained by our standards is if you practice our methods every single day.*

(*Additionally . . . once you are centered, it is like a properly and carefully laid building foundation, capable of supporting and sustaining a great deal of effort and pressure. You will no longer inadvertently kick anyone away, and you will be able to keep out intruders purposefully, rather than flail around wildly and uncontrollably, unpredictably, holding your breath in the hope that whatever it is will go away. Again, control only comes with practice . . . so the very first thing we will do is practice. Now that I can* talk *with you,*) she added dryly, (*it will go a lot faster, and you can practice over and over on your own while I sleep. Also . . . I apologize for sweeping in and taking control earlier, but there was no other viable choice in order to make the language transfer.*)

(*I will practice it in a moment,*) he promised her, holding up his hand with his knuckles to her, palm to himself. (*Your *skills are clearly superior. But we first* must *discuss what you know about me, and what that means, and what you may have already told the others.*)

(*I have discussed very little of what I learned with any of the others, your people or mine,*) Jackie said, holding both hands up palm out, Terran style for *I'm not going to harm anything, so please be patient with me.* They might not be talking out loud, but they were still talking, and posture and gesture were still a part of communication. (*We have rules about that, too. Rules which I try to follow closely, as much for my own sake as for yours, but no less for yours as a courtesy.*)

He eyed the gesture and nodded slowly, accepting her mental words. (*I shall accept that it is as you say, unless I should observe otherwise. But . . . They do not know who I am. I am uneasy about letting your government know. No offense to you is meant because I do appreciate being rescued by you, but I would rather not anyone decide that I would make an excellent hostage in an attempt to force concessions out of . . . my mother.*)

(*I will give you the right to discuss your lineage and political clout,* or *not,*) she conceded. (*However, I must also point out that Leftenant Superior Shi'ol Nanu'oc has been consistently acting in ways that my people will find rather rude at the start, and which will only be viewed as very offensive with repetition. Given your surprise at our communications ability, I will presume you do not have that capacity yourselves . . . and by how vehemently happy you were in pointing out its existence, I will also presume that you* need *our ability to communicate swiftly to win your war against those aliens holding you captive.*)

(No one *has your ability to communicate between stars where we come from. Save by actually traveling there,*) he told her. (*Even planets within the same system take hours, all of it at lightwave speeds, if they do not send a ship via faster-than-light means. But that still takes minutes, hours, and even days to accomplish. So yes, your technology* will *be crucially important,*) Li'eth agreed.

(*Then we are agreed that your people need our technology. This is our leverage over you. Not the fact that* you *are our guest,*) Jackie told him. (*Unlike Shi'ol, you have been polite and respectful enough from the beginning. I am certain you are wise enough to continue being polite and respectful. In my carefully considered opinion, it would be far better for you to use your civilian clout to handle this First Contact situation than to keep it silent, or to try to use just your military rank alone. It is still your choice, of course, and I will not discuss it among anyone else unless and until you do, but my people will look upon yours more favorably if you do all the talking and all the decision-making. Not her. Not unless and until she adjusts the way she presents herself, the way she treats the rest of us.)*

He rolled his eyes a little, closing them for a few moments. (*I knew she'd be a headache the moment she came on board . . . but I was still a junior officer to the Captain at that time and couldn't say no. Nor could I justify transferring her once I commanded the ship. She* is *good at her job, in the military.*)

That had her dipping her head in understanding. (*We cannot always choose our companions. Lieutenant Brad Colvers hates psis because his betrothed was one, and she abandoned him for a fellow psi. He is, however, an excellent engineer and pilot.*)

(*I wonder why you would tolerate him, then,*) Li'eth observed quietly, his gray and burgundy eyes open once again, studying her in thoughtful curiosity.

(*Because like you, I do not have nearly the power that my rank presumes to have,*) she replied with blunt honesty. (*I can wield it, and demand that he be removed . . . but that could waste my clout on something trivial. For the moment, he behaves, so he stays.*)

(*Then you can see why I am reluctant to wield mine. I have no way to prove it,*) he told her . . . but even as he sent that thought, Jackie shook her head.

(*I can sense the lie, Li'eth. You do have a way to prove it, by doing so in front of both your people and mine simultaneously. I can sense in your subthoughts that your crew's reactions would confirm it.*)

He studied her a long moment, then dipped his head in a sort of slow, acknowledging bow, keeping a wary eye upon her as he did so. (*I stand . . . float . . . rebuked, Great One. The legends are true, then; there is no lying mind-to-mind with one of such great power and control as you. I do have a way to prove it, but once revealed, I have not the means to conceal it again. Like you, I would not waste such a thing on something . . . trivial.*)

Jackie sensed an impression of some sort of substance which, when painted upon the skin, looked like skin, even allowed the tiny hairs to poke up through the skin, wrinkled like skin, yet could be tinted to be more opaque than skin. It could only be removed by highly concentrated alcohol, or by months' worth of time and daily bathing.

Her gaze dropped to his right cheek—the left side as she stared at him—where she could just make out a slight difference in his cheek under his eye, below the point where the lightning stripe ended. Or seemed to end. There was a thin strip of burgundy red hairs to his beard right where it began. Their guests still needed showers, their hair needed a thorough wash, combing, and trim, and the three men could all use a shave. Particularly since it showed the truth of where his *jungen* stripe actually ended.

This face-covering, she got the sense from him, was a substance used by actors to take on different roles, to disguise their current *jungen* marks and to apply new ones. It could also be used to fake *jungen* in those who had none, though permanent tattoos were more the usual solution. It lasted for up to three weeks, too . . . V'Dan weeks, since she didn't know the Terran equivalent . . . and he had applied a fresh layer the very morning of the day his ship had been lost to the enemy. All of that was in his subthoughts, which were open to her, mind-to-mind.

If the Salik had known who they had on board, they'd have taken "Captain Li'eth Ma'an-uq'en" straight to their homeworld in the expectation of being highly rewarded for their prize—and the warship's own commander, who would otherwise never dine in the presence of the grand generals for fear of becoming a meal himself for such hubris, could have even been permitted a single bite before being dismissed.

Yes, for the honor of capturing Imperial Prince Kah'raman Li'eth Tal'u-ruq Ma'an-uq'en Q'uru-hash V'Daania, thirdborn child of the Empress of the V'Dan Empire, the Salik would have done quite a lot.

(*You said you would not betray me,*) Li'eth repeated, following hints of her own subthoughts and leaping ahead to a conclusion.

(*No, I will not. The choice is still yours . . . but to quote an old piece of our culture, "These things must be done delicately."*) She mulled it over, withdrawing her mind slightly so that she wouldn't muddle his thoughts. (*I think the revelation should come, not on this ship, but when we are holding the first formal interrogation of your people,*) Jackie told him.

She made sure to flavor the word *interrogation* to mean *intense questioning session* only, and not, say, *threats and blackmail and possible torture would be involved*. For one, *she* would not put up with such things. For another, neither would the law, and the law was the law, with no one above its reach.

Li'eth in turn spent a few moments thinking. He finally raised his brows. (*You mean, when we are all together at once, being viewed . . . I should make my revelation and remove the cover-up, so that the reactions of my own crew to the truth will carry the weight of my proclaimed authority?*)

(*That was my thought, yes,*) she agreed. (*It occurred to me fairly early on that your jungen marks had to be covered up because they seem to be fairly unique, like fingerprints are unique. Particularly a stripe that covers and colors an eye.*)

(*It's not unknown for a mark to color an eye as well as the skin and the scalp, and my particular color is not uncommon,*) he pointed out in his defense. (*All I had to do was shorten the one mark on my face by almost a fingerlength, keep my beard shaved, and I was no longer an Imperial Prince . . . but then it has been the habit to disguise all of our bloodline when we go into the military, to prevent us from being used as leverage, being kidnapped for wealth or state secrets, or even being used to "support" an argument by our mere presence, simply when stationed involuntarily at some officer's side. I am lucky no one in my surviving crew has remarked on the line of red at the edge of my beard, yet.*)

(*I think I can scare up some sort of shaving equipment,*) she offered. (*Li'eth, I would not ask you to do this if I had any confidence in Shi'ol knowing how to treat the people of an utterly unknown culture with an initial offering of*

*respect, and the patience to learn our ways before making
any judgment calls . . . but she clearly cannot,*) Jackie stated,
shaking her head. (*That isn't appropriate.*)

Li'eth sighed heavily. (*No. It is not. She is too proud of her
Tier.*)

(*Whereas you are not?*) she asked gently.

He gave her a wry look. (*My first assignment as an ensign,
the captain knew who I was. The very first thing she did when
she called me into her cabin was to inform me bluntly that she
knew I'd been born into the Imperial Family, but that so long
as I was on* her *ship, she'd treat me like a common-born Fifth
Tier idiot until I could* prove *I had brains. That she would treat
me as a lazy deadweight until I could* prove *that I could work
hard—in other words, I was lowest on the ship, juniormost,
and that I would get no special considerations from her. She
then added how she had my mother's permission to demote me
to* enlisted *if I tried to complain.*

(*Not that I would, nor that I did,*) he added, sighing again.
(*I knew Captain Mer'it was well-intentioned . . . what is so
funny?*)

Jackie had to bite her lip to keep from laughing aloud,
though her shoulders shook. (*Mer-it . . . sounds like the Terranglo word for* merit,) she sent, carefully forming the word-
sound and plastering it over the packet of its definition
without muffling the underlying meaning. (*She was trying to
judge you on your own merit!*)

As soon as he got the joke . . . it provoked a rare smile out of
him. (*Yes . . . yes, she did. And I proved it to her. I cleaned the
filters, I scrubbed the deck—by hand when commanded, not
just with a cleaning robot—and I did not complain. I had to go
to the infirmary a few times for blisters and a bashed hand, and
twice for a broken foot when I dropped things on it, but I passed
her tests of my character.*)

(*My tests of character came when I was much younger,*)
Jackie found herself relating. (*My telepathy came on early,
barely at the edge of puberty rather than smack-dab in the
middle . . . and possibly even earlier, for I'd already learned
eight or ten languages quite fluently by then. Father tested me
for discretion on some rather juicy gossip overheard by him
and some of his clients—he's a polyglot translator somewhat*

like I am, though he's not an actual telepath or anything. I failed the first test but passed the second and the third.

(*I'm sort of the weirdling of the family, highly gifted in a family not known for anything other than speaking several languages on my father's side for the last five or six generations, and in being excellent managers and representatives on my mother's side. There were some famous psis in my father's bloodline—what you'd call Holy Ones or Gifted Ones—but that was several generations back.*)

(*I think I would like to meet . . . no. No, we are getting distracted,*) Li'eth asserted, disciplining his wandering thoughts. (*There was something you were thinking, when you were talking about the moment to reveal my full identity. Something about . . . ensuring your own people had to treat us with great respect and dignity.*)

(*Yes . . . that would . . . hmm. Let me see if I can explain a little bit about our government system,*) she told him. (*A long time ago—thousands of our years ago—there lived a group of people called the Greeks, who decided one day that they did not want an hereditary king to lead them. That instead each adult male who was a free citizen would have the right to a say—a vote—in their government. And one of their neighboring lands, the Romans, thought of a similar but different system, that the people would have individuals among them who would represent their wishes when it came time to vote. These lands strengthened, prospered, and perished. Monarchs rose and fell, empires grew and shrank, but eventually that idea of a democratic republic—the people voting to put representatives into positions of authority—created several different lands.*)

(*For the first time in a very long time, the people had an actual voice . . . but people being people, they could be easily swayed by a sweet tongue or a pretty face,*) Jackie acknowledged, shrugging as they floated there in the back of the central corridor. (*And while power, and indeed great power, can be wielded well by those who are wise . . . when those who scheme without wisdom to grab power get in control . . . a great deal of corruption soaked into the system, until 'politician' became a very dirty word.*)

(*But . . . ?*) he prompted her. (*There is always a 'but' because I can sense that you are not corrupt.*)

(*But . . . a great tragedy happened,*) Jackie admitted. (*Millions incinerated by a nasty massive weapon, millions dead or dying, diseased, rendered ill, great suffering . . . and the people of many, many nations were so upset by how poorly the whole situation had been handled by many, many governments, there was a massive uprising that ended in essentially a one-world government, ruled by people who had to take a test of competency in the law, in sciences, in basic Human compassion—for there were idiots who refused to believe the many facts of science laid before them on how their bad and often willfully ignorant policies were ruining things for everyone—and these representatives had to gain and keep a certain percentage of "votes of confidence" in them from the people they represented. More than that, the percentage would be raised every single term of so many years of service, to ensure that they would have to work* very *hard on the people's behalf to stay in power.*)

She broke off for a moment, marshalling her thoughts again. That unnaturally burgundy iris of his was a bit distracting, this close. So was his scent, still a bit ripe with sweat despite the body-cleaning wipes, which had no doubt been passed around at some point, because he smelled faintly flowery from them. The ship's air filters could only do so much without an actual bath, and zero-G showers were less effective than gravitied ones . . .

(*Go on,*) he encouraged her.

(*Well, today, in this era, we rely upon the proved ethics of our representatives. So if I were to make public promises to your people—putting* my *reputation on the line—in the name of hospitality, ensuring you would be well treated, ensuring that we would do our best to triangulate your home-star system, and promising to* return *you to your home, in the welcome-to-our-station speech . . . a publicly broadcasted speech . . . it would be very difficult for anyone to go back on what* I *promised in the name of our government. This would . . . be uncomfortable for those in the military who have mistrustful natures, those who would want to lock you up and study you, interrogate you—in the less pleasant sense—for every bit of information they could wring from you.*)

(*Ah! You seek to use that offer of hospitality-and-safe-return to ensure that I am* not *used as a hostage, given my birth,*) Li'eth concluded, smiling again. (*That's very clever.*)

(*Yes, thank you. While I am ethical, and must be so by the description of my job as Ambassador and my just-finished job as a Councilor—a highest-ranked representative of a certain section of my people—unfortunately, I am aware there are those who would* not *be ethical and moral in how they wish to treat you.*)

Li'eth studied her, his smile fading. (*Is this not colluding with a potential enemy, though? To let me know of your plans, to* arrange *them with my cooperation?*)

(*Perhaps in a very small way . . . but in most ways, this* is *the ethical course,*) she said. (*I must "save face," as we say, save it for my people by ensuring that no offense is given on either side. I must seek out and take the course of action that ensures that everyone is dealt with in a reasonably fair-for-all fashion. I must also—as it is repeated so very often in the Oath of Service, the Lochaber Oath—seek to act in ways that will benefit those whom my constituents—my people—will interact with, as well as my people themselves.*

(*As I am an Ambassador of the Terran United Planets, soon to be sent to your world to make formal First Contact, I must think from the very beginning of things that will* ensure *that your people and my people have a chance at getting along. I cannot* guarantee *that, of course,*) she added wryly, giving him a look to match, one brow cocked upward, (*but I must by my calling as a servant of my government at least* try *to arrange things so that no insults will be given . . . and no insults will be met unanswered.*)

(*. . . Unanswered,*) he repeated, dubious.

She flashed him a brief smile. (*Well, I don't plan on being a pushover, a rug for you and your kind to walk all over and wipe your muddy shoes upon. That, I could get from Shi'ol . . . and I would far rather pass on it. If she tries to take over these negotiations—if your* mother *is anything like her—then it will go badly for* your *people. I can guarantee you that,*) she finished softly. Soberly. (*I may need to seek out compromises that benefit the many . . . but I also carry and represent the pride and the respect of the many.*)

(*You will be a refreshing spring breeze in my mother's*

Court,) Li'eth told her. He studied her a moment, his eyes narrowed, calculating, then finally nodded. (*I will help you. I choose to believe in the Sh'nai prophecies, but I also believe that we must help the prophets' messages come true. Carefully, of course . . . The fact that you seem to live and breathe your ethics, and not just speak of them to anyone who would listen, is very convincing.*)

(*Not everyone is altruistic, back home,*) she warned him. (*But between you and me, we can cobble together a series of events that should ensure good negotiations will begin properly between our people. After that . . . it will be halfway out of our hands, if not completely at some point. And then, as both our peoples would say if I read your memories right . . . all we can do is pray.*)

(*Indeed.*)

(*Just . . . one more thing, Li'eth,*) she warned him. (*By the laws of my people, I* must *undergo a mental scan by my peers in the Psi League to ensure that my gift-based actions have been undertaken legally, with sufficiently high morals and ethics guiding them. The others* will *learn who you are, when those examinations take place. They will be bound by the same oaths not to divulge what they learn, but . . .*)

(*It would be easier for them to already know openly about it at that point in time, yes. I will think on it,*) he allowed, reasoning it through to the logical conclusion behind her warning.

(*Aside from that, I was wondering if I could have your forgiveness and permission-in-retrospect for having taken over your mind to teach you how to ground, center, and shield,*) she clarified. (*It wasn't exactly a life-or-death situation. I could have switched to try a translation transfer with someone else.*)

Li'eth considered her words, then shook his head. (*No, it was best for you to have approached me first and taken me over briefly in order to train me. When you did it, when I realized* why *you were doing it and what you were doing to me, I realized I* needed *your lessons . . . and if this is all we have to discuss for now, I will gladly undertake them again with your assistance. With a full range of vocabulary to draw upon for questions and answers this time, too.*)

Relieved, Jackie smiled and nodded. (*I will teach you quite happily, both the methods and the rules. If and when I go to your world, I'll consider it one of my duties to teach everyone else who is gifted, too . . . or at least get you all started with the basics. Having these abilities is considered a gift only so far; the rest of it is a pain in several body parts.*)

(*I can imagine,*) he murmured in agreement. And wondered, as privately as he could, what the Sh'nai priesthood would think of her, a Great One who was this overwhelmingly powerful in so many different ways.

Jackie carefully did not "hear" that subthought. A point of courtesy that ethics demanded from her, just as they demanded everything else. He had a good start on his mental shields now, and someone less than Rank 6 would not have heard anything through them, but . . . he wasn't yet trained into the full scope of his abilities like she was. Yet.

CHAPTER 8

JANUARY 31, 2287 C.E.
SOL SYSTEM

Admiral-General Vilhelm Kurtz did *not* like the idea of announcing to the entire United Planets that they had encountered alien races beyond the Greys. Admiral Nayak pointed out that it was inevitable, and that if they released the information slowly, the reactions of humanity—Terran Humans, that was—could be gauged and guided by further dribbles of information. But as to who should release that information, both men disagreed, until the Premiere stepped in and put his foot down.

"This, gentlemen," Callan stated over the group's joint commlink, his face occupying the far left of Jackie's central monitor screen, "falls under the purview of our Ambassador.

Contact and interaction includes introduction. Plus, she is a more well-known entity than any of the gentlemen or ladies you were suggesting. A well-known and well-*trusted* entity. Ambassador MacKenzie, I leave the introduction in your hands . . . but do coordinate with my office and with the Admiral and Admiral-General."

Jackie nodded. "I have put together a montage of carefully edited images from my helmet camera, sirs. Something that will convey both the danger and the, ah, *dignity* of the events that have been unfolding."

That was the discreet way to say she had edited out the undignified naked bits. There were still plenty of cultures that had nudity taboos, plus the five captives had not been very clean when they had been rescued, so Jackie had taken the time to carefully take pictures of them from the neck up after an admittedly awkward round of zero-G showers and shaving attempts.

Shi'ol had complained about the plebeian clothes they had to wear, and demanded something "in a proper V'Dan style." Lars, proving himself both helpful and multitalented, had taken a datapad with a sketch program in it and had conferred with the alien Humans in their midst. Jackie had then sent those sketches on to the manufactory bays on board the *MacArthur*, along with scans of their sizes. At least one set of V'Dan-style clothes per person would be ready by the time they reached quarantine sector alpha.

For now, they were drifting toward Earth under insystem-thruster power, having emerged at about the orbit of Mars but inclined upward by about seventy degrees from the system plane, their designated reentry position. Everyone on board—Terrans included—had been given a chance to bathe and groom themselves as best as one could in zero G, everyone had on clean clothes, and everyone was ready to disembark.

"Gentlemen, sirs," she said, "I am ready to broadcast when you are. Premiere, would you be willing to interrupt everything for my announcement?"

"A general broadcast on the emergency code?" Nayak asked her.

"A full broadcast, sirs, not a general one. It would be best to let everyone know, openly and honestly, what is going on, sir," she said. This was something she and Maria had discussed on the way home. "Not just newsfeeds and entertainment channels, but *every* channel, because these people are Humans. They carry a whole host of diseases that are new to us. That means we need to get everyone on board with worldwide and systemwide vaccinations. *That* means letting them know what has happened. Plus, by warning everyone about the Salik, it'll help prepare everyone in case they can somehow track us back to Earth. It didn't *seem* like they could, and the things the V'Dan told me suggest they have no idea what hyperspace even is, but . . . it's better to prepare people than be caught unprepared."

"Give me two minutes, then," Callan told her, and put his screen on hold. That left Kurtz's image in the middle and Nayak's on the right side.

"I want to know what will be in your speech, Major," Kurtz told her.

Jackie ticked off the elements on her fingertips. "The fact that we have made contact with a hostile alien race, that we made contact with a *non*hostile race, that the nonhostile race appears to be Human like us, but from a long-lost branch whose origin story we do not yet know, that—"

"Why *don't* we know that, soldier?" Kurtz asked her, interrupting.

"Because, sir, we haven't had *time* to ask origination stories. I've been putting priority on *my* crew asking Captain Ma'an-uq'en's crew about the Salik, their technology, their weaponry, their capabilities, that sort of thing. Those recordings will be downloaded to the *MacArthur* as soon as we've docked and the dataports have synched. As for myself . . . I've been busy giving almost everyone on board language transfers. That takes a minimum of three hours each person, with downtime required for recovery between sets."

"Almost? Who's left?" Nayak asked her.

"I have given language transfers to Li'eth, Dai'a, Maria, V'kol, Ba'oul, Ayinda, and Lars. I'm scheduled to give a transfer to Shi'ol as soon as I've made the broadcast. Much like Lieutenant Brad Colvers, she has taken a dislike to me and would not tolerate it if she wasn't now feeling very much left out of the loop while the others practice their Terranglo around her. After we arrive, I will be giving the language transfer to Robert as well."

"But not Colvers?" Kurtz asked sharply.

"Lieutenant Colvers has an aversion to psis," Nayak informed his superior. "His skills as pilot, gunner, and engineer were deemed more important than his aversion, plus his face did appear in the precognitive visions."

"The lieutenant has not yet made up his mind as to whether or not he'll allow me to transfer anything," Jackie stated calmly. Brad, minding the helm while Robert attended to nature in the crew cabin, glanced back over his shoulder warily. She met his gaze briefly, politely, before looking back at their superiors on her screen. "It is preferable for people to be *willing* to accept a language transfer. Of course, he is well aware that if he does not undergo one, he will not be eligible for piloting the ship that will return these people to their home, or be a part of the group sent to their homeworld to open formal contact with their government. I'm not going to pressure him to make up his mind right away."

The blue-and-gold logo of the United Planets vanished from the left third of her screen, interrupting whatever reply the Admiral-General would have made. Premiere Callan appeared in its place, seeking her gaze through his screen's pickups. "Ready, MacKenzie?"

"Ready when you are, sir."

"We'll have a fifteen-second interruption warning, then I will introduce you. In three . . . two . . . one . . ."

A flashing banner appeared along the bottom edge of her screen, along with an intermittent buzzing. It was not loud so much as it was annoying, designed to catch the attention of anyone with a speaker system. The flashing, scrolling banner read, *Incoming Announcement from the Office of the Premiere of the Terran United Planets . . . Incoming Announcement from the Office of the Premiere of the Terran United Planets . . .*

Jackie smiled to herself, seeing that. At some point, Premiere Callan had taken to heart her comment in one of her reporting sessions to differentiate *which* branch of Humans they were, by calling themselves Terrans. It wasn't a formal designation, but it had been discussed and approved in the past, should such a need ever arise from, say, a colony on Mars choosing to break away from the rest of the United Planets. Everyone came from

Earth, after all. From Terra, in the ancient Latin language that underpinned much of their sciences.

"Greetings, citizens," Callan stated, smiling slightly for the camera delivering the broadcast. "This is not a full state of emergency, but I would not interrupt everyone if this were not a vital message all the same. We will go now live to the exploration starship *Aloha 9*, and to the first Ambassador of the Terran United Planets, Jacaranda MacKenzie, former Councilor of Oceania, and a trusted government servant. Please give your attention to her message as you would one of mine. Ambassador?"

A red dot appeared along the top edge of her screen, letting her know she was being broadcast. "Greetings. As the Premiere has said, I am Jackie MacKenzie, a Major in the Space Force, a former Councilor for Oceania Province, a member of the Psi League, and a duly appointed Ambassador for our people—I still recite the Oath of Civil Service each and every day, so you may rest assured that I am doing my best to represent all of you truthfully and fairly.

"With that said . . . just a few days ago while surveying the Gamma Draconis System, which is located 148 light-years from our system, our ship encountered a *new* hostile race of beings." Checking her console, she tapped in a command. "These beings are *not* the Greys, with whom we are already familiar, and whom I have already faced down while serving in the military in the past."

Callan, Kurtz, and Nayak all vanished from her screen; in their place, she saw herself on the left, and the images she wanted to display on the right, a montage of the Salik in their pressure suits, their faces half-hidden by the orange glow of their ship's lighting systems, and their greenish-beige skins wrapped in beige versions of shipsuits.

"The race you see here is sentient, and hostile. They are called the Salik, and they are currently engaged in a war with several other intelligent races. As a Rank 15 telepath and a Rank 14 xenopath, I was included on board the *Aloha 9* in its exploration mission in case we did contact anyone. From the knowledge I have picked up from the thoughts of the Salik race, their plans include interstellar conquest, and . . . well, to be blunt, they prefer to eat live prey. They particularly enjoy eating live *sentient* prey.

"During our encounter with them, my crew and I learned several things. On board their ship, they had five captives remaining from the captured crew of one of their enemy races. They had brought *our* ship on board in order to figure out its unfamiliar technology and to take captive its crew, with the intent to eat *us* alive as well. They had zero intentions of initiating any sort of peaceful contact.

"As soon as I discerned these things, I decided that the correct course of action would be to free and rescue the five captives and extract our ship from the Salik vessel. The exact details of those actions will remain classified for now, though they will, of course, be released to the historical archives in due time. Suffice to say, we were successful in our rescue and escape attempts, and have on board those five former captives. I have given my word of honor that those five beings are considered to be guests of the Terran United Planets, and that they will be treated well, until such time as we can return them to their home territory . . . as soon as we figure out where that is.

"As to *who* and *what* our guests are, this is where it gets a little strange," Jackie continued honestly. "We do *not* yet know their origins, as we have been focused on exchanging languages and information on the much more important, immediate threat of the Salik race to both our peoples. We do not know how they came to exist as they currently do, nor why they should hail from a place that is not Earth. But we *do* know that our five guests are fellow Humans."

She stared straight at the tiny dot that was the video pickup for her monitor, keeping her expression sober, honest, and hopefully trustworthy while she paused, letting everyone watching or listening absorb that revelation. When a handful of seconds had passed, Jackie continued.

"Our onboard medic, Dr. Maria de la Santoya, has confirmed that they match us genetically as a species to the point of approximately one-tenth of a percent of difference, which is the average genetic variance for our current population. So they are Human. However, they call themselves V'Dan, as a race, as a planet, and as a language. They also have access to and an understanding of different kinds of technology that we

Terran Humans do not yet share. So it is important that we do welcome them as our honored guests, so that we can eventually exchange ideas, information, technology, and more between their people and ours."

Another touch of the console shifted the images to head shots of Li'eth, Ba'oul, Shi'ol, V'kol, and Dai'a, along with Terranglo versions of their names, spelled phonetically.

Jackie resumed speaking. "Because they *are* fellow Humans who appear to have been separated from Earth's humankind for several thousand years, we will be going straight into quarantine. Dr. de la Santoya, our mission medical specialist, has been monitoring and medicating both sides as best she can under our current conditions while our bodies adjust to each other's microbiomes, the various viruses and bacteria, benign and malign, that inhabit everyone. Once we are in quarantine, she and the medical staff on board *MacArthur* Station will be gene-scanning all possible pathogens and developing vaccines for them, both for our guests to survive our own versions of the common cold, the flu, and so forth, and for their pathogens to have antigens developed for widespread distribution to all of our own people.

"It is for that reason Premiere Callan has agreed to allow this broadcast to interrupt so many of you, to reassure you that the United Planets government is not only safeguarding all of us from potential new enemies but ensuring that we are able to give warm welcomes to potential friends. We want to reassure you that we are taking every step we reasonably can to guarantee that we welcome them in good health on both sides of the equation. In the coming weeks, as microbiome data becomes widely available, please cooperate with your local health officials to ensure global and intersystem immunization can be achieved once the antigens are ready for distribution. Because these are all illnesses which are new to us, the protection of 'herd immunization' is even more important now than it ever has been.

"Once both our guests and ourselves have had our immune systems inoculated and balanced against each other, it will be my pleasure to introduce our long-lost cousins to you, both over the vid channels and eventually in person. Until then, we will be busy learning all we can about each other, about the Salik as a potential enemy of the Terran United Planets, and about the *other*, non-Salik, non-Human, and non-Grey races that also exist out there, aliens who are allies of our new guests. Your patience is therefore deeply appreciated, as is your cooperation with our medical efforts. We may seem to be moving slowly, but we are moving with caution and respect for both sides of this important First Contact moment.

"In the meantime, if you have any questions, you may direct them to the office of Admiral Daksha Nayak of the Space Force Branch Special Forces, whose staff will be fielding all communications while we are in quarantine," she stated. "Thank you very much for your time, your attention, and your cooperation. I remain in service to my oaths, to the United Planets, and to you . . . and I apologize for the interruption in your various entertainments. May you all have a good day."

A third tap of her console switched the view back to the three men, two from Europe and one from the Indian subcontinent. The buzzer re-sounded through the speakers, and the banner flashed, though its text had changed.

This has been a broadcast of the Office of the Premiere of the Terran United Planets. For more information, contact: Admiral Daksha Nayak, Space Force Branch, at . . .

Jackie ignored the rest of it. She had a different, more direct way to contact Admiral Nayak. Instead, she made sure the little red light was no longer on and eyed the central figure on her screen. "I hope that was an acceptable broadcast, Admiral-General?"

He frowned a little. "I'd rather you hadn't mentioned bringing them down to Earth, nor returning them to their homeworld. That makes it sound as if you'll be doing it soon."

Callan beat her to answering that. Dark brows drawing down, he gave the head of the Space Force a chiding look. "Admiral-General, we are a *civilized* people. It is only right and proper that we *do* welcome them among us in friendship, then return them to their home within a reasonable amount of time."

"We will learn far more from them through open, peaceful exchange than we ever could by holding them here in isolation, sir," Jackie added. "By acting with honor, treating them well, asking for but not demanding any information they could give us, then doing our best to return them home safely—after giving them a reasonable tour of who and what we are, so that their people can question *them* about *us*—we will be showing our intentions are honorable and that we can be trusted when we give our word."

"That is the cornerstone of the foundation of proper government, and of ongoing government reform," Callan stated. "Honor, honesty, and integrity. Former Councilor MacKenzie lived and breathed it while in office, and she still lives and breathes it now. As a civil servant, she has my complete trust. As a military officer . . . she will know which things can be safely revealed to these guests, and which things must remain discreet for now."

Jackie nodded in silent agreement on that assessment. Admiral-General Kurtz sighed. "I shall have to remind certain of my intelligence officers that *they* are not in ultimate charge, once they start bleating at me for 'daring to allow' all of this. How long will quarantine last?"

"We don't know, but probably close to a month to be absolutely sure," Jackie told him. "Maria says it'll take a week or more to analyze, then synthesize the most important antigens in large enough batches to begin distribution, plus a couple weeks on top of that to ensure that everyone has had a chance to go through any symptomology resulting from inoculation— everyone planetside will have to endure various low-key sniffles and the sneezes," she joked lightly, "as will everyone in quarantine, but then we'll be free to bring our guests out of quarantine and show them everything. Within reason, of course."

"Of course," Kurtz agreed dryly, eyeing her through their commlink.

"If nothing else, Admiral-General—if the precognitive visions are to hold true—then we *will* be free in time for me to attend the Merrie Monarch Festival," she added. "That starts right at the end of Easter, which this year will be on the first Sunday in April. We should be planetside before then, at the very least."

"That reminds me of something," Admiral Nayak said. "If you'll excuse us, sir," he added to the Admiral-General, "I can start coordinating with the Ambassador *where* we will be taking these people once they get out of quarantine. Not just the locations, but any cultural or religiously significant visits should be discussed and selected in advance as well."

"We do have an opportunity to showcase the diversity of cultures and peoples of the United Planets, as well as climates and locations," Jackie agreed.

Kurtz mulled it over for a moment, then nodded. He eyed Jackie wryly. "I suppose you'll be *honest* about some of our ongoing problems as well as our triumphs?"

"Some of them. I won't ignore or hide any that come to their notice on any tour, and I am prepared to explain what I can . . . but neither will I draw their attention to anything," she stated dryly. "I—"

The cockpit door slid open, forcing her to break off what she was saying. Quickly holding up a finger, she turned to greet Li'eth. "Captain Ma'an-uq'en, is there something you needed?"

"I am amazed at how well you can manage the glottal stops of V'Dan, when your Terranglo does not have many," he murmured, pulling his floating body up beside her seat. "I came to tell you that Shi'ol has finally agreed to the language transfer. I . . . would tell you exactly how she phrased it, but I see you are communicating with people. Greetings."

"Is that their captain?" Kurtz asked, peering into his monitor.

Nodding, Jackie reached over and pulled gently on Li'eth's arm, getting his head into range of the pickups for the monitor. "Captain Ma'an-uq'en, the gentleman on the far left is Premiere Augustus Callan, the head of our entire government. The gentleman in the center is Admiral-General Vilhelm Kurtz, head of our entire military, the Space Force, which consists of four distinct Branches of service. And the gentleman on the far right is Admiral Daksha Nayak of the Space Force Branch Navy, who is the officer directly in charge of all the *Aloha* missions."

"This ship being the *Aloha 9*," Li'eth murmured. She gave him a nod in confirmation, and he in turn dipped his head. "Greetings, *meioas*—ah, *meioa* is a term from the Solarican race; it means 'Honored One' and can be used on anyone. I do not know of any equivalent in your language, but it is a very widely accepted greeting of politeness and courtesy among the member races of the Alliance. We have not yet had a chance to study the proper greeting protocols of your people, so I hope you will not take offense."

Premiere Callan smiled. "The newness of all of this is understood, Captain. You have been busy giving us more important tactical information about a potential enemy, so that we may prepare ourselves just in case they find us. Full courtesy can also wait when necessity cannot, such as your need to go into quarantine for about a month, but we will look forward to greeting you formally when everyone is ready. Ambassador, you will, of course, discuss the proper protocols while you all wait."

"Of course," she agreed. "Lessons in behavior and basic common laws will be part of the schedule that Admiral Nayak and I will arrange, for both during and after our time in quarantine. Captain, please tell the leftenant superior that I will be along in a little bit—let her know I am busy talking with the head of our government so that she knows there is a good reason behind my delay."

"I will. Please excuse me, *meioas*. I will be happy to speak with each of you later in more depth and detail," Li'eth stated before pushing himself back out of viewing range.

Jackie waited until he left, then sighed and shook her head. "They are very Human; some are more flawed than others. Thankfully, their captain has a good head on his shoulders. Premiere, Admiral-General, shall Admiral Nayak and I adjourn to a private channel now?"

Both nodded and signed out. Breathing deep, Jackie opened up a document file and prepared to start entering notes on what needed to be a priority in the first few days of their quarantine schedule, and notes on things that would need to be scheduled later on in the days and weeks ahead. *Anything productive to put off touching that woman's thoughts . . .*

MACARTHUR STATION

Her comment about preferring someone who was *willing* to go through a telepathic language transfer came back to haunt her. Instead of three or so hours, it took closer to five. Shi'ol resisted at every step of the way, refusing to share memories. Several times, Jackie had to break off and ask her did she *want* to sound like an untutored, illiterate child? The answer, of course, was *no*.

But for all Shi'ol consciously agreed she didn't want *that* . . . every time she came up against a cultural facet in the language-and-context transfers that was patently not V'Dan, Shi'ol's sub-conscious balked and resisted, and that dragged out the session. The nonpsychic blonde didn't quite kick her out as Li'eth's poorly trained mind had done, but she did resist . . . and since Shi'ol wasn't a badly trained psi, there was nothing Jackie could do that was even the slightest bit ethical to take over and force the language on her.

By the time it ended, Jackie had a throbbing headache and a serious dislike for the green-spotted blonde. What she wanted to do was lock herself in a room as far, far away from Shi'ol Nanu'oc, Countess of Bla'a-blah, as possible and ignore everyone and everything while she meditated to wash away any possible residue of the woman's overly annoying psyche. What she *had* to do was recite the formulaic words of, ". . . What was yours is still yours, Countess. That means I will not speak of anything personal without your permission, barring only extreme felonies—which you have not committed—so I will therefore try my best to forget all of it."

"See that you do!" Shi'ol snapped. In Terranglo, without noticing it. She shoved away—*grk*ed when the straps of the restraint harness kept her from leaving immediately—and disentangled herself as fast as she could. Jackie helped telekinetically, more than eager to get the woman away from her. She refrained from pushing on the rosette-spotted woman, however, focusing only on releasing the buckles. At her current level of annoyance, shoving might result in broken bones . . . and a telekinetic of her strength must *never* damage anyone without just and due cause.

The Salik had been a very clear-and-present danger. Jackie knew she had neither hallucinated nor imagined what they were thinking about doing to their Human—V'Dan and Terran—captives. Shi'ol . . . was the sort of danger one could only warn about, guard against, and hope it never happened. She disliked Jackie, disliked everyone on board, disliked her whole situation, disliked the lack of gravity and the clothing and the food and everything . . . but even Shi'ol would not have fed her hosts to the Salik.

Three explosive sneezes caught her attention. Kerchief

over his face, Lars poked his head out of the near crew hatch a few seconds after Shi'ol sailed through the far door. He sniffed, rubbed, and spoke. "Are you done? I have secured everything and *almost* everyone in here."

She caught his subtle eye roll. "Yes, we are finally done. I take it they've been waiting for us to finish before docking with quarantine?" Jackie asked. At his nod, she unbuckled her straps and started packing away both sets. Like virtually everything else on the ship, even these simple straps had to be stowed in a securely latched cupboard for ship maneuvers. It didn't take her long to roll, stuff, and latch—about as long as it took for her to speak, with the aid of her psi. "I'd better get up to the cockpit then. See that Shi'ol is strapped in, please?"

"Of course."

"Thank you for watching over them, Lars. Thank you for volunteering," Jackie clarified.

He shrugged and switched to Finnish, no doubt to avoid any accidental insults from any eavesdropping among their guests. *"One day, I will be a father. Herding our guests is like herding children, yes? Easier than cats . . . but only by so much."*

That made her bite her lip against the urge to laugh. Since her head hurt, she pulled herself forward through the cabin by her hands, now that the harnesses were stowed. Entering the cockpit, she found Li'eth seated at the geophysicist's station. He was reading something on a pad—etiquette rules, she realized. Robert twisted in his seat, peering back at her.

"All done?" the pilot asked, and echoed the nod she gave him with a sharp one of his own. "Good. We've been in a holding pattern with a crew on the *Aloha 23* on standby for the last hour and a half. The doc said it wouldn't be a good idea to interrupt your little mind-meld whatsit, but the other team is getting impatient. I'm certainly ready whenever you are."

"My fingertips were nowhere near her forehead, so it wasn't a mind-meld," Jackie shot back. Li'eth looked up at that. She maneuvered into her seat while answering his unspoken question. "Never mind, Li'eth; it's one of those classical cultural references that takes too long to explain. I'm just glad I'm *done* and don't have to do that again with her.

"Send the *23* my apologies for the delay, my thanks for their patience, and my wishes for a very smooth docking—oh, wait, that's *my* job," she quipped dryly, buckling the much bulkier cockpit harness into place. "Give me one more moment to strap in and find my headset, and I'll be free to do it . . . Done," she added, unclipping her headset and tucking it over her ear. Her hands touched the console, activating the comm system. *"This is Major MacKenzie of the* Aloha 9 *to the* MacArthur *and the* Aloha 23. *Please accept my apologies for the delay. The language transfer on the last of our guests is complete; they all know Terranglo and will be able to communicate, hopefully effectively, with everyone they meet while they are our guests. Again, please accept my thanks for your patience, and my best wishes for a smooth dual docking. Commander Graves will synch his helm with yours when ready."*

"This is Station Control; your readiness is acknowledged, Aloha 9, and thank you for finally being done. Commander Graves, Commander Yesetti, synchronization begins in five . . . four . . . three . . ."

On . . . *one*, both ships adjusted their seemingly static drift—relative to the station, not to the planet in the distance— and started circling around it. Both ships moved in the same direction, the spin of the center wheel, counterpoint to the smaller outer tori. They danced with careful pulses of the insystem thrusters at their lowest settings, and tiny hisses from attitude jets. The great torus of the center wheel rotated at roughly two minutes to the circle, but it was quite large, which meant the rim was moving relatively briskly.

Graves and Yesetti took their time, murmuring to each other over the comm channel; as they swung each craft into position, the conflux of centripetal and centrifugal forces started giving everyone the illusion of gravity. At this distance, Jackie had set the communications system to lightspeed, now that they were well within normal broadcasting distance. She also knew that amateur lightwave enthusiasts would be scanning for the bandwidths carrying the news of this momentous event, so she broadcast—on official channels—a picture of the interior of the cockpit facing forward, showing their ship drifting into view of the station.

Brad sneezed twice and sniffed hard to clear his sinuses, rubbing his nose against the sleeved forearm he had hastily moved into place to block the flow of droplets. But beyond that, it was a serene image of the cockpit crew working quietly and efficiently, with a view of the station seemingly drifting closer and slowing down, relative to their position, for all it was the other way around.

In her opinion, it was far better to conduct everything aboveboard and well within public sight, save only the most sensitive of negotiations. Since she had nothing else to do while the tedious process of docking took place, Jackie checked her messages. The system caches were filling up with queries from all across the United Planets, wanting to know if they were finally docking, if the "alien Humans" would be willing to give interviews, if they were indeed from a planet other than Earth, how they got there, who they were, what was up with those funny markings on their face . . . and, of course, the inevitable queries on whether these V'Dan were a threat, if they were here to steal resources, or perhaps just to steal sex partners for bizarre mating rituals . . .

Just skimming the subject lines alone was enough to make her roll her eyes and almost miss the *clunk* of grapples hitting their targets, from ship to station and from station to ship. Robert eased off the thrusters very carefully while the winches did their job. A quick check of her secondary left screen showed the *23* being reeled in at the same time, according to station cameras. The two vessels kissed one right after the other, the *9* followed by its sister ship within a second, second and a half. The hull *thunked* with secondary grapples, these ones attached to stiff telescoping arms, not to flexible winching cables.

Before them, the quarantine hangar doors slid open, and the ship was pulled partway into the close-fitted bay. When they hissed shut again, they did so by sealing around the ship just a few meters past the port airlock, which sat behind the cockpit. Station space was too precious to waste on a full-sized docking hangar just for quarantine needs, but neither could they let the ship sit fully outside the station.

Its hull had to be swiped and examined for microbial and other contaminants, and counteragents developed for anything potentially inimical. The rest of the hull would be swabbed and sterilized via spacewalking cleaner bots, which would do random samplings, so on and so forth, but they had to dock directly with the quarantine pods all the same.

Jackie was just glad they were firmly docked. She double-checked the hatchway seals—foam-based and similar to the primary material of a p-suit—to make sure there was no air loss while the modest bay space was being pressurized, then contacted the station. *"Aloha 9 to MacArthur, we appear to be green on the seals. Air pressure seems to be stable in quarantine alpha. Confirm, please."*

Telltales along the bottom of her screen showed the data conduits hooking up, switching from lightspeed broadband to direct-cable input, making the reply she received private instead of public.

". . . Confirmed, Aloha 9, you have achieved green hatchway seals, along with correctly coupled data and fuel conduits. You may disembark when ready. Be advised that as your crew is able-bodied—and we are pleased no one was harmed during your mission—your crew is responsible for basic postmission cleanup of the ship's interior. Let us hope your guests haven't brought along a bug that'll cause ship and pod to both be scuttled."

"If they did, we'd have to be scuttled with them, so I'm hoping right along with you," she quipped lightly before resuming a level of seriousness appropriate to the moment. *"But so far, we seem to be doing okay, beyond hints of common-cold symptoms among the Terrans, sniffles, watery eyes, and the occasional sneeze fits . . . and a lack of overt symptoms but matching elevated immune system activity from the V'Dan. Dr. de la Santoya is looking forward to having a proper lab for further research into these subtle differences."*

"The medical community await her results. Aloha 9 . . . you are now connected to station power. All conduits are active, all seals are green. Please shut down engines and transfer yourselves to quarantine."

"Roger, MacArthur. Major MacKenzie and the crew of the Aloha 9 are signing off . . . now."

"Are we actually free to disembark?" Li'eth asked, raising his brows as she punched buttons, shutting down her station.

"I'll get your things while you take them on the safety tour, *amiga*," Maria told Jackie. The doctor had already shut down her station and unstrapped her seat harness. She hopped down into the aisle between the seats and made her way aftward. "You're the host, so you get to play the tour guide."

"Thank you, Maria. Since you have nothing to collect, Li'eth, yes, you are free to disembark with me. However, I want to group up all of you for the tour of the facilities." Activating the intercom, she spoke. *"Shi'ol, V'kol, Dai'a, and Ba'oul, you are free to disengage from your seats. Please come toward the cockpit. I will be opening the portside airlock to the quarantine section of the station, and will be giving you a tour of the facilities. This tour will include explanations of safety features, safety drills and exercises, directions on where to go and what to do in the major categories of possible emergencies, and at the end, you will be issued datapads with further reading material, all of it in standard Terranglo.*

"This is a mandatory *tour for all newly arriving station personnel, both military and civilian alike, which means residents* and *guests. The rest of us have already been made familiar with these drills and lectures through our military training. Your cooperation and your careful attention as good guests will therefore be deeply appreciated . . . and may potentially save your life in an emergency. Jackie out."* Shutting down her station, Jackie unstrapped herself from her seat.

After several days of floating around, it was a little awkward to have to maneuver around the armrest and so forth, now that they had toroidal gravity to work with. Li'eth was in the middle of offering his borrowed datapad to Ayinda. The other woman shook her head, her dreadlocks resting naturally against her shoulders now that they were in simulated gravity.

"Keep it," the navigator said. "You can borrow it for as long as we're docked in quarantine. I loaded it with several hopefully useful things. Manuals on etiquette, how to recognize basic military insignia, even a timeline of Earth's history."

"Earth?" he asked, then checked himself. "Right . . . the name you use for your homeworld."

"You can hardly complain, partner," Robert said as he worked on shutting down the ship as instructed. "Your planet, people, and language are all one and the same word. We, at least, like a little variety. Or does everyone out there in the big, wide galaxy call themselves, their homeworlds, and their languages all the same thing?"

"No . . . it's . . . The homeworld name for the Salik is Sallha," he said, aspirating the *h* almost as if he was trying to clear something from his soft palate, not quite as harsh as if he'd been trying to clear his throat. "It means *Fountain* in their language. And the homeworld of the Gatsugi . . . it's easiest to say in V'Dan, which is the trade tongue we use. It means *Beautiful-Blue . . . blue* is their color-word for *happy.*"

"It could be worse," Jackie said. "We named the first planet in our system, an airless, star-baked rock we call Mercury, after a winged messenger-god, which is also what we call a very toxic metal that is usually found as a liquid at Human-compatible temperatures and pressures."

"Yes, and our second planet, an overly hot planet with a volatile atmosphere filled with sulfuric acid, is named after the goddess of love and beauty," Robert quipped. He flashed a grin over his shoulder. "By comparison, calling the one we live on *Earth*, as in mud or dirt, seems downright homey and welcoming, doesn't it?"

Li'eth chuckled and dipped his head, clearly amused by the commander's joke. "That, it does. If it's that marbled world nearby . . . it is a beautiful world. I look forward to seeing it personally, depending on how soon we can get out of this quarantine."

"That will depend on how soon we can vaccinate everybody," Jackie said, knowing that she had to be vague for the sake of all the doctors who would be poring over the medical data Maria would be sending them on each pathogen's shape, chemical properties, and genome patterns. Jackie might have the job of introducing these V'Dan to Terran humanity, but poor Maria had the job of making sure it would be a *safe* introduction.

Facing the airlock, she pressed her thumb to the scanner, then touched the button when the door beeped. The hatch retracted, allowing her to step into the airlock proper. The others filed in after her. They jostled a little, settling themselves into a semblance of rank, or at least seniority; while Li'eth was the undisputed captain, the others were all the same rank, Leftenant Superior, the equivalent of a Lieutenant

Commander. Li'eth, Shi'ol, Ba'oul, V'kol, with Dai'a standing at the rear. Double-checking the pressure readings on the panel for the outer door, Jackie thumbed the controls that would equalize the slight pressure difference between the ship and the station, and faced their guests.

"This will be your new home for the next month or so, while we make sure it is safe to expose you to our common pathogens and that it is safe for you to expose the rest of our people to yours," she added as the door panel beeped, letting her know the air was stable. Thumbing it open, she waited while the station's airlock cycled open as well. "May you enter and reside in the spirit of *aloha* . . . which is a single, simple-seeming, yet very complex word of my mother's people. It means compassion, caring, peace, mercy, affection, harmony, love, and more. It is the measure of how well we treat each other as we go through life, and we remind each other of this whenever we greet each other when we meet and say farewell when we part.

"So. *Aloha*, and welcome to the *MacArthur*," Jackie concluded, leading the way through the white-painted station airlock. "Which is the name of a famous war general. A bit contradictory, but the military is in charge of all interstellar interactions at the moment."

"Your mother's people?" Shi'ol asked as they stepped into the station's airlock and prepared to cycle through it. "Are they in charge, then?"

The question made Jackie's mouth twitch. She almost laughed, but confined it to a smile. For once, the other woman had not asked a snide question. Or at least not an overly-supercilious-sounding one. "The Hawai'ian Islands and its people *host* our government; they do not run it. At least, no more so than anyone else. You will have time to learn how the Terran United Planets runs itself. Let me squeeze past you so I can close the middle airlocks—that is the first rule of ship and station life, to keep the airlock hatches and section seals closed at all times when not in use.

"The second is what we call the Lock-and-Web Law," she said, launching into her explanations on how they were to live and pay attention while on board the station, "which is to secure everything while on a ship when it is not being used at that moment, to ensure it doesn't rattle around and damage anything. It isn't as important to follow on a station as it is on a starship, in terms of potential damage, but it is important to keep things tidy as we go. Obviously, we will not have any staff to perform common housekeeping chores while in quarantine, so we must do it all ourselves . . ."

CHAPTER 9

FEBRUARY 1, 2287 C.E.

Li'eth was rather surprised to see, on a military space station, so many *civilian* amenities crammed into the confines of this "quarantine" sector. Garden plants that were placed to be ornamental, though he had been told many were edible in one way or another. Furniture that could be easily cleaned and sterilized, yet was also comfortable thanks to some sort of closed-cel foam padding. Kitchen facilities that were a bit odd compared to V'Dan but included a "snacks cupboard," and not one, but two largish chambers for "recreational activities."

The first one was for lounging and relaxing, for playing board games and reading from data tablets, even for dancing, with a broad floor inlaid with thin strips of something called *bam-boo*. The second was for exercising, and included a small swimming pool just long enough for swimming laps, and just wide and shallow enough at one end for more playful activities, plus a smaller, pond-sized pool for soaking in heated water, and something which the tall blond male, Lars, exclaimed in delight over, a *sow-nah*, a sort of steaming room lined in an entirely different sort of wood, one with a scent somewhere between briskly pleasant and mildly pungent.

The floors were not carpeted, making them easier to clean and keep sterile. There were artworks hanging on the walls, some sculptures, but mostly a series of monitor screens that slowly rotated between collections of images—famous works of art representing many cultures and thousands of years, Ja'ki had explained. The wide variety certainly attested to that. None of the physical art items were originals, ". . . since the whole quarantine section has to be considered expendable in the event of a truly incurable, irremovable problem, which hopefully won't *be* a problem," but they were excellent reproductions from what he could tell.

On a military station in the Empire, while the common crew quarters might boast some personal artwork images, most of the interior would be utilitarian. The stations might have a little more leeway, but a quarantine section would not have nearly so many pleasantries. Ja'ki had an explanation for that, too. She and Robert, the short black-haired male, were demonstrating how to work the kitchen equipment while they cooked, but the actual work took longer than the explanation of it.

"I can understand why you'd be puzzled over the expense of decorating this place and making it comfortable," she said in answer to his question. "You see, it was decided long ago by our psychologists that people who had to be put into quarantine isolation would fare a lot better if they had pleasant surroundings. And they were right; pleasant, comfortable surroundings ensure the quarantined individuals emerge in a much healthier state of mind than those who are deprived of such seemingly insignificant comforts."

"Healthy emotions and healthy thoughts help encourage healthier bodies," Dai'a offered somewhat shyly. She and Li'eth were sitting on tall chairs in the kitchen, but while Li'eth was merely listening, the life-support officer had volunteered to chop vegetables. Some of which were familiar, the ones which his people knew were Before Time foods.

Ma-ree'a, their medical doctor, had appropriated the help of the second pilot, Brad—an easy name—in taking swab samples from everyone and in processing them in the medical lab at one end of the isolation unit. Lars and A-yinda were assisting Shi'ol, V'kol, and Ba'oul in the quarters positioned along the upper deck, helping the newcomers learn how their quarters' various facilities worked. As much as he wanted a real bath and a full set of clean clothes, including soft-sided shoes that would be comfortable to wear after so many days of being naked from his scalp to his toes, Li'eth wanted information. Well, information and food.

Except his hostess would not explain anything other than fairly trivial matters since she said she did not want to have to repeat the important things over and over just because a few of their guests were missing from the conversation. For the moment, it was just the four of them . . . and whoever might be watching on their camera systems, he knew. Had their positions been reversed—and probably would be—Li'eth could admit his people would be watching, analyzing, and dissecting everything their own foreign-yet-familiar guests were doing and saying.

For now, he followed her and Dai'a's line of reasoning with a nod. "That's a saying among the Sh'nai Holy Healers, who are the equivalent to your emotion doctors. We *have* psychologists as well, but the Holy Healers are a bit more . . ."

"Holistic?" Dai'a supplied, knife pausing while she looked up, before she bent her attention to her task. She seemed familiar with a good number of the unprocessed food items, though some were downright exotic to both of them. Then again, Li'eth only knew the basics of cooking; for the vast majority of his life, someone else had always done that chore for him.

Since that was the word he was looking for, he nodded. "Holistic, and more spiritually oriented. They are often preferred over the nonspiritual ones."

"We've separated a fair bit of religion from our own medical practices," Ja'ki murmured, stirring something in a pan. Robert was busy chopping vegetables with Dai'a's help, intending to make something he called a stir-fry, whatever that was, but Ja'ki was the one handling the meat dish.

The scents coming from her efforts were sweet yet savory, with a bit of vague familiarity to the meat. She stirred the food with her right hand and arm, dancing a spatula through the contents while sporting a thick dark band on her right wrist. Her left hand gripped the handle on the pan, utensils and actions that were essentially the same for V'Dan chefs.

Every single one of them, Terran and V'Dan alike, now had a similar band, a thicker, more complicated monitoring bracelet. Apparently, they had foods that could cause medical problems if someone was somehow sensitive to the contents, and the doctor wanted to make sure no one would suffer any problems, natives as well as guests. He couldn't imagine what sort of food could cause such problems and still be considered edible as a whole. Back home, there was a clear line between what was considered safe to eat and what was not. He tried not to let it cloud his opinion of these people, reminding himself there were always things that one just had to put up with from a particular colonyworld.

He wanted to ask her how her people ended up separated from the Empire but suspected she would avoid the question. Instead, Li'eth commented on the things he had seen. "If I didn't know we were in medical isolation, I would think we were enjoying a sort of . . . a cabin? The sort of building one could rent and use in a wilderness area, save that this wilderness is not found on any planet."

"Yes, I would never have expected all the art," Dai'a agreed. "The food certainly is wonderful—picked and prepared fresh instead of trapped in packets."

"Oh, we have plenty of those," Ja'ki warned her. "If anything upsets your bodies, you'll go right back onto the original packets that gave you no problems. And aside from eggs and the occasional fish, all the meat will be frozen or in canisters, and you'll get the fish fresh only because gutting a fish is far easier than gutting a chicken."

"Chicken . . . chick . . . *chika!*" Li'eth exclaimed softly. "*That's* what I've been smelling."

Dai'a nodded. "I smelled it, too, and so many of these plants are very similar to what we use . . . How can our foods be so similar, and our bodies, too? Are you a lost colony?"

Li'eth shook his head, answering before the Terrans could. "They have too many people to be a lost colony. There *are no* lost colonies. The Empire has carefully kept track of every expedition into space. These people are the descendants of the Before Time people, the ones who did not escape the great disaster yet clearly survived it anyway."

She peeked at him from under her brown curls. Unlike many V'Dan, her *jungen* had not colored her scalp and thus her hair. "You believe that these people are the members of the Lost Motherworld of the Sh'nai faith?"

"The prophecy about the Salik War, about finding allies came true, so why should there not be a kernel of truth in even the oldest of holy fables?" Li'eth offered. "If these people are the descendants of those who were left behind on the Before World, then that would make sense that they would have similar foods to our Before Time types, animals and plants alike. Roughly ten thousand years would not be enough to evolve many differences, other than maybe a lack of *jungen*, since we know that came along after arriving on V'Dan."

"You know, we *are* standing right here," Robert quipped dryly, scooping vegetable peels into what looked like a composting jar. He lifted his tanned chin. "Why don't you try asking *us* where our various species come from, rather than arguing whether or not we're from some lost holy world or some lost space colony?"

"Where *do* you come from?" Dai'a asked, taking the bait as she pared the last of some odd, orange root vegetable into thin oval medallions. It was supposedly a *ca'ot*, but the vegetable Li'eth knew was a rich purple, not luridly orange.

"Earth. Our species evolved on the planet we're currently orbiting," the pilot asserted. "We have genetically backed paleontological records of all our plants and animals spanning millions of years."

Li'eth sat back, gesturing at the pilot and the Ambassador. "There you go. They *are* the Before People, the ones who were abandoned to their fate when the World Was Wracked, and the Chosen People were taken to the Promised Planet."

"*That* sounds rather rude," Robert muttered, helping Dai'a scrape the medallions into his big bowl of mixed vegetables. "You make it sound like we were rejects. Maybe it was *your* people who were the ones put into exile, hm? And for that matter, *who* arranged your exile from Earth? And *when*?"

"It is currently the year 9507 in the Empire," Li'eth explained. "At some point in the month of *Sember*, which is either harvest or planting season, depending on which hemisphere you're in. So the *when* was nearly ten thousand of our years ago, though I cannot say in how many of yours. As for the *how*, the holy texts speak of how the High One, knowing that a great cataclysm was coming, spent years searching for the perfect new world. Once she found it, she prepared a citadel to house Her chosen people, and shipped many of the fruits and beasts of the field to that citadel in advance, before evacuating everyone She could get to move when the disaster struck—in other words, a carefully planned *d'aspra*."

Ja'ki choked. Coughing, she cleared her throat a few times, then asked, "Did you just say *diaspora*?"

"*D'aspra*," he corrected her. Then blinked. "What does your word mean? It sounds very much like ours."

She exchanged a look with her unmarked colleague before answering. "I suspect it means the same thing. The *diaspora* originally meant a dispersal of a particular ethnic and religious group, the Jews, from their holy land in a region we now call the Middle East, when conquerors came in and changed all the rules, effectively exiling them—I'm not up to date on all the details," she dismissed, pausing to clear her throat again while she stirred the food in the pan, "but basically the word means an exile to foreign lands . . . which, if your people were moved from *our* world by some means ten thousand years ago, means *you* were exiled. Except that word in *our* language has only been in existence a few thousand years at most."

"And you said *chika* earlier," Robert pointed out, rising from his rummaging through a cupboard, a curved, bowl-like metal dish in his hands, one with two handles on the rim. "Which sounds like our *chicken*. But that shouldn't be possible because if you parted company from Earth ten thousand years ago—never mind how anyone on Earth ten thousand years ago could have had any sort of interstellar technology back then—then how could you speak what sounds like an *English* word, the base language behind Terranglo?"

Li'eth and Dai'a both smiled. Gesturing toward Dai'a, Li'eth let his life-support officer answer the short, markless male. ". . . Because even *V'kol*, who refuses to believe in Immortals and Saints, knows that in the holy stories of the Sh'nai, the High One was sent back thousands of years through time to find, select, and protect the Chosen People. The V'Dan."

The looks Ja'ki and Robert gave them were bemused, amused, and disbelieving. Ja'ki shook her head quickly, the wisps of her dark reddish-brown curls bouncing a little. "Time travel is impossible. You can only go forward; you can never go back."

"The Feyori can," Dai'a informed her. "They are the only race that can achieve the squared speed of light. They are energy beings, not matter beings like us, or even the Salik," she added, picking up the cutting boards and knives to take them to the sink for cleaning. A lot of the fixtures might look a little weird to the V'Dan, but some things were just too common not to figure out easily. "They are very strange, very old, and very powerful. We call them the Meddlers."

"Energy-based?" Robert asked, heating up the round dish on some sort of radiant cradle and drizzling what looked like oil into the thing. "You mean, they're like a . . . a big pulsing ball of light?"

Dai'a shook her head, taking her time scrubbing the utensils. There was surely some sort of dish-cleaning machine, but no one had showed them how to use it yet. Even Li'eth knew the basics of washing dishes by hand . . . thanks to his time as a juniormost ensign on his very first ship.

"They are more like a great, silvery, mirror-smooth soap bubble. I was told by some Solaricans that the darker they are, the more hungry they are, because they are trying to absorb ambient radiation like we would eat or drink food. Electrical energy, stellar radiation, magnetics, thermal, you name it. And if they are silvery-bright, reflecting everything around them, then they are full and not hungry. But I do not know much more beyond that about their, ah, physiology? Is that the word?" Dai'a asked over her shoulder. "The way their body-forms work?"

Ja'ki nodded. She stirred her own dish a bit more, then helped her companion steady his pan while he added the vegetables, stirring rapidly with a wooden spoon as the oil sizzled and delicious smells wafted up out of the bowl thing.

"How very odd," Robert said, shaking the pan and stirring its contents.

As Li'eth watched, Ja'ki pushed a few buttons and covered her dish, then turned to the oven-thing and pulled out delicious-smelling loaves of bread. Bread was bread was bread. Robert leaned that way and inhaled, then sighed and grinned.

"Fresh-baked bread . . . or at least a facsimile of it," he explained. "The station's food-services crew pack up loaves that are *almost* cooked, then freeze them so they can be baked warm and finished—we're not allowed to make our own in quarantine, as the yeast culture would have to be dead on delivery. No live-culture foods are allowed outside of digestive microflora tablets, but we can still have the near equivalent of fresh-baked."

"Tell us a little bit more about these Fey-yor-ree, and the other races," Ja'ki suggested as she moved the pan to the countertop. He didn't know what her name meant in her own tongue, but *ja'ki* meant *bright stone* in his. A bit like the polished-to-a-shine granite rectangle she slid the bread onto, set between her and Li'eth. "Wait—one moment, please, while I call the others to supper . . ."

She moved off to touch an intercom button by one of the doors. Li'eth eyed the bread, wishing he could just reach over and pull off a piece. The rules for proper behavior and etiquette had been drilled in him from an early age. Dai'a, however, had no problem. As soon as she finished putting away cutting board and the knives, the logistics officer returned with a serrated knife, sawed off an end piece, and stuffed it into her mouth, chewing. She gave her captain a shy, mischievous smile as she did so.

"Would you please cut me a piece as well?" Li'eth asked her, giving in to the delicious smell. Nodding, she started separating that loaf into pieces. The look and the texture suggested a grain at least somewhat similar to *iit*. Biting into one of the rounds, he discovered the taste was very much like *iit*, if with a slightly odd, sour tang to it. "Mmm," he sighed, chewing and swallowing. "This is really good. Almost like home, but exotic at the same time."

Robert, still stirring and cooking, filling the air with a rich, peppery scent as he added herbs and spices to the vegetables, chuckled at that. "Everywhere you go, food is home to some and foreign to others. That version is what we call sourdough. Nearly every corner of the world has some form of grain or starch that forms a bread, whether it's a risen bread, a flatbread, a cracker . . ."

"Thank you for cutting up the bread, Dai'a," Ja'ki said as she came back to the group. She did so by swinging past a refrigeration cupboard, pulling out a couple things, and grabbing some dull-edged knives, the sort more suitable for spreading than cutting. "Here is some butter, and strawberry, blackberry, and orange *marmalades*—fruits sweetened and jelled for preservation. The chicken is stir-fried in rosemary, garlic, and thyme. And *now* you can tell us about the other races you know about."

"Well . . . at the moment, you know we are at war with the Salik. Or rather, they chose to go to war with us. And the Feyori . . . they are impossible to capture, impossible to stop, but they don't tend to interact directly, so much as they just . . . meddle. They have holy powers like you and I, but on a scale unseen anywhere else, and they can take on matter-based form," Li'eth explained. Only to be given more skeptical looks. "Dai'a is right; they are the only race that can achieve the squared speed of light, where energy and matter can be exchanged form for form. The fastest we can push our ships is the tiniest fraction past the speed of light, compared to that.

"Those are the enemy and the neutral races. The others are members of the Alliance. The Chinsoiy are perhaps the strangest of those who are our allies," he stated, accepting the dish and utensils Dai'a passed to him. "The rest are based upon the element of carbon as our primary component, and we breathe oxygen, but while the Chinsoiy breathe oxygen, they rely upon silicon as their primary element."

Robert turned off his heating cradle and brought over his dish to a different stone rectangle, next to where Ja'ki was setting hers. "How is that even possible? I'm not a chemist, but I thought that silicon reacts so much more slowly than carbon in chemical interactions. Comparatively speaking."

"They require types of radiation that would sicken and kill most V'Dan after moderate exposures," Dai'a told him. "Most of the other races, too. The Salik are being careful not to destroy too much of our colonyworlds in the attempt to leave our infrastructure intact—they are amphibious by birth, but they can use dry-land things like we do—but the Chinsoiy, they just bomb everything from orbit if they can. They are . . . how to describe them . . ."

"They have heads and torsos, and have two legs and two arms," Li'eth said, serving himself, "and in that much they are like us, bilaterally symmetrical, with eyes and mouths that can form V'Dan word-sounds, but the arms have extra-long fingers along the undersides, attached all the way down to the bottoms of their legs by large flaps of skin. Their homeworld gravity and atmospheric pressure are such that they can glide for distances, and I think the flaps also allow them to absorb enough radiation over the surface area provided to help the Chinsoiy with their metabolic processes."

"They mine a lot of rare ores and radioactive elements and their manufactured components for the Alliance," Dai'a explained. "They live easily twice as long as a V'Dan, maybe a little more than twice as long, and they are not always easy to understand, but everything living needs to eat, and everything sentient and advanced as a civilization needs tools to be created. There are things we can do which they find difficult because the manufacturing processes require *non*radioactive environments in the earliest stages."

"Their skin is very pretty," Li'eth added, scooping the chicken—which looked and smelled like ordinary herbed *chika* to him—onto his plate, alongside a very colorful selection of glossy cooked vegetables from the dish Robert had made. "Like the stone, *opal*? Like . . . milk mixed with water, different colors and slightly translucent. But the colors do not change, save by the angle and play of light and shadow. Unlike the Gatsugi."

"Gatsugi?" Brad asked, entering the kitchen. He had showered and changed into loose trousers and a short-sleeved shirt, both in a medium shade of blue. "What is that?"

"A race of sentient beings. They breathe oxygen like us, and are carbon-based. They have two legs somewhat like ours, if with much longer toes," Dai'a told him, offering him a plate as well. "But they have shorter legs, and their torsos are longer, with four arms. Both are thinner and a little weaker than a V'Dan arm, and they only have three fingers and an opposing thumb on each hand. But collectively, their arms are strong. We're told it's because they evolved to climb and cling out of the reach of predators, as the Chinsoiy evolved their wing-flaps to soak in the radiations of their overactive home sun."

"They have big eyes, too," Li'eth explained, gesturing with thumbs and forefingers curved but not touching in a circle over each of his own eyes. "Black and able to see into the infrared spectrum, where heatwaves lurk. They can see most purples, but not the ones close to ultraviolet . . . and I am glad we were given so many of your science words to explain many of these things."

"When I worked as a professional translator, I dealt a *lot* with scientists who were trying to explain things to government workers," Ja'ki said, stepping back all the way to the cooking counter, leaving the second pilot plenty of room to approach the island counter where the food had been placed.

Li'eth suddenly realized she had also subtly avoided bumping into Robert while cooking, swerving gracefully with a minimum of effort. This, however, was a much more overt movement, a clear *I will not bump into you* motion.

Of course, with the strength of her *holy powers, touching others must be uncomfortable, for it could share thoughts unbidden. I do much the same thing out of habit . . . though I feel a little safer after her training in how to guard my mind from others.*

He pulled his attention back to the topic, and the differences between the V'Dan—Humans—and the others. "While the Gatsugi are renowned as the race with four arms and two legs, their most famous and distinctive part of their appearance is the way their skin changes color. It is based upon their mood. If a Gatsugi is very happy, he or she literally appears a cheerful, bright blue. If they are frightened and sad, dull yellow. Anger is red, passion is purple, so on and so forth, with thousands of subtle shade differences, and even occasional mottlings—they prefer to conduct trade negotiations over a visual link, so that they can let their computer programs adjust their skin shade to appear a polite shade of calm, mild blue."

"Their word for *acting* is the same as their word for *lying*, and to be called an excellent liar is a high compliment," Dai'a added.

Shi'ol entered the kitchen, Ba'oul behind her; Dai'a moved to offer them plates and utensils as well. The two Terran pilots, Robert and Brad, politely moved into the dining chamber, with its long table and several seats, and long window overlooking the food garden with its racks of green, growing things in various stages of life. Ja'ki had explained that each of them would have to take on a set of chores to maintain the sector, from washing dishes to tending the plants, to sweeping the floors, wiping down walls, and, of course, keeping their own individual quarters clean. *Inspection ready* was the term she had used.

In exchange for manual labor, they had food that smelled delicious, clean clothes, a reasonable facsimile of gravity underfoot, and they were one and all very much alive. Li'eth was grateful that—

"Dish up my food," he heard Shi'ol order Dai'a, pulling him out of his thoughts. He blinked and frowned . . . and frowned deeper when Dai'a moved to do so. Shi'ol moved on, adding a second command over her shoulder. "Bring it to me when it is ready."

"Hold!" Li'eth snapped in V'Dan.

Both women stopped, Shi'ol swinging around to eye him in surprise, and Dai'a freezing with a spoonful of vegetables halfway to the plate in her hand. The only other person in the kitchen at the moment was Ja'ki, who also understood every word he said. But he did not speak in Terranglo to Shi'ol for her benefit. He did it so that those who analyzed the recordings of this moment would understand.

"Leftenant Superior Nanu'oc, you are *not* authorized to order Leftenant Superior Vres-yat about like an ensign on her first tour of duty, or some third- or fourth- or fifth-rank member of the military. She is *not* your servant. You will dish up your own food, clean up your own quarters, and accept whatever chore that will be assigned to you. If you do not know how to undertake a task, you will ask these Terrans for help, as it is their equipment, their territory, and their methods that need to be followed.

"You will not, at *any* time that we are here among these people, attempt to use your civilian status as a Countess of the Empire to wrest control of my authority, demand favors or services, or otherwise make yourself a poor example of the Empire among these people. Is that *clear*, Leftenant Superior Nanu'oc?" he finished, holding her gaze sternly.

Face flushing almost as red as her rosette spots, Shi'ol inclined her head stiffly. "Yes. Captain Ma'an-uq'en."

Without another word, she accepted the plate from Dai'a, loaded it with food, accepted the bundle of utensils the life-support officer offered next, and headed for the dining hall with a stiff back and a tightly clenched jaw. Li'eth held his own posture stiff and straight until she vanished from view. He didn't quite slump, but he wasn't the only one to relax, either; Dai'a blew out a breath, one that ruffled her curls.

A thread of thought brushed against his mind. (*Do you think she'd calm down if you revealed yourself?*)

He blinked twice, then dragged in a breath and managed a polite, even slightly humorous reply. (*I'm not sure which would be more dangerous. She* might *try to flirt with me. She seems the type.*)

(*Not interested in women?*) Ja'ki sent lightly, staying back out of the way as V'kol entered, chatting amiably with the other two Terran females, Mareeah and Ah-yinda, whose names he was still trying to figure out how to pronounce.

Her sending didn't have any sort of censure attached. Li'eth was grateful for that. A few minor cultural factions in the Empire disliked the thought of same-gender attractions, though the official stance on that sort of thing by the Empire was that if all of the people involved were fully informed, fully consenting adults, it was nobody else's business, unless a same-sex couple wished to hire a consort as an official child-begetter. Plus, there was one particular faction on the other side of the spectrum that actively encouraged orgies . . . and he cut off his line of thought right there, because it would be utterly *wrong* to picture his hostess . . .

(*No, just not interested in* her,) he asserted, reinforcing his mental shields while sternly redirecting his undercurrent thoughts back onto the topic at hand. (*I have obligations to my bloodline, but I still have the right to refuse any particular partner I dislike. She is a fellow soldier, nothing more—she is* good *at her job,*) he added, feeling compelled to defend his fellow officer. (*She is exceptionally gifted at Logistics, navigating the labyrinth of paperwork when requisitioning supplies, fierce in getting them delivered on time in the correct kinds and amounts, and when we had our ship, could have told within a handful of nuts and bolts exactly what supplies were located where without having to glance at a data unit.*)

(*Then I am glad she is an exemplary logistics officer,*) Ja'ki returned smoothly. Sincerely, as far as he could tell.

He glanced at her, suspicious, before scooping up a forkful

of food. (*Do you mean that? Or are you so skilled that you can lie in my mind?*)

The grin she flashed at him was carefully done so behind the others' backs. (*Even if I could, I wouldn't, and I'm not going to. No, I* am *sincerely glad she's good at something. Other than being an arrogant bit of nasal snot, of course—snot being disgusting to deal with and not something one exposes to polite company willingly.*)

He almost choked on the vegetables. He didn't, but it was a close thing. Biting his tongue to keep from laughing inappropriately, Li'eth chewed and swallowed with care. (*That wasn't in the etiquette notes I was reading . . . but maybe I just hadn't reached that part, yet.*)

(*It's something we teach to children; I'm afraid those notes were written for adults.*) She smiled as she sent it, her expression and her mental overtones apologetic.

(*Considering your people* look *like children, I'd think it would* be *in your books . . . I am sorry,*) he sent, breaking off that line of thought with a flush of shame the moment her eyes narrowed. (*That was inappropriate of me. Of course you are all adults. I should not let my inherent cultural prejudices blind me to that. I apologize.*)

(*. . . I still don't get why you think we look like children.*) Ja'ki sighed in his head.

(*You lack* jungen. *No marks means no maturity.*)

She dared to arch a brow at him. The others were just about finished collecting their food, and they moved, breaking her look for a moment, so she sent a question instead. (*Does that* really *mean that Shi'ol is perceived to be the mature one, while I am not? Because by my culture's standards, she is the one who is not acting, and thus* being, *mature. That is pretty much the only measurement system my people use.*)

(*I know that. I realize that. But . . . you would have to be raised V'Dan to understand how difficult that is to set aside. I had my eyes awakened to look beyond the surface and its marks a little while ago, but . . . not everyone has.*) He poked at his food with the fork, then looked up at her as she approached.

Filling the last plate from the stack Dai'a had set out, Jackie

served the food onto it, added utensils, and poured juice into
two cups. Li'eth watched her move with economic grace, and
remembered that, from her childhood images when teaching
him Terranglo, she had done similar things, commoner things,
for most of her life. That, too, would have to be something he
had to watch for and guard against, lest it prejudice his thoughts.

Then again, being in the military had already partially
erased some of that prejudice; there were far more officers of
the first as well as second ranks who were highly competent,
yet born of common blood—soldiers from the Third, Fourth,
and even Fifth Tiers who had proved themselves adept at
leadership—than there were nobles from the First and Second Tiers . . . and plenty of nobles who should never have
risen quite so high in their military ranks.

(*Come, we need to join the others. You can finish telling us
about the other races.*) She tipped her head toward the door.

Breathing deep to brace himself, Li'eth gathered up his
meal and followed her. The Terrans, he saw, had gathered at
one end of the table. The V'Dan sat at the other end. There
were a good six, seven seats in the middle that were available. Li'eth crossed to one of the middle ones and seated
himself, visually bridging the gap between the two. To his
pleasure, Ja'ki did the same thing on the other side.

"So, you've told us about the Feyori, who are energy-based
mirror-bubbles that like to meddle in the affairs of the others,
and we've met the Salik," she recited. "And then there are the
Gatsugi, who have four arms and whose skin changes color
depending upon their mood. And the Chinsoiy, who are
silicon-based and can glide with their wing-flaps. Who or what
else exists out there?"

"The Choya are the next race, and they were the youngest,
before meeting you—youngest in terms of having been members of the Alliance," Li'eth clarified firmly. "Like all races,
their culture and history stretch back for thousands of years, but
we only made First Contact with them a few decades ago."

V'kol spoke up, gesturing toward his neck. "They are like
the Salik in that they are amphibious; they are born with gills,
and with lungs, but unlike the Salik, they retain their gills
into adulthood, which they have to keep moist to keep them
from drying out painfully. They are built similar to us, or at

least more like us than like the squat, backwards-kneed Salik. The Salik can hold their breath for several *mi-nah*, which is . . . about seventy heartbeats per *mi-nah*?"

Li'eth noted how the Terrans exchanged quick looks on hearing the V'Dan time-unit word. One of the ones at the Terran end of the table muttered, "That sounds like *minute* . . ." but he wasn't sure which male had done it.

"I take it the Choya don't have to hold their breath, so much as they just close off their lungs and breathe through their gills," Ja'ki concluded. At Li'eth's nod, she shook her head. "I love to swim, but I can't hold my breath for all that long. I could wish for gills at moments like that, but I wouldn't want to be stuck with them. Do the Choya support the Salik in their war, being fellow amphibians?"

All of the V'Dan shook their heads. Ba'oul spoke up, his tone subdued and his words carefully chosen. "From what we have heard, they are being attacked along with the rest of us. Their blood is different, but the Salik do not find them impossible to . . . to attack personally, and . . . so forth, as they do the Chinsoiy. Only the Chinsoiy are being attacked from a distance with mass-destruction weapons."

"I'm sorry to hear that. What of the others? I seem to recall there are three more, from the language lessons," she added.

"I thought you were not allowed to talk of anything you learned," Shi'ol snapped stiffly.

Ja'ki dipped her head. "I am not allowed to talk of anything *personal*, you are correct. But this is common knowledge among all of you and thus not anything personal."

Tightening her mouth a little, Shi'ol picked up her fork and continued eating. The shapes of the utensils were a little different, the handles oddly curved, but Li'eth watched her handle them deftly enough to look about as graceful as the native Terrans. Arrogant, caste-conscious, but graceful.

"Well . . . for the remaining three, there are the K'Katta, the Tlassians, and the Solaricans," Dai'a explained. "The K'Katta look like giant . . . insect, is that the word? Arachnid? Arthro . . . arthropod?"

She didn't show any signs of her emotions visibly . . . but Li'eth got the impression Ja'ki was not pleased by that idea. He fumbled mentally toward her, and realized she was still holding mental hands with him. Using that link, he touched her, instead of letting her touch him first. (*Are you alright, Bright Stone?*)

(*I . . . what?*) she asked, blinking at him.

(*That is what your name means in my tongue. Are you alright?*) he repeated.

(*I hate spiders. I'm deeply afraid of them . . . and I have seen giant, freakish spider-people in all of your crew's thoughts,*) she said. He could feel her shuddering mentally. Outwardly, she merely put down her fork, barely listening while Dai'a explained their appearance.

"They have ten legs, two of which are shorter than the rest—they are about a body's length across, as tall as your Lars, or our Ba'oul," the life-support leftenant explained. "They have a dual skeletal system, bones on the inside, hard armor on the outside, because they evolved on a world with higher gravity than ours—this gravity is similar to our own. For many of the K'Katta, that armor is covered in a sort of fuzzy fur, which keeps them warm in cold climates, and which they can shed to make themselves difficult to catch and hold—they don't wear clothing like we do unless they absolutely have to, but they do make and wear the most beautifully woven sashes, as light as a feather puffing along on a gentle breeze."

"I have three K'Katta scarves at home," Shi'ol offered, joining the conversation for the first time without any arrogance. Pride, but not arrogance. "One I inherited from my grandmother. It is as blue as the sky in the northern latitudes of our motherworld, V'Dan. Like that blue in the upper right corner of that painted image," she added, nodding at the wall across from the big picture window.

Li'eth had to twist around to look at it. The blue in the upper corner of the painting on the artwork monitor had hints of violet to its tone. "It's a lovely color."

"Yes, it is," Shi'ol agreed, preening. "The Gatsugi—they communicate in *colormoods*—call that particular shade 'Deep Contentment.'"

"A good thing to know. May it always bring you that feeling, when you see or wear it," Ja'ki added diplomatically.

". . . Thank you." Shi'ol eyed the Terran Ambassador, then

returned her attention to her food. It was perhaps the first peaceful conversation the two women had held so far.

Li'eth found himself hoping the truce would continue. He changed the subject. "The next race would be the Tlassians. They are . . . lizardlike? I am picturing a word . . . the vocabulary escapes me. It is for a lizard, bigger than a V'Dan, but not quite the size of a small vehicle. It runs on two legs, with a tail behind it, balanced forward, longish arms . . ."

"Raptor?" Lars offered.

"Here . . . like this?" Ja'ki offered, and held up her hand, palm out. On the table between her and Li'eth, a strange glowing mist coalesced out of thin air, and shaped itself into a loaf-of-bread-sized version. It swung its head and tail, looking around, then "ran" in place, with bits of vegetation passing into and out of range of its body. Li'eth blinked, started, but it was V'kol who found his voice first.

"You have a technology that can project three-dimensional images?" the gunnery leftenant asked, peering at the illusion.

Ja'ki shook her head. "It is one of my psychic abilities— holy gifts—one which we call *holokinesis*. I am a direct descendant of a special bloodline, the great-plus-granddaughter of a woman named Jesse James Mankiller. We are hoping to escort you to the Moon when we are finally free to leave quarantine, to show you for yourselves the marks she left on its airless surface."

"Marks?" V'kol asked.

"She walked barefoot on the Moon, the one natural satellite that circles Earth. She did so without any kind of pressure-suit."

Shi'ol wasn't the only one to snort in disbelief. Ba'oul beat her, speaking first. "Impossible. If she was barefoot, then she would be dead. An airless moon would be freezing cold in the shade, the ground would be scorching hot in sunlight, and her blood would boil in the absence of atmospheric pressure. Therefore, she did *not* walk barefoot."

"She did. She used the power of telekinesis to envelop herself in a sphere for protection . . . the ability to move things with the mind, to create physical walls of force," Jackie reminded him. "An ability you saw *me* using during our escape. She also had had the gift of pyrokinesis, the ability to create and control fires, including not only creating heat but reducing heat, protecting her skin from the sun-heated sand. I could do *almost* the same as her, but I am not a pyrokinetic, so my feet would get burned in the sunlight and frostbitten in the shade. I am also not a biokinetic, so I could not heal myself of my injuries. I'd have to wear sturdy shoes at the very least."

"I have those abilities," Li'eth confessed. "My fire-calling gift is very weak, but in an emergency, I can light a candle, or a bit of wood or paper . . . and I can heal, but I cannot summon the ability to heal others save in dire emergency. I thought it was simply the will of the Saints that my gifts could be so erratic . . . but now I'm wondering if there is a way to train them to heed my control."

Ja'ki nodded. "We'll work on those. I may not have those abilities myself, but I do know some of the training methods, enough to ensure you at least get a start on getting them under control."

"You presume to teach one of our Great Ones how to use his abilities?" Shi'ol questioned her. The blonde's voice was more skeptical than arrogant.

"I presume, because from the Terran point of view, he hasn't had much in the way of training. There are *rules* about how those with these abilities must behave," Ja'ki asserted, tapping the table. "He must learn our ways of training so that he can follow our rules of behavior to the best of his ability. I am not here to hurt any of you or to watch you fumble, Shi'ol. I am here to help you navigate our cultures so that both sides achieve the best possible ends for our various goals. That includes training your captain in methods that should hopefully prevent potential problems, which could range from an accidental insult all the way through actual physical harm. Both are things I am certain Captain Ma'an-uq'en would like to avoid, the same as my people.

"Now, let us get back to these Tlassians," she stated, and held out her hand again. "Our precognitives—those who can catch brief glimpses of possible future events—saw creatures that looked like *this*." She concentrated, frowning softly, and the raptor-thing reappeared, before it shifted into a much more upright stance, with a more slender tail and more muscular arms. The calves thickened, and the thighs lost a good bit of their meat, though not all. "Is that a Tlassian?"

The V'Dan all nodded. V'kol gestured at it with his fork. "They have three castes; the priesthood have crests running around their skulls, either front to back like a fish fin, or ear to ear, like a balding hairline set halfway back on their skulls, or a sort of cross between the two, a curved peak that starts at the ears and joins at the front of the skull.

"The crest means they have holy abilities like yours . . . though none exactly like *that* one," he admitted, nodding at her illusion. "The warrior caste have flaps of skin alongside their necks, sort of muscular, which they can flex and flare outward in visible warning that you are making them mad. Wise travelers will avoid doing that because they can also spit a nasty, corrosive acid that can dissolve flesh and get into the blood, causing pain all over the body."

"Charming," Robert drawled, eyeing the being in its knee-length shorts and elbow-length shirt, the tail clothed halfway down as well. "And the third caste?"

"The priesthood is the smallest in number, maybe 10 percent, while the warriors are around twice that, but still relatively modest. The third is the worker caste, and it is about 70 percent of the Tlassian race," Ba'oul explained. "They are good people, hard workers. No crests, no neck-fringes or acid-spitting.

"They have a triumvirate for their government, a representative of each caste. The Priesthood dominates in times of peace, the Warriors dominate in times of war, and both must gain and retain the backing of the leaders of the Workers' caste to get *anything* done—*they* are the ultimate bureaucrats, as well as being farmers and factory workers, and more." The blue-marked man chuckled.

"I can imagine," Maria agreed, speaking up from the Terran end of the table. "Any other races?"

"The Solaricans are the last on the list so far. Locally, in this arm of the galaxy, the K'Katta were the first to achieve interstellar travel," Li'eth explained. "But the Solaricans come from a homeworld and a star system that is far overhead, well above the plane of our galaxy. They have colonized many sections around the galaxy, but each section is considered independent of the other, though all ultimately answer to the Queen of their kind. Oh, the Tlassians arrived among the Alliance worlds about fifty years before we V'Dan achieved interstellar space, which was two hundred years after the Solaricans and five hundred after the K'Katta."

"The K'Katta did not have faster-than-light technology," V'kol added. "They had artificial gravity, but nothing faster than generation ships. The Solaricans had a very awkward form of faster-than-light, which they refuse to share with the rest of us, though they adopted the V'Dan version shortly after encountering it over two hundred years ago," he told them. "So they, too, were traveling generation by generation. They have not said for certain, but I believe they have been traveling through space for almost a thousand years."

"Well, that's nice," Brad stated, flipping a hand at the far end of the table. "But what do they *look* like? We got giant bugs, lizardmen, frog-octopus people, more amphibians, flying whatsits—"

"Gliding," Dai'a corrected him. "They do not fly, they can only glide."

"Right. Glide, whatever," the copilot dismissed. "So on and so forth. So what do the Solaricans look like?"

"Felinoid," Ja'ki stated, remembering a mix of the precog's visions and the vocabulary-based memories of their guests. She let the illusion of the dinosaur fade since it was no longer needed.

Li'eth nodded. "Like *g'ats*. You would call them . . . *cats*, and there lies yet another word of ours which sounds very similar to the version you use in your Terranglo."

Ayinda sighed, shrugging. "I give up. Maybe time travel *is* involved somehow. Because the way *our* languages have evolved over hundreds and thousands of years suggest that there should *not* be so many lingering similarities."

"I agree," Ja'ki said. "The language, the very words being used, should have drifted wildly in most cases. Not in all, but most of them should have gone astray over the course of nearly ten thousand years."

"We have had ninety-five centuries' worth of our most formal language, Imperial High V'Dan, being taught in our schools," Li'eth told her. "Common V'Dan has drifted all over the place into various regional dialects, even to the point where they are now considered different tongues . . . but the mother tongue, High V'Dan, has remained the same. Or mostly the same. A few words have lost their sense of meaning as times and technologies have changed, but most of the words have remained known and stayed firmly the same."

"So it is sort of like *Hebrew*," Lars offered. "An ancient language with a group of people who learn it as a hereditary inheritance. They have been practicing it for thousands of years."

"Or perhaps like Latin," Ja'ki agreed. "Latin is one of the two backbones for the special naming vocabulary used by scientists, the other being Greek—we don't teach either as often as our ancestors used to, but the two color everything in the various branches of science."

"I will take your word for it," he told them. "And I shall let the others pick a topic to discuss now, as my food is getting cold." Forking up some vegetables, he dipped his head, and ate.

Ja'ki followed suit, picking up her own utensil—until she suddenly scrambled back up out of her chair, fork flying and clattering across the tabletop. *"Aah! Spider!!"*

She thumped up against the windowed wall, staring in horror . . . at a tiny, multi-legged dot no bigger than a finger-nail that was creeping hesitantly across the table near her plate. Letting out a sigh of disgust, Brad rose from his chair and crossed to her abandoned seat with a muttered, "You are so *bootless* . . ."

Gently coaxing the thing to crawl onto his hand, he exited the dining hall, carrying it away. About a minute later, he appeared on the other side of the window, thumped on the glass with his fist, showed Jackie the tiny arachnid—she shuddered and lurched away from the windowpane—and gently deposited the creature onto a leafy plant at the end of one of the multilayered growing stacks.

". . . Bootless?" Dai'a asked, confused.

Ja'ki shook her head, palm splayed across the tops of her breasts, no doubt to quell her pounding heart. ". . . It's a mild insult. Slang." Her other hand came up to rub at the bridge of her nose, massaging the frown pinching her tired face. "Something you only get by context."

"Slang or not, if you act like that around the K'Katta, you will *not* make a very good Ambassador to the Alliance," V'kol pointed out.

"I can be calm," she asserted, holding her hand palm out to him. "I can be polite. I just . . . don't like being surprised, is all. Besides, once we establish solid communication, more Ambassadors will follow—I can't be an Ambassador to each and every race individually, after all. And I will personally make sure that whoever is selected to be a representative toward these K'Katta is not the least bit arachnophobic."

Listening to their conversation, Li'eth made a mental note. If and when they returned to V'Dan, he would make sure she was warned in advance of an approaching K'Kattan wherever possible before encountering a member of that race. She could and clearly wanted to guide his crew away from making diplomatic mistakes; he could and should do the same thing for her side as well.

CHAPTER 10

Seven blessed, glorious hours of solid, gravity-assisted sleep . . . and two extra hours on top of that of utter privacy, even if they were split before and after that nap in her quarters, made Jackie feel, well, a lot more Human. A bit of privacy and real sleep seemed to have helped the disposition of the others, too, when they met for food, then parted again to do their own things before their formal introduction via commlink conference.

The Terrans had uniforms that had been sterilized and brought into quarantine for wearing, and the V'Dan had their single set of formalwear, tailored to a rough approximation of V'Dan military uniforms, plus the casual clothes supplied to everyone to wear. Those were tough, loose-fitting garments that could survive being boiled for five minutes on top of being cleaned by ultrasonic waves sloshing through the wash water. Jackie had pulled Li'eth aside a couple hours early, however, for yet more psi training. In her mind, that was too important to be easily set aside.

She and Li'eth now sat in cushioned chairs in the garden space, surrounded by faintly droning insects and the rustling of leaves in the artificial, ventilation-generated breezes. The air was warm, humid, and very much like home to her. She had donned heather-gray pants and a matching tee shirt, though later she would be wearing her formal Dress Blacks uniform, black jacket, black pants, silver-gray shirt, and gray and blue stripes down the sleeves and legs. A uniform that thankfully fitted these days.

(*Though I haven't done this, I've had it done to* me, *so I know the feeling,*) Jackie told Li'eth, meaning the use of bio-kinesis, his "holy healing" ability. (*You gather the green and gold energies into a coil, like a scroll instead of a ball, and you wrap it around the injured part of the body to stabilize the wound . . .*)

"There you are! I demand different clo— Why are the two of you holding *hands*?" Shi'ol demanded, striding up to them with a scowl on her rosette-marked brow. "He has already had his language transfer."

Her concentration aggravated out of its centered state, Jackie breathed deeply before answering. Twice.

"Well? Let go of him!"

"I told you, Shi'ol, he needs proper training, so that he does not accidentally cause offense. Which you are bordering on doing with your demands. I *told* you we hold hands to make the lessons go smoother and faster. I told *everyone* that I wanted an hour of privacy to concentrate on *teaching* your captain proper psychic protocols and behaviors, before dressing for the first formal interview the lot of you will be doing." She glanced at the digital numbers on the face of her health-monitor bracelet, and sighed again. "We have an hour and a half before that interview. What is the problem *this* time?"

"I demand better-fitting clothes. The waist on this jacket is too long," the V'Dan blonde told her. She gestured at the fitted, tapered, long-tailed military jacket she wore, dyed red and decorated in gold trim, with cream-colored lapels, matching trousers, and a cream shirt underneath. It was not quite Napoleonic in style, but it had something of that flavor to the design.

"That jacket was measured while you were floating in null

gravity," Jackie pointed out. "As a result, your spine had *lengthened* while in zero G. The tailor-bot program tried to compensate for it, but couldn't tell by how much you'd shrink once you were under the effects of gravity, spun or otherwise. It takes time to manufacture a new set of clothes, so be grateful you *have* something decent approximating V'Dan Imperial military uniforms. It will simply have to do for now."

"That is unacceptable," Shi'ol stated, lifting her chin slightly. "I am going to have to represent our people to your entire . . . whatever it is you have for a government. I need to be *properly* attired."

Li'eth had been sitting quietly through the exchange, until that. "Leftenant," he stated quietly, his voice edged with irritation, "I gave you instructions on how to behave. *I* will represent the Empire. *You* will remain silent until spoken to and make no attempt to seize authority while we are here. Unless and until the Empress herself grants you that power, you do *not* have it. Make a *good* impression."

"Besides," Jackie told her, "this will be a video-based introduction. Any flaws in the garments will not be as readily noticed as if we were present in person. I know Ayinda was helping Dai'a learn how to design clothes with the tailor-bot's programming system," she added, gentling her tone. "Since there will be many more meetings while we spend time figuring out where the V'Dan Empire is, and where to return you—by preference, to your capital so that we also can efficiently meet with Her Majesty on the same trip—you will have plenty of time to manufacture clothing that will fit a little bit better. I'd recommend living tailors to do the alterations, since that could be done within the time you have left . . . but we can have no unauthorized, unnecessary visitors while in quarantine. Tailoring clothes by a fraction for a slightly better fit just isn't necessary enough."

"It is Her *Eternity*, not 'Her *Majesty*,' whatever that word means. You have much to learn about Imperial etiquette," Shi'ol stated, looking down on Jackie.

"And you still have much to learn about Terran etiquette. It will be attended to in due time, Leftenant Superior. I know that Maria gave each of you a datapad with basic information on Terran etiquette to study over the last day. As you will need that information sooner than I will need yours, I suggest you study it. Now, if you will kindly take your leave, your captain and I need to get back to his lessons in self-control," Jackie stated as politely as she could.

Another long stare, and Shi'ol spun on her heel, and stalked off.

(*I don't think she's going to let the matter go.*) Jackie sighed. Reaching for Li'eth's mind was the easiest thing she had ever done. She attributed some of that to his lack of training and thus lack of shielding, but also because she hadn't entirely let go of him since first grasping his mind back on the Salik ship. Some of it, though, had to be from how quickly he was fine-tuning his skills. (*Shi'ol is going to try to bring up the fact she's a Countess to sway my people into paying more attention to her than to you . . . and yes, I overheard that as a thought, though I didn't want to. She's thinking it rather loudly. It's very much like trying not to overhear shouting through a thin wall.*)

(*I heard it, too, if not as clearly.*) Li'eth sighed and rubbed at the bridge of his nose. (*More clearly than I ever have in the past, save when my holy gifts fluctuated . . . What's your strongest drinking alcohol, and do you have it in quarantine?*)

(*Drinking alcohol . . . that'd be the Clear 180. Ninety percent alcohol, in fact. It's stocked as a backup sterilizing agent and a backup makeshift painkiller as well as a beverage. I'll get you some when this session has ended, a little flask you can carry, and a kerchief or something to apply it with,*) she added. She had to breathe deeply a few times to shake off Shi'ol's interruption (*Now, back to using your biokinetic abilities. I can only give you the basics, remember, but I can get you started. We can also get a biokinetic up here who is also telepathic, and see if they can help guide you, either after we get out of quarantine, or maybe from beyond an observation window . . .*)

The dining hall, Li'eth discovered, could double as a conference hall. It made sense, of course, since it was an efficient use of the space. It did require that the table be cleared, scrubbed, and draped with an elegant blue cloth to hide its utilitarian nature, but the real surprise was the screen that dropped down over the observation window, blocking out the view of all those leafy plants and vegetables on their carefully tilted tiers of shelving. His people used projectors, not screens, when they needed a large image. The screen was very broad, it was modestly high, and it divided itself into three repeated images. The logo, he realized, of these people's empire.

Some sort of oval-shaped map occupied the screen. A-yinda had explained that the solid portions of the logo's map outlined their main planet's continents on grid-striped water; in turn, the oval sat surrounded by curved branches from some sort of highly leafy, short-twigged, plant. The background color was blue, the overall images scribed in silvery white with a thin outline in black.

Those were auspicious colors for the Gatsugi, Li'eth knew. The colormooded aliens found the Imperial scarlet and gold of V'Dan a bit aggressive. The uniforms worn by officers in Gatsugi territory therefore tended to be made from creams accented with gold and scarlet, rather than scarlet with gold and cream, but these people were Terrans.

The V'Dan-style uniforms these Terrans had come up with were reasonably comfortable, and reasonably well fitted in spite of Shi'ol's complaint. True, the garments were a tiny bit too long in the body now that they were walking around in a reasonable facsimile of gravity, but not by too much. Li'eth had worn uniforms that were off by about that much, himself. The scarlet was a close match for trousers and jackets, the latter had cream front panels and lapels edged in some gold-like cloth, and there was plenty of braiding crossing the fronts, albeit a few more rows than expected.

Lars had said something about ". . . borrowing a classic *nuh'poly-on'ic* pattern for the base design," whatever that meant. Some sort of uniform design from a couple centuries before, apparently. But it was close enough to the real thing to make Li'eth feel comfortable. Even Shi'ol had only complained about the fit, not the extra frogging—a case of her trying to make demands and get special favors. Admittedly, such things someone of Second Tier or higher would always expect, but that was in V'Dan society, not Terran.

Even an approximation of the proper shoulder and sleeve-cuff insignia for their ranks had been manufactured for them, albeit none of their medals and awards had been made. Ayinda had stepped in again for that one, stating that they couldn't rightfully manufacture medals for a foreign military; that would be an insult to the V'Dan government. But she could make their rank insignia.

Li'eth could see her point about the medals. V'kol had grumbled a little over that one, since as a gunnery officer, his uniform had been decorated with the symbols of many enemy kills. But the four leftenants superior had been given steel triangular outlines to wear on their shoulders and cuffs, with the hypotenuse approximately the length of the first and second fingerbones, since they had no way to accurately translate units of measurement, yet.

His own triangle as a Captain was a solid piece of steel, no open outline. Polished to a bright shine, it came with a backing bar set with tiny, rare earth magnets to clip it into the appropriate spots on their jackets. That was rather clever in his opinion; the backing bars were flat, the corners carefully rounded and polished just enough for safety, with no real way to harm the wearer. The Empire still used actual pins for their insignia, and if you lost the protective clasp, you could puncture yourself. Or even just pick up some nasty bruises when taking a hit on the shoulder or wrist.

The undergarments were Terran in style, not too uncomfortable. The cream dress shirts . . . an approximation of V'Dan shirts, which in the current military style buttoned down one side, so as to avoid combat bruises on the sternum. They certainly weren't made from silken *qu'oleq*, which was a form of ballistics cloth meant to protect the entire torso while still remaining reasonably lightweight and breathable.

Then again, we are at the mercy of our Terran hosts, Li'eth reminded himself, waiting for Ja'ki to show. He was the first to arrive in the dining hall turned conference room, and had planned it that way. *If they really wanted to kill us, they could do so at any time . . .*

(*You know we're not going to do that,*) Ja'ki sent back to him, hearing his thoughts. She wasn't in the same room, but she had heard him. (*If we wanted you dead, we'd have left you in Salik . . . erm . . . hand-tentacle-things.*)

Anyone else, he might have flinched or demanded they not eavesdrop, but Li'eth knew he was still struggling to master his projective abilities. He knew she was watching him to help *him* know when he was thinking projectively instead of just thinking loudly. With her . . . it felt as easy as clasping and holding someone's hand. Someone he genuinely liked, the more he came to know her. It felt even more natural to just keep "holding hands" as it were, so how could he object?

(*Can you speak for every single person in your empire?*) he asked her instead, playing Saint's interrogator. (*I know among our own people, there will be radicals and mentally disturbed persons who will try to attack you just for being different. Can you say there will not be similar upset souls in this place?*)

(*I will not deny we have similar problems, though we have a very good mental-health system, invoking many different styles of therapies, both chemical and nonchemical in nature. There may be those who have slipped through the cracks who may try to harm you, but we will do our best to stop them. Unless* you *attempt to harm* us, *we have neither reason nor inclination to harm you . . . and the law says that unless circumstances prove otherwise, we must not do so.*)

He had an impression she was struggling to get her hair pinned up, though she knew she was running out of time. Now that they were out of null gravity, she didn't have to keep it pinned up, but it looked more professional to these people. His own were similar in preferring neatened hair, so he had used some of the grooming fasteners found in the toiletry drawers in his bathroom facilities. His locks had been pulled back into a braided queue, exposing every bit of his face for the formality of the moment. Now he waited with the flat little bottle of Clear 180 tucked into one of his pockets, wrapped in a kerchief she had found somewhere.

The others started arriving. Once again, the V'Dan gathered at one end of the table, the Terrans at the other. This time, Li'eth had hurried through his preparations in order to claim the end seat, the position of power. Shi'ol arrived through the door at his end of the chamber, the one not closest to the kitchen. She had to check herself and swing toward one of the other chairs. The logistics officer frowned a little, if not quite in his direction. Not with an implication of insubordination. Yet.

Finally, Ja'ki strode in, neatly dressed in one of these Terran military uniforms and carrying a box. Where Robert, A-yinda, and Brad were clad in somewhat dull, medium blue uniforms with black stripes down the pant legs and sleeves, buttons gleaming in silver, and where Maria and Lars wore gray uniforms with blue and black stripes, her uniform was stark black relieved by gold buttons down the front, and silvery-gray and medium blue stripes down arms and legs. She had given up on pinning up her hair and had instead simply twisted and pulled back the sides, confining her dark curls to the sides of her head before letting the mass of it spread out down her back, where it fell almost to her waistline.

When she set the box down on the seat of one of the chairs to her left, on the Terran side of the room, Li'eth noticed something else that a lack of gravity and then baggy clothes had hidden: The cut of her formal jacket showed off her figure. It was fuller compared to the other four women, the V'Dan included.

If one ignored the utter lack of proper marks, she looked very . . . adult. Ah-yinda was very modest in the chest compared to the others, while Shi'ol, Dai'a, and Mah-riia were moderate in their curves. Ja'ki . . . looked very adult. Li'eth had a preference for full-bodied women, and when Ja'ki—Bright Stone—moved, he wanted to . . .

Determined to erase the rest of that thought, Li'eth rose to his feet. His fellow V'Dan did as well, eyeing him in confusion. Rising was reserved for when a superior entered a room in formal uniform, but she wasn't one of theirs, he knew. Still, she was their hostess and deserved all the respect he and his surviving crew members could give. That meant he stood, and tightened his mental bubble to keep her from overhearing any less-than-formal, respectful thoughts.

She faltered a little, not expecting that, but finished walking back to the center of the table opposite the window-turned-viewscreen. "Thank you. Please be seated. Before we begin, I will give you a few instructions, and a bit of information; here are some pens and tablets of paper if you would like to take notes; you may make them in V'Dan or Terranglo, whichever you feel most comfortable with," she added, pulling notepads and Terran-style pens out of her box. "These notes will be for your personal use only, and will be destroyed if you wish it so—we still use paper from time to time because electronic data can be copied all too easily without noticing, and you can shield the tablets from any camera viewpoints with their covers. If you have questions, particularly once the proceedings are under way, then it would be good to write down your thoughts to help organize and refer to them when given a chance to speak."

"With that said," she told them, drawing in a deep breath, "you are about to face the full assembly of the Terran United Planets Council, which is our highest governing body. We no longer have royals or nobles who rule directly, in the sense of crafting laws as well as enforcing them; they do not work for the *legislative* branch of our regional governments, though they may serve as the *executive* branch, making sure those laws are carried out. The Council, as I said, is the legislative branch, with the Secondaire and Premiere being placed above all Councilors and governors, royal or elected. They function as the chiefmost members of the executive branch, trained through years of service in the legislative branch to understand the laws that are made, altered, or repealed, and thus how to implement them.

"The Council is elected through a system of tests, votes of confidence by the people, and a very strict ethical standard for its members' conduct," she continued, and tapped on a small datapad she pulled from her pocket. The viewscreen shifted in the center to a view of brown and green continents surrounded by blue ocean. "I myself served for five years as a Councilor for this particular region."

A swath of islands large and small, and a very large patch of ocean, lit up first in pink, then broke down into three smaller sections in beige, yellow, and orange.

"This is Oceania, which is composed of Polynesia—where I was born, which includes the island hosting our capital—Micronesia, and Melanesia. Other regions can cover entire continents, such as Australasia, or are broken up into many much smaller cultural and population-based regions, such as the continent of Europe, which has fifty-three distinct provinces. Those range from entire regions, such as the peninsula of Italy, to the megacity zones such as the eight lobes of Paris in the province of France. As you can see, there is a *lot* of diversity, both in environment and in cultural pressures, which you will be facing . . . but everyone on the Council speaks

Terranglo, so you should be able to make yourselves understood.

"If you cannot find a word or phrase in Terranglo which suits your needs, you may question me aloud in V'Dan, and I will do my best to translate. If they ask questions that we have not yet discussed, if you do not feel comfortable discussing it, simply state, 'That is yet to be determined,' or 'We have not yet discussed that subject,' or some variation along those lines. One more thing," Ja'ki explained, holding up a finger in caution. "There will be a group of people seated in a specific section of the Council Hall. Their seats are white, as are the section railings, and they will all be wearing short, sleeveless white vests."

A touch of the controls shifted the image on the viewscreen to an image of several Humans in various different outfits; each and ever one was wearing a sleeveless, white, waist-length vest.

"These people are *not* Council members, and are *not* trained diplomats. So if they ask a question which you deem to be offensive, please simply say, 'My culture considers that question to be inappropriate,' and please do *not* take actual offense. It will not be meant that way, I assure you," Ja'ki stated.

"Why shouldn't we?" Shi'ol asked, arms folded across her uniformed chest. "If they are going to ask us offensive questions—"

V'kol answered her, interrupting her. "We don't *know* their culture. People from the *Tarkonda* mountains wipe away their tears with their bare fingers, saying it is an offense to the gods to do anything else. People from the Capital cities would be offended at this unhygienic practice because it runs the risk of smearing bodily fluids onto various surfaces, or getting contaminants on the hands into the eyes. Capital residents prefer that a cloth be used, even if a sleeve cuff or a shirt hem is the only thing at hand. But when in Tarkonda, even the Empress might wipe tears away with her fingers out of respect for local custom."

Shi'ol snorted. "Her Eternity would *never*—"

"We are getting *off* topic," Li'eth asserted. He did not want to hear what the countess thought his mother would or would not do. "Who are these special people in the white-colored seats, Ambassador Ja'ki Maq'en-zi? Or rather, what are they?

What makes them special, and why might they ask odd questions and not the others?"

"The white-vest wearers are members of the Fellowship Lottery," she stated, and explained further at their blank looks. "Once every two weeks, a drawing is held across the United Planets. Every single province gets to select by random drawing two to four delegates, depending upon the local cultural diversity as well as its population density. Their immediate families are also allowed to attend, up to four additional people per selected Fellow, though only children aged twelve or older may accompany them, and only the Fellowship members themselves may attend the actual Council meetings and so forth.

"They must be adults—which is defined as anyone eighteen years or older—they must have lived and worked in the drawing region for at least one year, and they must have plans to continue to live and work in that region for at least another full year past their selection point. Fellowship members are drawn from all levels and kinds of life, whether it's cattle herders in central Africa," she added, pulling up a picture on the side of leather-clad, brown-skinned Humans in bangles and beads riding on four-wheeled vehicles through dry, yellow-withered grasslands among four-legged animals almost as big as the vehicles, "or the Sami people of northernmost Europe," another image of pale-faced, dark-haired people bundled in layers of clothing, riding strange beasts with branched horns among trees dusted with snow, "to the most street-savvy businessman or businesswoman of North Tokyo province, which is part of a megacity in the heart of the islands of Japan."

A golden-skinned woman with flattish, almond-shaped eyes and black hair, clad in a navy suit spangled down one side and sleeve, stood on a very busy street lit by colorful lights, with billboards, signs, and buildings towering all around her. She was doing something with a datapad. On the main map, different areas lit up to highlight the different regions being discussed.

"Each one of the Lottery winners is brought to the capital on the island of Kaho'olawe at the government's expense for two weeks," Ja'ki continued, her voice shifting in its accent on the name of the location. That, Li'eth finally realized, was the source of the slightly different accent she had, compared to the others. It was different from Maria's, from Brad's, from Lars' accent, from all of the other Terrans'. "And this is what the capital looks like."

He turned his attention to the map, where she was pointing. The pinpoint that she highlighted, Li'eth noted, lay within the uppermost of the broad, ocean-spanning triangle called Polynesia, within the region of Oceania. More images appeared, of a modest-sloped hill and crater on an island that was rather dry and desertlike, its reddish soil showing through though tufts of vegetation on its north-northwest side. On the opposite side, the south-southeast, bushes gave way to trees and greenery, interspersed with various buildings that blended in and complemented their surroundings. The buildings in the crater, located on the east side, were surrounded by more desert than by greenery, and stood out rather blatantly compared to the buildings in the thick foliage to the south.

"What are those structures?" Dai'a asked, pointing at one that looked like an unfurling flower, and another like a spire-tall clump of green crystals, and at a third like a series of stacked cubes in a rainbow of metallic colors.

"The green one is called the Tower, and it is the heart of the military. The rounded one with the suggestion of flower petals is the Council Hall, nicknamed the Lotus, after a type of flower found in ponds. It is the heart of the government in the sense that all the Councilors have their offices there, for it is where the Council meets. The sprawling one with different layers and colors is the Departments Building . . . which those of us in the government liked to joke is the 'Department of Departments,'" Ja'ki added wryly, humor coloring her tone. "While the Council Hall holds the offices for all the Councilors, every province, and even many prefectures, has an office as well for its representative and executive segment located in the Department of Departments. On top of that, all of the actual departments and bureaus of the government have their headquarters located there—the Department of Health, the Department of Agriculture, the Department of Ecology, so on and so forth.

"The north side of the island is maintained as a cultural preserve for the people of the islands of Hawai'i—my mother's people—and the south side is filled with residences for those who work on the island in the various service branches, for the Fellowship members and attending families of the Lottery winners, for Councilors, and for visiting dignitaries.

"As I was saying about the Lottery winners, the Fellows come for two weeks, and during those two weeks, they sit in on every Council session, they ask questions, they can challenge laws—they can *pause* those laws in the process of being made, forcing those proposing it or opposing it to present new data to justify said support or resistance, though they cannot *make* or *unmake* any laws—and they are there to serve as witnesses to all aspects of the highest levels of government," Ja'ki explained. "The United Planets Council does most of its business openly, with all sessions recorded and most made available for anyone to watch, and the Fellowship stands watch to personally ensure that reality matches those recordings.

"There are closed-door meetings where sensitive information is discussed—a lot of it pertaining to the military—but while the recordings of those sessions are almost never released, the current Fellows are still expected to attend. They must sign privacy and nondisclosure agreements, but they cannot be barred from attending those meetings once they do so.

"Most will not break their word," Jackie added soberly. "To be selected for the Lottery, to be granted the title of Fellow for two weeks and Former Fellow for the rest of their lives—unless it is stripped from them through the breaking of their oaths or the law—is to be given the rare opportunity to represent their local communities directly to the highest levels of power. This has a very great impact upon how their local region will be treated. It confers a *great* deal of prestige upon the people who are selected to attend. Former Fellows have been known to go into civil service after having walked the halls of the Department of Departments, and are often all the more valued for their comprehension of its workings.

"Anyway . . . These are the main three buildings that house the government and the defense of the United Planets. There is one more building involved in the government," she continued, "and it is this building here, which is called the Terrace, or the Blue Terrace."

The image that appeared was of a long, curved, blue metallic building set in the outer wall of the crater, not the inner. Ba'oul lifted his chin. "What happens there? It seems to be set apart from the other three."

"Deliberately so," Ja'ki confirmed. "This is where the Advisors interact with special interest groups. There was a serious problem with corruption a couple hundred years back, and in the wake of the tragedy following the destruction of the city of Vladistad by cultist extremists, the government reformation acknowledged that special interest groups would have to be handled a lot better than previously. Corporation representatives are no longer allowed to make closed-door deals with government representatives, nor can any other form of organization do the same. They must instead bring their proposed deals openly to an Advisor, who is a permanently retired Councilor—once you become an Advisor, you can *never* again be picked for office—and they review the case. *Anyone* can visit those petition meetings, but they have to request an invitation to attend, they must pay their own way, and they cannot stay overnight.

"Anyone caught petitioning outside of these areas, particularly in private, is immediately suspended pending a thorough investigation, including investigation by telepathic truth disclosure. Any corporation or interest group found attempting to influence the government directly can be banned from contact, including travel to the Hawai'ian Islands, the individuals directly responsible will be imprisoned, they and their corporation may have any associated assets seized, or even be disbanded and its ownership redistributed by law . . . and no one involved will ever be allowed to take office.

"The individuals directly responsible are also banned from being entered into the Lottery for the rest of their lives. Any Councilor *accepting* that influence is thrown in jail for a period of no less than five years and is banned permanently from ever holding any sort of office again. If bribery transactions took place, assets may be confiscated or frozen, so on and so forth. It's a very serious accusation. In fact, just *making* the accusation puts the accuser's motivations under tight scrutiny, too," Ja'ki told them. "They, too, will be investigated in the fullest measure of the law."

Surprisingly, it was Shi'ol who reacted the strongest to the Ambassador's explanation. Hand at the base of her throat, she blinked and stared at the structure of the Blue Terrace. "That sounds rather severe as a punishment. Perhaps even overly severe."

"We got rather sick and tired of the oligarchic corruption, the failure to enforce laws against corrupt activities, and the rampant ignorance polluting the histories of our late-twentieth through early-twenty-second centuries. After the city of Vladistad was destroyed, our ancestors finally did something about it," Ja'kie stated dryly. "On the other hand, to become a Councilor these days, you do not have to have served at lower levels of government, so you don't have to know the right people, or worse, pay the right people. You *do* have to pass a strict and rigorous series of tests covering the functioning of governance, all major common laws, and what we call STEM subjects, being science, technology, engineering, and mathematics.

"On top of that, you have to have a vote of confidence from your population, starting at 60 percent, and rising every five years by 5 percent with each attempt at a new term. The most popular of Councilors in this century was Rosa McCrary, who served for an unprecedented six terms—90-percent approval rating—before being requested to become the Secondaire to her predecessor, and then our Premiere. She just stepped down a few weeks ago as the Premiere, highest-ranked official in the land, and was replaced in turn by her Secondaire, Augustus Callan, who is now our Premiere.

"Just before her retirement, Premiere McCrary began authorizing the missions that resulted in the *Aloha 9* being selected to go on the mission that in turn rescued you. Premiere Callan took over her project at the beginning of this year and has been kept informed of all the pertinent details at every step along the way. So, on the military side of things, Admiral Nayak and Admiral-General Kurtz are my immediate superiors, yes. This makes me a midlevel officer at most. On the civilian side, as the Ambassador of the Terran United Planets . . . my only superiors are the Secondaire and Premiere of the Council.

"I no longer represent Oceania when I stand before the Council. I represent *all* of the Terran United Planets, every single person you have seen, and every single person you will see. Just as the Premiere and Secondaire must represent every single person, my constituency, my region, is the entire United Planets," she stated, finishing her explanations. "*That*, Shi'ol Nanu'oc, is the level of civilian authority I hold. I represent the needs and interests of billions of people. I suspect that places me at the equivalent of an Imperial Princess."

Ja'ki leaned on her palms, staring straight at the rosette-spotted blonde. Shi'ol blinked, but did not look away.

"Every single person you are about to meet—even the Lottery winners—in turn represents millions of people. That is my warning to *all* of you, to be respectful of that power," Ja'ki added, looking at the faces of the other V'Dan. Just as her gaze met Li'eth's, numbers started flashing on the screen, counting down from one hundred. "I give it in good faith because I honestly would like to see you V'Dan give a *good* impression of yourselves to my fellow Terrans. I give it as a warning because this will *not* be a secret session. You are about to be seen live by billions of people. *Billions*, many of whom are awake specifically for this momentous event, even though it may be their sleep cycle. Even though they may be at work, there will be very few who are not watching it right now, or who will not be watching it later when they have enough time.

"As I said, if you are unsure what to say, say nothing. Or if addressed directly, say, 'I am uncertain what to say at this time on that subject matter,' or some variation along those lines. Your honesty will be more appreciated than any lie . . . and lies *will* be found out, sooner or later, even if they're only the littlest of lies by exaggeration. We are a culture of honor, honesty, and personal responsibility." Straightening, she checked the time and tugged her jacket into alignment. "Now, we're about to go live to the whole world. If you are not sure where to look, just look at the eyes of the centermost person in any of the three screen sections. The camera will be behind that spot. Please take seats on *this* side of the table, so that you face everyone respectfully. There will be a very lengthy oath the representatives will recite, then the actual interview will begin."

That meant V'kol and Dai'a had to move, though both left a chair between the Ambassador and them. Li'eth stayed in his seat, but he did turn his chair somewhat to face the monitor screen. A few moments later, when the countdown of Terranglo numbers reached zero, the maps all vanished.

They were replaced by a seamless, visually curved image of a vast chamber lined with tiers of seats. One section, off to the far left, had the white-lined seats as promised; those were filled with people in a wide variety of clothes, each with the short white vest unifying them in appearance.

The rest of the seats were all edged and padded in dark gray. Every single one was filled with a Terran. Many held older, age-lined faces, some with youthful features, but all of them were clad in a sleeveless, calf-length robe. Each robe was a solid color, but they came in various subdued shades of the rainbow; most wore clothing beneath them that varied a bit less than the extreme ends of what the Lottery winners wore. A bit more subdued in style, a bit more formal, for all they were foreign to his eyes. The garments were not quite as layered or intricately cut as First Tier clothes, but the quality was still easily somewhere between Second and Third.

Had they been marked, the Terran officials would have looked fully adult to him . . . and the moment Li'eth caught himself thinking *that*, he firmly steered his thoughts away from that trap. *They are adults. They* are *adults . . .*

The audio portion of the communications link thrummed with the rustling murmurs of dozens and scores of quiet conversations, until a pair of white-robed figures strode into view from a corridor between the tiers of seats. Theirs were the only calf-length, all-white overgarments; Li'eth guessed it was a way to unify the two long-robed Councilors with the short-vested Fellows as well as the others.

A middle-aged, slightly graying man with a dark gray robe—the only color not in the seats surrounding him—stood and spoke into some sort of wire, an audio pickup. "Premiere Augustus Callan and Secondaire Jorong Que Pong have entered the Hall. Everyone, please rise for the opening ceremonies of this session, number 40,618, of the United Planets Council, taking place on this day of February 1, in the year 2287."

Everyone in the Council Hall—those who were seated— surged to their feet. Those who were already standing broke off their conversations and faced the center of the hall. So did the Terrans, standing as Ja'ki did. Li'eth, accustomed to the flow of ritual and protocol, chose to stand as well out of respect for their government since it was obvious the two clad in white floor-length vests were the Premiere and Secondaire she kept mentioning. Belatedly, the others in his crew stood as well. Thankfully, Shi'ol was the first after him to do so. She, too, was accustomed to the rituals of formality even if these people were not V'Dan.

The shorter, lighter-skinned of the two men in white, the one with the gray outfit that matched the silver streaks in his dark hair, lifted his hands palm upward almost exactly like a Temple High Priest would have. Li'eth found himself abruptly amused, since despite their plain appearance, those outer vest-robes were *sort of* like the formal outer vestments of the priesthood. Minus all of the embroidery, beadwork, and more, of course. A name flashed on the screen underneath him, scrolling from left to right in Terranglo lettering: *Premiere Augustus Callan.*

"We now begin this session, number 40,618, of the Terran United Planets Council with the traditional recitation of the Oath of Civil Service."

CHAPTER 11

The trio of Terran soldiers at the far end of the table immediately shifted, feet planting shoulder-width apart and hands tucking behind their back in an easy stance, the sort that could be maintained for long stretches of time. So did the doctor, and after a moment, the geophysicist shrugged and tucked his hands behind his back as well. Ja'ki, however, drew herself up square-shouldered and proud, her left hand covering her sternum, her right hand raised palm out . . . just as everyone else on the other side of the screen was doing.

Or rather, everyone *not* in the white-seated section. The Lottery winners, the Fellowship members, all stood, but only a few of them raised their hands; it seemed to be purely voluntary for them but mandatory for the rest. Certainly, everyone

else did, even the ones in the dark gray robes, which seemed
to indicate that they served as Hall staff of some sort. In a
mass of voices, high and low, age-grizzled and youth-smooth,
they all began their recitation.

The noise from the monitors was just that, measured and
paced, but very much the noise of hundreds of representatives speaking all at once. Ja'ki's words, however, were much
clearer and more easily understood. The only problem was,
it *was* a long Oath, very long, and it was a struggle even for
Li'eth, accustomed to long-winded speeches from youth onward, to keep his mind on what they were saying.

"I am Ja'ki Maq'en-zi," she stated, while all the others gar-
bled their names together, along with their locations, "and I
represent the people of the Terran United Planets." There was
a pause of so many heartbeats, waiting for those with the longest names for themselves and their districts to be said, then
with a slight gesture from the Premiere on the screen, she and
everyone else involved continued in a much closer version of
unison.

"Today, and for all the days ahead of me, for as long as I
shall serve my people and my government in any capacity, I
will cling to and abide by the following guidelines, laws, and
rules, keeping them carefully and fully in mind every minute
and every hour of every single day. I will believe in these
rules, and I will follow them to the best of my ability, as payment for the trust which the people have placed in me to represent them to the best of my ability in the halls of law and
leadership.

"I will treat every person I meet with respect, dignity,
compassion, justice, and consideration, regardless of faction,
gender, age, creed, culture, ethnicity, social or financial
status, or any other consideration. I shall seek to understand
viewpoints, and will not allow differences of opinion between us to alter how I treat them, save only where they have
transgressed the law. Even then, I shall still treat them with
dignity and justice, for I am here to represent them as fellow
citizens.

"I hereby acknowledge that I am not a servant of any one
faction, sponsorship, religion, creed, or group of any sort. I
am a servant of all of the people within my care, both with

those I agree and have such things in common with, and those with whom I disagree or lack such commonalities . . ."

The speech went on and on, hundreds of people reciting in lockstep vows of treating all with equality and consideration, of refraining from using or abusing drugs, alcohol, and other intoxicants both while actively working and while away from the office during one's term of service, oaths acknowledging that if they did not do their job as representatives, they would not get paid—which was a bit of a shock to Li'eth, since most of the higher-level government officials in the Empire were renowned for taking extra-long "paid vacations" whenever they thought they could get away with it.

It kept going. Oaths about not stockpiling resources, promises of understanding that the laws made applied equally to them as well as to the people they represented, that they were *not* above the law and could be subjected to arrest and all other such penalties the exact same as any other person, that *lying* was to be foresworn while in office . . . He began to understand *why* Ja'ki had coached them on what to say when they didn't want to answer a question. Following those things were vows to uphold the scientific process of seeking and acknowledging provable facts, relying upon consistent data gathered from multiple sources, and avoiding being swayed by falsehoods and bribes to believe otherwise.

And then they recited a vow of separating religion from government. Shi'ol and Ba'oul audibly gasped, Dai'a looked dismayed, while Li'eth felt shocked. Religion was such an entwined part of his life, of his *family's* life, it was hard to fathom a government system that did *not* lean upon the wisdom of the priesthood to guide it. Only V'kol, a proclaimed atheist, looked happy on hearing that particular part of the lengthy speech; in fact, he outright smiled at hearing it, and flashed that smile toward Li'eth, as if to say, *See? They're superior in at least* one *way to our people.*

Li'eth wasn't sure if he had mentally heard that, eavesdropping with his mind-speaking gifts . . . with his *telepathy*, as Ja'ki called it. More of the speech passed by while he struggled with that antireligious, or rather, aloof-from-religion statement, until he heard the closing words, and realized the Oath was finally coming to an end.

". . . Each day, I shall repeat these words not only with my lips and my mind, but with my heart and my will, acknowledging them fully in my mind, and accepting them as the truth and the price for the rights and the powers I now hold," Ja'ki recited. "Today, I shall serve, and I shall do my best to serve well and fully for the entire time I work. I am Ja'ki Maq'en-zi, and I represent the people of the Terran United Planets."

The Council Hall fell silent as the last of the oathspeakers gave their own regional identities. The man in white waited a few moments, then spoke. ". . . Thank you for reciting the Oath of Civil Service with me. You may be seated, now."

Everyone in the Hall, including the Secondaire, took a seat. The taller of the two white-clad men—his suit was a nice shade of dark brown—did so by mounting a dais to take one of two seats at a sort of desk arrangement; it looked something like what a judge would use back home, Li'eth realized, save that the desk surfaces sat to each side of the two chairs. The taller, brown-clad man took the lower of the two seats at that, while everyone else settled into their chairs in the various sections of the auditorium. On the station side of the monitor, the Terrans also seated themselves.

Ja'ki gave a downward press of her right hand toward the V'Dan, settling into her chair by the mysterious box she had brought in. Li'eth in turn gestured for his crew to be seated as well. It felt good to sit after standing for so long; the speech had gone on for several *mi-nah*, at least eight, maybe ten of them. Since the notepads were handy, blocks of neatly lined white, he pulled one close to him and made a note in V'Dan. *Remember to ask for a full copy of this Oath of Civil Service to study it in more depth.*

Maybe then he could get it all sorted out and properly contemplated. *This one speech,* he added, *seems to be the monotonously rigid driving force for how they conduct themselves as a government . . .*

"Ambassador Maq'en-zi," Premiere Callan stated. She rose immediately, hands at her sides, shoulders level. "We have all had a chance to review segments of the raw footage of your mission to the Gamma Draconis system, the events that happened, and the decisions you have made. Some of those decisions will be reviewed in greater detail, but for now, we wish to reassure you and your guests that it is the decision of this Council and its Fellowship that you have acted honorably and with consideration for our unexpected guests. Your decisions in these matters will be upheld, with full honor given to our guests.

"At this time, we wish extend our apologies to our foreign guests for the necessary restrictions of quarantine, and give them our reassurances that we are willing to meet them in person once the Department of Health has cleared both sides for physical contact. In the meantime, on behalf of the United Planets, Ambassador, please give them a warm welcome on our behalf, or at least as warm a welcome as you can, until they can visit us here on Kaho'olawe directly."

What does that *mean?* He didn't have much time to ponder it, for she nodded and spoke. "Each of our honored guests will be introduced in order from lowest rank to highest, based upon the seniority or longevity of their positions. This is because four of them are all ranked as *Sh'nol Kowehl*, or as we would say, Leftenants Superior, the equivalent of a Lieutenant First Class or Lieutenant First Grade. Dai'a?"

Standing, the life-support officer moved behind V'kol to join Ja'ki. She eyed the viewscreens, then asked hesitantly, "Should I introduce myself . . . ?"

"Yes, please," Ja'ki stated. "You know far better than I how you should be introduced, after all." Silently, she sent to Li'eth, (*Might as well give Shi'ol some extra rope to tie into a hangman's noose, as we Terrans say.*)

He had to bite his tongue to keep from smiling inappropriately. That, it seemed, was at least one idiomatic expression that translated perfectly. (*We V'Dan say something similar. Instruct Dai'a when she finishes to introduce the next officer up the line. That way Shi'ol can hang all her ambitions below my coming revelation.*)

(*I'll do that.*) Ja'ki gestured for the other woman to begin.

Squaring her shoulders, Dai'a stared at the wall of faces, finally settled on the white-clad man, and spoke. "I am, as you say, Leftenant Superior Dai'a Vres-yat, born on the colony-world of Du'em-ya—it is a world with domes, as it has no breathable atmosphere," she explained in a slightly nervous aside. "And . . . I served as the life-support officer on board the Imperial Warship *Wardrum Deathbeat*."

"The V'Dan name for their ship is pronounced *T'un Tunn G'Deth*," Ja'ki interjected, managing the glottal stops smoothly. Li'eth guessed she did that so that the ship's name didn't sound quite as threatening. "Do you have anything you wish to add at this time, Leftenant Superior?"

"I . . . like your plants," Dai'a stated. She pointed off to the left. "The scientist, Lars Thorsson, showed me all the plants. Your hydroponics . . . aquaculture? . . . is very well balanced. There are some species that look very similar to some of our own foods, and some which are very strange, but flavorful. I am not sure how your foods ended up on our world, other than what certain Sh'nai scriptures state, but those are religious texts and are written in sometimes indirect language.

"The science behind them is still being vigorously debated, since it is clear in our . . . our paleontological? . . . records that they did not evolve on our motherworld—the world where V'Dan first began to build civilized lives. Though now that we have reached what seems to be the Before World, it is clear where they come from," she added, smiling shyly with a slight duck of her tanned, beige-and-green-striped head. "I am looking forward to finding out all I can about your history, to see if we can learn where our two peoples split, and how. I am sure the rest of you are just as curious as I am."

Ja'ki wasn't the only one to smile at her sincere, ingenuous, if hesitant honesty. Many of the people on the other side of the broad monitor smiled. A few raised their hands, but were not called upon. Ja'ki spoke. "Thank you. May we call you Dai'a for the rest of this session? Or shall we call you by your kinship name, Vres-yat?"

"You may call me Dai'a," the life-support officer allowed, nodding.

"Thank you, Dai'a. Would you please introduce your next-ranked officer for us?" Ja'ki asked.

Dai'a blinked a little, but nodded. Ja'ki moved the chair with the empty box back, and stepped to the left a bit so that V'kol could stand and join them comfortably. Dai'a swayed in close, whispering a question to Ja'ki, who murmured back an answer. It gave the shorter woman confidence, and she nodded and squared her shoulders as a proper officer should when making introductions.

"People of the Terran United Planets, I present before you Leftenant Superior V'kol Kos'q of V'Dan—our governing planet—and the chief tactical and gunnery officer of the . . . *T'un Tunn G'Deth*. Leftenant Kos'q, this is . . . everyone. Terran," Dai'a stated . . . and blushed behind her green-and-tanned cheeks.

Again, there were smiles of amusement, but not unkind ones. Ja'ki gestured discreetly for Dai'a to take her seat, which the other woman did with palpable relief. In the six or so months he had served as her commanding officer, Li'eth had never known Dai'a to be comfortable with public speaking. She ran her life-support crew just fine, comfortable in her environment of air-scrubbing-algae tanks, agriculture bays, and more, but not in the environment of public speech. More than ten people, and she started to mumble and stammer.

V'kol gestured slightly toward the screen, and Ja'ki nodded, giving him permission to speak. "I am from V'Dan, but I should explain that I was born on the outermost of V'Dan's three moons, moved to the second one as a young child, then finally migrated to the surface of our motherworld as an adult. So I will have more of an affinity with those who live on your solitary moon, I think, for it is airless like our own. And I, too, am enjoying the novelty of your different foods. I suspect I will be of more use discussing military matters than of agricultural ones, however.

"And yes, you may address me by my personal name of V'kol, if you wish. After all," he added, smiling, "you have only five new names to learn. We are the first people to visit you from a very distant foreign nation, and I am aware you will want to know everything about us. I would rather start out friendly in the hopes that we shall all become friends. That, and I shall look forward with some amusement to my grandchildren asking me all about this day, and the ones to come."

"Thank you, V'kol. Will you introduce your next superior, please?" Ja'ki asked. He nodded and turned to face Ba'oul, who rose and joined them. More hands shot into the air, prompting the Premiere, who had retreated to his chair, to approach the podium to speak.

"Please hold your questions until after the introductions have been made, thank you . . ."

"Yes, with that said," V'kol stated, gesturing at the dark-skinned, blue-crescented man next to him, his own hot-pink *jungen* and light golden hide a contrast, "I present to you Left-enant Superior Ba'oul Des'n-yi, who if I remember correctly hails from Tai-mat in the Verlouss Archipelago on V'Dan . . . which appears to be similar to your Kaho'olawe, dry on one side of their mountains, dense and green on the other side. He has served us well as the chief pilot of the *T'un Tunn G'Deth* . . . before we lost the ship to an enemy attack."

Ba'oul nodded. "I look forward to seeing your world, as well. I am hoping to help figure out how to navigate between this system and the V'Dan home system, as I am a trained astronavigator. I also hope you will forgive me if I also seem eager to return home. Of all of us, I have been away the longest, nearly four years."

Once again, the Premiere spoke, this time out of compassion. "That longing is understandable; our soldiers in our Space Force are often deployed for long tours of duty as well, though we try to rotate them in and out as much as we can," he stated. "We do intend to assist you to our best ability in locating which star system we should return you to in the coming days. In the meantime, we hope you will be willing to linger long enough to enjoy our hospitality and hopefully answer some of our many questions."

Bowing a little, Ba'oul touched his hand to his chest, then uncurled his fingers, Archipelago style, in a gesture of thanks and obligation-acceptance that even the Gatsugi would have found graceful, to Li'eth's mind. "I will endeavor to enjoy that hospitality while I can."

He glanced at Ja'ki, then looked briefly at Shi'ol. The Ambassador nodded. Squaring his shoulders, he gave another slight bow. "I introduce to you now our seniormost Leftenant Superior, Shi'ol Nanu'oc, logistics officer of the *T'un Tunn G'Deth.*"

Rising, Shi'ol took his place as Ba'oul retreated. She faced the monitors, shoulders back, chin slightly lifted, a slight but polite smile curving her lips. Of the four leftenants, she was clearly the most comfortable with public speaking.

(*Bet you she'll seize it,*) Ja'ki sent quickly to Li'eth. He didn't reply, because Shi'ol began her speech.

"In the V'Dan military I am a leftenant superior. In the civilian realm . . . if I have been given the correct level of title in Terranglo, I am a Countess. In specific, I am the 373rd Countess Shi'ol A-kai'a Nanu'oc d'Vzhta ul S'Arroc'an. This is an important and fairly high rank among our civilians, being of the Second Tier, superseded only by those of the First and Imperial Bloodline Tiers," she not quite lectured. "We are what you would call a constitutional monarchy, ruled by our Eternal Empress, Hana'ka Iu'tua Has-natell Q'una-hash Mi'idenei V'Daania, direct descendant of War King Kah'el. As such, I am the highest-ranked *civilian* in this group . . . though I will of course defer during the length of our stay here to Captain Ma'an-uq'en, if that is your preference."

(*She seized it*,) Ja'ki sighed in Li'eth's head.

Sighing externally, Li'eth pushed to his feet. "That is inaccurate, Countess. I warned you not to make presumptions of rank during this meeting. Civilian or otherwise."

He reached into his pocket even as Shi'ol turned to frown at him. Withdrawing the cloth-wrapped bundle, he unfolded the kerchief, then twisted off the cap. The pungent scent of alcohol wafted up seconds later when he sprinkled the contents onto the white cloth.

"I said I would follow your lead, *Captain*," Shi'ol countered. "I am simply letting these people know which of us is more likely to have a better chance at carrying their questions, concerns, and so forth straight to the Empress."

Lifting the folded cloth to his face, Li'eth paused. "Again . . . Countess . . . you presume *you* have the most of the Empress' favor in this crew."

Pressing the alcohol to his right cheek, he started to scrub from just under his eye to a spot just above the corner of his mouth. The concealer had to be rubbed off firmly, and the high proof of the liquor fumes was strong enough to bring tears to his eyes, though they didn't quite fall.

Checking in the polished silver side of the little pocket flask, he scrubbed a bit more . . . and watched not only Shi'ol's jaw drop, but V'kol's, Ba'oul's, and lastly, Dai'a's mouths all sag downward from the shock. A check via the flask, a little bit more on the cloth, a bit more scrubbing, and the last of the concealed burgundy stripe came into view. Along with a bit of pink-scrubbed skin around its edges, but that would fade. The extra *jungen* did not.

He stared at Shi'ol evenly. "Please, *Countess*, introduce me *properly* to these people."

"*You . . . you . . . but you're a* Captain*!*" she exclaimed in V'Dan, her voice barely a wheeze but clearly overwrought.

Li'eth clung to Terranglo. "*Every* member of the Imperial Family must serve at least one year in the military. It is not, however, prudent to show our faces with our marks unchanged. Particularly when we are at war, Leftenant Superior . . . or I would not be here for this *prophesied* moment. Now. Introduce me. Formally, and fully."

She hesitated, golden skin flushing half as red as her rosettes, then turned to the monitors. It took the logistics officer a few moments to compose herself, during which she tugged on her slightly overlong jacket, and cleared her throat. "I . . . have the honor . . . of introducing Captain Li'eth Ma'an-uq'en . . . highest-ranked officer of the former Imperial Warship *T'un Tunn G'Deth* . . . and who is . . . actually . . . His Imperial Highness, Kah'raman Li'eth Tal'u-ruq Ma'an-uq'en Q'uru-hash V'Daania. Thirdborn child of Her Eternal Majesty.

"Give him now the respect this highest of Tiers is due."

Her voice hardened a little on those last words, cutting through the speculative murmurs that sprang up at her words. Li'eth reached for Ja'ki's mind, carefully restoring the cap to the flask. He set it and the now beige-stained square of cloth on the table. (*It seems she is still determined to wrest* some *sort of superior-than-your-people power out of this moment . . . even if I am the one now holding that power.*)

(*You have my sympathies. We only have to deal with our highest officials for five years at a stretch . . . and we only have to deal with* her *for as long as she is here,*) Ja'ki sent back. She fell silent, for the Premiere spoke.

". . . Your revelation is interesting," Callan stated. "From the shock and the lack of protest on your other companions' part, it seems they, too, recognize you. Because of this reaction, we will acknowledge at this time that this claim appears to be truthfully spoken. With that being the case . . . how shall we address you while you are a guest among us?"

Protocol. Li'eth knew it well, and could guess what he

should say in this foreign place. There were plenty of rules of etiquette for proper forms of address among the various Alliance races, and among their various ranks. He did not, however, think it was appropriate after three of the others had given leave to use their personal names. Nor, given what he knew of their government system, did it seem intuitively appropriate to be completely, rigidly formal.

"As the leader of your own empire, Premiere, you are the equivalent of my mother in rank, the equivalent of the leader of the Gatsugi Collective, and the equivalent of the Queen of Solarica. We are social equals. You may therefore address me—as may your Secondaire and your Ambassador, here—as Li'eth at any moment beyond the most formal of situations. The members of your Council, your highest government representatives, may also choose such informality if they wish. Otherwise, the proper way to address me as the leader of this group would be to continue to call me Captain, or Your Highness."

Callan bowed his head. "You grant us an honor with the use of your first name, Your Highness. I shall reserve it for moments of nonformality. This, however, is formal. How should we address the countess, your seniormost Leftenant Superior?"

"Please call her Shi'ol." There. That was a jab in her arrogance. "She does have some standing in civilian terms, as she says, but my mother will expect me to represent our people in all negotiations on the Empire's behalf. I cannot make any formal treaties at this point in time beyond a pledge of nonaggression, but I can represent the Empire well enough to give you an indication of how much she may or may not favor any additional ideas."

"That is good to know, Your Highness," Callan allowed, dipping his head slightly. "Nor would I or this Council expect anything more at this time. We are very curious about your people and wish to ask a few questions, if we may—please, be seated and make yourselves comfortable, both of you," he added.

A hard, searching look from Shi'ol met only a polite expression from him. The countess moved to take her former seat, and Li'eth picked the chair between Ja'ki and V'kol.

"Now, as you have our mission members available to answer your own questions at any time you so choose during quarantine," Callan stated, "we would like to ask you and your fellow V'Dan several questions of our own. Most have been compiled in advance and selected to be the most common or most useful at this time, but we hope to have an open question-and-answer period toward the end of this session, if that is acceptable to you."

Li'eth nodded. "We have all been expecting an interrogation of some sort."

The Premiere smiled. "Hopefully, this will be more pleasant than most interrogations. You are, of course, free to refuse to answer any of these and all other questions . . . though it is hoped you will at least answer the ones that will help us pinpoint where we can take you to return you to your people. Secondaire Pong . . . who is the equivalent of an apprentice to my position, and represents everyone, the same as myself and Ambassador MacKenzie . . . has compiled that list of questions. I hand the Council Hall floor to him—that is to say, I give him the command of all questions and answers—at this time. Secondaire Pong?"

Nodding, Pong stepped up to the podium as the Premiere retreated. He lifted the datapad taken from somewhere inside his outfit and read from it, looking up every few words to meet Li'eth's gaze through the monitor screen. His accent was a little thick compared to some, but his words were enunciated well enough to be understood. A musical voice, in Li'eth's mind.

"The first and foremost question on everyone's mind is . . . how did you, who appear in all respects to be Human beings like us, save for the, ah . . . colors spotting and striping your skin . . . come to exist on another world separate from Earth, the world that according to our own fossil records gave birth to the Human race?"

"It is not completely known, as the majority of our written records on the subject are almost entirely religious texts, but approximately nine and a half thousand years ago—the date in V'Dan Standard should be some point late in the month of *Sember* in the year 9507," Li'eth added in an aside, "a being of immense power managed to create some sort of gateway between what we call the Before World, and our homeworld of V'Dan.

"All of *our* fossil records point to a great *d'aspra*, a massive movement of people, herd animals, and plant matter—seeds and seedlings—all coming into existence on V'Dan approximately ninety-five of our centuries ago. Before that point, all of the records show nothing but plants and animals that had evolved for millions of years on V'Dan. After that point, some native species died out, while many Before World species supplanted them. On the motherworlds of the other sentient species of the Alliance," he stated, "their fossil records show how their own kind evolved over millions of years, but not on V'Dan.

"It has therefore been a great mystery for our scientists for the last four hundred years, ever since we reached into space and met the other races, as to why certain plants, animals, and ourselves simply appeared at some point. Our largest religion, the Sh'nai faith," Li'eth continued, "posits that we were taken from the Before Time Motherworld—which would be your world—by a benevolent immortal being who wished to save her chosen people from an immense disaster. She in turn—again, according to religious texts, which are not the most scientifically written documents—was stated as having come from 'the far-distant future.'

"These claims, of the *d'aspra* of her chosen people and of the Immortal High One's origins, have been repeated many times throughout the holy texts . . . but again, we have not been able to verify how or why, or even exactly when any of this took place. Other than fossil records supporting our sudden appearance and lack of evolving ancestors. Now that we have met you, we have hope that the Before World has been found in *your* world, supporting some of those religious claims . . . but it is still something that should be approached with minds open to science, not minds open to religion," he added.

Beside him, V'kol relaxed a bit. It was known the family V'Daania followed the Sh'nai faith, but not blindly. Religion was revered, but science was practical, and thus preferred. Li'eth hadn't bothered to make his policy on the subject as a commanding officer any different from royal policy, and knew his friend and junior officer was relieved to hear that policy was the same, as a prince.

The Secondaire paused, clearly thinking his way through the questions on the device in his hands, then asked, ". . . Do you know *why* your people were moved by this . . . immense being?"

"It is said in the holy texts that there was a massive series of disasters. The High One—our Immortal First Empress— was able to predict them," Li'eth explained. "According to those texts, she had advanced warning via a series of ancient prophecies, which she had carried from the future into the distant past. It was she who located the world we now occupy, she who constructed the portal, she who organized the *d'aspra*, saving her chosen people. It was said she ruled for five thousand years before the *d'aspra* removed us from the Before World, but that her kingdom was small. It *is* known as fact that she ruled for five thousand years after the *d'aspra* on V'Dan, before being challenged and removed from power by my direct, if distant, ancestor, War King Kah'el."

Several hands shot up, particularly among the rows of white-backed seats. A couple of the Fellowship even bounced in their seats. Pong glanced their way then sighed, and pointed. "The Fellow in seat number fifty-eight may ask a question at this time. Fellow . . . Blanding?"

The seat-bouncer, an elderly woman with white hair streaked in bits of gray, her pale face age-seamed, stood. She wore a pink sort of tunic over purple trousers, a wreath of flowers around her neck, and a purple, flower-printed belt. "Fellow Julia Blanding, Dakotas Province," she announced herself. "Retired schoolteacher of life sciences."

"I am honored to meet one of your teachers," Li'eth replied, and received a blush and a smile on that age-lined face.

"Well, thank you, Highness. My question is, if this female lived five thousand years as you say she did, and you have proof she did . . . how did she live so long? Was she a Grey One?"

"Ah . . . I am not certain how to answer that question at this time. I do not know what a Grey One is," Li'eth temporized. Virtually all of the arms dropped around the Council Hall, proving their questions were meant to be follow-ups to an answer he could not give.

"Ambassador Maq'en-zi, please visualize a Grey One for the prince," Premiere Callan instructed. "Your Highness, have your people ever encountered a being like this?"

Shrugging, Ja'ki held out her hand, narrowed her eyes in

concentration . . . and a spindly-limbed, vaguely humanoid being with a Gatsugi-teardrop head and Gatsugi-big or bigger eyes appeared on the tabletop, much as her raptor illusion had appeared. The skin was a sort of dull gray, the eyes black as a Gatsugi . . . but it bore no tufts of fluff-hairs on its head, it had a small body relative to that head, the torso was short and not very muscular, and the being had only two arms and two legs, not four arms and two legs. There were no clothes associated with the being, either.

She added a Human next to the Grey, proving the Human was not quite twice as tall, much more muscular, and almost complex-looking in comparison. Li'eth studied the image a long moment, then shook his head.

". . . I have never seen any being like that before, and I have met with all the known races of the Alliance territories. The High One was said to be a V'Dan in appearance, though she had all the tricks of a Meddler, a Feyori. Those are a very powerful, long-lived race of energy-based shapechangers. That . . . being . . . looks like a very physical, matter-based entity," he concluded. "But not one that I have ever heard about, let alone seen."

"Huh. Well, there goes *my* theory," Fellow Julia stated, and resumed her seat. Ja'ki released the illusion.

"It is good to know that we probably won't have to deal with the Greys when we head in the direction of your Alliance," Callan stated, his words mild but his tone suggesting the Grey Ones were not pleasant. "Secondaire Pong?"

The taller of the two white-vested men bowed a little. "Thank you, Premiere. Thank you, Fellow Blanding. Please be seated. Next question: Can you please inform us of what this Alliance is, and who else is out there that you do know about? You may each be seated for your comfort, and feel free to go into some detail, as we are all interested in hearing about other *friendly* races . . . and the unfortunate potential for unfriendly ones."

Prepared by the earlier questioning, Li'eth nodded and seated himself next to Ja'ki. "Then I will start with the history and structure of the Alliance, then explain as best I can what each race is. The Alliance was created by the K'Katta when they first encountered the Solaricans. The Solaricans have already established colonies around the galaxy, but each is considered to be a near-autonomous colony. As a rule, they prefer to coexist with other races rather than conquer or exterminate, as their method of interstellar travel, while unbelievably swift, is also extremely difficult and limited in its range to specific areas of the galaxy.

"Still, relieved to find peace-preferring aliens, the K'Katta proposed a series of trade agreements, and the two races established a set of common laws between the two species, centered around the basic ethics of not harming others in ways that are physical, financial, and so forth. It was not, however, a formal alliance arrangement at that time. When the Tlassians joined the interstellar community, the Tlassians brought into the growing Alliance the concept of a Charter, which is an outline of all major laws, all of which must be approved by the other groups, and which can be supported, even enforced by the other groups, should major transgressions of those laws happen and start to affect the other Alliance members.

"The reason for this is that the Tlassians have always had a three-caste system, physical differences which give rise to specific tasks and areas of control within both their culture and their government. The Worker caste's Charter is proposed by the Workers, then approved by the Warrior and Priest castes, and the Priest's Charter is approved by the Workers and Warriors, while the Warriors go through the same process as well," he explained. "Any rejections must have a solid basis, a set of reasons as to why, and none of the Charters can command any legal control over any other group, save lending support in enforcing infractions of the laws that start to disrupt other societies.

"This Charter system solidified the K'Katta version into a formal approach for the Alliance to accept new members. Individual colonyworlds could submit a governing Charter for their particular world—the Solaricans, Tlassians, and V'Dan all have similar enough biochemistry that we can jointly colonize worlds with relative ease, which made it an imperative for joint colonyworlds to come up with their own unique Charter agreements," Li'eth found himself explaining.

It wasn't just to hear himself talk, or to try to explain how the complexities of the Alliance came to be. No, he could *see* these Terrans actively paying close attention, looking interested, nodding along when they understood a certain point, or briefly raising a hand before lowering it again when he continued, adding a bit of clarification with each flash of enough palms.

They *wanted* to know these things, these Terrans. So he continued, trying to meet a gaze here, a look there, from the other side of the three-part screen. It was the closest he could get to answering them in person until quarantine was over.

"By submitting a joint Charter for that planet," Li'eth continued, explaining how colony governments were validated in the Alliance, "this outlines which parent government holds which responsibilities for support, defense, and so forth—which became rather important, if awkward as an understatement, when our current troubles with the Salik began . . ."

———————

(*Well?*) Jackie, asked, curious to know what Li'eth thought of the Council and its five hours of questions. Only five hours because the prince's voice started to give out, even with him deferring several of those questions to the rest of his crew to answer every so often. Which was why she asked her question telepathically.

(*Your people are . . . ruthlessly polite in their interrogations, Bright Stone,*) he sent back. At the moment, he was lying on an exam bed in the cramped but functional quarantine medical bay. Maria had examined his throat and was now formulating a restorative compound that could be injected safely. The doctor herself was beginning to sniffle with the onset of a cold, some sort of virus picked up from the V'Dan, but otherwise was fit for medical duty. (*They only pressed a couple different ways at most on questions we could not answer, before moving on. I'm also surprised they asked so many questions* not *related to the Salik. Some of them were a little . . . odd?*)

(*Can you pinpoint how?*) Jackie asked, as Maria sniffed hard.

Jackie was grateful she herself didn't have any sniffles, nor red eyes, nor sneezing—Brad would have had those symptoms since he was suffering from repeated sneezes when he wasn't taking an antihistamine. Robert had also taken an antihistamine for watering eyes and a suppressant for a cough, while Lars seemed to be fine for the moment, though he swore that was because he took a *sauna* session twice a day, now that he could.

Ayinda had watery eyes as well but no other symptoms, while the V'Dan showed no real signs of suffering from any shared common-cold symptoms.

There had been a bit of elevated temperature in Dai'a and Ba'oul earlier that morning, which they swore was something that should be taken seriously. According to Maria, they had been given their medicines for that before the meeting, however, and were being monitored remotely via their bracelets while they rested in their quarters.

(*Your people seemed more concerned with how soon the Salik might discover and reach this place than with their capabilities. They were interested in the* numbers *estimated for their fleet, but not their firepower or hull strength.*)

(*Hull strength and firepower is something we do not know how to measure, since your units are meaningless compared to ours at the moment; we simply have no basis for translation, and we're smart enough to know it and work around it,*) Jackie reminded him. (*It is also more of a concern for the Space Force to handle, not the Council. Which means I think I can explain why the Council were asking* what *they asked,*) she added.

His brows lifted. His face looked a little odd with the extra streak of burgundy down his clean-shaven cheek, a good finger's worth in length. (*And that is . . . ?*)

(*Budget meetings,*) Jackie sent succinctly.

He grunted and closed his eyes. (*Of course . . . I should've guessed.* Every *government is ruled by its budget. Even Mother must bow to the bottom line from time to time.*)

(*Just by encountering you, and by my choice of rescuing you—which was the ethical thing to do,*) she told him, (*I have thrown my people to the edge of war with the Salik. Now, it is possible that we could broker some sort of peace treaty . . . but considering they viewed me as just another walking V'Dan snack, despite my vastly different ship and its patently different technology . . . and given how I sort of bowled dozens upon dozens of them over during my rescue of your crew . . . I doubt that such would ever come to pass. Nor would I vote for it if anyone suggested it.*

(*So, that means the Council will be very busy discussing how much budget to allocate to the Space Force, how many ships to build, how many hyperrelay units . . . The Space Force already*

*has something of an idea of what things your people will need
from us first and foremost, but they will want to question each
of you in depth. Not so much your engineering specs as your
general capabilities, where your strengths and weaknesses are
in regards to the Salik forces—"you" being the Alliance races
as a whole, not just the V'Dan. From there, the military will
know better how to apportion our various resources . . . but the
Council needs to have an idea of the general scope of things so
that they can have an estimated idea of what the military's budget requests will be. Hence, budget meetings.)*

"Jackie . . . do you have any biokinetic ability?" Maria
asked suddenly. The question was so out of the blue, it made
the younger woman blink. The moment Jackie faced her,
Maria raised her brows "Well? Do you?"

"Of course not," Jackie denied, recovering from the shock
of the odd question. "Not even as a Rank 1, save whatever
biofeedback I can give myself for calming things like heart
rate and blood pressure, the same as anyone else can do. All
of my abilities are on file, and I know you've read that file.
Why do you even ask?"

"I am asking because both you and the captain, there,
have been showing neural energy patterns associated with
biofeedback, in patterns associated specifically with active
biokinesis," the doctor stated.

What the? Jackie blinked again. That should not have
been possible. *Li'eth* had biokinesis, yes, but *she* did not.
"Are you sure *I* have those energy signs?"

"Very sure. I've been combing through various medical data
sets to establish comparisons with V'Dan physiology. You mentioned that Li'eth is a psi. Does *he* have biokinetic abilities—
and no, *señor*, you do *not* get to answer aloud," the doctor
added, pointing at Li'eth, before glancing at her machines. "Not
until after you have taken the medicines that are still synthesizing, which will take another . . . seven minutes. We are not
straining your voice any further, today."

Jackie answered for him. "Yes, he is a biokinetic. But I
am not."

"Well, the monitors don't lie; your brain and body chem-
istry are elevated at rates associated with biokinetic healing,
self-healing. Not by a lot, but they are above basic biofeedback

levels. I suppose they could show similar readings caused by some other source . . . I'd have to hook up a KI monitor to each of you to be absolutely sure. Or give you a paper cut and wait to see if it heals fast," Maria joked.

(*We have been practicing those . . . biokinetic techniques of yours,*) Li'eth reminded Jackie, careful to use the Terran terminology. (*Would that do it?*)

She shook her head. (*Only to a mild degree in myself, to the same level as plain, ordinary biofeedback, since I don't have those actual abilities. I just know the basic training techniques . . . unless you're projecting, but I don't think you are.*)

All three of them fell silent. After a while, Maria suddenly laughed a little. It was a brief sound of mirth, but it caught both of their attention. Jackie lifted her brows. "You found something amusing?"

"Oh, it's just that the two of you are the first two Humans on each side to meet . . . and the first two psychics to meet," Maria joked. "Wouldn't it be funny if you turned out to be a Gestalt pair, too?"

". . . Not really," Jackie refuted, bemused by the idea— the logistics alone would be a nightmare because Li'eth wasn't a common sort; he was a prince. And she herself was an Ambassador. Opposite side of everything. "It would be very awkward. And highly unlikely. And very awkward."

"What is a Gestalt pair?" Li'eth asked aloud, looking between both women. His voice sounded raspy, and earned him a scowl from the medic.

"No sound out of you, *señor!* A Gestalt pair is—" A beeping noise from her machinery interrupted her. "*You* explain it," Maria ordered, flipping her hand at Jackie. "I know some of what it is, but you live it far more than I do. I specialize in trauma and general medicine, not psychic abilities."

"*Gestalt*, Li'eth, is a word from another language, German, and it basically means that the sum of the whole is greater than the tally of its parts. It's like adding two plus two and somehow getting five instead of four," Jackie explained patiently. She did so aloud for Maria's benefit as well as for their guest. "A Gestalt pairing refers to something similar happening between psychics. It's not common, but sometimes a pair will encounter each other and a sort of bond will occur. Something in their biology and in their psychokinetic makeup creates a link between the two. Gifts simply grow stronger even without training, and as the bond grows, the two can start sharing abilities."

He quirked his brows but carefully stayed silent.

Jackie nodded, acknowledging his unspoken question; she didn't have to sense his subthoughts, though they were there. "Yes, that means if one person has telepathy and pyrokinesis—mind-to-mind speech and the ability to control heat, even spark a fire—and if the other person has telepathy and clairvoyancy—mind-to-mind speech and the ability to see things at a distance without needing any equipment or being there in person to do so—then if they are a Gestalt pair, the clairvoyant would find themselves sparking a fire at some point, the pyrokinetic would find themselves viewing things remotely, and their telepathic capabilities would increase tangibly without much effort."

"The Psi League likes to say that every Human can train themselves up to four ranks beyond their base levels," Maria added, filling an ampoule with the medicine Li'eth needed. "Though even I know that in those who don't have any natural gifts, it can take years to reach Rank 4, and only in a few abilities, such as empathy, clairsentiency, or clairvoyancy . . . nothing flashy like pyrokinesis. But if you start out a natural Rank 3, you could, with enough training and practice, rise to a Rank 5, maybe even a Rank 6 or 7 after years of effort."

"Yes, that's how it works normally. But with a Gestalt pair, the boost just grows *without* needing practice. All it needs is proximity. And sometimes . . . sometimes the pairing displays a *new* ability, something neither of them had on their own," Jackie told him. "Like, they shared the telepathy to start, and they each can tap into a small amount of the other's fire-calling or remote-seeing, but then they suddenly also develop biokinetic abilities to heal themselves and each other, or even heal others outside their Gestalt. And when they combine together and join forces with other psis, those psis' abilities are also boosted to a small degree beyond what they should be, if not nearly as much as the Gestalt pairing's will.

"So the League encourages, promotes, and protects Gestalt pairings wherever possible . . . and the military wants them in their Psi Division," she finished, "because they're very good at irritating the Greys into going away."

That provoked another undercurrent question in the prince.

Jackie nodded, answering it. "The Grey Ones are vastly superior in their technology; they shrug off our weapons, they ignore our threats and pleas alike, and they do whatever they want when they drop by . . . except for one thing. For whatever reason, they are very sensitive to kinetic inergy, whatever it is that allows us psychics to manipulate the world in our unique, machineless ways. It seems to act like an acid or a poison on their nervous system, and so they will flee rather than remain."

"Which is very good for *us*," Maria murmured, giving the ampoule one last check before removing it from the scanner machine so she could scrounge up a hypospray gun. "Because otherwise we have no defense against their incredible tech level, and their bizarre preference for every so often coming around and trying to abduct Humans for experimentation without either seeking permission or giving an explanation. It is very rude of them."

"So that's why the Terran military loves psychics even though we don't always make the best of soldiers and are rarely rated for normal combat," Jackie finished, shrugging.

Moving over to the bed, the doctor touched the hypospray to the side of Li'eth's neck. She rubbed it first with the nose of the gun-like device to apply the combination of topical analgesic and antiseptic crème that came with the thing, counted to five under her breath in Spanish, then hit the button, injecting the medicine. "And that is that. You just rest, *amigo*. Let the medicine work. I'll let you up in ten minutes, but *no* talking for a full hour. In fact, it is now late enough in our day, you should be headed to bed after I'm done monitoring you. Both of you."

Li'eth nodded and relaxed on the padded bed. He eyed Jackie. (*What you describe, Bright Stone, is what we call a Holy Unity, and it is sacred, even magical—in the filled-with-awe sense,*) he clarified. (*I know you prefer scientific terms for describing all these powers, but . . . it is holy, this bond of person to person, mind to mind, and soul to soul.*)

(*Ours is not quite that reverently regarded. Well, it is in a way, but it's more of a secular reverence and understanding, yes. It's rare when it happens, but we know to keep such* pairings together. *True psis are actually pretty rare, around one in fifty thousand for the weakest registerable natural psi ability—I'm not counting those that have developed their sixth senses, such as peacekeepers who develop clairsentient "instincts" for searching for clues at a crime scene, or bodyguards who know when trouble is about to strike, doctors who have an intuition about what is really wrong with a patient,)* Jackie dismissed. *(I mean those who are verifiably psychic, with a nonsystemic ability such as telekinesis.*

(But the odds of you and I being a Gestalt pairing?) She shook her head, a small smile curving her lips. *(Not likely. That happens once in a hundred thousand psis—technically, once in* two *hundred thousand, since it takes two at the very least. I personally know of seven such pairings in the Space Force, and I know of them because I worked with them, back when I first served. As I said, the Space Force loves having them on hand.)*

(Well, I don't recall any exact wording of a holy pairing in the Sh'nai prophecies regarding this moment, but I didn't have the time to sit down and study everything in the holy writings before being captured,) Li'eth admitted. *(You'd think they'd mention it directly if it exists, given how some things have been blatantly described . . . but some of the prophecies are so vague, you only know it's come to pass after the fact, and after much examination. If you like, when we return to V'Dan, I'll look it up for you—all of the prophecies about this moment, I mean.)*

(That could actually be useful. Now, since you're lying here looking ornamental,) she teased lightly, *(we might as well practice your psyching training. You know the drill: ground, center, and shield . . .)*

(Yes, Teacher.) He rolled his eyes briefly at the ceiling, then closed them, breathed deeply a few times to prepare himself, and began the opening visualization steps under her watchful mental presence. They were halfway through his centering practices when Lars hurried into the infirmary, his hair still wet and tangled from a shower, his shirt and exercise shorts clinging damply to his body, and a datapad clutched in his hands. He was so agitated, the Finn immediately burst into his native tongue the moment he saw Li'eth on the exam bed.

"There you are! I've figured it out! I'm the first person to have figured it out! Look!" he added, thrusting the pad at Li'eth, who blinked and eyed Jackie, confused.

(*What is he babbling about?*)

"Lars, can you please explain in Terranglo?" Jackie prompted. "Or in V'Dan, perhaps?"

"Ah—yes, yes!" he exclaimed, switching languages to Terranglo. He shook the datapad in his hands, its image showing some sort of crude drawing of plants with watercolors tinting the leaves from the mottled cream of the background. "See? *See* it?"

"No speaking!" Maria ordered, pointing a finger firmly at the prince, who had opened his mouth.

Sighing roughly, Li'eth pushed up onto his elbows and lifted the pad, altering the angle for easier viewing in the glare of the overhead lights. After a moment, he blinked and looked closer, then lifted his gaze to Jackie, astounded. (*This . . . this is written in V'Dan! It's a dialect from the Valley of the Artisans! How did you . . . ? Did he write this? Ask him if he wrote this!*)

Jackie, not offended by the order, eyed the pages. It seemed to be a description of some sort of herb, including the precaution of being ". . . very, very, very careful not to taste its juices, as they are very, very, very poisonous . . ." A moment later, she frowned, squinted, and then widened her own eyes. "You're right! It *is* written in V'Dan! Lars, what is this? You didn't draw or write this yourself, did you?"

"No, no! *This* is the *Voynich manuscript!*" The geophysicist infused the title with all the awe of someone speaking of a long-lost holy tome. At their blank stares, he gave them an impatient look. "Please, this is the *oldest* manuscript mystery in existence! Aside from the Indus Valley civilization," he allowed in the next breath, tipping his head. A flick of it tossed his hair behind his shoulder again. "This is a medieval manuscript that was created several centuries ago, with a writing system that was clearly practiced and patterned like a real language, but no one could ever decipher what it meant.

"That's because it's written in *V'Dan*! I was practicing writing in V'Dan so that I could be prepared for discussing things with your scientists," Lars continued. "But there has always been something vaguely familiar about it. Then I went to go take a shower, and there was a leaf design on the shampoo bottle like *this* image—and that was when I remembered the Voynich manuscript! This is from the fifteenth century, and we are in the late twenty-third, so it is less than a thousand years old.

"*Think* about it," he added with wide-eyed, earnest enthusiasm. "If this Immortal of yours could open a portal from this world to your homeworld . . . perhaps she opened one from *there* to *here* at some point? This could have been written by *her*!"

Li'eth's jaw sagged. He looked between Lars, Jackie, and Maria. Jackie could feel his thoughts tumbling, but carefully did not interject any of her own. Finally, he placed his hand on the edge of the datapad and gently pushed down. "I suggest you keep this to yourself for now. We do not actually know if the Immortal wrote it, or if it was someone else. It *will* need to be investigated, though."

"And that is enough out of you. No. More. Speaking!" Maria asserted.

Lars, realizing he was interrupting something, pressed the pad into Li'eth's hands. "Here, you may study it while you rest. I can look at it on another networked pad—this is a very exciting mystery, though!"

(*He certainly has that right,*) Jackie muttered mentally, watching the tall blond hurry out again. (*Li'eth . . . if your Immortal cannot be killed, then where did she go when she was ousted from power by your ancestor?*)

(*Some legends said she lingered to give advice from the shadows, while some said she faded into the stars. But some said she went back to the Before World . . . This is odd. This manuscript reads more like a child's report, or diary or something, than a log written by a woman reputed to be well over ten thousand years old,*) he told her, sliding his finger across the screen to switch to a new page.

(*So maybe she brought a kid back to Earth for some reason. Or brought a book written by a kid?*) Jackie offered.

(*Either way, I will be glad when we have had a chance to compare theologies and histories, and hopefully find the truth,*) Li'eth said. Sighing, he eased back onto the bed under the doctor's firm stare. (*Though I have the feeling it will take our respective experts years to wade through all the myths, legends, and half-recorded information to get to the truths underlying everything.*)

(*Well, here's hoping that we live that long, then,*) she soothed him. Leaning against his bed, she angled her head so that she could read over his forearm.

CHAPTER 12

FEBRUARY 3, 2287 C.E.

Li'eth was in the showering unit when he heard a strange beeping noise. It repeated three more times, then ended. Since it wasn't an emergency signal for anything—those claxons and sirens had been used briefly but very loudly as a test of the various systems to show the V'Dan what to listen for and what each signal meant—he continued scrubbing himself with the soap provided. The cleaning facilities here on this *Maq'arther* Station were vastly superior to what they'd made do with on the shuttle-sized ship, which meant he was happy to indulge in the moment.

Showers were wonderful things, though at some point, he was determined to take advantage of what Lars had called a "hot tub" for a nice, long, indulgent soak. The *sauna* was semifamiliar; there were similar steam rooms available in the Winter Palace back home, and he had already used the local version in the tall Terran's company a couple of times. But for relaxing, he preferred a full-body soak.

Rinsing off and shutting down the flow of water, he let the drying nozzles blast his body with warmed jets of air. It felt like a Solarican shower, but he could understand that it was easier to contain the moisture inside the showering stall, recycling it close to the source rather than risking too much humidity escaping into the rest of the quarantine unit.

That, and it saved on towels for drying, though it wasn't too good for his hair. Stepping out when the system shut off, he reached for one of the towels he had set out and heard the beeping noise again. Without the pounding spray, the sound was louder though still indistinct in location.

Shrugging into the robe that had come with the small suite, he tied the material shut and padded into his sleeping cabin. The beeping noise shut off just as he pinpointed it somewhere near the bed. Unable to find the source now that it was silent, Li'eth gave up. Instead, he dressed himself in the casual style these Terrans preferred, undershorts, loose trousers, a tunic-like shirt with bicep-length sleeves, and toe-sandals, the kind that had a strap connected to the sole between the biggest toe and all the rest. The others in his crew had been issued shades of blue, but his were in a slightly mottled gray, something called *heth-ther*. There was a plant-image in his implanted vocabulary that was associated with the word, some sort of low-growing, tightly leaved bush, and an impression of a pleasant smell, but that was it.

The gray clothes, Ja'ki had explained, marked him as a psi on the station, while the blue meant "spaceship crew" for the others. That, and it would help him stand out as the leader of the quintet. Back in the bathroom, he pulled a comb—a comb was a comb, whether Terran or V'Dan—from one of the cabinet drawers and patiently started working out the snarls in his half-dried hair. Memories of his nanny El'cor intermingled with memories of Ja'ki's sister and mother, each patiently teaching them how to plait hair . . . which was odd because he shouldn't be getting images from *her* childhood.

The words *braid* and *plait* and *hair* should have come with generalized images and associations if he understood how telepathic language transfers properly worked. Not specific memories of her mother braiding her older sister's hair while her sister braided Ja'ki's hair, the mother standing, the eldest daughter seated on a chair, and the youngest perched on a footstool. They were . . . preparing for a festival? Yes, a festival, because next had come chaplets made from leaves and flowers, along with arm- and wristbands, and brightly colored strapless dresses with matching flower patterns.

(*. . . Li'eth?*) Ja'ki asked. (*Are you . . . ?*)

He blinked and blushed, thankful no one could see him. Well, no one but the monitors that were supposed to remain observed in retrospect only for medical reasons, here in each person's private quarters. (*I didn't mean to. I was just thinking about braiding hair, and . . .*)

(*Ah. I am braiding my hair as well, right now. I suspect that may have evoked the link between us.*) She sighed mentally, and he could almost see her as she worked to finish tying off the end of her braid, fingers wrapping the band back and forth deftly. (*I suppose I should end that link, though it's been handy for keeping tabs on you.*)

He flushed again. (*I want to protest that I am not some wayward child, to be put on a leash until I learn self-control . . . but I guess I am, aren't I?*) About to add more, he stopped when the beeping sounded again. (*What is that irritating noise?*)

(*What noise? Lend me your senses—ah. That's the vidphone. There's a tablet by your bed that functions for video and audio communications,*) Ja'ki explained.

He debated going after it, but a look in the mirror showed his hair a mess, and he had an obligation to look his best when representing the Empire. A vidphone meant visual communication, and that meant neatly ordered hair. The noise of the machine was bothersome, though. Irritation pulsed from him to her, prompting her to add on to explanation.

(*The screen on your desk also works—don't worry about missing it, Li'eth; if you don't get to it in time, it'll just go into the message cache. It's not like you're going anywhere, either. You can attend to whatever it is at your own pace.*)

(*Good,*) he grunted, resuming the task of plaiting sections of his hair to make the braid lie flat and neat along the back of his head. (*That'll be the third time it's interrupted me. The first time, I was showering.*)

(*That is a mental image I didn't need,*) she muttered back. (*I'm not supposed to be thinking anything along those lines . . . same as you.*)

(*What, me naked in the shower, covered in lather? Do you know how many women and men in the Empire would give up their fortunes for an image of me bathing?*) he joked. The beeping noise ended, once again after the fourth bleat from the machinery in the bedroom.

(*Probably several thousand times more than the Terrans who would ask for pictures of me bathing. Councilors are usually treated with a great deal of reverent respect. Not always; there are those who grow obsessed with someone famous, and God help them if she's pretty or he's handsome . . . I'm lucky in that I've only had a few offers to climb into someone's bed, or random marriage offers out of the blue—I'm afraid you might get a lot of those in person, people screaming out offers to "bear your alien love-baby," or "let me be your princess bride," though the military is currently screening all your calls and messages as a courtesy while we're up here.*)

Li'eth shrugged, his fingers now down to the simple wearing part of the plait's tail. He could only see his own face in the mirror, but inside his head, he could see her watching her own reflection as he watched his. (*I'd say you'd get the same reception on V'Dan, except you'll still look like children, so people won't be screaming, exactly.*)

(*Well, that might just be a relief, not having to deal with the sillier side of celebrity status,*) she allowed. (*But that does bring up the absurdity of someone taking a look at me and thinking of me as a child. I clearly have a fully grown figure, thank you very much. It's rather obvious, in fact.*)

(*Yes, I noticed.*) The confession slipped out of him. His face turned red in the mirror. Li'eth quickly worked the black stretchy tie into place on the end. (*Sorry. That was an inappropriate line of thought.*)

(*It's okay. Telepathy tends to lend itself to blurting out honest responses simply because there is literally no barrier of translating thoughts into actual, physically produced words. And . . . I'm flattered you noticed,*) she added carefully. (*I think you're handsome, too. A little odd-looking with those red stripes, but handsome nonetheless.*)

(*We shouldn't pursue that line of thought, however. You're an Ambassador, and I'm a prince. We both have to represent our people.*) Squaring his shoulders, he checked his face, then realized he hadn't shaved. Rolling his eyes, he stripped off his shirt and hung it on a nearby bar, then splashed his face with a little water and used the foam from a canister in the mirror cabinet.

Shaving was another trait Terrans and V'Dan shared, but it wasn't one that provoked shared images, telepathically. She was female, and did not need to shave her face, though she did shave her leg—*dammit, stop that.* Li'eth paused to breathe deep and practice his grounding, centering, and shielding visualizations, rather than any inappropriate visualizations. *Do not invade her thoughts, nor her memories. You* will *gain control over your ability to read others' thoughts. It is rude to do so in* both *societies without an invitation.*

He resumed shaving, trying to keep his thoughts tucked inside his own head. When he felt calm again, when his face was halfway-shaved, he reached out to her. (*Ja'ki, how do I open up the message cache for all these missed calls?*)

(*Want me to come visit your quarters and show you how to work the thing? I could do it telepathically, but it's . . . We should limit how closely we interact, mentally. I'm beginning to feel curious about things I shouldn't be thinking about.*)

(*As am I. Unless you want me to be curious about how you shave your legs,*) he returned. (*For that matter,* why *do women shave their legs in Terran society? Everyone knows it's something only hairy men do.*)

(*It's to project an illusion of youth, of the age when your legs don't grow much in the way of hair, and are instead still smooth and young-looking.*)

(*That's . . . very perverted,*) Li'eth finally said, firmly censoring several unflattering thoughts before they could surface. (*That's pedophilia. In V'Dan society, maturity is valued. Everyone shaves their armpits to cut down on odiferous bacteria since hairs give them extra surface area to occupy, and men usually prefer shaving their beards to look neatly groomed, but you don't shave the rest of your body unless you're so hairy, it looks bestial. Which is something usually only the men do.*)

She chuckled in the back of his mind. (*A refreshing outlook. We share something in common, though. Shaved armpits. About half of the men don't do it, but . . . they stink when they don't. And I can't stand the way how the hair tickles and itches in my 'pit, yecch!*) Ja'ki sent him a picture of herself making a face with that thought. In person, physically, she was already exiting her quarters and heading for his, just a few doors down in the tight confines of quarantine. He could sense her approach. (*But in the military, all men shave their faces so they can apply face masks in case of bad air. Most women don't have to shave their faces until old age and hormone imbalances cause problems . . . May I come in? I think you're still shaving, yes?*)

(*Yes to both. I'll be out there in a few more moments,*) he added, stroking the strange but effective disposable razor along his jaw.

Through the bathroom and bedroom doors, which were both standing open since they weren't sector seals, he could hear the hiss of the front door of his little suite open and shut. It felt odd to not have the end of his *jungen* stripe on his right cheek covered up with the concealer. His proper face, and yet not the face he had grown used to seeing over the last couple years. Just as well he didn't need to hide it; the concealer could last for many weeks without maintenance but not forever.

Nothing lasted forever. (*So many things are changing . . . So many more are about to change . . .*)

(. . . ?) Ja'ki sent in an inquiry.

(*Nothing.*)

He was just finishing the last needed stroke when he heard the door hiss open again, and a strident, familiar voice snap, "How *dare* you enter His Highness' quarters without his permission! I *thought* you said you were an adult, but this is exactly the kind of childish, juvenile, *disrespectful* behavior I'd expect from a *child*!"

(*Damn her!*) Whipping the hand towel off the rod with one hand and tossing the razor into the sink basin with the other, he wiped awkwardly at his face even as he hurried out of the bathroom and around the corner of the bedroom into the front cabin. "Shi'ol! *You* do not have permission to be in here. *She* does."

The blonde countess spoke even as she turned. "She didn't even *knock*, let alone press the door buzzer! I . . . you . . . *Highness.*" Shi'ol stared at his half-clad body, at his chest, streaked with burgundy lightning stripes. Blushing, she partly turned away, but her gaze lingered a little until she blinked and rounded on the dark-haired Terran, who was eyeing Li'eth with an equally bemused look. "*She* shouldn't be in here!"

"*She* asked for permission before entering," Li'eth stated flatly. He had forgotten he had removed his shirt. Face hot, he ignored his half-undressed state. "*You* are the only person who barged in here without asking for my permission, first."

"I . . . I was *protecting* your sanctity," Shi'ol protested. She not quite looked over her shoulder at him, then glared at Ja'ki, and hissed, "*Stop* ogling him, you little *Charuta*!"

Li'eth's eyes snapped wide at the insult. The story of Charuta was an old one, but it extolled the dangers of letting someone who was underage try to ensnare adults in sexual activities. It was *not* a compliment, and beyond acceptable when applied to their hostess. Their politically *powerful* hostess. Heat burned not only in his face but in his palms.

"*Apologize!*" he snarled at the countess.

"She's a *child*, and she—"

"*Wrong* answer!" He lifted his hands on instinct, heat bursting from his palms along with his roar—and Ja'ki yelped, flinging up her left arm. At the same moment, alarms started blaring. The holy fire—pyrokinesis—skittered across a wall of nothing, extinguishing itself, and her other hand slashed up—and so did *he*, thumping into the flat, white ceiling hard enough to provoke a grunt. It shocked him out of his burning-hot rage. Blinking, Li'eth felt the conflicting forces of rotational gravity versus the blanketing pressure of her telekinesis. Three seconds after he thumped into the ceiling, the fire alarm signal shut off.

"*Congratulations*, Shi'ol," Ja'ki snapped, rounding on the woman while he stayed pressed to the ceiling of his sitting room. "You have just created our *first* diplomatic incident!"

"All I did w—"

"*Shut* it!" the Ambassador ordered, thrusting a finger at the spotted woman's face. "You are confined to quarters until further notice. Your meals will be delivered if you have to wait that long, but you will have *no* contact with anyone until your captain and I have figured out what to do with you—*do not argue with me, you mannerless child*," she added in V'Dan, her back to Li'eth, but her tone conveying her anger without needing to see how it twisted her face. "*You may have spots on your face, but you acted with all the self-control and social awareness of a* toddler!"

"I didn't do anything!" Shi'ol protested, flinging up her hands.

Li'eth knew who was at fault even before Ja'ki replied. He watched, pinned and helpless, while Ja'ki Maq'en-zi explained in their own tongue just how bad things had gotten.

"You provoked His Highness into nearly killing you with his psychic—holy!—abilities," the Terran asserted, jabbing her finger again at the V'Dan standing in front of her. *"If he had kept going, the fire-suppression systems would have choked all of us with carbon dioxide gas. This is a diplomatic incident of the highest order, and you caused it because you did not think about anything but yourself and your own viewpoints.*

"Thanks to you, now I have to figure out how to avoid your precious prince's being charged under Terran law with attempted murder by psychic abilities, which is a very serious crime—I may look like a child, but you act like a child. Thoughtless, irresponsible, and untrustworthy. Had I the power, I would strip you of both your rank and your civilian title, for your actions are not worthy of either of them.

"Luckily for you, you aren't my problem. You are the Empress' problem, and I will be certain she hears in detail every act of thoughtless stupidity you have inflicted upon my people while a guest in our star system. Now, get to your quarters. I suggest you spend all of your time actually *thinking* about the consequences of *your* attitude problem, though I won't hold my breath over you," she ordered in Terranglo. "If I find you have deviated by so much as an *arm's length* in heading there, you will be punished further. Go!"

Shi'ol took a step back, toward the door, but then paused and looked up. "His Highness—"

"Not. Your. Problem. Not when all *you* do is make things worse. Do *not* worsen things any further, Shi'ol. Not today. *Go.*"

Backing up another step, Shi'ol looked up at Li'eth one last time with her mouth pinched tight, then turned and left. Ja'ki stayed stiff and tense until the door shut, then her shoulders slumped. Her palms came up to rub at her tanned, spotless face, letting out a weary-sounding sigh.

Li'eth cleared his throat faintly and risked a tap on her mind-shields. (. . . *I am calm now,*) he offered when she opened them to him. (*I can be set down safely.*)

(*I'm tempted to leave you up there,*) she muttered mentally, but lowered him anyway, swinging his feet down to touch the floor even as she turned to face him. She didn't look at him, though. Rubbing at her forehead, Ja'ki shared the thoughts roiling through her head. (*I don't know if charges are going to be pressed by the oversight committee, or not. They'll have visible proof of you attacking Shi'ol pyrokinetically on the cabin monitors—which they* will *look at, because the fire alarm went off; they are obligated by law to look at those video feeds because the alarm went off—but I don't know if anyone would charge you with attempted murder, or merely with assault . . . which can be anywhere from a misdemeanor up to a felony, a very serious crime.*)

(*Because you used your pyrokinesis, Li'eth,*) she explained, turning to pace a little, her palms having slid down so that only her fingers pressed against her mouth, (*this could be construed a case of aggravated assault, possibly even assault and battery, though technically you didn't touch her. But you did touch my shields. Psi law is . . . We've had a couple hundred years to work on it, but each case could be taken in so many different directions . . . And I am* not *a lawyer. I'm a translator. I've worked on legal cases before as a linguistics and cultural facilitator, but . . .*)

Watching her pace, Li'eth felt the urge to take her in his arms, to hold her and comfort her, to tell her everything would be alright. But it wouldn't be, even if this issue was resolved. And touching her? Holding her? Diplomatic suicide. Which led to a thought. (*At the moment, because my crew and I are inadvertent diplomatic representatives . . . do we have any immunity from prosecution?*)

(*Nebulous gray area,*) she replied, lowering her hands and shaking her head. (*Internally, there is no diplomatic immunity anymore. Such things only led to abuse and corruption. But you aren't a part of the Terran system. And your people are so blindly ignorant of our customs and culture and expectations, we almost* have *to give you immunity just because you're going to continue to trip and stumble over all the differences, no matter what we do—we need to discuss this* out loud,) Ja'ki amended. (*The others* will *examine this recording, and I cannot be accused of brokering a backroom deal. I only did so earlier because your people were blindly uninformed of how things work with my people, and Shi'ol would have offended the whole Council, putting your people in a very bad bargaining position. You've had enough time to start learning, though.)*

She gestured at his sofa, as if this were her quarters, not his. Li'eth tipped his chin behind him. "I need to put on a shirt, then we can discuss what happened. If that is acceptable?"

"Yes, please." Moving to the couch, she lowered herself onto it. He forced himself to turn away.

It didn't take long for him to check his face to make sure he had gotten the last of the shaving done, nor to rinse away the last bits of crème residue he had missed in his haste. Donning the abandoned gray shirt, he paused long enough to slip his feet into simple, canvas-sided shoes, then returned to the front cabin. A choice of seats lay before him. He could isolate himself in a chair—she could choose to move and isolate herself, too—but instinct said take the sofa next to her. It might be a bit intimate, a bit physically close . . . but they were in this together.

The Empire needed Terran technology to try to win a war they were on the verge of losing. The Terran United Planets needed V'Dan technology to get itself geared and ready for a Salik attack. Only by working together, by getting past all the differences between their two subspecies, would everything work out right for all. Moving to the sofa, he seated himself to her right and leaned his elbow on the armrest, chin on his palm.

It wasn't the most princely of postures, but if he had learned anything in the last few days, he knew there were a lot of very common gestures between their two peoples. Body language like his would be read as worried, pondering, and open in its emotional honesty. No, it wasn't the most royal posture, but it was honest. Switching to rubbing at his brow, he asked aloud in Terranglo, "What is the range of possible legal accusations I could face?"

"The worst would be attempted murder via aggravated assault with a psychic weapon," Ja'ki stated. She added aloud—no doubt for the recordings—what she had stated mentally earlier. "I'm not a lawyer, but I have served on legal cases in a linguistic and cultural translation capacity, including a couple incidents of psychic lawbreaking. At the absolute worst . . . it's attempted murder via aggravated assault with psi. And as psychic abilities are a form of weapon that cannot be removed from you without destroying parts of your brain . . . and even after two hundred years, we're still not sure *which* parts can be safely destroyed . . . you're lucky it was only *attempted* murder.

"But we don't want to invoke that end of the spectrum," she stated, cutting a hand through the air. "Particularly if word gets out about this incident. Right now, the only ones watching us are those who will check the recording to see what set off the fire alarms for a few seconds . . . and then their superiors, including Admiral Nayak . . . and the Admiral-General, who is the head of the Space Force. . . . and probably the Premiere, *maybe* the Secondaire. The only ones who could speak of it are those watching, you, Shi'ol, and me; the midlevels are bound by their oaths not to discuss anything once they've passed something like this up the line, and the higher-ups will realize as I do that invoking the worst accusations would not help this First Contact situation between our peoples.

"At the other end of the spectrum, you *could* try to invoke diplomatic immunity . . . but technically by Terran law, there is no such thing anymore." She looked at him, and waited.

" . . . There isn't?" he asked, a bit belatedly when he realized this was something that *had* to be discussed aloud.

"We haven't *needed* it since there are no foreign powers legally acknowledged by the Terran United Planets and haven't been for decades, if not centuries," she stated openly for the recordings. "We've abolished it within our own jurisdiction because it is believed that having it only leads to abusing it, and that leads to corruption over time . . . except obviously there *are* foreign powers now, powers strong enough that they have to be acknowledged. But your people are so blindly ignorant of our laws, you could break them all too easily without even realizing it—and there are too many laws, too many customs, which you haven't grown up *knowing*, so it would take years to explain them all under each and every context, in ways which *we* understand instinctually—not to mention things which the true aliens might not understand because, biologically and psychologically, they aren't Human."

"Well, there are common laws. Theft, murder . . . assault," Li'eth acknowledged honestly, wryly, knowing that it could damn him. But these people needed to understand why he reacted as he had, so he tried to explain in Terranglo the V'Dan viewpoint on such things. "What Shi'ol said was very, *very* insulting. Particularly to our hostess, and triply so to an adult woman of very high political standing. At the very least, she *should* be stripped of her rank as a Leftenant Superior, bumped down to Leftenant, even to Ensign rank . . . and if this causes harm to our future diplomatic maneuverings, I would advise the Empress to strip Nanu'oc of her civilian title in punishment for it, handing it off to one of her other relatives . . . but in *our* culture . . . Your people *do* look like children, Ja'ki."

"Children, children, children," she muttered, voice rising and hands flinging up. "I don't get this, Li'eth. *We* got rid of our appearance-based prejudices over a century ago! How can you be a technologically advanced, interstellar-traveling—interstellar-*colonizing!*—culture, and still lean upon something so stupid and . . . and *juvenile* as judging people solely upon their *appearance*? We have an age limit for achieving adulthood, yes, because the age of eighteen years is considered long enough for our children to have learned *some* basic grasp of maturity and common sense, but mostly, we judge each other upon our words and our actions. What kind they are and how well they mirror each other.

"And *don't* ask me to paint my face in spots or stripes just to satisfy Shi'ol's warped view of the world," Ja'ki added tartly. "If *I* had to paint myself just to get across the fact that I am mature, then you'd just go on to demand that the billions of people scattered across the entire Terran United Planets have to do that. I will *not* inflict the xenocultural prejudices of an entirely separate branch of Humans upon my own people. We may be Humans, but we are *not* V'Dan."

"I wouldn't ask you to," Li'eth told her. "We don't demand that the Gatsugi paint their skin, or the K'Katta . . . but because you *look* V'Dan to us, we *react* to you like you're V'Dan. Spotless, stripeless, *markless* V'Dan, who look juvenile to us. Underage. Not yet fully mature in a physical sense . . . which Shi'ol assumes means immature. *I* know that it does not, but I also know very few are going to take that first look at you and feel the urge to treat you as a fully grown-and-marked adult . . . and this is getting off the topic of what to do about what *I* did. We cannot fix a cultural problem in a single day. *This*, maybe we can figure out how to handle diplomatically."

They sat in silence for a little while, Li'eth rubbing his forehead and Ja'ki sighing once in a while, leaning back against the couch with her skull resting on its upper edge. Finally, she said, ". . . The problem isn't your getting mad at her. I know you understand that there are legal ramifications for doing so."

"I do regret acting as I did. I didn't *think*, though. I just . . . reacted to the insult she gave you," Li'eth explained. "Charuta is the name of a character in a story—an *underage* character, about the age of thirteen V'Dan years, maybe fourteen, having started puberty but still a couple years from her *jungen* fever. In the tale, she goes from adult to adult, seducing and ruining them socially, financially, culturally . . . as does her younger brother, Maruto. It is a very serious piece of slander when applied to an adult. Unlike Shi'ol, I *know* you are an adult, legally and culturally. I am doing my best to *see* you as an adult."

"This Charuta sounds something like our 'Lolita' character, but that was an underage girl seducing just the one fellow, if I remember right," Ja'ki said. Another sigh escaped her, and she rubbed at the bridge of her nose, thinking. "There is another option. There is a grace period given to psis when they are undergoing formal training. I have given you some instruction, and I blocked the burst of your power so it could do no damage. But it would have to be proved that you are *not* fully in control . . . but as I am not an official trainer, no one would take *my* word alone for it."

"So how does this make that an option to control the damage done?" Li'eth asked.

"If we presume that you acted without conscious control over your abilities?" she asked him.

"I didn't *intend* to burn her," he asserted. "I was angry, but I acted rather poorly because I reacted to her insult without thinking."

"Well, it's not common, but we can ask for a volunteer to enter quarantine with us. A certified instructor from the Psi League or the Witan Order, preferably one with pyrokinesis, biokinesis, and auramancy. That way, you'd get more training than I've been able to get you, plus we could certify through an independent observer that you are not consciously in control of your projection abilities—you're gaining a lot of control in your telepathy, but as I am not a pyrokinetic, I cannot gauge how well you're mastering that," she reminded him.

"I'm not," he admitted bluntly. "I cannot control when it happens. It just . . . *does*. On V'Dan, such things are understood and allowances are made. Legally, it would be considered . . . what is the Terran legal term . . . manslaughter? As opposed to murder?"

"Were you thinking of killing her before she insulted me?" Ja'ki asked.

Li'eth shook his head. "No. Absolutely not. Nor even during it."

"Involuntary manslaughter would be the term for it. Except that would require criminal negligence, which is willfully avoiding a course of action that would prevent death. You are *actively* agreeing to be trained, and cooperating with what training I have been able to give you, so you are not willfully avoiding that course of preventive action . . . so manslaughter wouldn't apply," Ja'ki reasoned. "It's not constructive manslaughter; you weren't committing an unlawful act when the attempt to kill her happened. In fact, you were reacting in defense of my honor, so to speak. That's not illegal in and of itself. So technically, you had provocation, and you were in a way acting in defense of another person."

"Well, I wasn't intending to use holy fire—pyrokinesis— upon her," Li'eth said, gesturing at the front door. "I will admit I felt like I needed to slap her, slap some sense into her as your people say it. Except I was burning up and just . . . It just came out of me *like* a slap."

"Involuntary loss of psychic control under aggravated provocation," Ja'ki rattled off. She looked over at him and sat up, nodding. "*That* is what happened. Now that I think about it, this is like a test case we had in my classes at the Psi League training headquarters in Honolulu—it's the capital city of the Hawai'ian Islands, though obviously not the capital city of the United Planets," she dismissed. "But in order to prove it, we need to prove you're not fully trained. That requires, as I said, requesting a certified instructor to join us in quarantine."

"What sort of . . . of diplomatic ramifications would happen with that particular claim?" Li'eth asked her, curious.

"Mandatory training sessions," Ja'ki revealed dryly, not quite rolling her eyes. "Which again would require pulling someone into quarantine with us, since it would require physical contact to enforce the psychic lessons with suitable impact. If you do not cooperate, as in *willfully* do not cooperate, you get a warning and you get watched. And if you keep doing it, you get a lobotomy.

"*That* would be a diplomatic disaster, in which case I'd suggest invoking immunity and shipping you home as fast as we can find your star system—not that I think you'd *do* that," she added quickly, holding up a hand when he opened his mouth to protest. "But that's the bad end of the spectrum for that lobe of the problem. If you cooperate, but make no progress, you may have to have a watchdog for the duration of your visit. That would require bringing in a psychodominant—a very strong sort of specialized telepath—who would watch you constantly for any projective abilities and 'sit' on you mentally until we could ship you home.

"If you cooperate, and make progress . . . then the only thing to add to your mandatory training is a slap on the wrist, as we say. That usually means making some sort of mild restitution and perhaps some sort of punishment without any severity to it, such as chores or repairs or the like. Actually, all of the different categories and options would require some sort of restitution, but since you don't have any resources to confiscate—money, property, whatever—plus there was nothing *physically* damaged, it would probably be limited to a series of apologies to Shi'ol as your target, to myself as your current instructor, to myself as the person who had to prevent the damage done, and to the government . . . which I currently stand for.

"Also, courtesy would demand you apologize to whoever your certified instructor would be, and give them the full breadth of your attention and earnest efforts in learning control of your abilities. Of course, we could defer demanding physical resources from you until such time as you have access to such things again . . . which could be strapping your government over a barrel for . . . Ahh, that's not exactly a diplomatic way to phrase things," Ja'ki amended quickly, chuckling a little. "Metaphorically accurate, but impolite and undiplomatic."

(. . . ?) he sent privately. She shook her head, but his curiosity was too strong, so he sent the query again. The image he got back, of a naked Human strapped over a barrel on what looked like an archaic sailing ship, with sailors lining up, unfastening their lower garments . . . He blushed red. ". . . Yes, we do not need to discuss such things undiplomatically."

"Then I guess we need to—"

The beeping came again, this time from the comm-unit monitor. Both of them jumped a little.

Ja'ki gestured toward it. ". . . Go ahead and answer it. Center bottom on the button for both audio and video feed."

"I remember that part," he grunted, pushing to his feet while the monitor beeped again, the screen displaying the blue-and-silver government logo. Touching the button as soon as he was within range of the screen, he found himself facing a trio of people. One of them was the military officer in charge of the *Aloha* missions. Admiral Nayak, that was it. Terran military rankings were very strange compared to V'Dan; an admiral, with no amendments to the title, was the lowest of the First Tier officers, not the highest as they were in the Terran system. It was all very strange. "Greetings, Admiral Nayak. What would you like to discuss?"

"Thank you for answering, Your Highness. I hope we didn't catch you at a bad time?" the admiral asked politely. "We tried reaching you earlier a few times."

"I was showering after exercising," Li'eth said, avoiding any mention of the holy-fire incident. It seemed the report hadn't made it up the chain of command yet, or the admiral would not be addressing him so lightly. "I am free now, for a little while."

Nodding, Nayak gestured to the left.

"This is Dr. Paurav Jain from the Pathology Institute of Jaipur, a city in the prefecture of Rajasthan, India." He gestured toward the slightly shorter man on his left, a younger, narrow-faced fellow with a hint of similar features. His hair was cut jaw-length while theirs was considerably shorter. It seemed to be the fashion among Terran males to have short-cut hair even outside the military, though women had hair of all different lengths. Or at least, the geophysicist Lars Thorsson was the only exception he had seen so far.

Then again, Li'eth had to admit, he hadn't seen everyone. On reflection, there had been a few men with long hair in the white seats of the Council chamber. Maybe he just hadn't seen a large enough sampling of these people, yet.

". . . And this is Dr. Jai Du of the University of Nanning, Guangxi prefecture, China," Nayak introduced while Li'eth was mulling that over. The officer gestured to the tallish woman on his other side.

Li'eth turned his attention to her, and blinked. Her face, somewhat squarish and flat with strong bones, but with more or less the same black hair and brown eyes as the other two, was mottled in a few patches of pale pink across her forehead, cheek, nose, and opposite jawline, with the rest of it a medium tan shade a tiny bit grayer than the golden hue of V'Dan coloring. The mottling wasn't exactly like *jungen*, more like one of those skin ailments that destroyed the natural pigments, he suspected, but . . . she was the first person he had seen so far who looked even remotely "adult" to his subconscious cultural sensitivities.

The woman, Dr. Du, spoke. "Call me Du, or Dr. Du, since Jai is similar to Jain, and I don't want to confuse you. We have been studying the microflora of your people—the small bacteria and such which live on your skin, in your mouths, even in a few samples of your excrement—and we have reason to believe we can create an immunization program for the people of Earth that will not cause significant health concerns in the vast majority of the population."

"However, Dr. de la Santoya is working alone on her side of the quarantine barrier," Dr. Jain added, "and as such, she is the only one working on the actual biota strains. We would like to volunteer to join all of you in your current isolation to systematically swab, sample, and synthesize the necessary vaccines."

"She needs to focus more on being a general practitioner and potential surgeon in the advent of an emergency, which is her area of expertise, and not on being a microbiotic specialist, which she is not," Dr. Du told him. She gestured past the admiral at her colleague. "We are those specialists, having been selected from a pool of highly trained microflora specialists who volunteered to handle this work. Courtesy commands that we ask you if this is acceptable since it would include medical exams and direct specimen sampling from each member of your crew. Plus there is a chance for additional exposure to any pathogens we might bring along in our own microbiomes."

"We would also like to observe in more detail your immune systems' responses to being vaccinated against our own pathogens," Dr. Jain stated. "This will help us tailor additional immunology treatments for the day we send an embassy to your people, so that they can be vaccinated against our own unfamiliar-to-them biota, as we have been inoculating you. One day, it is hoped that our two peoples will be able to travel freely without quarantines and inoculation measures, but to do that, we must dedicate ourselves to extracting, examining, and synthesizing."

Admiral Nayak lifted his chin, joining the conversation. "Including two more personnel in quarantine should not strain the system's capacity, and there are still a few open quarters without anyone having to share, if you have any concerns about that. As for their qualifications, Captain, both doctors are famous in medical circles for their work, and renowned for their ethical behavior and courteous treatment of their patients. They have the confidence of their colleagues backing them."

(*Ja'ki?*) Li'eth asked instinctively, glancing over his shoulder at her.

(*It would be a really good idea to bring in professional pathologists. But let me add more.*) Moving up beside him, Ja'ki nodded at the screen. "Admiral, Doctors."

"Major," Nayak acknowledged. The other two nodded, eyeing her in curiosity.

"Admiral Nayak, I would like to add at least one more person to this," Ja'ki stated, while Li'eth listened, gaze going back and forth between her and the screen. "His Highness needs more training for his psychic abilities. I cannot give him anything beyond the barest basics, but it is clear he needs more intermediate lessons, even some advanced training before we are released from quarantine.

"It should also be delivered by an independent person so as to confirm I have had no bias nor inadvertent influence on him, mind to mind. I realize this is short notice, but I can get you an analysis of what he needs and a recommendation of at least five League trainers within the hour. It's a subject that just came up, or I'd be more prepared."

"It would be best to operate the airlocks just the once," Dr. Du said. Again, she gestured at herself and her colleague. "We wouldn't be headed up there for at least a day or two, however, so if you can get this specialist ready in a reasonable time frame, I wouldn't object. Dr. Jain?"

"No objections here," he agreed, giving both women a nod.

Admiral Nayak shrugged. "Very well. Make sure you get me that list of candidates within the hour, Major."

"Sir, yes, sir," she agreed.

"That is, *if* Your Highness agrees?" Nayak added, turning his attention back to Li'eth. "The point of making this a request is to respect your people's body-rights while hopefully speeding the immunization process."

"As the representative of my crew, and a makeshift representative of our people, you have my permission, Admiral, Doctors. On one condition," Li'eth bartered. Making sure he had both doctors' attention, he said, "You have to share every scrap of data, every theory, every conclusion, and the formulae for every vaccine with my people, without demanding payment nor reserving any production rights."

"Done," Dr. Jain agreed immediately.

Dr. Du looked down her flattish nose at him. Just a little, but enough to give him a pointed, almost chiding look. "Only if *you* swear your people will do the exact same, with the exact same conditions."

"Agreed," Li'eth stated without reservation. He didn't have to be a medical professional to know that vaccines and immunization abilities were too important to condemn to a mess of payment plans, bureaucratic maneuverings, or trade restrictions.

"Can you *guarantee* your government will comply?" Dr. Du asked.

"Doctor . . ." Admiral Nayak admonished.

"It is a valid question, Admiral," Li'eth demurred. "The Empire's policy on medical needs is that widespread beneficial, preventive medicine has priority. So long as everything is shared openly on both sides and is engineered for aiding both sides, then there will be no hesitation in accepting these terms. Of course, I am trusting your people not to craft some sort of epidemic or plague . . . but then we are the same species, and the chance of it mutating to affect your own kind in return would be a bit too risky, I'd think. Especially as you don't know how fast we can synthesize a cure . . . and a retaliation."

The admiral frowned at that, but Dr. Du laughed. She had a hard, almost braying laugh, and pointed at the camera. "I like the way you think! You should go work for the Center for Disease Control when you get out of the military, Highness. Or maybe Disaster Prevention."

Li'eth dipped his head slightly, acknowledging the implied compliment. "My people would rather survive than fight, thank you . . . and I will not 'get out' of the military until our war with the Salik is over."

Despite the opened topic, the admiral did not press for more details of that fight. "I'm sure nothing harmful was meant," Nayak murmured instead. "With your permission as well, Ambassador, I'll begin the arrangements for sending three people into quarantine with you. Make sure I have your report within the hour, Major."

"Sir, yes, sir," Ja'ki agreed. The admiral touched a control on his side of things, and the screen went dark.

"Interesting . . ." Li'eth murmured. At the lift of her brows, he explained. "He treated you as someone in charge, possibly someone superior to him if not his equal, in requiring your permission to bring in outsiders to this quarantine situation . . . and then treated you as a subordinate in calling you Major and commanding your recommendations. That's a very sophisticated byplay of politics, parsing out the responsibilities and positions."

"We may not have artificial gravity, but we are an advanced society in many other ways," Ja'ki told him. "Before I leave to go write up that report . . . we need to figure out what to do with Shi'ol."

Sighing, Li'eth rubbed his eyes. "What I would do to her . . . as a prince to a countess, I'd have her fined and banned from the royal court for a set period of time, half of the fine to go to you, and half to the Imperial coffers. As a captain to a leftenant superior . . . I'd make her scrub the sludge filters for the sewage system."

She bit her lip, shoulders quivering and brown eyes gleaming. "Amusingly enough . . . if she were in the *Terran* military, that's what we'd do to her as well."

Thinking about that, he nodded slowly. "Then we are in consensus. She gets all the . . . what's the Terranglo word for it? I want to say sludge work, but that isn't it."

"'Scutwork'?" she offered. "Which is basically your sludge work, cleaning the sludge filters and other messy, nasty jobs."

"Yes, the scutwork jobs," Li'eth agreed. "Cleaning the filters, mopping up messes, sorting the garbage for composting and recycling, unclogging any drains, all of that," he decreed, sweeping his hand. "And . . . I should take on some of it, too, for losing my temper and losing my self-control."

She opened her mouth . . . hesitated . . . and bit her lip for a long moment. Then nodded. "Doing that would be looked upon with high favor among my people. Taking on personal responsibility is an important part of our culture, these days. Since there isn't enough 'sludge work' for two people to scrub all the filters . . . do you know how to scrub walls and wash dishes?"

He quirked his brows at her. "Wash walls and dishes?"

"Yes, by hand, not by machine," she said.

Li'eth shook his head. "No. I had no need or time for that in the palaces, and when I went into the military, cadets were punished with physical regimes or sludge cleaning, not kitchen chores. The most I ever did was keep my quarters tidy for inspection."

"Then you're going to learn. I'm going to have you laboring like one of your palace servants," she teased him.

Rather than being offended, Li'eth chuckled. "More like palace robots. But if nothing else, it should render me too tired to summon any powers. Unless our priesthood is wrong about too much exercise dulling the holy energies? Compared to your way of training, they've been wrong about many other things."

"Your priesthood is actually correct about that," she told him. "The Psi League mandates physical exercise for its trainees for several reasons. Disciplining the body helps discipline the mind, and it exhausts the energies needed to project anything. It may make someone more *receptive* to incoming information—telepathy, empathy, the ability to read the history of whatever you touch, even precognitive visions—but it reduces the energy to project anything."

"You keep mentioning this League, and another organization. You do not gather your psis into one organization to train and watch over them?" Li'eth asked her.

She shook her head. "We don't want any one particular system gaining ascendancy—we've stories from our past cautioning against . . . well, the phrase is 'putting all your eggs in one basket.' With more than one group being responsible, that means no one particular organization can go rogue and attempt to train their psis into an army. The other organizations will have enough psis of their own to go up against them and shut them down. So, when a psi has been proved to have actual powers, you're given a choice of several different organizations to join, which help train and monitor your abilities to make sure you're not committing crimes with them."

"That . . . makes sense. And is reassuring, even as it makes me reluctantly curious about those stories you mention," Li'eth said.

"Well, anyway, the Psi League is the most popular as a single organization because it's completely secular and doesn't require any sort of religious belief system, it doesn't couch things in occluded, mystical terms, and, at the same time, doesn't deny anyone their choice of faith," she explained, gesturing vaguely at the air. "The Witan Order accepts all faiths but presumes you *have* a faith system, so that it can put you into the correct subsect for training. It also requires that you are open-minded enough to accept that others have a right to their *own* faith systems.

"While it has as many members as the League, if not a few more—it varies from year to year—the Witan Order has several subsects that do all the training, and you are free to move among them or into and out of the League or the other, lesser organizations. The only requirement is that *someone* knows you're a psi, and that some legally recognized group evaluates you once or twice a year to make sure you're not using your abilities illegally. In fact, I know this one League member who was one of my mentors . . ."

She trailed off, lost in her thoughts for a moment. Li'eth wanted to reach out to her mind, to share those thoughts since the memories of the man in question brought a soft smile to her lips. He refrained, waiting patiently, and was rewarded with more information aloud.

"He had a sort of personal epiphany, a moment of realization, that led him *to* a faith system, and he eventually swapped over to the Witan Order as an instructor—actually, I should include him on the list," Ja'ki stated, glancing at Li'eth. "I don't know many of the trainers among the Witans, but he actually may be able to relate things more easily for you *because* he understands the faith side of things, the religious slant. I'm not the best choice for that."

"You don't have a faith?" Li'eth asked, curious. "At least, that is the impression you give me. I know Maria said she's a Catholic, and Lars said he's a Lutheran, and that both say these are subsects to your Christianity faith, whatever that is, but Robert called himself a 'neoclassical Buddhist meat-lover' when I asked, and . . . I got lost after that when he attempted to explain."

She chuckled at his words. "I've noticed both Robert and Lars like to pull little jokes on people . . . though Robert might be serious at the same time. I don't know. And I do have a *spiritual* side, but I don't follow any religion. I'll honor the gods and goddesses of my mother's side of the family when dancing the legends of the Hawai'ian *hula*, or expressing an occasional South Pacific *haka*.

"And I respectfully attend the occasional church service to placate my father's relatives . . . but I am what we call agnostic," she told him. "I believe something *may* be out there, a higher power we can only glimpse in the tiniest pieces here and there, but it is something that sentient life as we know it cannot yet fully comprehend. Because of this viewpoint, I can attend religious services of the various cultures I've represented as a Councilor, since it's all just facets of a greater thing. But to my way of thinking, that higher power is so far beyond us, it is unknowable, undefinable by traditional religion, which can only ever clip off a corner and worship what little they *can* understand. *I* simply cannot bring myself to put any limits on that higher power."

"Because if they focus on only a single corner, they will miss all the other corners that are out there?" Li'eth offered, and received a nod that made her long curls, caught up in a band like his, bounce a little on her shoulder. He wanted to reach over and touch her hair . . . and realized how dangerous that line of thought was. There was a cure for *that* kind of distraction, too. "Right. Physical exercise for punishment detail. Mopping floors and walls and such."

"I need to get that report written, first. I . . . hmm. Brad hasn't had much to do, other than cleaning the ship and taking pathology samples for the doctor," Ja'ki mused aloud. "I think I'll ask him to introduce Shi'ol to the joys of Terran sludge work."

"And who will supervise me?" he asked, curious.

"Lars, Ayinda, Robert, and Ba'oul are going over star charts," she counted off on her fingers. "Brad had offered to teach V'kol racquetball last I heard, but that could be put off . . ."

"He *did* teach us your racquetball sport . . . and beat V'kol and me both, even when we paired against him," Li'eth confessed, remembering the blond, markless male's athleticism. "That's why I needed a shower but didn't take one earlier this sleep cycle. I knew I'd get sweaty with whatever sport he had in mind."

(*Don't think about sweaty men, don't think about striped, sweaty . . .*)

Li'eth laughed, overhearing that. (*Maybe* you *need some review lessons on self-control, yourself?*)

(*Oh hush . . . and yes, I'll consider it.*) Out loud, she said as she stood up, "After racquetball, he usually goes swimming. He's probably still in the pool. Let's go set up his oversight, and inform Shi'ol of her punishment detail. You will join Shi'ol for now in her punishment detail, so that she understands you both acted wrongly. Once that's settled, I can leave you to it and get those recommendations to Admiral Nayak."

Nodding, Li'eth gestured at the door, letting her take the lead. As far as lawbreaking punishments went, mopping a floor or cleaning sludge filters were mild versions at best.

CHAPTER 13

"Master Sonam, it's so good to see you again," Jackie greeted the third member of the trio that had just stepped through the airlock. She moved forward to embrace the red-clad, wrinkled man, stooping a little because he was shorter than her by several centimeters. (*Such a pleasure, my teacher,*) she added telepathically. (*Thank you for coming up here.*)

(*It's an adventure, and I am still hale enough for a mild one like this,*) he added politely, returning the hug with strength despite his age, somewhere in his late seventies. (*Plus being a biokinetic didn't harm matters, I am sure—Dr. Jain is eager for me to pursue things psychically where the pathology of these V'Dan is concerned.*) Out loud, he said, "It's always a pleasure to see you, Jackie dear."

(*And what does Dr. Du think of you?*) Jackie asked

(*She doesn't have patience for "mental twaddlings," though she will, of course, accept my findings if there's a way she can replicate them scientifically.*) He grinned at Jackie, brown eyes gleaming with mirth. (*I have been trying to convert her to Tibetan Buddhism. Alas, I shall learn the patience of a bodhisattva before I will convert her . . . but I am told it is good for my karma to be patient as I try. Now, introduce me. Which one is my pupil? This is the prince, yes?*)

"Master Sonam, I present His Highness, Li'eth V'Daania," Jackie introduced, gesturing toward the waiting, burgundy-striped man. "Li'eth, this is Sonam Sherap, a Master Trainer of the Psi League, the Witan Order, and a monk of the Buddhist religion. Their monks wear robes that vary from sect to sect, but are usually some shade of saffron yellow through crimson red, with other shades being less common."

Maria, who had just finished greeting the two patholo-gists, moved over to speak with Jackie. She gave a nod to the monk as she did so. "Greetings, Master Sonam. Major MacKenzie . . . I know we have a good variety of vegetables thanks to the aquaculture bay, but can we sustain a vege-tarian diet with the proper ratio of amino acids while in quarantine? Did anyone remember to address that?"

Sonam smiled and bowed a little in her direction. "Doctor, you are kind to be willing to go to the trouble of not only pro-viding vegetarian meals but healthy meals. I am, however, a Tibetan Buddhist. Our karmic balance is countered by our teachings, our meditations, so it will not be necessary to deviate too much in creating special meals for me. As my meals in quarantine are paid for by the government," the red-robed monk added lightly, "it is also more of an alms-giving than anything, and thus not prohibited. Nor was it packaged in advance specif-ically for me, which helps alleviate karmic concern in that di-rection. I do *like* vegetables more than meat these days," he added, patting his red-draped stomach with a chuckle, "but I think it is more a case of my digestive needs as I age."

(*Dietary restrictions? That sounds like it happens all year long for him,*) Li'eth sent to Jackie. (*We have some minor reli-gions with similar lifelong constraints back on V'Dan, but in the Sh'nai faith, diet cycles with the seasons as to what is available. With modern agriculture and transportation providing things all year-round, the seasonal foods are therefore merely re-served for special meals, such as holy days, natal celebrations, and such. I would like to know more about this faith of his, that his specific sect doesn't have such restrictions yet clearly most of the other related subsects do.*)

Sonam eyed the two, one brow quirking upward. (*Did he just send something to you?*) he inquired. (*Telepathically?*)

(*I'm sure he'd be willing to discuss religions with you,*) Jackie sent to Li'eth, before parsing a separate sending to her former teacher. (*Yes, he did. Is he leaking? As the only one here, I haven't been able to tell. He doesn't leak to the nongifted, at least.*)

(*Yes and no. He leaks a little. It was wise, I think, for you to have called for an expert instructor,*) Sonam told her.

(*I am strong, but I do not teach for a living; I know my*

own limitations,) Jackie promised him. He mock-touched his heart, as if staggered by her confession, along with a pulse of faked shock. (*Hush,*) she shot back. (*I need you to verify he is not yet fully in control of his abilities.*)

(*Oh?*)

(*We had an incident. I need an expert opinion to place him firmly in the category of—*)

(*Firmly in the category of the still as yet untrained, yes. I don't need to know the details of what happened in order to evaluate him for that. I do need to know the gifts involved,*) Sonam reminded her.

Jackie sighed. (*Pyrokinesis, predominantly.*)

(*Oh joy. That's the one that went rogue? Training* that *one on a space station will be fun,*) he sent back, and patted his chest with the fingers of the hand still covering his red-robed sternum. "Well, we had better show me to my quarters. I was informed that there is just enough room for privacy per person?"

"We'll still have a couple cabins left over, Master," Jackie stated aloud. Now that he was a Tibetan monk, the proper term for teacher should have been *lama*, but as the lessons being sought were not in Buddhism, it didn't feel right to address him as such. Jackie wasn't asking him to teach Buddhism to anyone, after all, though he would be free to answer questions on it. "You'll even have your choice: a view of Earth or a view of space."

"I call dibs on Earth," Dr. Du called out, breaking off her conversation with the other two doctors in the entry cabin just beyond the quarantine airlocks. She shuddered a little, her bony frame quivering for a moment. "I don't think I could stand looking at the void of space without something at least vaguely familiar in view."

"Then I shall concede my rights to an Earthly view," Sonam stated.

Jain smacked Du lightly on the shoulder. "He has seniority as an elder, Du. You should let him have the view."

"Please, gentles, we have *plenty* of cabins on the Earth side of the station, enough for one for each of you if need be," Jackie quickly soothed.

"Well, *I* will take a spaceside cabin," Dr. Jain told her. "I do not need to look at the planet to know it is still there."

"As you wish. As soon as you have picked up your things from the sterilizer bins," Jackie added, nodding to the machinery off to the side, "I can take you to your quarters and get you settled. There will be a drill on the various emergency alarms and procedures in half an hour, which will be directed by Commander Robert Graves. It is mandatory for everyone in quarantine to attend, but you should have at least a little time to settle in, first."

She switched to speaking telepathically as the trio moved to gather and pack their things in the carrying bags provided.

(*The prince is doing fairly well at controlling his projection and reception telepathically, as far as I can tell. His other skills will need work, though. You did read the profile I sent?*)

(*I cannot help train his auramancy outside the context of biokinetic healing, as that is not one of my skills, but within it, I should be able to give him a solid evaluation, and I know enough of the discipline to guide him in the right direction for self-teaching,*) Sonam informed his former pupil. (*I should also like to test your telekinetic and holokinetic progression from the days when you were my pupil. How long will this emergency tour last?*)

(*Half an hour or so, but right after that, I'll be eyebrow deep in trying to practice long-distance with the Honolulu University Hula Team. I was supposed to be on the surface, retired from being a Councilor and thus free to put on a joint show during the Merrie Monarch Festival,*) she added.

(*Ah, yes, I heard through both my high-ranked friends in the League and the Order grapevines about precognitive visions of you dancing in front of oddly painted strangers . . . and lo, we have oddly painted strangers among us. I look forward to seeing the performance,*) he told her, smiling as he worked to put his few personal belongings, mostly sterilized clothes, into his carry bag. (*Any chance we'll get to eat at a lu'au? I love the raw ahi dish—poke? Silly name, but delicious. And the ground-roasted pork, and the poi with soy sauce and brown sugar on top . . .*)

(*Master Sonam? You're drooling all over my neocortex,*) Jackie pointed out, trying not to laugh.

He chuckled aloud at that, if seemingly to himself.

FEBRUARY 10, 2287 C.E.

The instant Jackie felt polite mental tapping for her attention, she opened her inner shields to her old mentor. At the moment, she was sorting through yet more invitations for the "Human Aliens" to come visit various locations around the United Planets. So far, only Mars, the Moon, and Earth had been included. Nayak wanted her to assess the cultural value of taking the V'Dan to one of the mining or research stations farther out in the Sol System.

(*I thought you said he was growing quite skilled in his telepathic control,*) Sonam stated without preamble.

(*He clasps mental hands with me almost like you do,*) Jackie told him, lifting her gaze from her monitor. (*Like a seasoned pro.*)

(*He has the fumbling touch of a thirteen-year-old,*) Sonam scoffed.

(*I'm telling you the truth; clasping mental hands with him is like clasping hands with a close friend,*) she stated.

(*And I am telling* you *the truth; he hasn't mastered more than a third of what he's supposed to be doing.*)

(*Maybe . . . maybe he doesn't like you?*) she offered. (*Oh, don't laugh,* someone *eventually won't.*)

(*True, that high-strung female, Shee-oll, doesn't like me,*) Sonam admitted. (*She only likes that Dr. Du, the one with the melanin pigmentation. But this Li'eth does like me. He just has no finesse. But I believe you when you say he does, so I should like to observe the two of you interacting if you have the time.*)

Sighing, Jackie gave up trying to pick the best sites. (*Give me a few moments, then . . .*)

Thinking quickly, she pulled together a rough list of twenty locations and used a random number generator program to come up with three of them. *Peregrine* Station Depot just inside the asteroid belt between Mars and Jupiter . . . the *New Lunnon* Mining Station orbiting Jupiter . . . and the *Terran Lagrange 3 Astronomical Array and Hydrorefueling Station. That last one will be helpful in assessing the star charts, I suppose, even if it's not exactly the most entertaining of sites to visit.*

It's also on the far side of everything from us, even the as-

*teroid belt, though it's technically within range of the belt . . .
so . . . the Moon first, where they'll get to see my ancestress'
footprints in the lunar soil, plus the Tranquility Base historical
museum, though they won't be able to stay long.* Her fingers flew
over the keys of her workstation, typing up the proposed itinerary as she peered at the system chart showing the relative locations for everything. *Then all the way out to Jupiter and the* New
Lunnon—*it is a new station compared to the* MacArthur, *so
they might enjoy its design, and the miners will certainly get a
thrill—then to the* Peregrine *since it's opposite Mars and more
or less on the way from Jupiter. From there, we can swing
around to the L3 Array, then to Mars and visits to its three main
domes, and spiral back in to Earth. Maybe even a quick trip to
Saturn somewhere in there to show off the rings . . . ?*

She put in a note to ask their guests if they'd like to see
the rings of Saturn up close. They might have to visit Jupiter
and Saturn by short-hopping on an OTL ship in order to fit
it into the schedule, rather than one of the slower but much
more comfortable military ships that patrolled the system,
but with Admiral Nayak's permission, she could line up a
series of ships to be in position for personnel transfer around
the system. Or even better, have a specific ship assigned to
escort them so that they could . . .

Someone tapped again on her mental walls. Sonam Sherap.

(*Do you have that time, Jackie?*) the monk asked politely.
(*It would be helpful if you could join us for part of today's
session.*)

(*I will, in just a few more minutes. I'm sitting here, hoping
I made the right choices for the pre-Earth tour,*) she added,
sighing again.

(*I'm sure you did, and I am just as sure everything will
be fine after you have taken the necessary precautions.
Various ones,*) Sonam added.

(. . . ?) she sent, more than half of her attention on finishing the paperwork needed to send the proposed itinerary
to Nayak.

(*Oh, yes, there have already been at least fifteen recorded
fights of . . . what is the term . . . ah, yes. Of "nubile"—as in
marriageable aged—ladies and gentlemen brawling over
getting to be the Imperial Prince's companion. Various sorts*

of "companion" that is, ranging everywhere from legally wedded Imperial Princess Consort, to common bed warmer and mattress tester, both the paid and unpaid varieties,) he told her. That snagged her attention, as did his next revelation (*Honestly, Jackie, it's been all over the news. There have even been comments about women and men wanting to know if the V'Dan countess is single, as well as lesser numbers salaciously salivating over the other sentients in space . . . I love alliteration, it's so much fun . . . Anyway, as someone who is at least partially asexual by nature and thus happily celibate by inclination, I've never been motivated to have children, so the whole concept of people screaming to "bear their alien love child" is a bit odd to me . . .*)

(*Rrrrgh—not you, too! I was hoping our people would be a lot more dignified than that. Fine, I'll up the security against that as well,*) Jackie muttered mentally. She added a note on that to her recommendations before sending it off to her military superior. (*I admit I haven't been paying as much attention to the news as I should; I'm not naïve, but I've been mostly sticking to Council reports, not gossip rags.*)

(*I detect undercurrents of annoyance with hints of either . . . envy or jealousy. Is there something you'd like to share with your old teacher?*) Sonam asked. (*Off the record, of course.*)

She could deny it—Jackie had been denying it to herself for all manner of reasons—but it was hard to lie mind to mind with someone as skillful as Master Sonam. Taking a deep breath, she organized her thoughts, then sorted her feelings. (*I preface this with the awareness that nothing will ever happen, because of our respective political, social, and other situations. But . . .*

(*I find His Highness to be gorgeous,*) Jackie sent, thinking of his long blond-and-burgundy hair, those intriguing stripes. She lingered for a moment on her memory of the body that— even naked and dirty from lengthy captivity—had been strong without being overly muscular, the sort of body one would love to see surfing in the sun and the wind . . . (*The more I chat with him, Sonam, the more I genuinely like the man. I've rarely been so quickly at ease with anyone, particularly telepathically. Touching him only magnifies the . . . the comfort of it. If*

*he's having problems connecting with others telepathically,
well, he's having very few of them with me, and I with him.)*

*(Hmm. Well, the sooner you can come help, the sooner I
can pinpoint if it's just me, or just you, or . . . well, we'd need
a third telepath, or possibly a willing nontelepath.)*

*(I'll be there to help in a moment, but I don't think we can
get anyone else into quarantine.)*

*(It was just a thought. Between the two of us, and maybe
a nonpsychic volunteer, we should be able to get him trained
well enough. Poor fellow doesn't realize I've been going
easy on him so far. The truly intense sessions are about to
begin,)* Sonam added, chuckling in his head. And in hers.

Li'eth's head hurt. From the inside out, not from any external
blow. In fact, it felt like his skull had been used by *guanji*
birds, the brown-and-red-feathered ones with the long,
skinny, yellow, mud-digging beaks.

Guanji birds liked to kick and chase shelled water bugs up
and down among the tide-ditches and the chest-high roots of
the mangora trees along the southwestern shores of the Caenna
continent. They even had a sport named after them, *guanjiball*.
The Terrans had a similar version, albeit without the obstacles,
football, but they could only kick the ball around with their feet
or bunt it with their heads; like guanjiball, they couldn't carry
the ball for most of the game, but they weren't allowed to
smack it as the V'Dan version could.

He hadn't seen a guanji bird in person, but he had seen
documentaries on their life habits and ecosystem impacts on
the coastal mangora forests. They had almost gone extinct because of pollution nearly a thousand years ago. According to
what he was slowly learning of Terran history . . . well, they'd
had their own plethora of man-made extinction and near-
extinction events.

But it wasn't any trio or quintet of guanji birds trampling
through his brain, kicking around shelled, rotund meals. No,
this pain was reserved for these abominable *psychic* lessons.
At first, the short, wrinkled, red-robed Master Sonam had
been gentle and understanding, answering his questions in

more and more depth, prodding lightly into his mind, stimulating him carefully and slowly into learning how to project, how not to project . . . and then . . . hell. Intense mental hell.

Lesson after lesson after lesson, stressing and straining and pushing his limits. Slapping mentally when he tried things the wrong way, exacting demands that he repeat it again the right way. Practice, practice, practice, and more practice, making him long for the days when Ja'ki had prodded him just three or four times a day, not fifteen and eighteen and twenty-five times or more.

Pulling the damp, nubbly washcloth from his head, he flapped it a little in the air of his cabin, then reapplied it to his eyelids and the bridge of his nose as soon the evaporative movement had cooled the cloth a bit more. The air wafted around by the flapping smelled of candle wax and a hint of smoke.

Apparently, the tiny flames of mere candles did not set off the fire alarms on board this station. There were only a few on board since they apparently ate too much oxygen in large numbers, but a small box had been found in the kitchen area, some sort of holdover for a ritual called "birthday-cake candles." With the monk ready to suppress and constrict his powers, Li'eth had eventually succeeded in lighting one of them under his conscious control instead of as a reaction to a powerful emotion. He had to repeat the process several times before Sonam had pronounced himself satisfied. For now. That "for now" carried with it the implication that several more days' worth of literal headaches lay ahead.

Ja'ki had assisted in his lessons today, and it had been odd, watching her take on yet another subservient role. She normally spoke and acted like someone who was used to being in command, making tough decisions. In her military-based deferences, there was a subtle impression that she had gotten *out* of the habit of reporting to superiors, yet she had slipped into the role of junior-to-the-master readily with Sonam.

But she was gone, now, leaving him to recover. Master Sonam was busy mixing up some sort of psychic-headache-easing tea in the little kitchenette in his quarters. Li'eth shifted the damp cloth again, letting out a soft moan of pain . . . but not soft enough.

"You will get used to it, Highness," the monk stated soothingly in Terranglo. "Considering how awful your training was when I found you—and how much Miss Jackie said she had seen you improve—then you have nothing to be ashamed of. Your progress is remarkable."

Li'eth managed a grunt in response and pressed the wash-cloth into the inner corners of his eyes, where the heat was worse. The worst was directly behind his forehead, just above the bridge of his nose, but that was inside his skull. His eyelid corners, those he could reach with the damp, cool cloth.

(*Of course, you are even better with Miss Jackie, tele-pathically,*) Sonam stated. Privately. (*How do you feel about her? As a man, I mean. Not as a prince.*)

That . . . was not an expected question. And it was a bit invasive. (*I thought, according to your Psi League's rules, that my thoughts would remain my* own, *and thus private,*) he returned, wincing a little because his mind-voice felt bruised and strained. This wasn't a conversation to hold aloud, how-ever. (*Regardless of what my answer might be, such a ques-tion is intrusive.*)

(*I ask because it affects your abilities, and thus will affect your training. Your status as a prince has nothing to do with your abilities as a psychic, young man,*) the mark-less but clearly elderly monk chided. He carried a mug over to the couch where Li'eth lay, along with a fresh damp cloth. "Here, trade this one for that, sit up a little, and sip this. You can hold the cloth with your free hand . . . there we go . . ."

(*My abilities as a psychic have nothing to do with my opin-ions of her "as a man, not as a prince,"*) Li'eth retorted men-tally. The tea was awful, an odd herby tang to it, "improved" by some sort of sweetener. He could tell through his holy . . . through his *biokinetic* senses that it would be good for his aching head, though, so he forced himself to swallow.

(*Actually, they might.*) Sonam settled himself on the coffee table as if it were nothing more than an elongated stool. Hands clasped in front of him, he looked like he was praying, but his mind clearly wasn't on anything religious. (*I may be a monk, but I am not ignorant of the ways of mind and body. Both must work together, and both must be healthy and well for a person to be at their best. Denying or refusing to acknowledge one kind of hunger is much like denying or refusing another. In denial,*

there is no action taken toward an easement of the trouble. Life
may mean pain, but it is our goal to ease that pain, for ourselves
and others.

(*In other words, if you are drawn to her, or if you hate
her, yet you refuse to deal with how you feel—however you
feel—then that will cause your mind and your body to be out
of balance. Your abilities seem to be very much easier for
you whenever she is near, when she is involved, and particularly when you and she physically touch—an aspect of the
body which affects the mind, among psychics. Physical
touch almost always amplifies abilities, you know.*)

(*Yes, she mentioned it several times. But . . . whether or
not the body and/or the mind are interested, I cannot and
will not approach her as a man approaches a woman. There
are too many cultural unknowns, too many cultural
differences—taboos, even—and too many political reasons
to even think of such things.*)

(*So you do find her attractive?*)

Li'eth held his answer in check, pondering how to explain
his feelings. (*She looks like both a child and a woman to me.
I am striving to treat her, and you, and every other markless
Terran as an adult . . . yet I have found myself trusting more
in Dr. Du's opinions than anyone else's, just because her
face is mottled in its pigmentation. As if this somehow makes
her more adult than anyone else. Yet she has admitted she is
younger* than Bright Stone. Ja'ki. Jackie,*) he managed, sensing Sonam's underthoughts for a moment on how he was
treating her name. (*It is not easy being a V'Dan among you
Terrans because of these subtle differences.*)

(*What do you think of* her?) the monk stressed lightly.

(*Ja'ki is . . . beautiful,*) Li'eth admitted. (*Exotic. There
are few people among the V'Dan who look like her. And she
has, ah, a figure which I find appealing as a man. But she is
not someone to be considered in such ways. She is a political
entity far more than she is a person.*)

(*And this disappoints you,*) Sonam stated gently. He did
not question it.

The man was a master of subtleties, and of subthoughts.
Li'eth had to admire his interrogation skills. (. . . *Yes. In a way.
My duty comes first. My duty to return to the Empire, regardless*

of her presence or absence. My duty to represent the Empire, of which she is not a part. My duty to see to the best needs of the Empire, which she could oppose as easily as assist. So I try not to think of her as a man thinks of a woman he is . . .)

(He is . . . ?)

(Attracted to,) Li'eth admitted simply. *(She is attractive, and I am attracted to her.)*

(Yes, there is a difference between the two,) Sonam agreed. *(It is wise of you to recognize it.)*

(Part of me is yelling at me for being drawn to a seeming child. Part of me is trying to tell that part to learn to see things the Terran way—that we should be judged by our actions, not our appearances. Part of me is succeeding. Part of me is failing. And my head is hurting the longer I talk like this. Is there a point to this interrogation? I'll presume you're keeping it silent out of privacy's sake.)

(There is a point beyond privacy's sake, yes,) the monk agreed. *(But it is nothing that will be solved, or even uncovered, in a single session. Drink your tea. When it is gone, you may have cool, clean water to drink. It's best not to eat anything solid until the tea has had a chance to settle in your stomach, and the water a chance to wash away the flavors. That will take at least ten, fifteen minutes, then you really should have something to eat. I will fix something soothing and gentle for your stomach. If this suite is like my own, it should have some packets of soup for boiling . . .)*

(Thank you, Master Sonam,) Li'eth offered, reaching out to the elderly man. *(For helping me learn self-control.)*

(You will find it very much easier to learn than our ancestors did,) Sonam told him, moving off to begin making that promised snack. *(They had to figure all of this out by trial and error. Through scientifically methodical experimentation over a long and painfully slow-progressing period of time. Something which your own people have not settled down to manage . . . but then even though I am of the religious-minded Witan Order these days . . . I will admit the Psi League's atheistic, purely secular, science-based approach sped up quite a lot of what used to be years' worth of mystical training techniques even among those mystical orders that did have something of a clue on how to proceed.)*

(*So which part of those is this interrogation on how I feel about Bright Stone as a man?*) Li'eth asked. (*The mystical training, or the secular?*)

(*I have not yet decided. More empirical evidence must be gathered first . . . if the Gods allow it.*)

That struck the recumbent prince as funny. A purely scientific viewpoint on how to progress, with a deity-based plea for success. Unfortunately, laughing hurt his head. Quelling it with a deep breath and sigh, he asked, (*How long until this tea of yours takes effect?*)

(*Soon. Start counting backwards from 150, and you should feel fine by the twenties. If you count slowly. I will stay and watch to make sure it and the soup bring you no harm before I leave.*)

Sighing, Li'eth picked up the cloth, flapped it a little to cool it off, then tucked the damp little bit of toweling back over his eyes. Counting silently backwards.

"How is he?" Jackie asked, letting Sonam into her own quarters.

"I gave him enough tea to sleep it off," the monk told her. "With his monitor bracelet, and from the signs that I saw, the tension leaving his body . . . he will be fine. Besides, these couches are remarkably comfortable for napping." Sonam grinned at her. "I have already tried them out myself a few times, and each suite is identical, yes?"

"You have more energy than some people half your age," Jackie joked back. "So. Do you think he'll have sufficient control by the time he leaves quarantine?"

"Yes," Sonam stated, sobering a bit. "He *was* a danger to himself and others. I should like to have firm words with those who supposedly trained him . . . but I suppose they cannot help it. They are much like we were, before our kinetic inergy machines proved that some people do have these abilities, and that they can be trained methodically, and much more efficiently than mystically. There is a time and place for mysticism, but it is not when gaining control of an ability that can kill—I will make that an official report, how he is not yet in control, but that he should be by the time we are free to leave."

Jackie's shoulders slumped, tension leaving her body. "Good. I wouldn't want to have this First Contact with his people marred by any legal accusations of deliberate attempted murder. Awkward doesn't even *begin* to describe it. The Council knows that misunderstandings happen, and that the untrained, or undertrained, cannot always control what happens—there was a message on that waiting for me, today. They held a closed session to discuss the situation, and they will abide by my determination that he had no control over what he was doing, but that he *is* trainable if your report indicates it was so."

"It was so. It *is* so," Sonam added. He gestured toward her furniture. "Now, as your mentor, I'd like to have a private consultation with *you*, young lady. The prince's training takes precedence, but you have been under a great deal of strain, encountering murderous aliens, rescuing strange, lost Humans, translating languages, and having to balance the needs and perceptions of two disparate factions. *Your* mental health is of some concern in all of this, psychic and otherwise . . . and I should like to think I can qualify as a friendly shoulder, if nothing else."

"Considering half of my class went to you for advice and not just to our official counselors?" Jackie quipped. She gestured for him to take his choice of seat, then curled up into the corner of the sofa next to the padded, vinyl-covered chair he selected. (*So, what did you want to discuss?*)

(*The fact that, when you were assisting him, Li'eth performed much better than whenever he struggled on his own.*)

(*I wasn't helping him!*) Jackie protested mentally. Then checked herself. (*Well . . . maybe, a tiny bit . . . I tried not to,*) she sent firmly. (*You know how ephemeral this can be, sometimes—you* want *to help someone do something, and the next thing you know, you're projecting that help.*)

(*I know,*) he reassured her mildly. (*Jackie, I have had the privilege and honor of teaching students for over fifty years, now. Almost sixty. And in my half-century-plus, I have seen, and taught, and interacted with . . . eighteen? Yes, eighteen Gestalt pairings.*)

She choked on a misdrawn breath. Face flushing, she covered her mouth and coughed to clear her throat. (*You . . . are* not *implying . . . ?*)

(*I am.*)

(*I ruled that out!*) Jackie protested, blinking at him. (*The odds are astronomical!*)

Sonam looked at her calmly in return. (*Dai'a and I have been exchanging tales of our religious interests. She is intrigued by the stories of the gods and goddesses of India and of Tibet, and by the Enlightenment of the first Buddha. I, in turn, am intrigued by the idea of a physical person being considered immortal, unkillable, and capable of traveling through time. We have been exchanging a lot of information along those lines.*)

(*She is convinced—and frightened by the possibility—that she is not only a witness to, but a participant in their Immortal High One's prophecies regarding the return of the Motherworld.*)

(*I'm not too comfortable being the center of precognitive visions myself. Too much can go wrong,*) Jackie confessed.

(*Yes, well, among those prophecies,*) the monk continued placidly, (*is a small subset of stories regarding some of the battles that will take place. One involves a Holy Pairing—which she describes as two psychics who are "married mind to mind"—saving one of their capital cities from destruction.*) He lifted his brows pointedly. (*That sounds like a Gestalt pairing to me. The power to save an entire city—a presumably large city, as a capital—does not lie within the span of any two normal psychic minds alone. A Gestalt, however, might summon that kind of strength.*)

Her head reeled with denial and implications. (*It . . . it could be deflecting a single missile, which is what a strong telekinetic could do—it doesn't have to be a Gestalt pairing.*)

(*No, but there were other stories, she said. I got the implication she read them because of some implied romance between the two. Male and female, each one from a separate, mighty faction . . . Don't groan mentally at me, young lady,*) he chided. (*I can* feel *your eyeballs rolling upward.*)

(*But the odds . . . !*) Jackie protested, slumping sideways so she could drop her head onto her forearm.

(*The universe has been known to do even odder things with far lower probabilities of success. Such as sparking and evolving life to the point where it can question the universe about its own existence,*) Sonam reminded her. (*But if you look at it another way,* they *had precognitive knowledge of this meeting, and* we *had precognitive knowledge of this meeting—his people's prophecies apparently mentions one of the royal blood being involved, and ours very clearly showed your face . . . so maybe the probabilities weren't so much astronomically against it, as* guided *into it.*)

(*Ugh . . . it's one thing to serve a precognitive purpose. It's another matter when all that guidance is going to lead to a potential nightmare of disgrace, ridicule, and being barred from civil service. And that's just on* my *side of things. For all we know,*) she added, flipping her hand in a circle to encompass life, the universe, everything involved, (*he's got some arranged marriage waiting for him, even if it only exists in his mother's mind as of yet.*)

(*That is a possibility,*) Sonam allowed. (*We simply do not know.*)

(*Most probably, we'd face some social or cultural rules against making the equivalent of a marriage with someone not approved of by said mother/Empress. Or even just the highly likely scenario that they won't understand it's nothing we can control or prevent, and will therefore attempt to dismiss and ignore it, causing us untold problems. If* it's *a Gestalt.*) She let her fluttering hand flop on top of the forearm supporting her forehead.

Sonam sent her a mental shrug. (*I'm not their Empress, so I could not say. Of course, this is all still merely speculation . . . and still in its earliest stages. Even the existence and evolution of life itself had to take a great deal of time to grow and blossom, with several setbacks along the way. We have time to decide what to do, if anything should need a decision. But I want you to try something, in the coming days.*)

(*What?*) Jackie groaned, with an undercurrent of *what now* to her thoughts. The implications and their consequences were crowding out the doubts, bringing with them fears of failure, accusations of impropriety, being banned from civil service, her dream job—having any decision she'd been involved in during this whole stretch of time doubted and reexamined, possibly to the detriment of Terran-V'Dan relationships . . . !

(*Oh, do stop panicking and overimagining, child. Just try to light a candle. You know from observing and assisting Li'eth today with his pyrokinetic self-control how it feels when he successfully lights one. I want you to try, and practice.*)

He didn't add that he knew she could technically light a candle by crudely rubbing two bits of flammable matter together telekinetically. It wasn't her area of specialty, but she could do it if she had to, even if that version was exhausting from the sheer amount of concentration and control required. Li'eth's ability was based on thermal manipulation, not mass movement. But wavelengths could be considered holokinesis, the manipulation of light . . .

(*How will that prove anything? I could be doing it telekinetically, or even holokinetically,*) she protested, lifting her head from the couch arm so she could look at her mentor physically.

Sonam tugged the slipping folds of his shawl higher on his shoulder. (*Because I know your skill, and know you haven't practiced in those regions. And because I don't want to test you for biokinetic healing by having you hit or cut yourself. Your doctor would wound me severely with her tongue, if not her scalpels, if she found out I asked you to do that without her supervision. She gave Lars hell this morning for spraining his ankle on the running track, then for trying to run some more on it rather than putting his foot up and resting as a sensible man should.*

(*So. Try it Li'eth's way. Gather the feeling of heat in your hands, then leap it to your target and focus the heat on the tip of the candlewick,*) Sonam said, leaning forward to place a modest, blue-and-white-striped birthday candle on the glass-topped coffee table in front of their seats. (*When you can do that like he can do that, then we will test for biokinetic ability in you . . . and in the meantime, see if you can sense and see auras like he can. That is another skill you do not have.*)

(*Is it wise to pursue trying to learn whether or not I have a Gestalt bond with His Highness?*) Jackie countered.

(*Denying a Gestalt bond is psychologically unhealthy,*) Sonam said. (*Depression, anxiety, even paranoia and other potentially severe psychoses can result—remember, I started out thinking I would go into a parapsychology career before being asked to teach psychic abilities by the League, not just counsel those with gifts. I am fairly well trained in these sorts of things . . . even if I never did get more than a master's degree in it.*)

(*But it doesn't mean we* are *bonded,*) she said.

(*No, but it doesn't mean you are* not. *Practice trying to light the candle as His Highness does it. Practice trying to see auras. And should you pick up a small cut or a bruise . . . practice trying to heal that as he does, too,*) Sonam instructed her. (*I shall see if he can cast images of light and sound, and move small objects, and so forth.*)

(*Being in a Gestalt would complicate things beyond calculation,*) she argued.

He smiled slightly as he rose. (*Growth comes from the struggle to overcome pain. Without pain, there is very little growth.*)

(*You are a very odd Buddhist. Aren't you supposed to be easing pain?*) Jackie accused.

(*I am supposed to teach others how to manage their pain . . . which cannot be done unless you first acknowledge and confront it,*) Sonam Sherap stated formally, giving her a bow. (*It is time for me to retire and relax with a nice book and the last of those little spiced nut-candy things Dai'a made for dessert the day we arrived. She insisted I take the last of them with me to my quarters, since I enjoyed them so much.*)

Sighing, Jackie rose and bowed in return, her from-childhood lessons in courtesy coming to the fore even though she just wanted to stay flopped on her couch and not move, or think, or have to do anything. "Thank you for the counsel, Master Sonam," she stated out loud. "I shall take your advice into careful consideration."

(*Do try to figure out whether or not you are* before *we leave quarantine. This is not a Shakespearian play, and you are not from the families of Montague and Capulet,*) he stated silently. (*And even if it turns out you are, there are ways to avoid all the silly miscommunications and problems that they faced in that tragic farce.*) Aloud, Sonam added piously, "May you be Enlightened into the best path through the troubles and pains that lie ahead."

"May your own burdens be light and easily alleviated," Jackie returned politely. She watched as he left, then dropped back onto the couch, which hissed slightly as the impact of her weight compressed the spongy material of the cushions. She stared at the candle for several minutes, brooding, then rose and fetched a cup from the kitchenette area. Propping the candle more or less upright in the bowl of the teacup, she sat down again, rested her elbows on her knees, held up one hand, and concentrated.

Imagined heat from her body pooled into her fingertips. She didn't feel much of a difference, but from what she had sensed through her link with Li'eth, not much was needed. Concentrating, focusing that intense warmth into—

Smoke curled up from the wick, and a tiny red ember appeared. *Exactly* where she focused that sensation of heat. Shocked, Jackie broke off and sat back, blinking rapidly. The ember winked out, leaving a slightly thicker but still tiny curl of smoke to dissipate just above the cup-propped candle.

"Boot me," she whispered, blinking and staring. She *knew* she hadn't invoked telekinesis or holokinesis. And yet, it had happened. She could smell the candlesmoke, pungent and distinct from the cotton and paraffin wax involved. The pristine white-and-waxed-blue wick had blackened just a bit at the tip.

It. Happened.

Which meant she had to figure out how to deal with it, if it *was* a sign of a forming Gestalt. If it really was . . .

Just boot me off the whole station, right now.

CHAPTER 14

(*Holy yak turds!*)

Shocked, Jackie fumbled and dropped the basket of leafy greens she'd been harvesting in the aquaculture bay. "What?"

Ba'oul and Dai'a, who were on garden-tending duty with her, peered respectively over and under the tiered growth shelves between them.

"Ja'ki? You said something?" Ba'oul asked, his brow furrowing in concern.

Jackie held up her hand to quell him and reached out with her mind. Tapping carefully on Sonam's shields, she waited for a response.

(*Jackie—you just—he just . . . Sorry, my mind is startled. I apologize for my epithet. But . . . His Highness just used holokinesis to show me the auras he was seeing around his friend V'kol—and it startled the annoying female into shrieking,*) he replied. (*I nearly did as well.*)

With the term *annoying female* came an association of blonde hair and green rosette spots. In other words, Shi'ol. Jackie couldn't argue with the description. Crouching, she started plucking spinach leaves off the deck. (*So it wasn't just him sharing his viewpoint telepathically?*)

(*No, it was an actual holokinetic projection. The annoying female is about as mind-blind as the average Human can get,*) Sonam stated. (*It had to be a physical-world manifestation for her to have seen it and reacted.*)

Leaning forward, Jackie braced her head against the nearest support post, groaning softly. (*Great. Just great. Gestalt.*)

(*Most likely, yes.*)

"Ja'ki?" Ba'oul asked again. "Is something wrong?"

Dragging in a deep breath, she tossed the last few fallen leaves into the basket, then picked it up again. "Telepath stuff. It's just a conversation with Master Sonam. He said something that startled me, but it's nothing for you to worry about."

"I like Master Sonam Sherap," Dai'a confessed, reaching up to carefully select several leaves of kale for lunch. "He answers my questions with a lot of patience and loves asking me questions."

"I think he enjoys your company, too," Jackie reassured the somewhat shy outworlder.

"I like most of the people I have met, and the food is . . . good," Dai'a allowed, tipping her head to the side. "But, I miss the flavors and sounds and . . . and faces of home."

"I miss the entertainment programs," Ba'oul said. "I like yours, some are very imaginative and different, but . . ."

"It's simply not home," Jackie supplied without censure. "I do understand."

"No, it isn't," Dai'a agreed. "And thank you. I just wish I knew how much longer it'll be."

This, Jackie had an answer for. She nodded at Ba'oul. "We're sending out ships in the direction of the star systems you and your fellow astronavigators think might be some of the ones in the Alliance. But there are a *lot* of stars out there, and the farther you go from your starting point in space, the more interstellar drift has altered the positions of the exact stars being sought. Even at our fastest, we still have to stop and take corrective readings, and that takes time."

He nodded, eyeing the green onions he was carefully easing out of the fine gravel beds. "There are thousands of uninhabited stars scattered through all the reaches of the Alliance. Most are too small and near-dead to support habitable zones. Not enough stellar radiation for power cells to make cheap energy, very few planets in a stable temperature zone for dome building, never mind other forms of construction . . . and very few worlds in that temperate zone capable of sustaining our form of life, with breathable atmospheres, the right level of air pressure, and natural resources with which to build colonies—we don't ask for much," he added, joking.

"Agreed," Jackie quipped back. She resumed picking spinach leaves.

"It's hard to find habitable worlds . . . which is where interest and resources will be focused. Which is where you will find space stations, starships, lightwave broadcasts, and other easily identified signs of Alliance life," Ba'oul concluded. Changing the subject, he held up a clutch of green tubes ending in small white bulbs. "Is this enough of these baby onions?"

Jackie eyed it. "Add four or five more. Sonam likes lots of onions, especially the spring ones."

A mock-heavy sigh escaped Dai'a. "He is a very wise man, but his wisdom has not saved him from the soul-deep flaw of having onion breath."

All three Humans chuckled at that.

FEBRUARY 14, 2287 C.E.

(*The fourteenth of your month of February,*) Li'eth observed, sharing the thought privately with Ja'ki. (*A day reserved for celebrating romance, correct?*)

(*In some cultures, but not all,*) she sent back. They were in the kitchen, sharing the chore of cleaning up after making breakfast. (*It is a facet of the dominant culture, yes, but there are groups that don't consider the day special—entire cultures—and groups that celebrate different things instead. The Council and the military celebrate it as Love Bot Day, for example.*)

(*"Love Bot" Day?*) Li'eth asked, amused.

(*Nine years ago, the Love Comm Satellite was launched. It was an unmanned probe and communications hyperrelay unit sent to Proxima Centauri, our nearest stellar neighbor, in preparation for manned spaceflight. We sent the unmanned probe to scan the system and send back telemetry on everything it could sense, so that when we sent a manned vessel, it would reduce the risk of running into anything,*) she explained. (*By mass petition, the name of the satellite was given in honor of Saint Valentine's Day, and the first message sent and received was "We love you, Sol." The reply we sent back was, "We love you, too, Proxima Centauri."*)

(*Seriously?*) he asked, blond-and-burgundy brows raising.

(*It was a test message. The important data started streaming immediately afterward. But that's how the probe got the nickname Love Bot. Any probe launched on the fourteenth has since been tested with those two messages.*) She finished stacking the dishes into the crate and sent it into the high-powered scrubber. The sounds from the machine were buffered somewhat by its insulated walls, but it was still noisy enough that even telepathy needed a little mental boost to be heard. (*We can be, and usually are, quite serious as a government . . . but we do know how to relax and make jokes once in a while.*)

(*That's good to know. We have four days a year where we celebrate love. Saint's Love, which is in the spring, Beloved's Day in the summer, Self-Love Day in the autumn, and Stranger's Day in the winter. Saint's Love is for all manner of love—love for no other reason than someone exists—but usually it's a time to celebrate one's love for family and friends. Beloved's Day is obviously for romantic love. Self-Love Day is the day where you are encouraged to do something nice for yourself. And Stranger's Day is the day you find someone you do not know and express some sort of affection or kindness toward them—usually an act of kindness through charity. It's held early in the winter season in the northern hemisphere, so it's often used as the day to give warm clothing to the homeless, food to the hungry, so on and so forth.*)

(*Fascinating. We have Mother's Day, and Father's Day, even Grandparents' Day, but not Different Types Of Love Day . . .*) She shook her head. (*I think I like your idea of celebrating different facets of love throughout the year.*)

(*Bright Stone . . . if we are a Gestalt . . . Saints, that thing is loud.*) Li'eth sighed as the machine shut off for a moment, then switched to jetting hot air over all the dishes to dry them. The noise was reduced to a dull roar during this phase, but still a bit of a roar. (*If we are a Gestalt . . . that will complicate things. A holy pairing is a sacred thing if it is proved and acknowledged. You—and I—would be accounted living saints by my people. We would have a great deal of cultural power under normal circumstances. My mother would be pleased at the honor of having a holy-paired son. But . . . culturally, you don't look like an adult. That would taint the whole experience.*)

(Again *with the mark-means-maturity thing!*) Ja'ki rolled her eyes. Grabbing a cleaning rag, she dampened it and started wiping down the counters while the air jets dried the dishes. (*No offense, but from where I stand, that's just such a . . . a stupid measure of maturity. Maturity has virtually nothing to do with one's looks, save for biological maturity. Mental and emotional maturity are what matter most. The only way those all pair together is by giving someone enough time to grow up physically, and hopefully over that time span have enough learning experiences to mature themselves mentally and emotionally. But the color of one's skin, or hair, or eyes, none of that matters.*)

(*It does to the V'Dan,*) Li'eth countered. He quickly held up a hand, sensing her forming mental protests. (*I'm not saying you don't have a point. You do. But to the V'Dan, that's what maturity means.* Jungen *marks . . . because as you yourself said, that is usually considered the point at which a youth has lived long enough to develop maturity . . . and once they develop the marks, they are* expected *to behave as they look. Mature.*)

(*Impasse,*) she stated. (*Get out the mop and mop the floor. The walls don't need to be wiped down today, I think. Li'eth, I cannot change V'Dan culture overnight. I know I can, but not overnight. But don't even think about asking me to fake marks, like those I've seen in your memories. I mean the ones born without the ability to gain any marks, have to in order to be viewed as adults. I won't do it. I won't do it on behalf of the billions of Terran Humans who shouldn't have to do it, just to be treated as adults by your people.*)

(*Impasse,*) he agreed, moving to the supply closet. (*I'll sweep, first. There are some peelings that need to come off the floor before it can be mopped . . . and what my family will say when they find out I've learned to sweep and mop like a Fifth Tier janitor, I don't know.*)

(*My mother would say, "It's about time!" She and Father insisted we learn a wide variety of skills so that we could appreciate the career of every person we met. Father says if you don't understand what a particular task is like, you're more likely to misjudge how much effort and time it takes and dismiss those who do that work. Every field of work has some importance to it; otherwise, it would not exist and would not need to be done.)*

(*What, even assassins?*) Li'eth asked dryly, dragging the broom across the black tile of the floor. (*That's a field of work I do not think should exist.*)

(*In certain rare cases, it is easier to assassinate a brutal, ruthless tyrant, sparing the lives of many who would otherwise be lost in open rebellion,*) she pointed out. (*Though for true change to take place, it is more likely to firmly take place if the people rise up as a group, even if lives are lost along the way. Especially if.*)

(*You have actually considered such things?*) he asked, pausing midsweep to look at her.

(*Every psi is required to take an E&E course, Ethics and Expediency. And every would-be government official must also take and pass the E&E course. This is not to say that all psis would make good officials,*) Ja'ki allowed, tossing the used rag into the bin that would be taken to the sonic cleaner for cleansing. She fetched another one and started wiping down the flat ceramic cooking surface. (*Nor are all officials psychic by any means. But they are required to undertake similar lessons and train in balancing ethics and expediency. As much as we wish to be idealists, sometimes one must balance the one against the other. Though ethical behavior is always preferred.*)

(*When would it not be preferred?*) he asked, resuming his work.

(*If someone has a weapon that could destroy a bunch of people, and they are holding those people hostage, ethics says that you should try to save everyone, including the criminal holding them hostage. But that way is risky, for he may be unstable and liable to use his weapon at any moment. Expediency says if you can eliminate him and his threat through killing him, you will save a lot of lives by taking his.*) She gave him a wry look over the island counter between them. (*It is never an easy choice, but there is almost always a choice.*)

(*So what does your Ethics and Expediency training have to say about this Gestalt problem?*) Li'eth asked next, curious.

She sighed and switched to a coarse scrubbing pad, along with some cleanser from under the sink. (*Ethics says that, in acknowledging the Gestalt bond is forming, that it exists, I should step down from being Ambassador so that I do not cast any doubts upon any decisions I may make as Ambassador, which could harm the interrelations of both our peoples. There is a potential for a conflict of interest. Ethics also says that if I step down, removing myself from the equation as it were . . . I will put the Gestalt bond at risk, potentially harming the two of us . . . but only the two of us. Removing myself from being Ambassador means having no more contact with any of you, after all.)*

(Not necessarily. What if you stepped down from being Ambassador, but remained on hand to be in the holy pairing with me?) Li'eth suggested.

She shook her head. *(It might still be seen as a point of undue influence. Ethics and expediency both say I should do the least harm, which on the surface would seem to be to step down and step away—hurting just the two of us but no one else. And at this point in the Gestalt, we barely even know each other. The damage would probably be mild, and thus bearable.)*

(But what if your stepping down and going away causes far more harm? To my people, a holy pairing is just that. Holy. Inviolable,) Li'eth told her. *(To rail against it, to tear it apart, is a sin of high magnitude . . . once a pair has been proved to be blessed in holiness, of course. There have been attempted cases of fraud.)*

(Score one for the kinetic inergy machines; they confirm or deny use of actual psychic abilities.) Finished with her meticulous scrubbing, she tossed the scouring pad into the bucket and fetched a fresh rag to wipe down the cooking unit. *(We don't have one in quarantine, but a couple could be scrounged up once we're out to prove/disprove a Gestalt-based ability to lean upon the other person's psychic abilities.)*

(How so?) There was nothing like a machine that could sense such abilities back home. Li'eth knew the communication satellites were of paramount importance, but these "kinetic inergy" machines would also be important, eventually.

(Easy. You put two people in two separate rooms a good kilometer or more apart—since the machines have a limit to the sensitivity of their range—then you have the person who does not normally have that power attempt to do something

with it. Like my holokinesis, which you apparently used when trying to show Sonam what you see when you read auras,) Ja'ki pointed out. *(If it's just you developing a new power, only your machine will register any kinetic inergy being used.*

(However, if it's you leaning upon my holokinesis, and I am very carefully doing nothing, then my machine will show a spike at that exact same moment. But again, that has to wait until we're out of here. MacArthur Station may have a KI machine on board, or it may not, but it'd only have one, and the station itself is not big enough to separate us by enough distance.)

Li'eth could sense a subthought of hers. *(But your Psi League facilities do?)*

(Yes, down on the planet.) She chucked the last of the rags into the bucket, then heaved up the bucket, muttering under her mental breath. *(All the advantages of the twenty-third century, and we still have to do so much by hand . . . but at least it gives us something to do while stuck in quarantine . . .)*

(Wise planners, to occupy both body and mind. That's why I'm not objecting to doing physical labor,) Li'eth agreed. *(On top of accepting it as my punishment for losing emotional control of my abilities, that is.)*

(I know. Getting back to the problem of Gestalt,) Ja'ki sent, disappearing through the doorway to go run the rags and scrubber through the cleaning machine, *(the tangle of it lies in the fact that it is potentially politically dangerous for you and me to allow a Gestalt bond to progress between us. It could be personally dangerous not to allow it, or it could be personally dangerous if anyone on either side decides that verbal objections to our bond aren't vigorous enough and tries to eliminate the side they don't like.)*

(Every time I think your culture is optimistic to the point of naïveté, you assert something highly cynical. You constantly surprise me, Bright Stone,) Li'eth told her.

She sent him a pulse flavored with a heavy sigh. *(That's another thing. My name is Jackie. Jackie, short for Jacaranda, as in the jacaranda flower, bright violet-blue when it's in bloom, can't miss it. Not "ja'ki" as in "bright stone." What in the name of boot polish is a "bright stone," anyway?)*

(Usually it's a reflective crystal of some sort, most often a

type of gemstone that flashes when sunlight reflects off its polished surface, such as a diamond or a quartz crystal,) he admitted. He finished scooping up the debris from his sweeping into the pan, and painstakingly sorted through it, as instructed, to make sure it was all biodegradable. (*The others, their personalities don't match any V'Dan words similar to their names, but you are bright and sunny, yet your ethics are stone-hard. Like a diamond, you are a bright stone. But I am not the only one mismanaging names.*)

(*Oh?*)

(*You call me* Lieth *when you speak aloud. Not* Li'eth. *You are good with the glottal stops—better than most of your people I've met, particularly in formal introductions—but you keep missing a few when speaking casually.*) Dumping the detritus into the composting bin, he put the broom and pan away, and moved to wash his hands. (*Lieth means "beloved," while* Li'eth—*my name—means "Year of Joy." Not that I mind you calling me "beloved," but truthfully, we do not know each other well enough to begin calling each other that, even if we do end up as a holy pair. Gestalt pair.*)

(*Then I apologize for the mispronunciation,*) she replied, giving him the mental equivalent of an apologetic bow.

(*I said I don't mind,*) he repeated. Fetching the mop—which looked nothing like a V'Dan mop, since this Terran version required special, solution-soaked, felt-like sheets strapped across a flat board thing—he started assembling the parts. (*The more I get to know you, the more I like and admire you. Your sense of ethics is very strong, yet it is tempered from time to time by expediency. I'm not sure I could stomach someone who had to be rigidly ethical all the time. If you don't mind me being blunt.*)

(*I don't think I could stomach that, either,*) she admitted. (*Inflexibility leads to things breaking when pressure is applied. The trick is to spring back as soon as you can and make sure you're not permanently bent that way.*) Ja'ki . . . Jackie sent him an image of herself made out of a metal cutout being pulled back partway, then *twanging* upright once more.

He chuckled, applying the mop to the floor. (*You are definitely not a* ja'ging, *a "bright* spring." *Though I'm sure whatever metal you'd be made from would be both flexible and strong.*)

Moving to wash her hands at the sink, she shook her head. (*If I were that strong . . . Damn. I have to do it, don't I?*)

(*. . . ?*) he sent, lifting his head from his work.

(*I won't be going with the rest of you when you leave quarantine and start the tour of the system,*) Jackie clarified.

(*You won't?*)

She shook her head again. (*I cannot. Not and be true to myself. I have to go to the Premiere and . . . and confess that Sonam and I think that you and I are forming a Gestalt. The possible negative consequences have to be acknowledged, as soon as possible. There's no point in doing it while we're stuck in quarantine together,*) Jackie added, drying her hands. The air jets in the dishwasher had shut off; she crossed to it, pulled out the crate, and started putting away the dishes. (*It's too sensitive to just blare it in a vidchat, which can be hacked. As soon as we're set free, I have to go down to the capital and discuss the matter in person.*)

(*As far as uncomfortable tasks go, this one isn't too bad,*) he offered in comfort. (*You don't have to shoot anybody.*)

(*Just my career. It's pretty much my everything. I mean, it's not as if I have a husband or kids to fuss ov . . . oh.*) She stopped midstretch, then absently put the bowl in her hands on the higher shelf and sank back down onto her heels. (*Oh . . .*)

(*Oh, what?*) Li'eth wondered. Her mental undercurrents were swirling too fast for him to sample accurately.

Physically, she kept her back to him. Mentally . . . he could feel her blushing even if he couldn't see it, like a warmth against his own skin. (*Oh, as in . . . if we are a Gestalt . . . then I could have . . .*)

. . . A husband and children.

(*Oh.*) His own face heated. (*That . . . that would be expected of a holy pairing back home, whatever the gender match. That they . . . we . . . would bond emotionally as well as, ah, psychically. Indeed, if the pairing is male/female, then it's expected that the pair should marry and breed, in the hopes that their children will be born with similar powers . . . and usually they are.*)

(*Exactly. Further complicating everything. It is possible that we'd merely become the equivalent of best friends, platonic and so forth . . . but I'm heterosexual, and I'm pretty sure you are, too. At least we aren't in a triad. They're very rare, but the bond sets within all three at the same time. There's no third psi in our group.*)

(*I didn't know three people could bond,*) Li'eth said, distracted by the very idea. (*They can?*)

(*We know of only five Gestalt triads in the history of the Psi League. The last triad died a good eighteen years ago, but I remember reading about it in my classes on psi history. They had volunteered to be constantly biometrically monitored, to try to see if anyone could crack the code on what makes psychic abilities work. They grew old—as everyone does—and one of them had a stroke. A blood vessel popped in his head. The other two, both ladies, each had a heart attack within seconds of him and each other. Then the first fellow had a heart attack a few moments after that . . . and that was that. All three dead, near instantaneously.*)

The undercurrent that went with *that* thought was easier for him to pick up. (*I take it most Gestalt pairings tend to die in similar joint ways?*)

(*If one of the partners is endangered, if it's from an external source, there have been known cases of one or the other teleporting to their partner, either away from the danger, or toward it. Particularly if it can be stopped by them working together on the scene,*) she offered, resuming the unloading of the dishwashing crate. (*But . . . yes. If they've lived in the Gestalt for several years, the odds go up that when one dies, the other dies within hours, if not minutes—decades of being bonded equals death within mere seconds. Less closely bonded pairs can take days, weeks, or months to pine away without their partner.*)

(*How sad,*) he murmured.

(*Theorists propose that, whatever it is within a Human that allows us to tap into kinetic inergy, the brains of two Gestalt-bound psis become entangled on a quantum-like level. I don't know if your people know about quantum theory, but quantum entanglement means that, no matter how far apart the entangled particles are taken, they remain linked. If you can measure the spin of one, you automatically know what the spin of the other is, and vice versa.*)

(*We have similar theories,*) he reassured her. (*But they*

haven't been applied to holy powers, obviously. I'm trying to think of any stories of how holy pairings have died . . . but mostly the ones that are reported are the ones that die in spectacular ways, defending each other, their companions, their homelands . . . they had external reasons for their deaths.)

("*May you live in interesting times,*") Jackie quipped. (*Rumor says it's an ancient Chinese curse, but it's actually from England. The nearest equivalent in Chinese is "Better to live as a dog in an era of peace than a man in times of war."*)

(*Charming. And appropriate, given how we're embroiled in a war right now.*) Li'eth warned her, mopping in her direction. (*The V'Dan, that is . . . and simply by association, you will be, too. Now that the Salik know a separate branch of V'Dan exist, they'll come looking for you. I don't think they'll find you anytime soon, but they'll come looking, and then you'll have to be a man—or woman—living in war, instead of a dog living in peace.*)

She pulled out the silverware from the bottom of the tray and neatly stepped over his mop without looking at it. (*I guess that's a good thing because I'd much rather lie down with a fellow Human than lie down with a dog . . . and I'm sure you would, too.*)

She'd meant it in a lighthearted way, but both of them stilled, suddenly aware of the intimate implications. Of her lying down with him. Cuddling . . . and more. Blushing, Li'eth focused his attention firmly on the floor. The felt pad needed rinsing, so he moved to deal with that, while she sorted the utensils into their spots in the drawers. His task was unpleasant enough, it resonated through their telepathic link, cooling their straying subthoughts. Mostly.

(*I . . . find myself curious about your courtship rituals,*) he finally said. (*V'kol said he'd managed to find his way through your computer networks to data caches of, uh . . . sexuality in action. But while he said everything looked and acted pretty much the way we V'Dan know and . . . uses similar, ah . . .*) He cleared his throat, even though he was speaking mentally, not physically. (*But he couldn't find as much on how you court each other.*)

(*It varies from culture to culture, and it can vary wildly. Some areas still try to arrange marriages for their children; the prospective bride and groom don't even see each other until they marry, though the Council is always trying to enforce our universal law against unwanted or underage marriages. Although underage marriage isn't nearly the problem it used to be ... but we were talking courtship, not just marriage. Some areas, beloveds exchanged "soiled" or "scented" undergarments. Some areas, that's considered bizarre, and they instead exchange messages, or, flowers, candies, little gifts.*

(Most often, the way we find our life-partners is through shared experiences, compatible cultures, common interests, curiosity, and willingness to learn new things, and of course an underlying foundation of similar ethics and principles ... and like a circle, we're back to the ideals behind Valentine's Day,) she observed wryly, smiling as she sorted the different types of spoons that had been used and cleaned.

(Jackie ... what increases a Gestalt bonding?) Li'eth asked her, returning the rinsed felt mop to the smooth-tiled floor.

(Physical touch, actively trying to use each other's abilities, telepathic communication—if the bonded pair have no natural telepathy on either side, then they usually have at the very least an empathic connection—followed by sexual interactions, pure physical proximity, and communication, in that order,) she listed, closing the silverware drawer. Then amended, *(At least, as far as we know.)*

(Wouldn't sexual interactions be listed under physical touch?) he asked, crouching so he could work the mop under one of the counters. If he was going to mop the floor like a servant, he was going to do a good job of it.

(Most of it is, yes, but I'm talking about things like masturbating simultaneously while not touching each other, just communicating. Like during a vidcall.)

He straightened, shocked by her blunt revelation—or tried to, thumping his head into the edge of the table. *"Aiy!"*

"Need an ice pack?" she offered aloud.

"No," he muttered aloud, gingerly touching the top of his head. "It's just a little bruise. I'll be fine." Silently, he said, *(Your people truly have turned this into a science if you've conducted enough studies on how to strengthen a holy pairing that you know which activities are the most potent for it.)*

(*Well, even with the KI machines, a lot of this is maybe observed phenomena, but much of it is still ephemeral, anecdotal, and intuition-based observation,*) she allowed. (*We've created machines that can sense the energy involved, but in over 175 years of experimenting, nobody's been able to create a machine that can generate psychic energies. Whatever it is, it's outside the electromagnetic spectrum . . . and even creating the machine was more of a serendipitous accident than anything else.*)

(*Maybe it cannot create them because psychic energies have to come from a living being?*) Li'eth offered. At her sharp look, he shrugged and straightened, taking the mop to be rinsed again. (*The words of the Immortal have suggested as much—though only indirectly, I'll admit. It's because of this that we've ruled machines do not have souls; there is no way for them to emanate holy power.*)

(*A coincidence, since the League has made a similar ruling: No matter how sophisticated the Artificial Intelligence, it is not alive, does not have a soul, is not truly conscious and sentient, so on and so forth . . . which is what led to the AI War just over a hundred years ago, but that's a whole 'nother story.*)

(*Yes, another story. Let us stick to the one we have . . . though I'm still a bit skeptical of machines that can detect this energy . . . kinetic inergy,*) he corrected himself.

(*That's only fair; I'm having a hard time believing in someone who is immortal,*) she replied, lifting a hand toward him. (*We have plenty of legends and myths about such things, but in reality nobody lives forever. Even the Greys can die. I've killed at least one of them, personally.*)

Li'eth still didn't quite know what a Grey was, but he believed her; Jackie's underthoughts swirled with the sort of grim memories that could only come from causing an actual death. Not wanting her to dwell on uncomfortable memories, he returned the subject to the things they needed to discuss now. (*Never mind about the Immortal, then. We have plenty of time to share lessons in history and religion. If what you're saying is true . . . then we shouldn't even be talking mind to mind, because that will increase the Gestalt.*)

She shrugged, leaning back against the counter by the

sink. (*There were a few case studies of people attempting to resist the Gestalt. Of them separating and going their own ways, or of being requested to stay separate . . . or of being forced apart. Only if the bond was very new were they able to stop its growth for a while. Both sides of each pairing had emotional difficulties, however. Despondence, depression, despair. Agitation, anxiety, paranoia. A lack of joy in what they were doing . . . and in at least one documented case of separated pairs, for all they'd been separated for a good six or more years . . . when one of the subjects died in a vehicle accident, the other went into a decline, eventually suffered a stroke, and died within just a couple months.*

(*But that was in a very lightly set bond. In cases where the bond had been allowed to deepen, prolonged absence only increases the depression, agitation, and anxiety in each half of the pairing.*)

(*So we literally cannot live without each other?*) Li'eth summed up. (*If we are?*)

(*Pretty much. And in every case studied, the farther away a pair gets from each other, the higher the distress. Meditation helps somewhat, and in all the telepathic cases, once a certain level has been achieved, there's no distance at which a bonded pairing cannot communicate—telepathy can ease the distress—but again, it's only been tested by the length and breadth of the Sol System, here. Or rather, by a fraction of the Sol System. I think the farthest apart has been from Earth to Jupiter, and both pairs each time eventually had to be sedated to calm them down until they could be brought back into proximity.*

(*And, of course, there are cases of extreme distress even here on Earth; partners being forcibly kept from each other growing more and more despondent and reckless in their thwarted attempts to reunite. Luckily, the easiest way to fix the problem is to allow the pair to physically touch.*) She gave him a wry smile. (*The military even had two cases of spontaneous teleportation, before they wised up and wrote up new policy to keep Gestalt pairings firmly together. No enforced separation means no distress. Constant contact is all it needs.*)

(*Including telepathy, which strengthens the bond, as you*

said,) Li'eth recalled. He dug the flat mop into the last corner of the kitchen.

(*Exactly—here, if you're finished with that, we can toss it into the sonic cleaner,*) Jackie offered. (*I haven't run it yet, but there's a bleaching agent in the machine that'll help kill whatever muck got onto that. The others are supposed to be busy wiping down all surfaces on their checklists for the public areas. After we're all done with morning chores, Dr. Du suggested a game of charades.*)

(*Yes, that's right, ladies versus gents—and miracle of miracles, Shi'ol agreed to it,*) Li'eth half joked, peeling off the felt and handing it over. (*Dr. Jain will still be asleep, since he volunteered night watch on the antigen cultures, plus that fellow of yours, Brad, declined to play, so that leaves us evenly paired, six and six.*)

(*Oh, he is* definitely *not my fellow,*) Jackie denied flatly. She headed for the laundry room while he put the shaft and head of the mop thing back in its cupboard. (*He hates psis because his betrothed was one, but she dumped him for a fellow psi, and he insists on painting the rest of us with that tarred brush.*)

(*Tar?*) he asked . . . and received a thought-burst, a complex image that started with what tar was—some sort of sticky resin derived from plant life—all the way through a cruel ancient practice of brushing or splashing it on someone, and then smacking them with fistfuls of feathers. (*That . . . is a very bizarre custom.*)

(*It's a punishment not practiced in hundreds of years, thank goodness, but it's too vivid not to keep in mind,*) she agreed. (*Anyway, that is the actually point of not bothering with stopping our telepathic interactions. If we're bonded, then we're bonded. The advantages of being able to share packets of information as quickly and tidily as that—telling you what "tarring a reputation" means—is far more valuable to ensuring each of our respective societies understands each other than preventing a Gestalt bond from deepening.*

(*If we're not a true bond—and all signs so far say yes, we are,*) she allowed, (*then it won't matter if we communicate telepathically because it won't strengthen a bond that does not exist. If we are, then it is an inevitability that the bond will exist whether we want it to or not. The strength of the bond becomes irrelevant in a way . . . though at the same time, we shouldn't engage in any activities that would strengthen it rapidly.*)

(*Which would be physical touch, and telepathy, and . . .*)

(*Not singly.* Stacking *them is "bad,"*) Jackie countered when she caught his undercurrent implication. She put the mental sense of air quotes behind the word as she came back into physical view. The sonic cleaner hummed and sloshed nearby, filling with water, but not nearly as noisily as the dishwasher had. She didn't use a mental image of herself making them, nor did she hold up her fingers to make the writing marks midair, but she kept the sarcasm and sardonicism invoked by them. (*The "worst" kind of physical touch is lovemaking, sex on top of touch. Lots of nonsexual physical contact is also an intensifier—so hand-holding isn't good, true, but full-body cuddling is even worse, almost as bad as sex.*)

(*Jackie, I am getting . . . undercurrents of your thoughts, with that word,*) Li'eth stated, leaning back against the sink counter.

(. . . ?)

(*Sex,*) he clarified. She blushed, the change in color mildly visible on her tanned, markless face, but he pressed on. (*I'm getting the impression you've never really cared for it. Putting aside all the political ramifications—though they are the biggest concern, I agree—is that why you're reluctant to deepen the bond? You don't like lovemaking?*)

(*It's . . . good. I've had good experiences,*) she allowed, folding her arms and leaning against a different counter. (*I've achieved orgasms both on my own and with partners. A few. But . . . it's never really been exciting for me. Attention-grabbing. I'm nowhere near as asexual as Master Sonam—I'd never take a vow of chastity,*) Jackie clarified. (*But when you're a telepath of my strength . . . stray thoughts are very distracting. It takes a lot of concentration and effort to achieve, well . . . true mindlessness. The kind of mindlessness where you can just let go and enjoy a climax.*

But I wouldn't say it's the reason for avoiding physical intimacy with you.) She gestured at him with a hand before tucking it back into the other elbow. (*If anything, all reports of Gestalt pairings, whether between a male and a female, or two males, or two females . . . or even a female and two males, whatever . . . by all reports, the sex is booting* fantastic, *if you'll pardon my crudeness. The bond apparently makes it* easier *to enjoy sexual activities for a strong telepath because it encourages both minds to focus on those activities. Rather than, say, a grocery list, or wondering if you remembered to wash a certain shirt, or . . . All of which has been my problem in the past—the other person thinks of something outside the moment, and the moment gets ruined for me. I'm not a virgin, but . . . I'd need the right partner, really.*)

(*Well, I'm not a virgin either,*) he confessed. (*In fact, it's a required course of instruction, back home. We're given practical sexual instruction as well as theoretical after we've gained our marks and are considered adults. Formal training ensures that a member of the royal family cannot be easily seduced and thus persuaded or even blackmailed into some harmful situation by a putative lover.*)

(*How very pragmatic. I was given hands-on training in how to enjoy sex without projecting my reactions to it all over the place telepathically—or losing control of my other abilities, such as my telekinesis. And how to use it midcoitus,*) she added, smirking a little. (*After all, it's amazing what positions you can taken when gravity and flat surfaces are no longer a concern . . . but that takes a lot of concentration and makes it that much harder for me to achieve a climax. And I'm not into bizarre positions plus exhibitionism if one asks another telekinetic to take over the support system, so to speak, so there's no point in making love like a circus acrobat every single time.*)

(*I'm glad we agree on that much,*) he indicated, with an undercurrent about avoiding exhibitionism . . . though he didn't hide the thread of curiosity about "floating" while making love, either. Dragging in a deep breath, Li'eth folded his own arms across his chest. (*So . . . no lovemaking while we're still figuring things out. No full-contact cuddling.*)

(*Which stinks,*) Jackie admitted frankly. (*I like hugs. Lots of hugs. I just . . . don't get them very often because physical contact amplifies my ability to read thoughts, even if I'm shielding against eavesdropping. If we are a Gestalt . . . I'd want lots and lots of hugs with you.*)

(*I don't get many hugs either because I'm the prince. On top of that, in the last few years, I've been a senior officer, or the commanding officer,*) he agreed. Li'eth couldn't help the touch of longing that colored his underthoughts. (*Just holding your hand has been . . .*)

(*We're not going there right now,*) she asserted, holding up a finger. (*We're not going to accelerate the Gestalt, no matter how much either of us longs for . . . for that kind of physical closeness, comfort, and affection with another person. I'll continue to help you understand our culture, and seek a better understanding of yours, because the benefits outweigh the disadvantages, but for now, that's it.*)

(*I can see you have a very strong inner will.*) He sighed, and received a slight, wry smile in return.

Her reply was broken off by the appearance of Dr. Du, who poked her mottled head into the kitchen.

"There you are! Time for charades, you two," she told them. "Splitting it ladies and gents ensures that there's a chance that a particular cultural gesture will be understood by one of the members of that culture, but with only five players, it's kinda boring. So come on! We're playing for extra desserts and trading off chores, so hurry it up; Maria says she'll be making flan, and I *love* flan, so I'm going to be fighting fiercely to win."

(*No sharing suggestions telepathically,*) Jackie warned him, pushing away from her counter. (*No matter how tempting it might be to help each other.*)

(*Another one of your exercises in self-control?*) Li'eth asked Jackie as she followed the pathologist toward the main lounge.

Jackie snorted, smiling. (*No, I'm like Dr. Du, there; I just want to win a doubled dessert.*)

Amused, Li'eth followed both women out of the kitchen.

CHAPTER 15

By the time she arrived at her sister's townhome in Kahala, Jackie was bordering on exhausted. Parting from the V'Dan had therefore been a matter of staying with them until they boarded the shuttle for the TUPSF *Katherine G*, which would take them on their starter tour around the pre-vaccinated stations around the Sol System. At that point, she had been free to head back down from the station's spindle to fill out paperwork while waiting for her shuttle down to the planet. That, and a decontamination shower to reduce chances of introducing pathogens early, though distribution had already started on Earth with the capital, the islands, and all the major cities. Quarantine had ended a little early, just a few days after the vaccinations had gone into production and distribution well ahead of schedule.

Landing hadn't been a problem, either. Clearing the spaceport-security measures at Aloha City had been, however. Not because of the decontamination procedure—she had all her certification stamps for speeding that up—but because of the throngs of people who had somehow found out that the Ambassador of the United Planets was coming down to the capital. Hundreds had flocked around her as soon as she had gotten past the security checkpoint, all calling out questions, shouting them, demanding them, shyly requesting them, all wanting to know about the "alien Humans" that were here, or going to be here—anywhere on Earth, really. And then she had faced it again on her way into the airport section to catch a commuter flight to Honolulu . . . and on the aircraft, where she had to repeatedly request her nearest seating partners to just leave her be . . . and again coming out of *that* airport's security checkpoint.

Jackie had been forced three times to resort to holokinetically "disappearing" from everyone just to be able to continue her trip . . . which could have gotten her in trouble with spaceport security, but at that point she hadn't cared. It was late, she couldn't stop for a bite to eat at the spaceport, there were too many people trying to talk to her at the two airports, and even her hovercab driver had given her more than one double-take looks. Particularly after insisting on visiting a storage unit first for more civilian clothes before making the trip here. She'd paid him double the rate on the meter with an order to ". . . forget you ever saw either address, so my family and things aren't mobbed by any insane stalkers trying to get to me."

Most people out here on the islands were laid-back, but they were still prone to plenty of curiosity. Thankfully, the driver seemed inclined to obey.

Kit bag over her shoulder, suitcase at her feet, she pressed her palm to the front door's security panel. She hadn't even approached this specific door in the block of five townhomes until the hovercab had lifted off and soared away, engine thrumming quietly. The lock looked new; she hoped her palm-print profile had been transferred to it. The machine sat there silently for a few seconds, making her sweat in the humid warmth of the night . . . then it buzzed and unlocked the front door. A soft chime rang through the stone-and-plaster house, announcing her entry; it accompanied the gust of delightful coolness from the air-conditioning system. Hefting her suitcase handle, Jackie stepped inside, grateful her sister and brother-in-law had kept her profile on hand.

Thumping footsteps came down the stairs. "Lani-Lani, Lani-Lani!" Jackie had barely enough time to set down suitcase and kit bag, and had to brace herself telekinetically as the young girl flung herself at the psi. Wrapping her arms around her aunt's belly, Alani Haunani Bennington squeezed with palpable strength. "Auntie Jackie Lani! *Makua kane!* Aunt Jackie is here! Lani-Lani, Lani-Lani . . ."

"Lani-*Nani*, Lani-*Nani*!" Jackie chanted right back, grinning. She lifted the twelve-year-old off the ground in a bear hug aided by a touch of telekinesis while the door swung shut behind her, relocking itself, then—making her niece giggle—opened her arms wide, letting go as soon as Alani let go. The young girl wafted up and hung in the air, supported half a meter off the floor by her aunt's mind alone. "It's so good to see you, Alani! Look at how big you've flown!"

Alani giggled, happy to be held aloft.

"*E komo mai*, Jacaranda Leilani," her brother-in-law called out, descending the steps at a slower pace, his tone slightly chiding. "You're late; we were tucking the *kaikamahine* into bed."

Alani pouted and crossed her arms; her legs and torso, wrapped in dark blue shorts and sleeveless top, were caught in her aunt's grip and could not move, but the rest of her could. "I'm *twelve*. I *should* be allowed to stay up."

"It is nine o'clock, and you still need a lot of sleep, so you can grow up big and strong like your mama," Maleko Bennington admonished his daughter. He started to point up the stairs, then sighed and flicked a hand. "Oh, *fine*. You can stay up half an hour. *Only* half an hour," he added, as his daughter squealed and clasped her hands together. "Then you go right to bed. Put her down, Jackie. You fly her around the house, she won't go to sleep for hours."

Jackie complied, doing her best to ignore the soft, pouty "*Awww!*" from her niece as her bare feet touched the stones of the floor.

"I'll go surfing with you tomorrow," she promised her niece. "I'll be here for a week, probably—thank you for putting me up, by the way. Sorry about being so late. I was hounded at the airports."

"Eh . . . *aloha kāua*," her brother-in-law relented, giving her a hug as well as the warmer greeting. "Not your fault you couldn't keep your apartment," he said, letting go so he could pick up her bags. "Hm, you're traveling light this time, no bricks packed inside . . ."

"I *can* carry those myself, Maleko," Jackie told him, following him toward the downstairs office that doubled as a make-shift guest room. It had a daybed couch that was comfortable for napping or sleeping, and to get to it, one had to go through the family room.

Her nephew, eighteen and tall and lanky, pushed up from the couch and came around, arms outstretched. "Hey, Blue-Butt!"

"Ahe!" his father reprimanded. "Be nice."

"Hey, Tuna-Breath," Jackie shot back, not at all offended. Jacaranda trees were renowned for their blue flowers, and she'd sort of started the nickname-calling years ago. *Ahe*, which meant "soft breeze," was a play on the slightly similar-sounding *'ahi*, which referred to either the bigeye tuna or the yellowfin tuna fish. She hugged her nephew, until he dug his chin into the top of her head. "Ow!"

"Short squirt," he teased, shifting from using his chin to using his hand, mussing what he could of her braided curls. "You look like you shrank at least three centimeters in space from your last visit."

"And *you* just flunked astrophysics," his father, a biology and life sciences teacher, shot back. "People grow taller in space, not shorter, when their spines decompress from the lack of constant gravity."

"That, and it's more like *you* grew a couple centimeters while I was gone," Jackie retorted, reaching up to ruffle his hair. "It's only been two months, you know." She got attacked again from behind as her niece Alani wrapped her arms around Jackie's waist.

"Are you gonna tell us about the *malihini*, Lani-Lani?" Alani asked, mind boiling with curiosity, forcing Jackie to tighten her mental shields.

"Are we going to get to *meet* them?" her nephew asked more pointedly. "That's more important."

"They're not coming *here*, are they?" her brother-in-law asked with a touch of alarm, looking up from tucking her suitcase and kit bag inside the office door. "I don't want a whole bunch of gawkers trampling all over the lawn."

"Not to the house, though we're thinking of giving them a proper beach *lu'au* so they can experience *casual* Terran life, not just formal tours and such," Jackie reassured Maleko first. She eyed her nephew next. "As for meeting them, Ahe, you might be able to, or you might not. Nothing's completely decided yet. I *can* bring a few special guests to the formal reception at the capital, but I have a long list of relatives all demanding tickets, and only a small handful to give. I might have to do it as a lottery."

Ahe huffed a breath and folded his arms, slouching in disappointment. His father eyed him, then smacked him lightly on the bicep. "Stand up straight. Be calm and composed like an adult, not pouting and pubescent. Alani, you, too. Hyacinth should be home soon; she had a town meeting tonight, about the strangers coming and what it might mean to tourism for the area, to have a bunch of strange Humans from a distant world showing up."

"Town meetings about tourism? Already?" Jackie asked, quirking her brows. "It's going to be years before that becomes common."

"Which is all the more reason, given the general laziness of Earth Humans, to get started on making plans *now*," Maleko reminded her.

"Terran Humans. The Council has decided to call us the Terran United Planets, to differentiate us from the V'Dan Humans," Jackie told him. "Speaking of the V'Dan, I did bring a couple gifts."

"You did? From them?" Ahe asked, raising his dark brows. Like a lot of Polynesian young men in the current era, he had left his hair to grow long, almost waist long, but had taken to trimming his eyebrows to make them look sleek and stylish, not bushy. "I thought they were rescued from some sort of alien prison and didn't have anything."

"Rumor has it they were *naked*," Alani added in singsong.

"They were, and be respectful, both of you. Ahe, you were telling me at Christmas that you still needed something to do for a senior sciences project," Jackie reminded him. "For you and your father, I've brought printouts of medical data—the declassified common stuff, with their permission—from three of the V'Dan, from the dark-skinned *kane* with the blue crescents, Ba'oul; from the dark-haired *wahine* with the two tones of stripes, cream and green on tan, Dai'a; and from the tall blond with the long spiral stripes in hot pink, V'kol."

She started to say more, but felt a touch of telepathic familiarity against her mind. It wasn't the first time today, either; at Sonam's suggestion, she and Li'eth were going to keep checking in with each other, to see how far a casual telepathic contact could reach before actual effort was required.

(*Jackie? The banquet is over, and I've been shown to my quarters. They're very small, compared to quarantine, and I have to share with V'kol and Ba'oul. I could almost wish we were still on the, ah,* Katherine Gee.)

(*They would be. That's the original Lunar Dome you're staying in. On the bright side, you're near the Sea of Tranquility, and the Mankiller Site, so your tours won't take too long getting there.*)

"You were saying something?" her brother-in-law prompted her. "Or did you get lost in your own thoughts?"

"Someone else's," she quipped. "Just a little telepathic conversation. I was about to say I also have written down copies of children's stories from the V'Dan culture for Alani to present a paper on at her school," she said, reaching behind her to ruffle her niece's hair since Alani was still clinging to her from behind in a comfortably slouched hug. Since her niece was simply thinking happy thoughts about listening to Auntie Jackie talking about the alien Humans, the prolonged contact was bearable. "Maleko, I figure you can use the data I brought for your son to discuss microflora divergence and evolution over thousands of years, plus the potential health concerns and consequences, and the steps one can take to ameliorate the risks in your biology and life sciences courses."

"What does ameelee . . . uh . . . something mean?" her niece asked, letting go of Jackie's waist so she could peer up at her father.

Her brother moved around behind Jackie and plucked his equally slender but much shorter sister fully off the ground. Biceps flexing, he curled her belly-up. "*Ameliorate* is a big fancy word that means to make things better. And *raspberry* is a word to—"

"*Eeeee! Nooo!*" Alani shriek-giggled, squirming in Ahe's grip as he tried to lift her belly into range.

"No shouting indoors, both of you," Maleko warned his kids. Ahe lowered his sister out of raspberrying range with a mock-sigh.

Jackie stuck a finger in her ear and wiggled it. "The last time

I heard anything that loud and high-pitched, it was a test of the emergency claxons on the station." She started to say more, but her stomach rumbled and gurgled. "Sorry, but I haven't had anything to eat in about nine hours. Can I raid the kitchen?"

"I'll do you one better; I'll cook you up a meal," Maleko offered. "I was going to anyway, once Alani was in bed. Hya will be wanting something when she gets home."

"So what will you be doing while you're here for a week?" Ahe asked, following them. He had shifted his sister into a piggyback carry on his back, with her hands fisted in his age-worn tee shirt and his arms under her knees.

"Well, I *was* supposed to go with the V'Dan on their tour, but I'm also still scheduled to perform with the Honolulu University Hula Team at the Festival," Jackie allowed, moving to sit on one of the barstools on the far side of the cooking island from the kitchen proper in the back room. The back room was kitchen, dining room, and conservatory in one, built with a greenhouse-like glass wall that let in sunlight—or starlight and citylight at the moment—and had screened window sections that could let in cooling breezes now and then. "So I'll be practicing with them tomorrow.

"That is, in the afternoon," she amended. "I'll be going surfing in the morning since I checked the tide reports, and they looked good for it—and I'll also be spending time sharing the V'Dan language with other polyglots all week long. Some will be official translators for the Department of Transcription Services, but particularly with the other telepaths who know how to do language transfers. They'll be flying into Honolulu all week long. I'll be spending my energy either practicing with the university team, or using one of the linguistics department's conference rooms to teach people the new language. Also . . . a couple days from now, I have a very important meeting with the Premiere."

Her brother-in-law eyed her carefully as he pulled back from the refrigerator, ingredients balanced in his arms, but merely shrugged. "Sounds like a busy start to the week."

"After that . . . it all depends on how the meeting turns out. I'll probably have more stuff to do with the Psi League, and more meetings, and more practices . . . and more *surfing*," she joked, careful to keep her tone light and playful, rather than hinting at any of the gloom of possibly losing her position and her job up ahead. "But most of the later-in-the-week bits depends on my Tuesday meeting with the Premiere. And no, I cannot talk about it."

"But after that, we can meet the V'Dan, yes?" Ahe pressed, his brown eyes alight with eagerness. "I'd be the envy of everyone at school . . ."

"I will make no promises at this time other than that I will see if it can be done," she replied calmly.

Machinery rumbled somewhere nearby, and Alani squirmed to get her brother to let her go. "Momma's home! Momma's home!" As soon as she had her feet on the ground, she pounded off toward the hall that led to the basement garage, calling out, "*Aloha kāua, makua hine!* Daddy's letting me stay up 'cause Auntie Lani-Lani's here . . ."

"Alani, she can't even hear you yet, if she's just now pulling in!" her brother called out after her. Ahe sighed and settled onto one of the other barstools. "Children . . ."

Jackie chuckled. Reaching over, she ruffled his hair. "You were just as excitable at her age, or close to it, when I was voted onto the Council."

He nudged her hand away, she tried to fuss with his hair again, he countered it, and the two of them exchanged mock-attacks and blocks until Maleko cleared his throat. "No fighting in my kitchen."

Subsiding, Ahe and Jackie attempted to look innocent. In the back of her mind, she felt Li'eth reaching for her again. (*Oh! That makes sense—I was wondering about that . . .*)

(*About what?*) she returned.

(*Robert just explained that the name of the ship carrying us, the* Katherine G, *is short for* Katherine G. Johnson, *a scientist who plotted the mathematics involved in your earliest space explorers' reaching this place. I think that's a wonderful thing, naming your military ships after famous persons. Ours are all about sounding tough and fierce, and thus are boring in comparison because there is no deeper meaning.*)

(*Oh, we have ships like that, the* Valiant *and the* Victory *and so forth . . . but any ship with a person's name is usually named after a tough-warrior type or an important civilian whose efforts should not be forgotten. Like how* MacArthur

Station is named after General MacArthur from a major war a couple hundred years back.)

Ahe changed the subject while she and Li'eth were thinking at each other, seizing on what his aunt had said. "Now that's something I don't get. I thought everyone liked you as Councilor for Oceania, Auntie. Even my political sciences teacher said you've been very conscientious, a model modern politician. Why did you step down? Everyone was poised to vote for you. You didn't talk much about it at Christmas when you visited."

Jackie shook her head, fingers intertwining and playing over each other. She answered while watching as his father started paring and slicing several vegetables, two fruits, and some scraps of fish, preparing to fry them up in a spicy-sweet sauce with Japanese characters all over the label. Plum sauce, probably. "That's because there wasn't anything to talk about. Now I know that it was because the precogs were all having glimpses of the coming days, and that my face was present in several of them, working alongside the V'Dan."

"Oh. I suppose that makes sense . . . *Aloha, makua hine,*" he added as his mother came into the room, Alani trailing behind. "Did you have a good meeting?"

"We did." Hyacinth, an older, slightly plumper version of Jacaranda but with a bit more of their mother's features in her face, went straight to her sister and hugged her even before Jackie could stand up from the stool. "*Aloha, kaikaina.* You're here for a week?"

Jackie nodded. She realized her hands were fiddling together, twining and untwining, clasping and twisting. That wasn't like her; she gestured—everyone gestured when they talked—but she didn't normally fidget. Pulling them apart, she dismounted from the stool and embraced her sibling. "*Aloha,* Hyacinth. Yes, I am. I'll be commuting a lot, so I'd like to borrow one of your hovercycles while I'm on O'ahu. It's cheaper to park it at the university or at the airport than a whole car."

"You can take Ahe's," her brother-in-law offered.

"Hey!" Ahe protested, frowning.

(*It is time to sleep, here. I am glad we can still communicate from this far away,*) Li'eth told her. (*The others are good company, but it feels strange to not have you here.*)

"*You*, young man, have midterms to study for, so you have no reason to go flying around town," his mother reminded him, poking her son lightly in the arm. "Taking the school bus won't kill you, either."

(*Agreed. Sleep well, Li'eth,*) she told him.

"It could ruin my social status," Ahe argued back. "Having to take the *bus*?"

(*And you.*)

Not able to let that one go unanswered, Jackie scoffed at her nephew. She was used to multiple conversations taking place on different levels, and even in different languages, though thankfully there were only two to follow at the moment. Or rather, just the one now. "Hardly. Not when *you* have actual data on the V'Dan. You'll be beating off the science geeks with your surfboard by the end of the week. Girls *and* boys."

He blushed. His mother eyed him, then hugged him with an arm, pecking him on the cheek. "Go help your sister get ready for bed."

"Awww, but *makua*!" Alani whined.

"Don't 'but mother' me. Off to bed with you. If you want to go surfing with your auntie in the morning, you will need your sleep," Hyacinth told her child.

"*He'e nalu 'apopo*, yaaaay!"

"I suppose you'll need a proper *papa he'enalu*?" Ahe asked, nudging his sister toward the front of the house and the stairs to the upper floor. "I got that new one for Christmas, so you could use my old 'board. If you're going to use my hovercycle, you might as well use my 'board. "

"I was going to ask you if I could," Jackie agreed. "Thanks, Ahe. *Aloha po,*" she added, as the pair disappeared down the hall.

"*Aloha po*, Auntie!" Alani called back before they vanished from hearing range as well as sight.

Maleko exchanged a look with his wife. The spatula in his hand danced through the diced vegetables, fruit, and bits of fish in the lightly oiled pan, filling the air with a fruity, spicy, seafood scent. Jackie's stomach rumbled again. Her sister moved to fetch her a glass of juice, poured it, and set it on the island counter, and looked at her husband.

He spoke quietly as he cooked, pointing briefly with the

spatula at her once-again-clasped hands. "You hid it well from the kids, but something is worrying you about the future."

"Oh?" Jackie asked, picking up and sipping at the grape juice.

"You normally have a very clear idea of your schedule," he said. "And you almost never fidget with your hands."

Hyacinth sat down next to her sister and tucked her arm around Jackie's shoulders. "Is there anything we can do to help?"

Sighing, she leaned into her older sister, absorbing the pure, loving concern that filled Hyacinth's subthoughts. "Just be my family. I've spent three-plus weeks confined in close quarters with people who don't necessarily like me—and by that, I mean in particular a certain unnamed Terran who dislikes all psis for reasons beyond my personal control—and I just need . . . *normalcy*. The rest of it . . . nobody can help with. It's just something I'll have to figure out how to get through."

"Well, if you're still here next weekend, you'll get plenty of *'ohana* here. My brother and his wife's family will be coming to Honolulu for a vacation," Maleko told her. He turned off the heat and moved to get a bowl from the cupboard, along with a pair of chopsticks and a bottle of soy sauce from the fridge. "Almost too much *'ohana*, if you ask me. *Eighteen* people are coming. I'm glad they'll be staying in a hotel down the road."

"Eighteen?" Jackie asked, eyes widening, accepting the chopsticks and the soy sauce. "That *is* a large family."

"A lucky family," Hyacinth explained. "They've won the third-child lottery for three generations. The great-grandparents had three kids, two of the three had three kids of their own, and about half of those nine also had three kids. Not everyone is coming, but still, eighteen." She hugged her sister again, kissing Jackie on the cheek even as her husband scooped the stir-fry into the bowl and set it in front of his sister-in-law. "We love our own third in the family, though. Lucky you, getting to meet with *nice* aliens."

"Well, it does make a nice change from having to face down not-so-nice ones," Jackie admitted. Settling the chopsticks just right in her fingers, she plucked at the food in her bowl . . . and hummed happily at the flavors contained in that first bite. Swallowing, she gestured at the medley of foods. "I don't know how you do it, Maleko, but *every* time you cook and I get to eat it, it always tastes so *good*."

"Sprinkle a little soy on it, if it's too sweet," he advised. "It'll help kill the chili peppers, too, if you're out of practice."

"Commander Robert Graves is from West Texas," she countered. "He cooked us a Terlingua recipe for *chili con carne* on a dare, five nights ago. I managed to outeat Lieutenant Colvers . . . but then I was smart and dumped cheese into mine, after the first bite."

"Did any of the V'Dan cook?" Hyacinth asked, curious.

Jackie nodded, grateful neither her sister nor her brother-in-law were pressing for what exactly was bothering her, leaving her indecisive about what her schedule was going to be. Food was always a safe topic, anyway. "Dai'a did a fair share of it. She's their life-support officer, and she recognized about half of the plant-based foods, some of the spices, and some of the meats. Because of that, she was able to throw together things that she and the others said were close approximations of V'Dan cuisine . . ."

MARCH 1, 2287
COUNCIL HALL, ALOHA CITY, KAHO'OLAWE

The offices of the Premiere of the—now Terran—United Planets was not a quiet, placid place. Staff members came and went, flowing through the waiting room where Jackie had been directed to sit and rest. Some guided Fellows in their short white vests here and there, a couple times into the Premiere's office but mostly to other locations nearby.

Li'eth's presence wasn't even a whisper anymore. Very early this morning, he had reached out to her, waking her from her sleep while reboarding the *Katherine G.* By the time she boarded her flight for Aloha City midmorning, he was already at the edge of casual contact, sped along by the insystem thrusters of the large patroller. And now that she was here, awaiting a prelunch meeting with the Premiere, he was somewhere halfway to Jupiter. If she tranced, she could reach out to him, but—

"Madam Ambassador? The Premiere is ready to see you now." The aide who had approached lifted the tablet in her hand.

Jackie obediently rose from the chair she had taken not quite half an hour ago. Nervously, she smoothed the flowing skirt of her black, flower-edged dress as she rose—civilian attire, not military, because this was not a military concern. A glance at the clock on the wall proved she was being let in five minutes ahead of her scheduled appointment, which suited her; she had arrived half an hour early on the off chance Callan could see her early. There was no telling how long this meeting would last, after all.

Unlike Jackie, the aide was clad in a beige outfit of trousers and a soft-sleeved blouse, the sort of tasteful outfit meant to help one blend into a background. Given that most of the walls were painted in cheerful shades of cream accented with white, her outfit went well with the décor. Given that much of the furniture ranged from brown to deep beige, the woman's classic Egyptian good looks went equally well. A lot of staff members were wearing shades of beige and cream and brown.

In contrast, Jackie felt like she stood out in her dress, with its flowers painted in bright tropical colors at the flared hemlines of cuffs and skirt. That was supposed to be a good thing, psychologically; black meant seriousness, and bright meant she didn't want this particular problem to be easily dismissed or conveniently overlooked.

It might not *be* a problem—hope springing eternal—but if it was, it needed to be faced and addressed. It was, however, a more feminine look for her, but again that was deliberate; this *was* a personal matter for her even as it was a political issue.

"Will you be wanting anything to drink?" the aide asked as they walked through a final security arch and down the last corridor.

"Not unless this goes over half an hour," Jackie demurred.

"If it does, you'll be invited to lunch, I'm sure."

The Premiere's office lay at the end of a modest hall, in a room nicknamed the Dome. It did not have any windows that were real since it was built into the bedrock of the caldera, but it had a hemisphere of monitors that functioned like windows, set to overlook live images from certain locations around the world. They covered the back half of the room in a wide-paned, faceted curve, with the front of the chamber being more square in shape and painted over in a pleasant mix of blue and cream with a subtly patterned cream carpet underfoot.

She couldn't place the current projected view on all those carefully positioned monitors; it was in the northern hemisphere somewhere, given that it was a nighttime view of some snow-covered, parklike meadow, ringed by bare-limbed trees and some evergreens, what looked like a bit of iced-over river, and a span of many buildings in the distance. Park lamps lit the view, along with the gleaming orbs of the city in the distance, and tiny little streaks of sparkling white let the viewers know that it was snowing a little, wherever the scene might be.

Looking neat and professional in a blue-toned gray suit, Augustus Callan caught her focus on his dome display and smiled as he stood. "Novosibirsk, Siberia. It's been a warm week here in the capital, so I was hoping for a little visual cooling." He came out from behind his desk, switching his attention to his aide. "Thank you, Tangira; unless it's a disaster, please hold all calls and messages for the duration of this meeting."

"Of course, sir." She withdrew and shut the door, leaving them alone. Not completely alone; everything in this office would be recorded, of course, but they were as alone as one could get in politics these days.

The Premiere offered his hand to Jackie, clasping hers in a quick, friendly shake. "Thank you for being patient about not being able to meet with me until today. I've had too many commitments to get out of the way in anticipation of the V'Dan finally visiting Earth, so my schedule has been packed."

"Thank *you* for being willing to see me in private on such short notice," Jackie returned. At his gesture, she took one of the cushioned seats in the conversation corner of his office.

"Considering your original intent was to accompany the V'Dan in order to smooth over any questions, queries, concerns, and so forth, I felt it was worth opening a bit of time in my schedule to see you," he said, settling into the chair across from hers. Crossing his legs, he braced his elbow on the padded armrest and flicked his fingers at her. "Now, what could be so overwhelmingly urgent, or at least important, that you couldn't make that trip?"

"If you will recall, I requested that a psychic-instruction

specialist be brought into quarantine to increase the quality and speed of instruction for the V'Dan prince," Jackie stated.

"Yes, Master Sonam Sherap, who has served with distinction in the League and among the Tibetan Buddhist sect of the Witan Orders," he agreed. "I want to thank you for smoothing over that, ah, diplomatic incident you experienced. It would not *be* diplomatic to accuse the son of a powerful foreign leader of murder, however accidental."

"Master Sonam agrees with my assessment that Prince Li'eth did *not* have conscious control over his pyrokinesis. He has since *gained* some conscious control, though of course only ongoing practice will make it reasonably reliable," Jackie said. "But that particular incident is not why I am here."

"Is this meeting then in regards to the ongoing . . . cultural differences . . . which the V'Dan logistics officer, Shi'ol, has displayed?" Callan offered, gesturing vaguely.

"No, sir. *That* problem cannot be addressed and fixed here on Earth; it can only be addressed by the V'Dan, on their capital world. This visit is in regards to a different potential problem," she told him. At his gesture, she drew in a deep, steadying breath, and relayed it. "Master Sonam has come to the conclusion—and given the evidence, I must concur—that while the odds may seem astronomically against it . . . the odds also appear to be high that Imperial Prince Li'eth V'Daania and I appear to be developing a psychic Gestalt."

He blinked at her, hazel brown eyes dazed for a moment. Their focus sharpened with a soft frown. "A psychic Gestalt? Between the two of you? The odds of that . . ."

She nodded quickly. "Yes, it *seems* astronomical, but both Li'eth and Dai'a, who apparently is one of the most religiously spiritual members of their remaining crew, have confirmed that there were prophecies regarding *us*, just as we had precognitive visions of them. In these forewarnings, it was said that a member of the Imperial family would be involved in bringing about the return of their 'Before Time Motherworld'—meaning Earth, and the Terran United Planets—and that there are additionally subset stories of a 'holy pairing' or 'holy unity' of two strongly gifted individuals bonding together and performing miracles. If one strips away the religious mysticism and hyperbole," Jackie admitted dryly, "it does start to sound like a Gestalt bond is being described by their precogs."

"I see. Our precogs did confirm that the face of the prince, after he revealed his identity, was the one seen in the majority in their visions . . . and that you will be involved in those visions at his side. Apparently in a large number of them," Callan muttered. He dragged in his own breath and let it out on a sigh. "That *would* complicate things, though, if you are forming a Gestalt."

"Indeed. If I were *not* in the position I am in, a precognition-chosen Ambassador to these people," she clarified, "then I would be stuck in the awkward position of having to prove not only that the Gestalt exists, but that my presence would *not* cause any harm or conflict of interest between Terran-V'Dan relations. As it is, I am stuck in the even more awkward position of not only having to prove the Gestalt exists, if it does . . . but having to figure out how *not* to have my presence as a Gestalt member unduly influence or compromise Terran-V'Dan relations."

"Which could ruin relations, or make them seemingly better, only to have accusations of favoritism flung about like the mudslinging of old," Callan murmured, studying her.

"Yes, sir." Just thinking about it made her feel uncomfortable. Saying it out loud . . . she could feel her blood pressure spiking with a touch of adrenaline. Fight-or-flight. Except this wasn't something she could physically fight, and it wasn't something she could physically flee.

He studied her thoughtfully. "You, Jacaranda MacKenzie, have presented me with a quandary. A very awkward quandary. And that's just looking at this from our point of view, our side of things. We don't even know how the V'Dan would react."

"Master Sonam did perform some indirect queries of Dai'a, and I made direct inquiries of His Highness," she admitted. "According to the predominant theology of V'Dan, their Sh'nai faith, 'holy pairs' of two gifted individuals who bond mentally and psychically, are considered to be the holiest of holies outside of their four topmost high priests. To split them up, to interfere in the Saints' divine plans for them . . . or something along those lines . . . is considered anathema.

"But first you have to *prove* it's a true holy pairing," she added, flicking her hand out. She swept it toward herself next, then clasped her fingers. "The problem on *top* of that is because I do not have their *jungen* marks, I will not be viewed consciously and subconsciously as an adult . . . and pedophilia is a serious social taboo, from what I've gathered. Countess Shi'ol Nanu'oc and her reactions to our lack of *jungen* is apparently only the tip of the iceberg, though we won't know how bad the bias is until we send an actual embassy to them."

"Nor will we know how they'll actually treat holy-pairing members until we do send an embassy to them," Callan agreed. He rubbed at his forehead. "The next question is, therefore, are *you* going to be a part of that embassy? In an official capacity, that is. If it is a Gestalt . . . I'm not up to date on what all that entails, but I have heard that it's a bad idea to separate such a pair."

"It can lead to increasingly severe problems, yes," she agreed. His gaze dropped from her face to her lap. With one elbow on an armrest, the other clamped at her side, that meant her fingers were . . . twisting and fiddling right where he was staring. She hadn't been aware of it until now. *Is this a sign of mere nervousness? Or is it a sign of impending agitation from Gestalt-separation?*

"If I remember correctly, there is another problem with Gestalt pairings," Callan added. "In specific, separating them for great distances or great lengths of time—I am not sure which—causes extreme stress on the bond." He looked up at her again. "If you are developing a bond, aren't the V'Dan on their way to Jupiter at this very moment? To the *New Lunnon* Mining Station? How many kilometers away is that?"

That was an annoying question. "Measuring distances in kilometers is useless at intersystem distances, Premiere. They are in the middle of an eight-hour trip from Earth to Jupiter at the *Katherine G*'s preplanned cruising speed. I lost easy contact with the prince not quite an hour ago. He will still be within my telepathic range if I should concentrate or even trance, however."

"I presume you know how to *confirm* whether or not you have a Gestalt?" Callan asked her. He tapped the end of his armrest. "Any decision made will depend upon that."

"There's a KI machine on the *New Lunnon*, sir," Jackie confessed. "I looked it up. It's a new station, an upgrade from the other five circling the gas giant, and their infirmary therefore has every bell and whistle they could want, so they can serve all the stations in the area for any possible condition. With Master Sonam already going along on the tour as a hedge against the prince's psi getting away from him again, he can operate the machine, instruct the prince on displaying his power while I am in a League facility being quiet, then we can switch, with him doing nothing while I attempt to use *his* gifts."

"The mark of a Gestalt being the ability to lean upon and use the other half's powers," the Premiere murmured. "Can you?"

She looked around, stood, and crossed to a low bookcase near his desk. Ignoring the falling nighttime snow, she plucked a tissue from the dispenser and returned to her chair. Using up some of her nervous energy, she twisted the soft paper sheet into a tight column, held it up . . . and focused heat into the tip of it. Between one breath and the next, the twisted bit of paper caught fire . . . exactly where she focused.

Callan blinked. Jackie extinguished the flames with telekinetic pressure, and offered him the brown-and-black-edged bit of tissue. He held up his hand in polite refusal, shaking his head slightly. The scent of burned paper spread out, slowly fading in the air currents of the large, temperature-controlled office. The flame hadn't existed long enough nor been large enough for the automated fire system to have a nervous fit. Then again, this wasn't a space station; this was a place where fire could be escaped by simply running outside. Crumpling up the tissue, Jackie settled back into her seat. "I've also tested myself for biokinetic ability. Dr. de la Santoya confirmed that I am able to heal a minor laceration at two and a half times my normal, natural speed. That's already the threshold for a Rank 4. With more practice, I could do a lot better. For obvious reasons, I am reluctant to experiment further."

"You have no interest in moving on to a paramedical career?" Callan asked, his tone amused.

She didn't have to guess why. It was well-known that Jacaranda MacKenzie was a dedicated public servant. Jackie smiled wryly. "No, thank you, sir. I have no interest in subjecting myself to more pain than absolutely necessary. On any given day, that is. I *will* train this new ability since it is my responsibility to master it, but I'm in no hurry to do it all at once; nor do I care to learn more than the basics of nonpsychic first aid."

"Forgive my ignorance, not being a psi, but . . . If you are aware that you are now a biokinetic and a pyrokinetic when you've shown no aptitude before now, what is the purpose of the two KI machines?" Callan asked, frowning softly in puzzlement.

"If Master Sonam can confirm that Li'eth is not using his abilities at the exact moment that I am leaning upon him, *but* the KI machine still reacts as if his gifts *are* being triggered, then that is definitive proof that we are in a Gestalt. It will prove I have not spontaneously developed two extra abilities. Conversely, he could test for telekinesis, which Sonam says the prince can already use to the tune of shifting around small screws and bolts, and if I am not using my abilities here on Earth, but the machine registers kinetic inergy activity emanating from me, then it's double confirmation. He would be leaning on *my* gifts. If this is merely a display of innate new abilities, there would be no simultaneous confirmation of KI activity at the opposite location."

He tilted his head, giving her a dubious look. "You want him to be at *Jupiter* for this test."

"That would be the soonest we could be tested, yes," Jackie confirmed.

"Surely the distance involved . . ." he muttered, mulling it over.

Jackie shook her head. "Distance is irrelevant. The theory is that Gestalt pairings are quantum entangled. Tests performed here on Earth at distances of thousands of kilometers have confirmed that both psychic activity and kinetic inergy emanations take place in both locations simultaneously. Entangled molecular research has been tested at thousands of light-seconds apart, as well as thousands of kilometers. I don't see why it should be any different for psychic gifts if it is a Gestalt bond."

"Except the two of you could be out of range, if you already cannot communicate telepathically," he pointed out.

"I said we could not communicate *easily*, Premiere," Jackie had to correct him. "And the bond is still in the lightweight stages. If and when it sets, telepathy can work simultaneously—as proved by hyperrelay communication—between Gestalt partners over insystem distances. Astronomical units. Or at least between Earth and Jupiter in previous pairings . . . which is as far as *this* pairing is being separated. If nothing else, we can try it, and if we receive no confirmation, we can wait until the V'Dan come to Earth and try it again at a more reasonable separation distance—thousands of kilometers instead of thousands of light-seconds, to be absolutely sure one way or another."

"If I remember correctly . . ." He lifted a finger and pointed it at her. At her lap, and the hands twisting and fidgeting just above it. "Signs of agitation are also a possible indicator. Yes?"

Jackie glanced down reflexively. Bits of white tissue speckled her mostly black lap since the colorful flowers rising from the hemline stopped at about knee height. Her hands had not only crumpled the tissue but had essentially shredded it from twisting and worrying the material. If she stood, bits and pieces of mangled facial tissue would scatter over his office carpet. She blinked and looked up at him, remaining carefully in place. "I apologize for the mess. I don't normally fidget."

"You didn't seem the type to fidget at our last meeting," he told her.

"Is there a recycling bin . . . ?" she asked. He pointed to a set of low cabinets with flap-style doors near their tops. Jackie carefully gathered up all the little pieces with her telekinesis. Adding the remaining bits of mangled tissue from her grip, she sent it all wafting to the bin he indicated. "Thank you. Again, my apologies."

"For mangling the tissue? Or for mangling your job as our first Ambassador in over a century?" he asked wryly.

"Yes." She didn't clarify. Didn't need to clarify which, really.

"If you're *not* a Gestalt . . . then this is all just newly found abilities and cautious speculation. Your coming to me to 'confess' is the appropriate action to take, with very little harm done. An appropriate, honorable action," he added. "I could continue to keep you as Ambassador, because your integrity is without par. And if you are in one . . . your honor as a public servant is without question. You have placed the welfare of the

United Planets above your personal interests . . . because if you are, I *could* have you stripped of all rank, authority, and power."

"If you did that, sir, it would only reduce any possible accusation of undue influence in either direction. It would not completely remove it, and it would not solve the conundrum of the two of us being a bonded pair. If you ban me from his presence, it is a known fact that parted Gestalt partners suffer emotional difficulties, even at the earliest, lightest levels of bonding. Past a certain threshold, these difficulties can endanger the health and well-being of both partners. And at a certain critical threshold . . . spontaneous teleportation.

"If you send him back to V'Dan—once we find it," she allowed, "but send him home without me, there is no telling what would happen. Agitation, teleportation, perhaps even grievous physical harm. Nobody yet knows because the farthest we've ever parted a pairing was Earth to Jupiter . . . which is why I knew we could be parted in relative safety for a limited span of time."

"The severity of that harm would be difficult to gauge without knowing just how far along in the Gestalt the two of you have grown. You haven't . . . ?"

She shook her head. "Not even a physical touch once I realized it was a possibility. Telepathic contact, yes, because there has been an ongoing need to explain unique aspects of each side's culture. It is the grease needed to keep the gears rolling, rather than risk any bout of ignorance damaging the diplomatic machine."

"Yet you risked removing yourself from 'easy' telepathic range to come here?" he asked sardonically. "It *is* good you haven't taken this anywhere fast or too soon, but you in essence have abandoned your job as a diplomatic envoy."

"At this point, they need a tour guide more than they need an Ambassador," Jackie defended. "They're busy learning about us, not busy trying to figure out what sort of things we could trade with each other. Besides, Master Sonam did go with them," she pointed out, flicking a hand skyward. "He is just as adept at delivering contextual thought packets as I am. He's not the polyglot that I am, but I did give him V'Dan, and he can act as a Terran cultural interpreter."

"I am grateful he volunteered for that. It is needed right now," Callan agreed. "Particularly to smooth over any more possible 'incidents' before they can get out of hand. But later on . . . If you were to remain with the group, if we sent you to these people's home system, even if you weren't Ambassador at the time, your constant 'packet sending' could be construed as undue influence. We don't know how the V'Dan would react to that."

"I know, sir. I am literally reading the thoughts of their leader's thirdborn offspring," she agreed grimly. "They don't know our rules for ethics and integrity. Until they come to understand us and have faith in such things . . ."

"Yes. They certainly don't know how closely you in particular follow such rules. Not perfectly—no one is one hundred percent perfect every single day—but closely, yes," he praised briefly. "Under simpler circumstances, I think I could in good conscience send you with your rank as Ambassador intact . . . except you also do not know how strongly this Gestalt bond could affect *your* judgment via his influence upon you, not just yours upon him. Nor do we know how much bias they will infer through their own cultural lens on that point. It could be a good thing, it could be a bad thing. We just don't know."

"To play devil's advocate, sir? On a positive note?" she offered. "If I went as Ambassador and performed properly, responsibly, with honor and integrity intact, it could *show* them more than mere words that we are who and what we say we are. A display of Terran maturity to counter the lack of fancy marks on our skin. By being up-front about the fact that we know about the Gestalt, yet you—the Terran government—have faith in me to perform my duties honorably and ethically in spite of the Gestalt state, it would show them stronger than words that we *are* mature because we *act* mature."

"Devil's advocate on the downside, it could be seen as an act of hubris, of arrogant belief in your self-control," the Premiere pointed out, waggling his hand. "It's a gray area, and it depends very much on how the V'Dan will react. Which, again, is something we simply do not know."

"Which is why I am here, trying to figure out all the possible permutations and ramifications, and not making any unilateral decisions, sir," Jackie told him. "I cannot make this decision on my own. It isn't my own decision to make, for all that my life may be permanently affected by it, one way or another. More than my own happiness and comfort—or even His Highness'—is on the line, here. The future of the Terran United Planets in the interstellar arena is on the line.

"I may still barely be able to fit into my original uniform, but I was a soldier ten years ago, I still am a soldier to some degree today, and it goes against my every bit of instinct and training to put the United Planets needlessly at risk." She looked down at her hands, which were twisting mindlessly together once again, and sighed. Untwining them, she brushed back a few stray wisps of her hair. That aide had worn hers in a stylish, off-the-shoulder cut, low fuss, low muss. Maybe it was time to change her own waist-length mess. Except she didn't know if Li'eth liked short hair or long—*Wrong line of thinking, Jackie.* "My opinion is potentially biased and thus potentially compromised."

"Except you are aware that it could be compromised, and have taken steps to ensure others are apprised and are able to assist you in making good decisions." He studied her, falling silent for a long moment. Her hands started to twist together again, drawing his gaze once more. "I can literally see how much this is bothering you."

Pulling her fingers apart, Jackie flipped them in a shrug. "I don't know why my hands are doing this. It could be for any number of reasons." Reclasping them, she tried to keep them still. "Devil's advocate number three . . . I could be a *positive* influence on Terran-V'Dan relations. As could His Highness. The bond would force us by its very nature to get along, to cooperate and seek out understanding and effective compromises from and for each of our respective governments."

"You know, we haven't had to face down more than minor pockets of rebellion and attempted independence for far too many years," Callan stated out of the blue.

". . . Sir?" Jackie asked, confused by the sudden change in subject.

"There is the question of just how *closely* aligned Terran and V'Dan interests might become. They apparently have settled several star systems, whereas we have barely begun exploring our nearest stellar neighbors, never mind establishing colonies . . . though it would be a deep relief to have the room to expand, and not have to limit our population growth anymore," he murmured. "But would they insist upon absorbing us, as a one-system entity? Would we—*should* we—instead insist that, as *we* evolved here, we are the parent and they are the child, and consider having them join *our* government?"

That made her shake her head, letting out a half laugh. "Oh, I doubt that'd ever happen. They're *very* proud of their nearly ten thousand years of history, and their idea of a one-world government, ruled by a specific bloodline, has apparently lasted more or less unbroken for nearly five thousand years. They're very proud to be monarchists and aristocrats and . . . and reciters of lineages thousands of years long. In comparison, we're merely a meritocratic republic of common plebeians—I may be wrong, but I don't think merging the two governments is going to happen the moment we meet up with them."

"No, but from what we've learned already of their technology, they are in many ways more advanced than us. Merging may be an option for swifter integration of various benefits. It *is* an option to be considered," he stated.

Her fingers were wringing each other again. Jackie stilled them, hope for her chosen career rising a little. "I . . . wouldn't need to know and consider that possibility if I *weren't* going to be the Ambassador . . . would I?"

Callan shook his head. "I cannot make that decision right now. I agree with you that this is a decision, a situation, that is too important to handle lightly or casually. If you are Gestalt, it would not be good to separate the two of you permanently. The long-term consequences are either a severely depressed or possibly dead Imperial prince—as well as how it would affect you—but we won't know for a while.

"For now . . . so as not to cause undue speculation in the population . . . we will assert that you came back to Earth to get in some practice for the Merrie Monarch Festival and to deliver to me a personal evaluation of the V'Dan and the possible impacts of this First Contact situation. Which you will do more formally later in the week to the whole Council," he told her. "This will be after you have attempted to establish the Gestalt all the way from Jupiter. For that matter, you will undergo a second series of testing when he comes back to Earth, under full Psi League supervision."

"Understood, sir. In the meantime, my status is . . . ?" she asked.

"'Innocent until proven guilty,' of course," he offered with a soft smile. "I see no need at this time to alter your status as our Ambassador. You are still acting with due diligence despite all the possible negative ramifications to yourself and your situation . . . which is *all* we can ask of each other, as civil servants. We do not expect perfection, but we are expected to at least try with a whole and willing heart." Rising, Callan offered her his hand. "Thank you for bringing this information to my attention, *Ambassador.* I look forward to your next report and any revelations it may contain."

"I'll make sure to schedule another meeting before I leave the Council Hall, sir," Jackie agreed, rising and clasping hands with him. It . . . felt wrong to be touching him. Not because of anything on his side of things; he was an honest, honorable Councilor, with solid reasons behind his being trusted and liked by so many within and without the Council Hall. But because of all this talk of Li'eth and . . . a chain of thoughts that brought up a good question. "Sir, should I let things progress at a natural pace, or attempt to delay the maturation of any bond that may exist?"

"What does your sense of ethics tell you?" the Premiere asked, arching a brow.

Jackie sighed, since there was only one answer she could give in good conscience. "Delay it."

"And that is why I trust you to be an effective Ambassador. For now." He gestured toward the door out of his office, indicating their meeting was now over. "Please try to keep up the good work, Jacaranda."

"I'll try, sir," she promised, though she realized her hands were once again wringing and twisting together.

CHAPTER 16

Strangers. Surrounded by strangers. Gawking, juvenile-looking strangers. Li'eth sat in the chair indicated by Master Sonam, putting up with the wired cap and the matching forearm bands. Ever since parting company with the Ambassador, he had felt increasingly adrift. Lost. Abandoned in the wilds of this backwater system with its "top-of-the-line" space station that still required rotation to create the illusion of gravity underfoot.

He had nothing to anchor himself in the alienness of these Terran surroundings. All of the equipment was new; the only impressions he could feel from their past were senses of them being crafted and installed, bland, utilitarian memories. On board the military ship that had brought him and the others here, it was similar, nothing but creation, installation, and spacefaring soldiers going about their daily routines. Nothing felt truly familiar. Nothing felt safe. He didn't like this sensation creeping into him, that he was adrift with no safety line, no anchor, nothing he knew how to cling to for relief.

Nearby, a communications unit snapped to life. He couldn't see the screen comfortably from where he sat, but he could hear the voices. ". . . Sonam, you old son of a psi! How is it *you* go into retirement and land a cushy, prepaid tour of the system, while I'm still stuck on the ground?"

The aged monk moved over in front of the screen, smiling warmly at it. "Ah, Jonesy, if we knew how the twists and turns of pure chance could evolve in advance, then it wouldn't be chance, now would it? And I know you enjoy a lucky gamble once in a while," the red-clad monk stated. A soft sound—a growl?—came through the speakers. Sonam sighed, a smile in his tone. "And you do still owe me sixty from our last card game, if I remember right . . ."

"Aren't you monks supposed to refrain from gambling?" Jonesy—whoever that was, someone male from the sound of the tenor voice—demanded.

"I was not yet a monk when we last played cards. How is dear Jackie doing?" Sonam added, moving back to the machine that was supposed to monitor Li'eth's holy powers.

Jackie? Bright . . . Blue Flower, he corrected himself. He had seen pictures of jacaranda trees in bloom, and they were very lovely. He twisted in his seat, hoping to glimpse her in the monitor, but there was just some dark-skinned male on the screen.

"She's already hooked up and has been testing each of her rankings."

"Any signs of improvement?"

"Actually, yes." Jonesy's report had the monk straightening from adjusting the controls on the KI machine next to Li'eth. "Her telepathy has strengthened half a rank. Considering her age and her constant, advanced use of it, she shouldn't have gone up even a tenth of a rank, once past her late twenties."

"*Half* a rank, already?" Sonam murmured, surprise in his voice.

"What does that mean?" Li'eth asked, worried over the way the two men remarked on these Terran rank things. "I know you rate your abilities based on their kinetic inergy output, but I was told those abilities aren't completely static. That with time, and training . . ."

Sonam nodded, checking the fit of the armbands. "Yes, yes, with time and training, you can improve up to four ranks beyond your normal peak—just as you can have muscles of a certain size and strength as a normal Human, but with time and training, turn yourself into a bodybuilder or a master martial artist, all covered in bulging muscles and fast-striking tendons. But, Li'eth, when we speak of that, we speak of those who are like *you*: untrained or incompletely trained."

He tapped Li'eth lightly on the nose, smiling, then adjusted the cap with a soft frown. "This would be easier with shorter hair . . . thank you for unbinding it, by the way. The braid confines the locks, making it harder for the electrodes to touch the skin—we would normally just aim it at you, but I wish to eliminate the possibility of my own kinetic inergy signals being picked up, never mind those of anyone else on this station. That means using the cap and armband sensors. I will also not be able to touch the machine once it is working since sometimes the silly thing picks up inergy emanations right through the casing."

Li'eth frowned and rubbed at his nose. The man was kind, but he was not used to being casually touched. "So if we're not talking about someone untrained . . . ?"

"We usually talk about youths in these circumstances, since most psi abilities emerge in puberty; the stress of hormones, the final connections being made in our neural networks, that sort of thing. If they are given training right away, and are diligent about it, if one starts at the age of, say, fifteen and keeps exercising that ability on a regular basis, not just a casual one . . . peak strength will be achieved by age twenty-five. Or say we have someone of your age, a man in his early to midthirties who blossoms unexpectedly—usually out of a trauma of some sort—it would take anywhere from three to seven years to get you up to full strength in each and every ability. In your exact case, someone who has never had true training, it would take the same amount of time if you are diligent.

"But in every case, in every single one," Sonam lectured with an upraised finger as he moved back to the machine, "unless they suppress their gift and refuse to use it—and it *will* atrophy if you don't, though it will never completely go away— it will hit a peak *natural* ability within roughly five years of emergence and standard, diligent training. That is if you only use it casually, and have had that basic, standard instruction. It will improve from that natural, lazy baseline if you are diligent and consistent in exercising and training your gifts.

"*You* have not been properly trained, and so your rankings will be all over the place, unsettled for the next few years to come. It is the act of consistent, ongoing, willfully intensified training that can move your mental muscles from 'realistic and reasonably fit' to 'muscleman' of the mental world . . . which, for a prince, would give you a distinct useful advantage as you go along through your princely life."

He flicked a switch, and Li'eth felt the machine next to him come to life. It took him several seconds to realize he was trying to read its history, and that the machine was reading his *attempt* to read it, which in turn was altering what he was sensing from the thing. Experimentally, he tried narrowing his search to just the armbands, to the history of the . . . people who had unpacked it and installed it in its cupboard on the station, one of them a shortish woman with shortish, curly hair, earrings in her lobes, a gray coverall with hints of a peach-pink shirt underneath—Gatsugi colormood hyper-in-the-face-of-tension, oddly enough—and she was thinking about . . . meat loaf? Meat loaf on that night's menu.

"Hm . . . Fascinating. Whatever you are doing, that is a Rank 8 ability. What *are* you doing?" Sonam asked him.

"The woman who unpacked this machine," Li'eth told him. "She had medium brown skin, gray coveralls, a . . . light peach shirt. And she was thinking of meat loaf on the menu for the evening she put this machine into the cupboard."

Sonam smiled for a moment, warm and proud. "Ah, your psychometry, your object-reading, has been activated. And I am pleased to see it is around the rank I thought it might be. Now, clear your mind, young man," the monk added somewhat sternly. "Deep breath, relax your attention, relax all thoughts . . . think of nothing but a single flower from your homeworld."

"I'm signaling Jackie to calm down and power down on this end," Jonesy stated through the still-open monitor.

"Clear your mind . . . think only of a single, simple flower . . ."

Li'eth closed his eyes. He summoned up the thought of a crysollam, a delicate, many-petaled flower. The innermost petals were thin and transparent, sending the warmth of the sun's light down to the seed chamber to warm the burgeoning seeds once they were fertilized; the outer petals were a more shimmery, translucent white. He had seen designs on clothing and some actual images for a *chrysanthemum* flower that were somewhat similar in overall shape, but its petals were solid, opaque, and apparently came in different colors.

Those colors were gold, and red, pink and yellow, purple, and even a few that were blue. Blue flowers that rose up on stems with dozens, seemingly hundreds, of slender, individual petals, not slender trumpet blossoms with lobed ends that dangled from tree branches, the flowers that Jackie said were what she was named for, the delicately inked ones surrounding the blunt, odd eye symbol on her shoulder, which in turn were surrounded by three rings of shark teeth, which she had said were a symbol of her protecting the Earth three times from Grey invasions, and yet she was the one who was back on Earth, safe and surrounded by everyone while he was stuck here on a gas mining station of all places with a bunch of strangers and he just wanted to reach out to her . . .

Sonam touched his nose. "What are you thinking about?"

The touch and the question interrupted his chain of thought. Li'eth opened his eyes. ". . . Flowers?"

"A bit more than flowers, I'd think," Sonam chided lightly, pulling his hand back. "You were thinking about something that spiked the KI meter just now."

"Sonam, what was the exact time stamp on that spike?" Jonesy asked through the commlink.

The monk moved over to the machine. "Since we have not established what time it is there versus what time it is here, I will simply say that it was . . . thirty seconds ago . . . *mark*."

"We had a spike at that point, here. What was he thinking about?"

"Yes, what *were* you thinking about at the end of your meditations, young man?" Sonam asked.

Li'eth felt his face heating up a little. He hesitated on actually admitting it, though.

"Were you thinking about . . . her?" Sonam asked, his brows raised but no trace of censure anywhere in his tone or his expression. Li'eth nodded slightly, embarrassed anyway. "Yes, that would do it. I registered a Rank 5.4 at that point. Your end, Dr. Jones?"

Jones? Isn't his name Jonesy? Or . . . oh. Nickname. Right.

"It was 3.4 on this end. A mere two ranks in differentiation would be fairly strong for this early on—presumably early—in a bonding," Jones relayed, his tone suggesting he was distracted. "According to what Jackie told me, they haven't done anything more than moderate amounts of telepathy and mild hand-holding. They should be at a three-rank separation at least, not merely two."

"They did engage in a three-hour mutual-language-transference session," the monk pointed out. "Then again, even for this early, she shouldn't have gone up half a rank," Sonam replied. He touched a couple controls on the machine, then instructed, "Initiate test 3a on subject one."

Li'eth didn't know what that meant. He leaned forward a little, catching a glimpse of the lever. It wiggled, then swayed up along its arc a little. "Three plus a bit . . . ? Is she thinking of me?"

Even as he said that, hope rising inside, the needle jerked and swayed upward, past five.

"And there it goes, he's thinking of her," Sonam sighed. "Calm yourself, Your Highness. What is your favorite rock?"

"My . . . what?" Li'eth, distracted by the non sequitur, realized after a second that the needle had dropped back down. He wasn't thinking of—

"Type of rock. Crystals, sandstone, granite, hot glowing lava . . . your favorite kind of rock," Sonam interrupted him.

"Ahh . . . crystals. Quartz," he added, dredging up the Terranglo word for it. "Simple, common quartz. Smoke quartz, the gray-colored ones. And amethysts, when they're found in a big geode. I like how they look like a cave from some magical children's tale."

"It's 3.4 on this end," Sonam reported.

Crystals were easier to talk about, except . . . *Bright Stone*. Only she wasn't bright stone, she was blue flower, indigo, bluish-purple . . .

". . . And another spike. You really need to control your thoughts better, young man," Sonam chided mildly. "Jonesy, implement test 17b on subject one. What temperature of water do you prefer to bathe in, young man?"

"Water . . . ? Fairly hot if I'm to soak. For a shower, I prefer to ease into it, mildly warm, then increase it toward the end. Unless it's a cold day," he added honestly. "If the bathing chamber isn't warm, then the shower needs to be steaming hot to compensate."

Sonam chuckled. "I think we all have that feeling. I know that as I get older . . ."

(*Li'eth?*)

(*Jackie!*) He reached out to her, seizing her mind in his as he would have seized her hands had she been physically there. (*I've missed you. I need to—*)

(*You need to calm down and focus your thoughts,*) she sent to him, her mental fingers shifting to his mental shoulders. Somewhere in the real world, outside his head, Sonam was making observations, but Li'eth didn't care. He strained to listen to Jackie even though her sending wasn't the happiest thing in the world. (*We both need to keep our minds focused during these tasks. I have missed you, too, but . . . I am under orders not to accelerate any bond between us.*)

(*I . . . I realize that. But . . . I feel like everything is too foreign without you here to reassure me,*) he confessed, shifting his own hands to her waist. (*Like I'm on a spacewalk outside a ship, but without a tether or a maneuvering pack.*)

She smiled, one hand touching his cheek. It wasn't an entirely happy smile. (*I know. I'm showing some signs of anxiety, too. But you must be strong. Meditate, strive to calm yourself, and follow Master Sonam's testing instructions as exactly as you can. Now, I am going to end this conversation, and then . . . I think Master Sonam will ask you to speak telepathically with him. Do not reach for me. And do not worry; when the tour is over, we will be together again. There won't be such a great distance to try to bridge. Can you let go, so we can begin?*)

Hesitating, Li'eth pulled her into a hug. A mental embrace, knees to shoulders, arms spread across her back. She returned it after a moment, and for one beautiful, peaceful mo— something *zapped* through him, jolting him back into his own physical body. Blinking his eyes open, Li'eth found the monk withdrawing an odd, ridged rod.

"Mild electrostatic shock wand," Sonam enlightened him. "It's useful for pulling students out of a trance without giving them any actual damage, just a little zapping pain to ground them back in their bodies." He nodded to a tray on a cart that had been rolled over. On the tray were some gauze pads, a scalpel sealed in a packet, and antiseptic spray. "Are you ready to begin demonstrating your biokinesis?"

A sigh escaped him. Li'eth nodded. This, he was familiar with by now. Sonam had forced him to practice on himself both in quarantine and on the journey here.

Biokinesis, according to Terran techniques, was often trained in a major medical facility, where the students worked under close supervision to ". . . encourage the body to do what it would normally do on its own, which is to heal itself and return to good health." Injuries and illnesses often made the job harder for the tissues in question to handle everything; the energy to heal had to come from somewhere, and if the injury or illness was severe, it meant resources got tied up, slowing down the healing process. Biokinesis sped that process by giving extra energy to that system, among other things, but like every gift, it had to be practiced to strengthen and speed the ability.

Reaching for the antiseptic spray, a move he had performed dozens of times in the last few weeks, Li'eth squirted it onto the top of his forearm and started rubbing it into his skin. He suspected he wasn't going to be asked to do anything other than shallow cuts, the sort one got from a pet *g'at*, or *cat* in Terranglo, but the top of his arm would hurt less than most other locations. It just needed to be cleansed of the potential for infection, first.

MARCH 5, 2287 C.E.
ALOHA CITY, EARTH

". . . But that means we're still not sure what the rank cap will be, since Li'eth's own abilities haven't reached their fully trained potential. It's highly probable that both of us may turn out to be Rank 16 or even Rank 17 as telepaths when acting individually. An increase of two ranks, on my part . . . which, when you get into the teens, is pretty powerful, since the scale is somewhat logarithmic."

"Somewhat?" Callan asked. "I'm getting thirsty. Would you like some water?"

"Yes, please," Jackie agreed.

He rose to fetch two cups of water from the dispensary unit in one of the square corners of his office. Today's wall-windows at the other end were showing a view of Gibsons Beach, South Isle, New Zealand. The great, surf-rounded rocks near the cliffs contrasted with the fine gray grit of the sand near the waterline. A man and his dog were running along the firm-packed sand halfway to the surf's edge. It might have been past sunset up in the Hawai'ian Islands, but daylight still reigned down there, and the slanting summer sun of the southern hemisphere looked refreshing.

Pulling her fingers apart, Jackie murmured her thanks as she accepted the water. Today's dress, or rather, a skirt and sleeveless top, was another black ensemble, this time decorated here and there with hibiscus flowers. In an odd coincidence, one of the blush-pink flowers on her outfit went with the Premiere's shirt, though his slacks and the jacket thrown over the back of a nearby chair were a muted purplish gray, not basic black.

"By somewhat logarithmic, what did you mean?" Callan repeated, expanding his question as he reseated himself across from her.

"The power scales aren't a simple base-ten progression, each following number being ten time the value of the number before it. I'm not an expert, but I believe the way it was described back in my classes years ago is that it's more like a base-six logarithm tied to a foundation of base-eight mathematics. Which I didn't study," she clarified. "I was more into actually using my gifts, learning new languages. Practicing the occasional feat of holotelekinetic legerdemain, but mostly focused on being a polyglot translator like my father."

"Did you ever think you'd follow in your famous ancestress' footsteps? The stage-magician ones, not necessarily the Lunar ones," he clarified.

Sipping on her water, Jackie shook her head. "Father says I look more like Jesse James Mankiller than I do Mother—Hyacinth, my sister, looks more like our mother than I do—but while I entertained the thought a brief couple of times, holokinesis has always been more of a hobby. Languages and learning about cultures, that has been the big fascination. Some people keep trying to tell me I'm wasting myself on civil service when I could be earning a fortune as a stage magician, but that's just not what I want in my life. I have it,

I train it, I use it from time to time, but it doesn't define me. And it shouldn't have to define my choices in life."

"Well, it looks like you could be learning and speaking a whole slough of languages and cultures, soon. We can't exactly endanger the emotional and mental well-being of the son of the head of an entire major government by denying him the presence of his Gestalt partner," the Premiere allowed. "At the very least, you will go to V'Dan in one capacity or another, because of that."

"Thank you." She didn't take offense at being placed lower on the priority list, the way he put that. It was the truth, after all. Terran government hadn't been parted from autocratic-government styles nearly long enough to have forgotten how territorial those autocrats—monarchs included—could be over the well-being of their nearest and dearest. She looked down into her mug, plain white on one side, stamped with the seal of the Premiere of the United Planets Council on the other side. "However, the big question remains. Am I the Ambassador, or am I just a tagalong?"

"Oh, never just a tagalong," Callan dismissed, briefly lifting his hand in denial of that thought. "At the absolute very least, since you've conducted yourself ethically, I could arrange to have you listed as an official translator for the embassy. Or even appoint you to the V'Dan government as an adjunct linguistic-and-cultural translator, offered to their royal court or whatever for their edification."

"*Don't* play with my career aspirations, sir," Jackie said flatly. She set her mug on the table and rose, pacing. It was bad enough she missed Li'eth. That brief telepathic connection, which required trance-concentration, hadn't completely eased her separation anxiety. She caught herself midpace, stopped, breathed deep, and apologized. She didn't have to be empathic to know what she had said was inappropriate. ". . . I'm sorry. I *know* you're not playing with them. I know without scanning you in any way that you are honestly trying to offer viable suggestions."

"Is your career more important than the well-being . . . ?" He trailed off when she turned to face him sharply.

"No. Ask for my resignation, and I will give it. As I gave it to your predecessor," she reminded him. "Rosa McCrary?

Last Premiere? Your mentor? I've already been through this pain once. I can endure it again."

"Pain . . ." He narrowed his eyes, studying her.

"Failing to serve. I honestly thought she was right, that enough of my constituents had complained that I should step down, that they had *legitimately* complained. That's a failure. A failure of the trust my people placed in *me*," she added, thumping her chest with her fingertips, "to represent *them*."

She flung out her hand at the monitor-windows. At New Zealand, which only failed to be a part of Polynesia because it had a large enough population base to be its own province, with its own representative in the Council. Technically, the Maori, the original inhabitants, were a part of Polynesia. Many had called her an "honorary Councilor" for her willingness to stand up for aboriginal rights and needs, too, as a neighbor to their Councilor's constituency. But that was then. This was now . . . and now she had her place as an Ambassador, the ultimate in representatives, being *toyed* with . . .

No, not toyed with. Stop thinking like that, she ordered herself sternly.

"So, what am I going to be? A mere translator? Less than that? I . . . I'd be free to be a woman," she added, gesturing at herself, at her outfit. "I could have a love life. Something I never thought I'd bother with. But I wouldn't have a career. I don't *know* if I'd have a career. We don't know how the V'Dan view such things. Particularly not at their highest levels of society." Her hand slashed out at nothing, at everything, and she started pacing again. "We have the word of a handful of people, one palpably biased against us, one with legitimate reason to be biased *for* us, or at least for me . . .

"But no matter how many times His Highness reassures us of this or that, it still isn't *official* policy. It's . . . wishes and hopes and dreams. It's all ephemeral. Nothing exists anymore—it's like being set adrift on the sea without sails or paddles or . . . or outboard motors . . . !"

"Jackie. *Calm* yourself," Callan stated, rising to his feet. He held up his hands. "You are becoming agitated."

"I can't help it! I don't *want* to feel this way—do you think I *want* to feel this way?" she demanded. "I did *not* go on that trip expecting to . . . to . . . to *bond* with *anyone*!"

"Miss MacKenzie, please—"

"Oh, so now it's *Miss* MacKenzie! I'm not the Ambassador anymore?" Jackie asked, flipping her hand at him, anger and anxiety, especially anxiety, rising sharply within her.

"Please, you must calm down . . . what was it that message said . . ." the Premiere muttered half to himself.

"Calm myself? When my entire career and aspirations for public service are on the line, and you can't even call me by my *title*, giving me an *anxiety* attack—"

"What was it . . . what was . . ."

"—and now you're *talking* to yourself like a half-witted *lunatic*, and you want *me to calm*—"

He darted in and bopped her on the nose with his fingertips. Jackie reared back, stopped midspeech in sheer shock at the nondamaging, nonbruising, non sequitur attack. Callan eyed her warily, straightening slowly. Behind him, the door opened, and a security officer peered cautiously inside.

"Are you alright, sir?"

"You booped me!" Jackie exclaimed in a near whisper.

"Yes," Callan said, addressing her even as he held out his hand to the agent at the door. "That's what the message one of my aides received from Master Sherap said to do if you got . . . hysterical."

"You *booped* me."

"Yes. On the nose. He said if I did that, it should break the feedback loop of your . . . your agitated emotional state," the Premiere repeated.

"Sir, is everything alright?" the security guard repeated. There were three more crowding the doorway behind him.

"Well? Is it?" Callan asked her.

"Yes, of course! . . . Why are you even in here? Surely not because of me raising my voice a little," Jackie added tartly.

The guard eyed her and pointed with a gloved hand to the right and to the left. "We registered a KI spike, ma'am, on the machines monitoring this office. We just want to know if the reason behind it is a threat to the Premiere, ma'am."

Jackie looked around her . . . and realized she was still levitating a few papers, a couple pens, a potted plant . . . and the coffee mugs and coffee table. "Oh. Sorry." Carefully, she started lowering everything neatly back into place. "I . . . I haven't done that in a while. At least I didn't *drop* everything when you booped me."

"I'm rather grateful it was just peacefully levitating things, and not flinging them around the room, myself," Premiere Callan stated, adjusting his shirt cuffs.

"That's because I *don't* throw things when mad," Jackie replied, setting down the coffee table and their mugs of water last. She hadn't even spilled a single drop of their contents, just lifted them into the air with the tension in her mind. "In fact, that was the hardest lesson I had to pass, learning to throw objects at people with the intent to harm. I almost couldn't do it . . . until the military assigned me a combat instructor who *wanted* to harm me. It turns out my telepathy was getting in the way, since the moment I got into range, I was 'pretesting' them for hostile intent. I . . . broke the poor woman's leg when she chased after me with a knife in her hand and the free-willed intent to carve her initials three inches deep in my inner thigh. A direct threat to my femoral artery and the very clear possibility of killing me."

"What did you fling at her, to break her leg?" Callan asked.

She looked at him. "I didn't. I broke her leg directly so she couldn't keep running after me."

"*Sir*, is everything okay?" the guard repeated for a third time.

Callan faced him. "Everything is okay. Everything is perfectly okay. Everything is okay."

All four guards relaxed, accepting the coded way he spoke. The lead guard nodded. ". . . If you say so, sir. Sorry for the interruption, ma'am," the lead one said. "Just don't spike the monitors again. We'll have to come back in again because that's in the rules and regs, ma'am."

"I'll try to keep myself calm and under control," Jackie told them.

They withdrew—and someone else came running up. Tangira quickly reached them, a datapad lifted in her hand. "Sir! Premiere Callan!"

Callan sighed and beckoned her in. "What is it?"

"Sir, they've *found* it," the aide reported, handing over the tablet before swiping a hand through her dark curls to tidy them from her run. "*Aloha 22* found a *known* system based on the

V'Dan astrophysics descriptions. All the planets their pilot Ba'oul could remember, *and* signs of space stations and starships. They were spotted in the general configuration sketched by our guests for both Gatsugi and K'Katta design. No sign of a V'Dan vessel, but we've sent the images to the *Katherine G.* The V'Dan pilot and gunner, the ones who have worked the hardest on describing their known systems, are currently in a sleep cycle, but they are being woken up to help confirm it."

Jackie lifted her chin, anxiety warring with relief. The latter, because it meant Li'eth and his companions would finally be able to go home . . . eventually. Anxiety, because her own situation was still up in the air. "They've already described how they line-of-sight navigate, then sail from system to system, one system at a time, so this means *we* can trace their path from star to star how to get to the V'Dan homeworld."

"Yes, and we already have all the markers for doing *that* straight from their pilot," Tangira agreed. "*Alohas 1* through *8* are on standby, ready to jump out and start laying a trail of hyperrelay probes along the known vectors, which Leftenant Ba'oul gave us. They're just waiting on your word, sir, and Project White Pebbles will forge a trail to the V'Dan homeworld."

"White Pebbles?" Jackie asked, quirking her brows. "The project has a name, now? I thought it was just Project Find V'Dan."

"To the public, that's what it is. Internally, it's got a few extra layers. The name comes from the old Hansel and Gretel story—the first trail they laid was of white pebbles so they could find their way back home again," Callan told her. "Only in our case, we're the birds laying the pebbles for the V'Dan to find their way home again."

"Didn't those same birds eat the bread crumbs on the second trip?" Jackie asked, wary of the project name's analogy.

"Yes. If they try to 'eat' the pebbles, they won't get very far," Callan said, hands resting on his hips. "They'll vanish like bread crumbs. All five V'Dan are still amazed and awed by our near-instantaneous communications system; that much awe means it's currently our biggest bargaining chip. We may be ethical and honorable, but we won't give away our biggest assets for free. Do you have an objection, *Ambassador* MacKenzie?"

She folded her arms across her chest. "*Am* I?"

"For now," he allowed. He held up one finger. "But this is a situation that is still fraught with a *lot* of potential land mines, political and cultural. A lot of unknowns on the V'Dan side of the equation. We know now that you are a Gestalt, and we know that *we* know what that means . . . but we still don't know how the V'Dan government will react to it. Which means *I* cannot make this decision a permanent one. Not alone."

"*Boot* me," Jackie whispered, closing her eyes as she caught the loud thought. "You're putting it to the whole Council, aren't you?"

"Fellowship and all. When the prince comes to Earth, and has had a tour of the planet, he and his companions will be welcomed in person to the Council Hall . . . and that is where the two of you will be cross-questioned. You can reassure us he's an Imperial prince, and he can reassure us, and his companions can as well . . . but even if *they* believe it's the truth, even if it *is* the truth . . . we *don't* know if he's going to be a favored son returning home safe and sound, a prodigal son returning home with lingering problems to be overcome in spite of the joys of having him home again, or an entirely unwanted headache returning home. Particularly with a bunch of culturally perceived children in tow," Callan finished.

"Great." She pulled her fingers apart so that she could rub at her brow. Her head hurt, as if a great pressure was building behind her skull. "And when he returns . . . what do I do about the bond, between his return and his . . . our . . . appearance before the Council? Do I join them? Do I stay away? Do I join them but stay away from *him*?"

Callan flicked his hand around his office. "Given your little display just now, I think I shall follow Sonam Sherap's advice. I would like you to go to the Psi League University and stay in their testing-facility quarters. If you get agitated again, I want them able to shut you down. Make you fall asleep. I'll have word sent to the *Katherine G* to have watchers set on the prince as well. That, I am told, is the correct procedure for separated Gestalt members who get agitated beyond reason. Beyond nose-booping."

She nodded, lowering her gaze. "It is. Master Sonam knows all the steps and all the tricks for controlling his students." Her head hurt worse now, though it shouldn't have. She hadn't taxed her telekinesis in any way. Pushing against the pain, she thought through the ramifications. "You'll need to have this explained to the prince in advance . . . and have him appoint their pilot as next-in-command. Make it an official order. You don't want Leftenant Nanu'oc in charge with her captain sedated."

"No, we don't . . . and it has thankfully already been suggested, when I realized on your last visit that you were showing signs of distress. Focus on calming yourself . . ."

(. . . *no you don't! You don't do that! You don't touch me, you don't talk to me, you get away from me! I know you did something to her, and I—*)

Surprised by the anger, the paranoia behind that mental shout, Jackie blinked twice . . . and then collapsed at the feel of something stinging her in her cheek. She reached up with eyes that no longer saw the Premiere's office even as she fell. A mix of the Premiere, his aide, and people who weren't even there shouted at her, lunged toward her, but then it wasn't *her* fingers that pulled the dart away from the face that wasn't *her* f . . .

CHAPTER 17

TUPSF *KATHERINE G*
INSYSTEM SPACE

"Good morning, sleeping princeling . . . no use hiding under your eyelids; all this fancy Terran biotech is telling me you are now wide-awake."

Li'eth cracked open one eye, feeling disoriented, dizzy. His brain was finally used to translating Terranglo, so to hear his friend and chief gunner speaking in V'Dan confused him for a moment. He answered in Terranglo, still trying to focus on his friend's pink-marked face. "Not wide-awake . . . head feels like the ball in . . . a guanjiball game."

"Well, hopefully you won't go off again like you did a couple hours ago," V'kol stated, switching to Terranglo as well. He held up a pair of fingers. "Just two hours, so it's not actually morning, but you were asleep for a while. They dosed you with enough anesthetic or whatever to put you out for four to six hours, but that red-robed old fellow and this machine over here," the leftenant stated, patting the KI machine, "both say your biokinesis has been chugging along like mad, burning right through the stuff."

Li'eth grunted and lifted his hand to his cheek. He remembered pulling something off his face, small, metal-and-fletched, red with a long . . . "Needle. They shot me."

"*Ya.*"

"Why?" he asked V'kol, who was busy touching something on a tablet in his hands.

"You started getting paranoid right after we were woken up with the good news. You mentioned having suffered some nightmares about being in those damned Salik pens, then ranted about our hostess being stressed. Then you started accusing people of deliberately harming her," his friend added.

Li'eth frowned, trying to remember what good news his friend meant. Seated in a tallish, rolling chair by the infirmary bed, V'kol had his boots up on the bedcovers. Clean boots, of course; they hadn't worn them on any planet yet, and all corridors they had seen so far were regularly swept and mopped. Except for the three Luna-surface tours, but those had involved pressure-suits with their own footwear, and the Lunar dust had been left in the airlocks.

"Master Sonam wasn't around at that moment to bring you down out of your . . . whatever it was . . . your little fit, so the Terran crew had orders to tranquilize you," V'kol added blithely.

"Tranquilizer . . ." That would explain the dizziness, and the trouble he had remembering everything. It would come back as his head continued to clear. Patches of the drug were being processed in his bloodstream in uneven amounts . . . which that monk had told him might happen, regarding his barely trained biokinetic abilities.

"A bit crude compared to Salik stunner weaponry," V'kol acknowledged, "but effective. Oh, and you're officially on medical leave, and I am officially in charge of you. Ba'oul isn't available, so it fell to me. Shi'ol's madder than a dry *trask* right now. The Terrans have told her flat out that they do not, and will never, accept her in a position of authority. She's fuming in her quarters."

"Where's Ba'oul?" Li'eth asked, pushing up onto his elbows with rising worry. "Am I stuck here? Where's Dai'a? What are they doing to—"

V'kol reached over midspeech and pushed on the prince's nose like it was a door chime. He even made a little "*ping-ong!*" noise, grinning as he sat back. "I am officially under orders to 'nose-boop' you, as they call it, each time you start to get agitated. Master Sonam's in the bathroom, or he'd have been here on hand when you woke up. Something about fiber and an elderly digestive tract."

Easing back onto the bed, Li'eth let out a sigh. "As a distraction method . . . it is undignified. Effective, but undignified. What's on the tablet?"

"The bridge has set up a communications link on standby with a similar room on their main world. Your little paranoia attack—which they don't blame you for; they say it's all just part of being a Gestalt pair—caused your lovely, if unmarked, partner to collapse when you were tranquilized."

His eyes snapped open. "Jackie . . ."

"She's *fine*. Relax. They'll be . . . ah, there we go." Kicking his feet off the bed, he reached up and dragged over a monitor screen on a smooth-floating arm system. The screen had gone from black to blue with the silver-white logo of the Terran Space Force. "Connecting you to her observation lounge in three, tw—whoops, off by a second. Greetings, Ambassador," V'kol added, angling his body so that he was beside his recumbent captain. "How are you feeling?"

"Peachy. Black eye from when I fell. Or . . . oh. Possible Gestalt sympathetic biofeedback echo," Jackie muttered, using a jumble of words that Li'eth half understood. She had a soot-eye, her right one . . . which was on the side Li'eth had been shot.

"Is my eye sooted, too?" Li'eth asked V'kol, touching his cheek. He couldn't see his own face; there were no reflective surfaces nearby, but he could feel with his fingertips. The scratch from the tranquilizer dart was more or less gone, but bruises often took longer to fade, even with holy healing. With biokinesis. V'kol nodded. So did Jackie.

She spoke, recapturing his full attention. "Because of the severity of the link—I dropped literally when you did—we are now authorized to communicate every day telepathically to maintain . . . psychic emotional stability. Since you're already most of the way to *Peregrine* Station, I am being shipped out to the L3 Array tomorrow, and will meet up with you there. So it'll just be a few more days before I rejoin the tour group. Can you stay calm until then?"

Embarrassment at his behavior made his face feel a bit hot. "I . . . I *think* so. I didn't *mean* to—"

She held up her hand palm out, Terran style, forestalling him. It was so strange to realize he was literally on the far side of this system's star from her, yet they were able to communicate pretty much instantly with each other instead of waiting tedious minutes, even hours, for lightspeed communications to transmit painstakingly composed messages.

"It's alright, Li'eth. We *do* understand. Even *knowing* what could potentially happen, even I got a little stressed and accidentally floated several objects in the Premiere's office. The guards were a bit nerve-wracked by it when it set off their KI monitors."

V'kol frowned in confusion and pointed at the machine to which Li'eth was once again wired. "You mean he has one of these things attached to him?"

She chuckled and shook her head, which had its own cap applied over her loosened hair. The sound was somewhat relieving to Li'eth, to know she could be happy instead of stressed, but not quite enough to alleviate his anxiety.

"You don't *need* the cap or the armbands to detect KI activity, period. The machines can be aimed in a direction and just . . . pick up general psychic activity. It's one of the many security measures you don't see going on behind the scenes in any major government office. When I was a Councilor, they pretty much had to shut mine off, send in adjustment techs, and aim them *around* my office to keep my own abilities from triggering the things—my telepathy was constantly aiding my linguistic capabilities in the course of my duties, which meant they were constantly setting off the monitors. Oceania is the one representational district on Earth with the *most* languages spoken, period. Africa as a continent has more languages overall, but it has many Council provinces dividing them up into considerably smaller units, linguistically."

"Jackie . . . you said we could communicate telepathically? To feel calmer?" Li'eth asked. The door to his infirmary room slid open, and Master Sonam stepped inside. He smiled warmly at the prince, happy and tranquil as ever.

On the screen, Jackie nodded. "I'll be reaching out to you shortly, but I wanted to wait until the anesthetic is out of your system. I woke sooner than you—I wasn't drugged, just suffering from the backlash of your brain reaching out to my brain, and then feeling the backlash when yours was shut down very quickly. You, ah, *will* forgive them for their precaution, yes?"

"You must accept my own apologies," Sonam added, approaching the bed. He had to do so on the side with the KI machine since the gunner was more or less occupying Li'eth's left. "I was not there to calm you down and reassure you that what you were feeling was not actually what *you* were feeling. I should have been there."

"What do you mean, it's not what *I* was feeling?" Li'eth asked, wary.

"He means it's a combination of what *both* of us were feeling," Jackie interjected. "I was getting agitated—I'll tell you later—and that made *you* agitated, which fed back to *me*, and I sort of shoved it back onto *you*."

"It wasn't just you," Li'eth told her. "I was having bad dreams about . . . about our time on the Salik ship, waiting to be eaten alive. I think that may have leaked to you, despite the distance."

"It very well could have been part of the cause," she allowed. "Anyway, that's when you were tranquilized, with a fast-acting anesthetic to ensure you couldn't trigger any of your gifts. You're still relatively undertrained, and on the tight confines of a spaceship, pyrokinesis is *not* something to take lightly. The military have their orders: *All* pyrokinetics serving on board Space Force vessels know that they can be tranquilized at any time if it looks like that gift is going to trigger. Other psis with potential ship-damaging abilities also know that they can be tranked.

"In fact, a few pyrokinetics have been known to shoot *themselves*, after warning the others," she added, tipping her head. "Same with metrokinetics, because they can mess with the atmosphere, and the same with electrokinetics, because they can mess with the equipment keeping everyone alive. Telekinetics, sometimes we're under watch, but not as closely as the pyros. Usually, though, psychics with those abilities aren't allowed on board any ship until they can demonstrate a high level of self-control, but we all know things can happen. Things can just . . . get out of control, even with the best of intentions," she reassured him. "You aren't being blamed for a perfectly normal reaction to a very stressful situation. Which will be remedied, I promise."

He believed her. He could even almost *feel* her, just looking at her. Li'eth realized in that moment that he had slowly lost his trust in everyone around him over the last few days, thanks to her absence and the distance separating them. "Telepathic contact will . . . Will it cure this anxiety-attack thing?"

Both she and Sonam nodded. The monk spoke. "I hope you will forgive me, but this is literally the farthest apart we have parted a Gestalt pairing in twenty-three years, so I should like to continue to monitor the two of you with similar machines as time goes along. You won't have to wear them when we're in transit, of course, but I will be seated at your side to 'boop' you to get your attention refocused."

Li'eth held up a finger in warning. "There will be *no* nose-booping when we return to V'Dan."

"I'm sorry, but there may still be some nose-booping, for *both* of us," Jackie countered. "Though Master Sonam will not be going along."

"Riding along at insystem speeds is as fast as I care to go. I'm not sure that hyperspace is safe for someone as old as I am," the monk added, sighing. "I am told it forces the body to live a little too fast. I have lived a little too long for that. Nothing I do anymore is fast. Except think."

V'kol chuckled. "If we can get you passage from Earth to V'Dan on one of our nice, safe, faster-than-light ships, then you should come to V'Dan anyway. Nobody ages too fast on one of those, no hunger or nausea or disrupted biology . . . and I think you would get along with my great-uncle just fine. You remind me of him."

"Which one, Jo'kol, or that funny fellow, Do-gri?" Sonam asked.

V'kol grinned. "Do-gri, of course, though he is a bit funnier than you . . ."

(*Reach for me, Li'eth,*) Jackie called out to him, distracting him from the byplay of the other two males. On the screen, she was still smiling, but she was lying in her propped-up bed with her eyes closed. Trancing to reach him over the gulf of physical distance between them.

Closing his own eyes, Li'eth reached for her. The noises of Sonam and V'kol chatting and chuckling faded. He opened his inner eyes onto the dark, vast chamber lit by that sourceless light from above, the first place they had met mind to mind . . . and stepped straight into her arms. Pulling her against him, Li'eth wrapped his arms around her clearly adult body. Not in some sexual embrace—though he was glad she *felt* adult to him—but in a purely relieved hug.

(*I don't like being apart from you. I feel like I can't trust anyone when you're not nearby, reassuring me on everyone's motivations and meanings . . . but I fear for what that means when we head to V'Dan.*)

(*It means you're in highly unfamiliar territory, which spikes your adrenal instincts, which aggravate your Gestalt-parted anxiety levels,*) Jackie soothed him. (*It's simple biochemistry working against you. I'm considerably more calm about the people and things around me because they are familiar. I am in my own territory. When I get to V'Dan, I'm probably going to have an equally hard time trusting everyone around me if we're not in frequent contact, reassuring each other. I may also be calmer about it because I am more aware of what's going on because of my many years of training and experience . . . but I'll still feel the stress. It's not a case of me influencing you, nor will it be a case of you influencing me. We're both too strong-willed for that. Too dedicated to each of our peoples.*)

(*I don't know when we'll be going, but . . . I am anxious to get home. Every day we delay here is another day the Salik could be attacking a system in force, whittling down its defenses. Landing troops on our colonyworlds, and those of our Alliance neighbors.*)

(*Oh!*) She pulled back a little in their head-space hug. (*Tangira—the Premiere's aide, one of them—she came in just before I collapsed, said they found a known Gatsugi system.*)

Li'eth was so startled by this, he pulled out of their link almost all the way. "Ba'oul! Is that why he's missing?"

V'kol and Sonam broke off their conversation to blink at him. The monk leaned in with a kindly look, and said, "We're not a part of *that* conversation, whatever it is. You'll have to use a few more words to clarify what you mean, young man."

"The star charts—the Gatsugi system," he added, turning to V'kol. "They found one?"

"Yes. They found the star system with what looks like the domeworld mining colony of Paper-Skies-Heavy-With-Lead," his third officer . . . technically second officer, with Shi'ol suspended . . . relayed. "Ba'oul has been busy helping plot and correct courses from there through known territory to the Empire for the last two hours, trying to triangulate. If they hit two, maybe three more in the chain that they can recognize, then they'll be able to coordinate that with the star maps we tried to delineate. That's why *I'm* in charge of you. Ba'oul's a bit more important than you to these people. Right *now*, at least."

"I am *happy* he is a bit more important than me right now. I'd thank Shi'ol if she could find our way home," Li'eth muttered

"Just so long as you don't kiss her in thanks," Jackie ordered over the commlink, reminding them it was still open. "Now get back in my head. We need at least ten minutes, maybe twenty, to calm our link. Sonam, you'll watch the monitors on that end? You'll know when it's safe to come knocking on our mental walls."

"I shall stick to a nose-boop, once the biofeedback numbers look close enough to normal. You're both still very stressed, so the more time you spend in the link, the better. I suspect I should take advantage of this opportunity as much as I can right now, before I lose all such privileges when His Highness returns to his people. Even if I do get to go visit them some day before my death, I suspect I won't be able to boop his nose with impunity once he goes back to his home," Sonam added. "That, and my range isn't quite what it used to be. Jupiter to Earth right now is a bit out of my reach, so I cannot telekinetically boop yours, young lady."

With his paranoia soothed, Li'eth didn't like the thought of losing the elderly male. "I'll send a ship, specifically to pick you up and bring you to the Imperial Palace. If one can be spared. I don't know how much damage they're taking nor how much time is left."

"We'll talk about it when the time comes. I'll be with you for most of the tour, after all," Sonam reminded him, patting the prince on his blanket-covered leg. "Go back to mentally hugging your partner."

"How did you . . . ?" Li'eth asked, blushing. At his other side, V'kol raised his blond-and-pink brows but carefully did not say a word.

"The two of you make Gestalt pair number nineteen for me," Sonam said, patting his leg again. "I counted them up, to be sure. I *am* experienced in watching over younglings like you. Eventually, it will get easier for you."

Li'eth relaxed, accepting that this wasn't a rare, odd anomaly for these people. Mostly accepting it. He did, however, have a question as soon as he reached out to meet Jackie's mind. (. . . *Your government has plans to tranquilize people?*)

(*We try to be honorable and ethical in our actions in this day and age. We have far too many examples of dishonesty, corruption, and worse in our history,*) she replied, even as she looped her arms around his shoulder in that odd, blank, warehouse-like space. (*But being honorable and ethical is* not *the same thing as naïve. No one is above the law . . . but we are well aware that there are plenty of those who still try to break it.*)

(*Duly noted. Is there any place we can go in our minds that doesn't look like* this?) he asked next, sweeping his hand at the concrete floor and vast darkness beyond.

She smiled and "booped" his nose by rubbing it with her flatter one. (*Anywhere you like. Let me show you what a good surfing beach looks like.*) She turned her head, and suddenly they were standing on a wooden platform shaded by an open-walled structure with lashed-together fronds for its roof, thick bundles of pale, narrow leaves yellowed by their time in the sun. A wind blew steadily from off to one side, and the sun gleamed off the pale beige sand. (*A lot of the best surfing is in winter, and it's getting toward the tail end of the season, but with me along, we could ride a wave out there.*)

Li'eth looked where she nodded, at the blue-green-white curling waves rushing slowly, steadily toward shore. They looked to be taller than him, if he was judging the distances right. (*You ride that? The waves?*)

(*These are just little ones, good for beginners. And yes, I ride them. I will show you surfing. Hawai'ians invented the sport hundreds of years ago, if not longer. You don't have that on V'Dan?*)

(*We have three moons. They're small compared to your Luna, but the tides are rather complicated because of it,*) he told her.

(*I look forward to finding out—yes, I am aware that surfing is dangerous,*) she added, catching his thought packet. (*I've been knocked off a board more than once. My telekinesis is trained to wrap around me in a bubble,*) Jackie reassured him. (*If I lose my board, if I lose my orientation—even in zero-gravity training in the military, anyplace I lose my focus—my bubble pops up. Sometimes full of water, but it gives me a chance to orient myself, find the tug of gravity, and go up.*) She smiled and held him in the cool shade, heat radiating into their shelter from the sand outside. It was a very good illusion. (*You'll see. It's in the schedule, a day at the beach. With sunscreen crème, surfboards, and cordoned-off privacy.*

(*Ah, relative privacy, that is. There will be guards everywhere. Mostly to keep the V'Dan groupies away, though. They still give me a bit of trouble at airports, but I've been calling ahead to Security to get me through quickly. It'll be even smoother for you,*) she reassured him.

(*Good. Thank you in advance for the sunscreen. Jungen burns just like the rest of our skin, but with burgundy and other reddish colors, it's sometimes hard to tell. And good, about the guards,*) he allowed. (*I'm not sure what sort of tour our people will put together for yours, but there will be honor guards.*)

(*Good.*)

(*Where is this place located?*) he asked her, lifting his chin at their surroundings. (*It is a real place, right?*)

(*We're just down the beach from a place called Diamond Head. It's an old volcano cone which shelters the south end of O'ahu, just right for producing little waves about the height of a Human. My grandmother lives a few blocks away.*)

(*Will you still be the Ambassador? Or . . . ?*)

She sobered a little; the sensations of sun and wind faded correspondingly. (*I don't know. The Premiere says there are too many variables that could adversely—or positively— affect Earth and its colonies . . . such as they are, so far. He's going to open it up to the Council to discuss.*)

That made him wrinkle his nose. (*Rule by committee? Making complex decisions by committee? That's a recipe for . . . what's that term you Terrans use . . . bureaucratic red tape swamp-bog stuff. Disaster by slow, stifled death. Robert used a phrase the other day . . . "Nibbled to death by ducks." I think it applies. It is not exactly an image to inspire confidence in your government system.*)

(*We have rules to speed up the process,*) she promised him. (*Now, let me introduce you to the pleasure of lounging side by side with me in a tropical hammock. Even if it's only in our minds.*)

He followed her into the envisioned sunlight and down the beach a little ways, toward an object strung between two of the odd, tuft-topped, scale-barked trees shading the shoreline. (*That, we have. We definitely have two-person hammocks.*)

MARCH 8, 2287 C.E.
TERRAN LAGRANGE 3 ASTRONOMICAL ARRAY AND HYDROREFUELING STATION

Jackie touched the interactive map on the main console. Not to adjust the view, since there were only two views being conjoined on the holographic pane above it—one from the *Aloha 31* and one from the hyperrelay it had dropped off ten light-minutes away to get sufficient parallax on the system they were observing—but instead to adjust the volume on the data streaming through the system at lightspeed.

The video feed was still causing them problems. Teams of computer-language specialists were racing to crack the code for that. A monetary prize had been posted by the pooled resources of seven different communications corporations for the group that could do it first, *and* the group that could do it best. At stake was not just the ability to communicate essentially face-to-face with the V'Dan, but for the corporations to have whole new worlds, literally, of potential viewers for entertainment and advertising programs. Jackie didn't envy the Advisors who had to deal with *that* proposal, ensuring everything stayed clean and aboveboard. Or any Advisors faced with Terran businesses clamoring to get their hands on a piece of the V'Dan pie. Even if they didn't know what they were waiting for, nor what the V'Dan might already have and thus not need.

The audio feed was mostly cracked. A small prize had already gone out to a team of audio engineers working in southern Africa—and by small, only in comparison to the full feed being successfully decoded. Each of the nine-member group that had given them the baseline translation program for digital audio streaming had become multimillionaires under the United Planets Credit system. It wasn't a perfect match, but while there were bits of static interrupting now and then, the audio feed was discernible.

If one spoke V'Dan, it was even intelligible. She had arrived two days early, and aside from her time spent contacting Li'eth to keep both of them relatively calm, she had spent a good portion of her time teaching V'Dan to several key personnel. The Astronomical Array had the databanks to process all the visual information coming in from the *Aloha* searches, but anything text-based plus the audio needed a linguist's touch.

With the *31* finally parked in what they thought just might be the V'Dan home system, they needed someone who understood V'Dan. The other eight souls she had transferred were still trying to settle into the language. She had been living it for a few months, which meant being in this room, monitoring the incoming data.

"Well?" Commodore Mokope asked, dark hands resting on his blue-clad hips. As the commander of the station and overseer of all military missions that docked with it, he was technically now her immediate superior, Space Force–wise. "Can you understand them, Major?"

"Of course I can understand them," she murmured.

"And?" he asked, gesturing at her to continue.

". . . And they're talking about mining operations. Or at least, that's the only chatter within the last few hours at light-speed. Not exactly the most awe-inspiring stuff," she replied, gesturing at the table console, which had a flat map sketch of what the system should look like, courtesy of Ba'oul. The *Aloha 31* and its hyperrelay probe were tucked behind the second asteroid field not far from the system's edge, relatively speaking. "That's not the sort of conversation that screams, 'Congratulations on reaching the heart of the Empire, bootsie; welcome to the V'Dan system, the *lu'au*'s at seven.'"

Three of the technicians, two males and a female, burst into laughter. Even the commodore grinned. He shook his head. "For all we know, the local lobster on their homeworld is six feet tall and takes home as many crabbers as the crabbers take. Keep listening. The *Katherine G* will be here within half an hour, maybe a little earlier. They're trying to outrun a chunk of CME."

"Coronal mass ejection," the tech opposite Jackie explained. His accent was Scottish, like her grandfather's, though he was short and stocky, not tall and lean. The curly light brown hair was similar. "The new insystem thrusters are a bit picky about how they kick back the particulate matter. Better for the ship to be on our side of the CME, aiming it away from us, rather than bombarding the Array with high-temperature, high-speed molecules as she comes in. Ceristeel can stop it, but it can still damage the sensor panels."

"Which are currently wide open. This is not the only project we have," Mokope reminded the others. "Just one of the most important right now."

"Hang on, what's that?" the female asked, lifting her blue-dyed hair. From the rather faded state of it, she had dyed it long before the V'Dan had come to the Sol System. She lifted a hand, pointing at the hologram monitor. "That object—holy!"

The hologram flickered; the image was definitely being seen by only *one* sensor array, not two, making the feed program struggle to compensate. Mokope squinted. "Which is that coming from, the *Aloha*, or the satellite?"

"Satellite, sir," the Scots tech replied. "Switching to monocular view. The system will continue to record in parallax on the main channel, don't worry . . . There."

The blur slowed over several seconds, drifting into close view. A magnified view, Jackie realized, as the image backed up a bit under the third technician's touch. Either way, when the lenses finally focused, when the ship slowed enough to recognize it, the configuration was very much V'Dan.

"Major?" Commodore Mokope asked.

She nodded, her attention more on trying to translate the name she saw than anything else. "Imperial War Fleet. You can see the nameplate there; it's barely lit by the stars at this distance, but it's there. *V'Cotse T'aranguul* . . . 'The Coastline Whirling Bladesman'? No, that can't be right . . . coastline . . . border guard? 'The Whirling Border Guard' is probably the closest translation for that name, since 'dervish' has a religious slant to it. Let me contact the prince . . ."

"Considering they've found our satellite, I suggest you do that fast, before they try to pick it up and look inside," Mokope warned her. "Try to get some sort of contact protocol out of him. MacLeod, is that half-assed audio broadcast program uploaded yet?"

"Uploaded and checked," the Scotsman confirmed. "You can broadcast when ready. Kaampe—ah, good, you already got the headset. Getting her patched in?"

The tall, dark-skinned male nodded. He handed the headset to Jackie, who absently hooked it over her ear with her physical hands. Her mind was busy reaching mental hands toward her partner. (*Li'eth?*)

(*Almost there. I think I shall break the normal sort of stuffy Imperial protocol and just hug . . . wait, what's going on?*) he asked, sensing her thoughts. (*You've found something?*)

(*The V'Dan have found something, rather. Just under an hour ago,* Aloha 31 *made it to the system we think is the V'Dan homeworld,*) she told him. (*Unfortunately, while we were sitting beyond the second belt, getting oriented, a V'Dan midclass cruiser spotted the hyperrelay probe and is now drifting up to the unit. Is there any call sign or code word that'll get their attention swiftly but peacefully which I could use?*)

(*Everything I know is out of date, and I don't have the current codebook. That was destroyed the very instant the Salik first boarded our ship, as per standing orders,*) he revealed to her.

"You are live to the system," Kaampe murmured. He swiped

a control-pad program into reach on the table console. "Standard comm keys, press that button to activate the link or to mute it."

(*Give me what you can,*) she urged.

(*Give me a moment to think,*) he retorted. (*It's been months since I memorized the last set of protocol codes.*)

Lifting her chin at Mokope, she asked, "As you are the seniormost officer within reach, Commodore, and this could end up in a rather one-sided firefight if we stay silent . . . permission to open communications with the encroaching vessel?"

"Permission granted, Ambassador." Mokope braced his hands on his hips. "All hands, keep your eyes to your boards, your thoughts on your tasks . . . and your ears open to history being made."

Nodding, Jackie checked the controls. Thanks to her training for working on the *Aloha 9*, she was able to open six different frequencies. Hopefully, one of them would catch the cruiser's attention. A check of the time stamp showed they had a good three seconds one-way of communication lag. Switching to V'Dan, she spoke into the mic on her headset.

"*Attention, Imperial Warship* V'Cotse T'aranguul, *you are approaching the* Aloha 31 Alpha, *a satellite probe transported to your system for the purpose of peaceful communication. Please respond on one of these channels. I repeat, attention, Imperial Warship* V'Cotse T'aranguul, *you are approaching the* Aloha 31 Alpha, *a satellite probe transported to your system for the purpose of peaceful communication. Please respond on one of these channels.*"

It didn't take long for them to respond. The audio was a bit scratchy, but otherwise intelligible. "*This is the V'Dan Imperial Warship* V'Coste T'aranguul *to the unidentified object. Who and what are you, and why have you entered V'Dan sovereign space?*"

"*Greetings,* V'Cotse T'aranguul. *I am Ambassador Jackie MacKenzie of the* Terran *United Planets,*" she stated. "*You are speaking with me through a communication device with a turn-around time of approximately six V'Dan resting heartbeats. Please be patient and allow six heartbeats of time lag in all communications with this device. Do you understand?*"

Several seconds passed while the Humans on the other end of the line no doubt consulted with each other. A new voice came through, male and deep. *"This is Captain Superior Cha'kon V'kuria, commander of the* V'Cotse. *We do not know of any Teh-ran United Planets."*

"I am aware of that, Captain Superior. My people encountered some of your people on board a Salik vessel a little while ago. They were being held as prisoners of war. We liberated them, and have been hosting them while attempting to find your homeworld so that we can peacefully and safely return them to your Empire, along with an embassy to begin opening peaceful negotiations with your people."

A bit of static made them all strain to hear the next question. No doubt the V'Dan on the other end were having the same problem. *"Why is this communication audio-only?"*

"We are still having difficulties translating the programming languages used for visual communication by your people. It takes time to reconstruct such systems. Please forgive the current poor quality of the translation program."

Again, more than six seconds passed. *"... You speak flawless V'Dan. How did you manage this?"*

"I am what your Sh'nai faith calls a 'holy one,' gifted with the ability to learn languages swiftly and the ability to transfer them to others."

"Yet you cannot speak the language of a simple communication system?"

She rolled her eyes. Non-psis didn't always think things through. *"Computer languages are vastly different from spoken languages, Captain Superior. It takes a very special gift to be able to communicate directly with machines. One that I do not have. My abilities apply strictly to biological beings only."*

(*I've got it!* Ten g'at dance with a double-spring moon,) Li'eth enunciated carefully in his mind. (*And when he asks for confirmation, tell him* Ten g'at dance with a double-summer moon.)

(*Got it.*)

"What are the names of the V'Dan you say you rescued?" she heard. Grateful for the lag delay, she reached for Li'eth.

(*Oh boot me ... Li'eth, this Captain Superior Cha'kon V'kuria wants to know your names. Which one do I give?*) she asked.

(*Captain Li'eth Ma'an-uq'en. Do not use my title at any point,*) he warned her.

(*Right.*) Out loud, she stated carefully, "*We have rescued five V'Dan. Four are leftenants superior from the Warship* T'un Tunn G'Deth. *They are life-support officer Dai'a Vres-yat, logistics officer Shi'ol Nanu'oc, gunner V'kol Kos'q, and pilot Ba'oul Des'n-yi.*"

"*Did you say* T'un Tunn G'Deth?" the unseen officer asked. "*Who else survived?*"

"*Ten g'at dance with a double-spring moon,*" she stated, guessing this was the moment to use the security code Li'eth had passed her. She waited patiently for the message to get there and a reply to come back.

"*Did you say . . . ten g'at dance with a double-spring moon?*"

"*That's what I said. Ten g'at dance with a double-summer moon . . . and yes, the person who told me to say that knows how old that code is. He is the fifth survivor, Captain Li'eth Ma'an-uq'en. Unfortunately, he is not available at the moment, as he is currently in transit to this location, but he will be available within the hour. We were hoping he'd arrive in time and be on hand before you discovered our communication device.*"

"*Where is your ship located? Our scans are looking for the sourcepoint of your broadcast, but it seems to emanate only from this . . . machine.*"

Mokope moved off, muttering instructions into his own headset. "*Get the 31 out of there now, Lieutenant Commander. You are not authorized for First Contact. Retreat to the fallback position.*"

Jackie ignored that side of the table. "*Our communication in your system is relying upon lightwave broadcasts. As there could be Salik vessels lurking in the system, passively scanning for any information . . . that information is Classified, and shall remain Classified for now. I repeat, ten g'at dance with a double-spring moon. Ten g'at dance with a double-summer moon.*"

"*So what do you want us to do?*"

"*Well, whatever you do, Captain Superior, don't try to touch or take apart the device you're looking at. Right now, it is the only way we have to communicate with you,*" she reminded him dryly. *"In the meantime, it would be nice if you could confirm whether or not the system you are currently occupying is the home system of the planet V'Dan."*

"Why do you need to know that information?" The static was a little coarse, but the tone was wary, almost belligerent.

"Captain Superior, please think these things through. We rescued Salik prisoners. Prisoners who had nothing on them, not even clothing, when they were rescued," she pointed out. *"We have no V'Dan devices with which to synchronize star charts, no ability to make measurements in V'Dan units, and until now, no contact with any of your people who do have access to clothing and star charts and V'Dan measurement systems. We have been searching star system by star system, at great cost and expense, tying up many resources with our fleet just trying to find the V'Dan homeworld,"* she told him. *"It would be nice to confirm we have reached the correct system so that we can turn that exploration fleet home, and start building up the resources needed to ship home the captain and his leftenants. Exploration, even when it is focused, is expensive."*

"I will have to consult with my superiors. That will take time. Hours, if not days."

"That's alright. We are aware of your current level of communication ability and its logistics difficulties. If you feel you cannot inform us directly, then with luck, our V'Dan guests will be able to confirm it from what we've ascertained of your current system via passive lightwave readings. Once they arrive, that is. I was just hoping I could tell them with certainty when they do arrive that we have found their Imperial homeworld. But no matter," she dismissed lightly. *"It'll get done one way or another. While we await their arrival, do you have any non-Classified, non-sensitive questions you'd like to ask?"*

". . . Not at this time, Ambassador. Will you keep this channel open?" he asked

She checked which frequency was being used. Two of them, technically. *"We should probably reserve power, but if you send a signal on either of these two frequencies, it will open communications, and someone will be standing by to accept your call. For absolute certain, I will be back with Captain Ma'an-uq'en when his ship arrives and he has been settled on board."*

"The T'un Tunn G'Deth *survived? Wasn't it destroyed by the Salik?"*

"Technically, he is on board one of our *ships,"* Jackie clarified. *"His ship was indeed lost to the enemy. I apologize for being imprecise."*

"Then we will gladly await his arrival, and escort our soldiers home."

Jackie bit her bottom lip to keep from grinning too much. So much for not having any other questions. As soon as she felt she had her voice under control, she said as smoothly as she could, *"Captain Superior V'kuria, we are* nowhere *near your current star system. Nor can we immediately deliver them as you imply. As I said, we are still putting together the resources for an embassy as well as the means to return our guests to the V'Dan Empire. The distance between our two locations is vast, so for efficiency's sake, we'd like to bundle everything together when we ship it all to you, all on the first try. Which takes time and planning, as I'm sure you're aware.*

"In the interest of First Contact, we have arranged for our five guests to have a tour of our own little empire here, after which—when we have confirmed the correct star system—we will see that they are escorted safely home . . . where they will no doubt be interrogated by your people as to everything they have seen and learned while they were here. Which we know you will do, which is why *we're giving them that tour."*

"Sir, the *Katherine G* has begun braking," one of the techs at the edge of the room stated. "Their pilot estimates they should have a shuttle docked within eighteen minutes."

Jackie nodded when Mokope glanced her way, indicating she had heard. (*Almost here, I see.*)

(*I can't wait. Did you get a reaction on the code I gave you?*) he asked. She had a sense of him walking onto the shuttle that would make the transfer from the cruiser to the space station.

(*Not yet, but I'm pretty sure he has to carry word all the way to your home planet before he'll get a really big reaction,*) Jackie pointed out.

(*True.*)

"You seem remarkably open on some subjects, yet very closed on others."

"We are not prepared at this time to draw Salik attention

toward ourselves. For now, the location of the 'Before Time Motherworld' will remain a secret," Jackie explained.

"*The* Before Time *Motherworld? You're jesting.*"

Jackie leaned her palms on the table. Today was a uniform day, not a civilian-clothes day, but not anything formal, just gray slacks and a matching button shirt. It wasn't a slovenly outfit, but she felt it was a good thing the feed wasn't set up for video yet, just audio. Between her lack of formality and the need to flex her legs to keep them and her feet from getting tired with all this standing, her current appearance was a bit too casual for something momentous. There had been too many cases of "joke" outfits ruining portentous moments in the past . . . but it wasn't as if she could take the time to put on a full Dress uniform or a nicer civilian outfit. So long as the *V'Cotse's* crew wanted to talk with her, she had to stay at her post.

"*I assure you, I am quite serious, Captain Superior. I don't know all the particulars, since our guests did not arrive with religious texts in hand . . . again for obvious reasons. But if you like—since I have a few more minutes before their ship docks—I can fill you in on a few things that we've pieced together since their arrival in our care.*"

"*. . . We're listening.*"

"*The first revelation is one of great importance. I cannot stress this enough. We are the same species. I realize you may be doubting that, but I assure you, we are the same species. Our finest medical doctors have confirmed we are the same species down to the molecules in our cells. And unlike your world, whose history begins just under ten thousand of your years ago . . . our history, our fossil records, stretch back for millions of years . . . so the planet our guests will be touring is the birthworld of our mutual species. We call ourselves Humans . . . and though we are the same species, we are not V'Dan. We do not have the* jungen *virus, we have never had it, and as a consequence, we do not have the* jungen *marks which your people bear.*

"*Please understand that this is very important, Captain Superior. To your eyes, we may look like children because of this silly lack of stripes and spots . . . but we are not children. Please do not overlook, dismiss, or cling to this notion. It has already caused one major diplomatic incident . . .*

which we in our maturity and generosity have decided to overlook. It would be best if your people do not cause any further such incidents. That takes forethought and care.

"On the bright side," Jackie continued, watching the feedback of the V'Dan ship still slowly drifting closer to the probe, *"this means your people have been properly fed, clothed, and are living in an environment well suited for our joint species. On the* downside, *as my people say . . . this means we will have to ship various vaccines and antigens to your world to help ensure your people's ten-thousand-year isolation from* our *list of natural diseases does not cause massive problems among your people.*

"We have already synthesized and distributed antigens for most V'Dan diseases among our own population, but we will need to ensure and stabilize your own people's immunity to what we call the microflora *that share space in and on our bodies. We are also interested in sharing medical knowledge on the ones our guests weren't carrying when we found them. We understand that this may require quarantine procedures—"*

"Ambassador, please," Captain Superior V'Kuria interrupted, speaking over her. *"I am* not *authorized for most of this discussion. You may sound V'Dan, but without video confirmation, I cannot be sure of that. You are suggesting I take Sh'nai holy stories as the absolute truth, and I cannot."*

"I reassure you, I am not asking you to take those holy stories as complete and total truth," Jackie stated. *"I don't even know most of those stories. I am admitting, however, that there seems to be a grain of truth at their center. We are both the same species, we will need to watch out for bacteria and viruses that may have evolved far enough to cause problems, and we are willing to cooperate and work with your people to hopefully ensure that they don't. Because the third point of all this, Captain . . . is that you do need at least some of what we have. It won't be given away for free, but neither will we gouge you needlessly."*

"I'm going to have to think about this, Ambassador. We all will."

"Take as much time as you need," she told him. *"I'll set this frequency to await a signal from your ship if you need me. If not, I will go greet our arriving guests, and put you in contact with Captain Ma'an-uq'en directly within a short while—we don't know the exact conversion rates for seconds, minutes, hours and so forth, but we do know from what our guests have observed that our day cycle is close to what they're used to knowing. Since we both apparently use twenty-four-hour time units . . . I'll be back in touch within an hour. In the meantime, please leave the communication satellite alone. It would be a pity if you broke it before our guests had a chance to hear a fellow V'Dan speak to them after so long."*

"*. . . Understood.*"

"*Ambassador out.*" Tapping the controls, she stared at the monocular view of that ship, then sighed and removed the headset. Her free hand rubbed at the bridge of her nose. "First Contact. One of the messiest constituencies I have ever been assigned."

"Even after having served as Councilor for all the fiddly factions of Oceania?" the Scots technician, MacLeod, asked her.

"Even after that. Thank you for setting everything up and for keeping it all monitored," Jackie stated. "I'm going to go up to the spindle to welcome our guests."

Mokope pointed at the headset still in her hand. "You should keep that on, in case they call again."

"Right. Itchy things," she muttered, fitting it back into place over her right ear. "Particularly this model."

"It's what we have on hand, Major," the commodore told her, spreading his hands. Jackie suspected the use of her military title was to remind her that the Space Force couldn't always pick and choose what it got in supplies. "You want something more comfortable, go pick it up on Earth."

"Then I'll keep it in mind for when we put together the embassy's supplies." With a wave of her hand, she headed out of the room, on her way to the nearest spoke.

CHAPTER 18

Master Sonam, discreet and kind soul that he was, kept the others on the shuttle so that Li'eth could disembark first. Pulling himself through as soon as the shuttle crew confirmed the seals were good and unlocked the hatches, Li'eth soared into the far corridor, hands reaching out for the woman waiting for him. The moment Jackie caught him, skin against skin, fingers gripping forearms, an odd sort of shock rippled through his system.

It wasn't anything painful, but it did feel like some sort of inner component clicking into place. A misaligned joint regaining its proper position. Like the damned guanjiball game inside of him was finally tumbling to a stop. He wanted to wrap himself around her, to drink in her scent, her warmth, her *presence*, as if it were the waters of life itself.

(*Easy, I got you,*) she murmured mentally, steadying the force of his forward movement with body and mind. Their bodies touched in a floating, awkward hug, but their inner senses, those intertwined like tangled vines. (*I feel the same way. I just can't . . . I can't let go of you. That . . . Wow, I didn't realize how strong this would be. Damn—here come the others. We need to move, Li'eth. We shouldn't do this in public.*)

(*Why not? Or rather, why in private?*) he asked. Instinct had him bending his elbows, pulling his body closer to hers. His stomach muscles tightened, adjusting his torso to be in line with hers.

(*Because Shi'ol is going to kick up a bootload of feces all over us if we touch like we apparently need to,*) she warned him. (*I want to wrap my legs around you, to just meld with you, but that's too intimate for public, even if it'd be fully clothed.*)

(*She needs to grow up. I feel like I need to press my whole body against yours, too. Strip both of us naked, and just . . .*

It's not sexual,) he asserted. (*It's just a . . . a need. I mean, there* is *sexual attraction there, but this is deeper.*)

(*It's the Gestalt bond. Our personal kinetic inergy fields probably need to realign or recharge or resomething,*) she muttered mentally, trying to think through what they needed versus what they could get away with. He was wearing a short-sleeved tee shirt; she, a long-sleeved dress shirt. Jackie concentrated on the buttons of her cuffs. (*Let me roll up my sleeves. Wrists to wrists, elbows to elbows. That should be enough skin contact without making the other V'Dan uncomfortable.*)

"What are you doing?" Shi'ol demanded within moments of coming into view. Predictably.

"They are repairing the holes in their souls," Sonam replied poetically, coming to the rescue. Or trying to. "I believe Miss Dai'a referred to it as a 'holy pairing,' the highest of blessings for holy ones in the Sh'nai faith. Our people call it a Gestalt, and it is very important to the Terran military because of the various advantages it brings. This way to the lifts."

"She shouldn't be touching him!" the green-spotted blonde protested.

Jackie drew in a breath to speak, but again her old mentor beat her to it.

"To interfere in this pairing is to go against the will of your Saints," Sonam stated, his gentle tone turning stern, even chiding. "Not to mention it goes against several dozen precognitive visions on the Terran side, *and* prophecies from your own people that are literally older than your entire bloodline, young lady. Keep moving."

That made Jackie relax, glad she didn't have to look away from Li'eth's eyes, one gray, one burgundy. Forearms bared, she laced her fingers together with his, palms and elbows pressed, her telekinesis holding them carefully still, and carefully out of the way of the others. Repairing a hole in her soul might be a bit poetic, but *something* was easing the tension that had kept her hands fidgeting and fumbling within days of Li'eth's absence.

"She still shouldn't . . . wait, I'm moving—how am I moving?" Shi'ol protested, drifting past the alcove where Jackie and Li'eth floated.

"I may not be the very strong telekinetic that the Ambassador is, but I can still throw around my own weight mentally," Sonam clarified, moving both of them out of the airlock zone. "On the ground, back on Earth, I could not fly. Here, in zero gravity, I can even make you fly. And here you are, free to soar like a bird, or plummet like a brick. I should like to hope you are not as *thick* as a brick, Miss Nanu'oc . . ."

(*Don't think of her. She's not important,*) Li'eth dismissed.

That made her smile a little. (*No, she's not. Though she is still an annoyance. I'll recommend strongly to the Council that she be banned from being allowed to set any policy involving the United Planets or its citizenry. Not even if your own mother commands it.*) She nuzzled his nose with her own, then hugged him closer, breathing in the scent of his braided hair. (*I missed you unbearably.*)

(*I missed you, too. Maybe now I can sleep through the night. I had too many nightmares when we were far apart . . .*)

Another voice intruded on her ears, words spoken in a mutter. "So. You're just like *her* after all."

It took her a few seconds to process what had been said. By the time Jackie pulled her gaze away from Li'eth, Lieutenant Brad Colvers had already disappeared into the doorway that led to the spindle's lifts.

(*What was* that *about?*) Li'eth asked.

(*. . . I think he just compared me to the fiancée who dumped him for a fellow psi. But* she *had a choice. I don't.*) Jackie met his gaze, feeling his undercurrents rippling at her words. (*You know I don't mean that in a bad way. It's just . . . this isn't something we* choose *as free-willed beings. It just . . . happens, sometimes. We will have to deal with it, first before the Council, then later, before your mother and her people.*

(*In the meantime . . . first, we have to deal with the captain superior of a certain warship. We'll confirm whether or not we've found your home system, then I'll need a little while to confer with Commodore Mokope on setting up a series of resupply points on the way to your people. After that . . . I have a very small but private cabin.*)

(*I don't feel comfortable engaging in sexual . . . oh. You just mean getting enough time to just hold each other, without the others thinking it* is *some sort of sexual embrace,*) he corrected himself, catching a little more of her underthoughts. (*Not that I wouldn't eventually like that, ah, sort of thing, eventually. Because I would, but . . .)*

(*It wouldn't be politically wise,*) she agreed, finishing his thought for him. (*Self-restraint and self-control are marks of maturity. Adulthood.*) Bringing their clasped fingers to his cheek, she rubbed the slightly stubbled skin with the edge of her forefinger. (*We also don't know each other well enough. We may both be Human, and I'm pretty sure it all works the same way . . .*)

He blushed and chuckled softly, ducking his head at her gentle teasing. (*I'm pretty sure it does, too. But it's not about that. Something like that can wait. We just have too big of cultural gaps between us, still. And too many responsibilities to ignore them. We do have that in common, our sense of duty.*)

(*Then we're agreed.*) Jackie sighed, disappointed but determined to be responsible.

(*Duty before pleasure,*) Li'eth confirmed. (*We'll have plenty of time to get to know each other better, both here in your system and when we finally get to mine. In the meantime, I have a ship to contact, don't I?*)

(*Yes, you do.*)

(*The relay-satellite thing—can their ship move it? I keep getting the image that—*) He fell silent when she shook her head.

(*Too many safety features. Instead, we'll send in a ship with a spare relay and drop that into your home planet's nearspace. Once we have* permission *to do so, and only when we do. The one that's out beyond the second asteroid belt, we'll leave it there for now. If nothing else, it'll be a backup in case the closer one gets destroyed by the war.*)

(*Contingency plans for everything,*) Li'eth mused, disentangling one hand so that they could pull themselves—or rather, soar with her telekinesis—toward the doorway that led to the lifts. That was much more convenient than trying to use one's arms, he had to admit. (*Is there a scenario you haven't got a plan for, in all of this?*)

(*Me, personally? Plenty. I try to look over everything, make sure all the major points of concern have good core plans laid in advance, then plan for flexibility beyond that because that's all you can do. Anticipate the major stuff, try to be ready for the most likely minor stuff, then get ready to be flexible. Come on, I'll take you straight to the scanner room, where they've got the connection set up with the relay probe.)*

———

"And that . . . is all I can do," Li'eth sighed, switching back to Terranglo. Removing the headset, he placed it on the console table on an unused spot, then reached for Jackie's hand. She clasped it willingly enough, which helped him to relax. "The *V'Cotse* will be on its way to V'Dan within the next few minutes, where, after a few hours of transit, Commodore V'kuria will be able to make his report to the First Tier officers in his chain of command.

"They will no doubt come back to the probe in due time with a whole host of questions, but since I gave V'kuria a special code that will alert my family that I am indeed the real thing, and still safely alive . . . you'll be able to begin preliminary negotiations within just a few days' time. That means not only will we be returning with your help, but we'll be returning with an official Terran embassy ready to begin negotiations between our peoples."

"It's a good day's work," Mokope agreed. "I'll call up Admiral Nayak personally with the good news. Unless you'd rather do it, Major?"

"Captain Ma'an-uq'en and I still have Gestalt recalibrations to perform," Jackie hedged. "Master Sonam recommended we do so up on the life-support ring, so that's where we're headed next. Something about the healing energies of plant life making it easier to rebalance our inner senses." She shook her head. "It makes me very glad I focused on languages, not on teaching."

The commodore nodded and eyed the view of the V'Dan ship. Sure enough, it was now firing its attitude thrusters, turning itself slowly around so that it could head back to the inner system. "You two go on ahead, then. I haven't dealt personally with a Gestalt pair before, but we do have one psi on the Array team—she's good at intuiting mechanical failures—and I do remember the briefings on what to do with Gestalts.

"I'll contact the Admiral, then keep an eye on this ship of theirs while we process more stereoscopic data on that system. Then I'm going to see if we can prod the teams working on decrypting the V'Dan video feeds into working a little faster. Not that I *have* a cattle prod that's two AUs long and can go straight through the Sun to reach Earth," Mokope added wryly, hands on his hips, "but I'll do what I can verbally. Audio is okay, but there's a reason why the old cliché is called '*seeing* is believing.'"

Jackie nodded in farewell and guided Li'eth out of the operations room. It didn't take long to reach the nearest lift, though they did have to wait awhile for the car to make its way back down to the full-gravity level. On the Array, unlike *MacArthur* Station, there were two small life-support bays in the main ring, with a midway ring holding the most food and so forth, plus a selection of living quarters that could be used in an emergency. If anything went wrong all the way out here, it would take a lot of effort to evacuate the station. More than that, the midring helped supply a lot of food for patrols on the far side of the Sun from Earth; the life-support and aquaculture system aboard the Array was therefore huge compared to the *MacArthur.*

All of that, Li'eth had learned in the lectures they had been given while traveling to this place; the Terrans were methodical about giving information and instruction for each new living space they visited. As soon as they emerged on the midring, seeing the bays thick with greenery and the colorful foods being grown, hearing the clucking of edible fowl, the water trickling and splashing and draining from upper beds to lower ones, he had to appreciate the ingenuity of these Terrans. They did so many things differently from the V'Dan even though both cultures had similar greenery spaces on their ships.

It was also a popular place for people to go, he realized. Benches lined the tiled, curved floor, spaced here and there for station personnel to use. There were even a few joggers following a winding track among the planting beds . . . and more than just joggers, he realized. Tugging on Jackie's hand, he halted her before they could get very far along the right-hand side of the upper level, spinward. (*That looks like Shi'ol in the distance, on that bench. Someone's with her.*)

(*Well, it's a big station, she's welcome to go anywhere that doesn't say "Restricted,"*) Jackie pointed out. She blinked, frowned, and peered. (*Huh. That looks like Brad sitting with her.*)

(*Strange. I would've thought she wouldn't want anything to do with any of you,*) Li'eth mused. (*Particularly after he put her through her paces while she was being disciplined for triggering the incident.*)

(*Except for Dr. Du,*) Jackie pointed out. (*She liked the doctor. But Du went back to Earth to work on coordinating and monitoring the vaccine-distribution efforts.*)

(*Maybe Shi'ol's finally learning to get along with the other Terrans?*) Li'eth offered. He tugged her away from the pair, back toward the left.

(*Maybe. Though she did throw a little fit when you boarded the station,*) Jackie pointed out.

(*I am still an Imperial Prince, and she is a Countess, whereas you are not even a member of the Empire. She probably feels some impropriety between you and me because of that.*)

(*Hey, if you go back far enough, I am related to royalty,*) Jackie told him.

(*Really?*) he asked. (*How far back? I thought you got rid of all your royals a couple hundred years ago.*)

(*Most royals, but not all. Father's side of the family is related through the French bloodline to the famous King Charlemagne from over a thousand years ago. And my mother's side of the family . . . they don't count it by the centuries, but rather by the generations. If you go back eighteen or so levels in the genealogy, I'm descended from a royal princess. The* moku-pini, *or island, of O'ahu was originally divided into six* moku, *or sections of the island as determined by water availability and the ability to support a population. My mother's family comes from all over the Isles, but the royal bloodline was from a* moku *on the east side, very lush and green, very easy to make a living. I might have time to show you the valley watershed where the princess was said to have lived and worked.*)

(*Eighteen generations ago?*) he asked. (*That's a long time, but I suppose it's closer than a full thousand years.*)

She nodded, nudging him toward a bench that had a good view of three sets of "waterfalls" from a trio of growing shelves set side by side. (*Don't make me recite the whole lineage—my mother's lineage. I can only do it from memory if I'm doing a* hula *at the same time, and I haven't practiced that one in a while. My father's side of the family, I'd have to find a copy of the family tree. They never had a history of orally preserving family lines of descendance, though they did have an extensive written history at certain points.*)

Straddling the backless bench she had picked, Li'eth put his back to a support strut at one end and pulled her close, so that she straddled it in a way that allowed her to use his chest in turn for her own backrest. (*I won't make you do that,*) he promised. (*That is, if you in turn don't make me try to recite the whole family lineage myself. Forty-five centuries is a lot of memorization to manage.*)

(*On the bright side, you'll please my mother's mother if you can. She won't be truly impressed with you unless you can recite at least thirty, thirty-five generations—family, what we call* 'ohana, *is a big deal to Hawai'ians. Not as big on Father's side of the family, but he was able to show her family trees going back the forty generations needed to prove he was related to Charlemagne, which satisfied Grandmother enough that she gave her warmest blessing to their marriage.*)

Li'eth twined their fingers together and wrapped their arms lightly around her waist. (*Marriage. That's something we'll have to discuss. I was expected to make a politically advantageous marriage with one of the noble families once I got out of my mandatory service in the military. But then the war happened, and we found ourselves far more concerned with fighting for our lives. You haven't said, but the implication is that Gestalt pairs marry, yes?*)

(*They don't have to, but it is considered a form of marriage. Not legally, but psychologically, even biologically. Or rather, it's more like marriage is considered a mere formality,*) Jackie clarified. Off in the distance, something bleated. Probably a goat. (*If a member of the pair is already married to someone else, the courts have set up an easy "No Fault" format for divorce.*)

(*In V'Dan terms, that first spouse would automatically be granted the title of Consort Nanny if there were any children already,*) he told her.

Jackie could sense a complex layer of marriage types behind the words *Consort Nanny.* Something about ensuring an heir in the event of infertility of one spouse or the other, in the event of someone wanting to marry their own gender, or even for political reasons or money but not love. She wanted to explore that, curious, but went back to her own explanations for now. (*The military has also put pressure on Population Control to ensure that our Gestalt pairings get to have at least three children, sometimes more, because the odds of their children also being psychically gifted are very high, and the military likes having psis spread all over Earth, to help thwart Grey invasions.*)

(*Which you've already told me about,*) Li'eth sent, settling himself a little more comfortably against the support strut behind him. That allowed her to slouch just a little bit more and sigh in contentment. He adjusted his arms around her, and rested his chin on her curls. (*You're right; this isn't a very sexual embrace, but it is a very satisfying, soothing one . . . exactly what we need.*)

"Mmhmm," she sighed out loud. (*Just what the instructor ordered. It's not what I want, which is to crawl into a bed with you, naked, but it is what we need.*)

(*Let's not think about that,*) Li'eth countered, quelling the urge before his body could do more than halfheartedly respond. (*Let's discuss and compare the similarities and differences in marriages. If it's considered a foregone conclusion that a Gestalt is in essence a sort of marriage, then we should at least have the Terran versus the V'Dan version discussed and settled. It would certainly be expected that there be some sort of formal marriage if you are to constantly be at my side yet not be considered a professional consort.*)

Jackie nodded, soaking up the warmth of his chest. The stations were always just a little bit on the cool side for her tastes. (*At some point, yes, it'd happen. Let's start with the Terran versions of what marriage is about. Plural, since we have so many different cultures . . .*)

MARCH 12, 2287 C.E.
LANDER 3 STATION DOME, MARS

The insistent chiming of the doorbell for his tiny, cramped quarters in the Martian Prime Dome settlement dragged Li'eth out of restless sleep. Sitting up—wobbling a little from the lighter-than-normal gravity—he struggled to bring his brain out of the damned Salik prey-cage he had been reliving. The bell chimed again. He knuckled some of the sleepsand out of his eyes, then reached up and tapped the intercom button on the door, which sat within arm's length of his bunk. *"What is it?"*

"Apologies for the interruption, Your Highness," a man called on the other side, *"but two things have happened. Literally within minutes of each other. We have received word that* Aloha 31 Alpha *has been contacted by the Empress of V'Dan, who is requesting that she speak with you immediately,* and *the video teams believe they have cracked the V'Dan programming language for your visual broadcasts."*

"The Empress?" Li'eth repeated, blinking as the adrenaline of that news jolted him wider awake.

"Yes, sir. If you can get dressed as fast as possible, we're in the middle of uploading the new language parameters now. We can have you talking face-to-face with Her Majesty within minutes. Hopefully. We still have to test the program between Earth and Mars, here, with the newest feeds we've been receiving."

"Where will that take place?"

"Observation Room 4, sir. I'll be standing out here ready to escort you."

"Have you alerted the Ambassador?" he remembered to ask, rising and twisting to dig into the cupboards where his clothes had been stored. Not casual, no, but the Terran version of his formal uniform. Hopefully, the Imperial Army would forgive the fact that it *wasn't* an official, proper version . . . but better to be dressed in his best than to be seen in casual clothes.

"Yes, sir; an ensign was dispatched to her quarters, too."

"Good. I'll be out there soon," he promised, and hurried to get dressed.

Spurred by adrenaline, getting dressed didn't take long. Nor did it take long for him to make his way along the dome's stout, stone corridors to the room in question under the escorting junior officer's guidance. Observation Room 4 was a chamber with a great clear ceiling showing the Martian sky, and a series of monitors, stations, and console tables meant to observe and coordinate all the activity going on around the imperfectly colonized planet. Jackie entered the chamber from a door at the far side, still tucking in her uniform shirt under her open jacket.

Someone handed her one of those over-the-ear devices, and she hooked it on before buttoning up her gray coat. Li'eth accepted one as well, every scrap of his uniform already neatly in place.

(*Did they tell you about the—?*)

(*Video? Of course. I'm sorry it's just my Dress Grays, but I didn't bring my Dress Blacks, and only my minimum of awards and honors. How does my hair look? Yours is a mess,*) she added, trying not to smile visibly.

She had taken the time to comb and braid hers. Li'eth . . . hadn't. He grimaced. (*No time for it now, I suppose.*)

Digging into her pocket, she fished out a little black loop, a hair tie. Lifting her gaze to him, she narrowed her eyes thoughtfully. His hair prickled from the feeling of a thousand tiny fingers sorting through it in rapid downward strokes from the ends on up to the roots, detangling the strands, then he felt it swinging this way and that, pulling taut. Releasing the hair band, she sent it floating across to the tail of his neatly woven plait and telekinetically tied it off with a grin.

Under the astounded looks of the technicians, she blushed and cleared her throat. "Telekinetics—particularly those with long hair—like to practice simple-seeming things like hair-braiding as a way to fine-tune our skill. A lot of us did it in the League dormitories while we were being trained. The best hair-braider I know was barely a Rank 4, but he could do all sorts of things with hair. Last I heard, he was running an upscale styling salon in North Los Angeles."

". . . Right. If you're done grooming, are the two of you ready?" Admiral Nayak asked. He had joined them on Mars yesterday and looked like he had been awake for a few hours, unlike his guests. Jackie had already given him a language transfer, and knew he had gone to bed early to sleep through the aftereffects. He looked fine now, no signs of a post-transfer headache as he lifted his chin at the upper display screen. "The video translation has been tested, and we have the V'Dan Empress waiting impatiently on the line. Hope you can do this without coffee."

Li'eth hid his flinch. He had tried the nasty stuff. It was wonderful for waking up the senses, yes, but horridly bitter compared to the nicer, gentler V'Dan *caffen*, which was some sort of close botanical relative. One of the Before Time plants, but clearly bred in a different direction than the Terran version. No, he could do this without *coffee*. "I am ready, sir."

Jackie nodded as well and turned her attention to the controls at Nayak's gesture to proceed. (*You'll want to stand at my side, Li'eth. The pickups are up there,*) she added, giving him a pulsed awareness of where they were located. (*This is strictly flatpic transmission. Your people don't use holograms . . . though given how advanced your tech seems to be, I'm rather surprised you don't.*)

(*They give both the K'Katta and the Tlassians major headache equivalents. Out of courtesy, we use flat video feeds. That, and they cost far less to transmit. Smaller data packets, shorter transmission time, less energy . . . though we fill up half the datastream with redundant repeats to make sure it isn't lost when the signal spreads out over distance.*)

(*Redundant—? Is that* what's been slowing us down, cracking the programming codes?)

(*I don't know; I'm not a programmer,*) he shot back. The overhead monitor—a clear panel—swung down level with their position on its robotic arm and flicked into full-color life . . . which wobbled once in a while, but otherwise presented a strong signal, an image of the V'Dan Imperial Seal.

A pang of homesickness ached in his chest at the sight of that red-and-gold symbol. Two curving, mostly vertical lines, closer at the top than the bottom, crossed by two straight horizontal lines, the top shorter than the bottom, with a short vertical line descending partway from the bottom of the two horizontal bars. Painted in red, limned in gold, on a plain white background, it represented everything that said *home* to him. A home he had not seen in far too long.

"That's . . . kind of nice-looking. Is that your people's symbol?" one of the other soldiers in the room asked. Though there was a civilian government of sorts, Mars was still a series of testing grounds for domeworld-colonization efforts, and therefore staffed as much by the military as by civilians. He lifted his chin at the screen. "Kinda looks Chinese."

Li'eth nodded. "I was told that it is not an actual Chinese symbol . . . or any linguistic symbol with which Ambassador MacKenzie is familiar . . . which is very good to know. I'd hate for it to somehow accidentally translate into 'broken chunks of elephant dung' in one of your languages." A few chuckles broke out around the room, and he dipped his head in acknowledgment. "Dignity is important in the Empire."

"Then we will be dignified alongside you," Admiral Nayak asserted. Instantly, the soldiers who were still grinning sobered their expressions, turning their attention back to their work.

Movement caught his attention. Li'eth stiffened, straightening his shoulders, for the image of the Imperial symbol wobbled, then shifted. A woman with silver-gold hair pulled back in an intricate braid appeared on the screen, her brow caught behind a circlet shaped like a pair of miniature swords stretching out around either side, conjoined at the hilts by a pommel made from a very large crimson gem. She looked like she had gained a line or two beneath the short burgundy stripes angling down the right side of her face, but otherwise looked nearly ageless. Someone had once remarked to him that there was good bone structure in his family bloodline, an artisan from the Valley.

Jackie, standing on Li'eth's right, took in other details. Studying the waist-up view, she assessed the older woman's demeanor and appearance. What the Terrans had approximated in their guests' uniforms had been perfected in hers. In fact, it looked like cloth of gold to Jackie. Not lamé, nothing flimsy or brassy, but actual thin strands of gold spun around sturdy threads, which were then woven together. Where the V'Dan officers' uniforms were scarlet with cream facing under the frogging, her uniform was gold with scarlet. That jacket looked well tailored, on a figure that seemed trim and fit. No spare signs of aging or waste. A finely crafted sword, in other words.

This, then, was the Empress serving in her capacity as War Queen. She looked formidable. Given the circumstances, the ongoing war her people faced, Jackie approved.

Those gray eyes moved, flicking over her son's face . . . but she did not address him as such. *"Captain Ma'an-uq'en. It is good to see that one of our loyal officers survived."*

"Greetings, Empress," Jackie stated in careful V'Dan. *"Please understand that there is a six-heartbeat delay between messages; three to reach you, three more to return to us with your reaction, and the other way around as well."*

The Empress spoke when she paused for breath before going on. Or rather, the Empress interrupted three seconds prior to her message reaching Jackie midspeech. Jackie paused politely. *"We will speak with Captain Ma'an-uq'en."*

The audio was still imperfect, as was the video. Li'eth kept his expression calm. Stoic. *"They know who and what I am, Eternity. You need not hide it."*

"I will not endanger our good Captain by broadcasting such knowledge in a war zone . . . though we are puzzled as to why we cannot find the vessel you are on, nor any sign of your broadcast reaching this machine left in our sovereign system."

"Greetings, Hana'ka V'Daania, Eternal Sovereign and War Queen of the V'Dan Empire," Jackie interjected smoothly, restarting her introduction speech. Those gray eyes shifted to her, and a faint frown pinched that otherwise mostly smooth brow. *"I am Ambassador Jacaranda MacKenzie, and represent the* Terran *United Planets. I assure you, we are nowhere near your home star system, and have seen zero signs of Salik capacity to trace our method of interstellar travel, so far. We are actually transmitting this message from hundreds of light-years away. You cannot find us because we are not actually there."*

"Impossible." The Empress' denial was flat, clipped, and neutral.

"Very possible, Eternity," Li'eth countered, recapturing his mother's attention. *"This is but one of the advantages which these* Terrans *will bring to the Alliance very soon . . . just as the* Book of the Immortal *prophesied they would."*

A few heartbeats after his statement, those gray eyes narrowed. *"How soon will you be bringing them?"*

Jackie fielded that one. *"If construction of our supply chain remains on schedule, Eternity, we should arrive at your system in approximately thirty more of our days . . . which should be around twenty-eight of yours, if we have calculated everything closely enough. Our scientists look forward to getting their hands on actual V'Dan units of measurement for better ease of conversion rather than relying upon rough estimates and careful guesses."*

The Empress narrowed her eyes a tiny bit, glancing briefly at Jackie. The movement was subtle, something that might have been missed if her son had blinked. He had not, and could guess what was going through the royal mind.

"Their government will be discussing the details of who exactly will be free to come to the heartworld of the Empire in a few more weeks," Li'eth stated. *"These people are honorable, open, and I believe them to be trustworthy."*

"How long have you been in their care?" the Empress asked next. *"You and your four surviving bridge officers."*

"Several weeks, now."

Jackie spoke up again. *"We first had to isolate them—and the crew that rescued them—to discern and counter any potential dangers from various pathogens. Our medical specialists have confirmed that there have been approximately ten thousand years of separation between your people and ours, and so we have been taking careful precautions to ensure that our diseases and your diseases will not cause massive medical problems across each side. This is but one of many things we are interested in trading; in fact, there are a lot of scientists, spiritualists, and historians who would love to get their hands on any V'Dan records from your earliest beginnings, to try to piece together how your people ended up leaving the world where our joint species was born, Eternity. My people look forward to exchanging what we in turn know about our mutual origins with your people, and all the history you have missed."*

". . . I would like to speak with someone in charge," Empress Hana'ka stated after a pause that was longer than the six seconds of turnaround time between their two worlds.

Everyone in the room around them stiffened. Li'eth spoke firmly, gesturing to his right. *". . . Allow me to reintroduce this* woman, *Empress. This is Ambassador Jackie MacKenzie. At this moment, she is the third most politically powerful* adult *in the Terran government."*

His mother stared through the screen at the two of them, her mouth pressed shut.

(*Can we turn those pickups so that she sees the whole room?*) Li'eth asked Jackie. (*I think she needs to see every unstriped face in here.*)

(*Agreed.*) Touching the controls on the table, Jackie activated the panel's servos. They swept the monitor around in a slow spin while her Gestalt partner spoke, explaining the shift in view.

"*This is what every Terran looks like, Empress. They do not have jungen. They do not rely upon visual marks to discern those who are mature from those who are childish. They rely solely upon physical age, actions, and words. In this regard, they are very much like the other members of the Alliance. They may look like us, Mother,*" he added, making her frown, almost flinch briefly. It was not proper protocol to acknowledge the relation in such a formal moment. "*And we are the same species, separated by ten millennia . . . but these people are not V'Dan. Every single person in this chamber is an adult.*"

"*With respect, Eternity,*" Jackie added, bringing the monitor back to its starting position. "*Make that clear in your mind. The Terran culture, and its government, are not V'Dan. The correct course of action is to treat us with full respect as a separate nation and a separate culture.*"

The Empress stared through the screen a long moment, then addressed her son. "*You informed them of your identity. You trust these . . . people?*"

Jackie had the impression Li'eth's mother censored the word *children* at the last moment. She waited for Li'eth to answer her, holding her own tongue.

"*With my life. With your life. And with the lives of the Alliance. I will bring home the Motherworld, and the means to end our war, as prophesied,*" he told her.

Empress Hana'ka narrowed her eyes in thought for a moment, then shifted her gray gaze to Jackie. "*You. Ambassador.*"

"Yes, Empress?" she asked politely.

"*You will be held personally responsible for His Highness' safety.*"

"Such threats are not necessary, Empress," Jackie replied smoothly. She even managed a polite smile. "*I already hold his life as precious as my own. He and his fellow survivors will be returned intact to the Empire. I plan to come along in person for many reasons. The foremost one is that we hope to help establish a Terran embassy on V'Dan. Your people and mine have many things to discuss, ranging from ways we can be useful in your war to things we can trade once peace has been achieved. But as His Highness advises . . . please do not make the mistake of viewing us as you view the markless among your own people. We are not V'Dan, and we will not respond as V'Dan."*

The Empress frowned, a look more of puzzlement than annoyance. *"I am not finding much of confidence in your technology. Your communications equipment appears to be malfunctioning."*

"I repeat, Eternity, we are not V'Dan," Jackie explained patiently. *"It has taken many days of effort among our top specialists to decode and create a translation program to smooth over the differences between V'Dan and Terran communications systems. We are doing so with zero help from V'Dan source materials. Ten thousand years, give or take a few centuries, is plenty of time for divergent technologies to be developed, and to do so in ways that have zero ability to communicate with each other. In fact, less than an hour ago, you would not have had any visual contact. Less than a week ago, you would not have had audio.*

"Be glad you have more than audio when speaking with your son. Speaking of which," Jackie added, *"the current location of Aloha 31 Alpha, the unit which you have approached, should remain where it is as a backup communications system. We would like to transport a similar satellite into V'Dan nearspace, into an orbit arranged by your people. These units have been guarded against opening and tampering, as the technology is proprietary to the Terran government . . . so it is not advised that anyone attempt to move, open, or otherwise damage any of them.*

"If you do not like the thought of one of them being placed in planetary orbit around your capital world, we can arrange to have it dropped onto the surface of your innermost moon, which we understand is both airless and tidally locked, with one side constantly facing your homeworld. It will increase the lag by approximately two seconds due to the constraints of lightspeed broadcasts, but an eight-second turnaround to be able to communicate near instantly would still be worth the trouble, compared to a couple hours' worth of lightspeed lag.

"Technicians, scientists, and medical personnel on both sides of the interstellar divide will have many things to discuss

in order to make a visit, and the establishment of an embassy, a success for both sides . . . starting with exchanging units of measurements and other technological background knowledge, so that we can improve the video feeds, among many other things," she added.

"We will consider it. When is the soonest such a device can be delivered?"

"That depends, Your Eternity," Jackie allowed, tipping her head a little. *"If you are willing to put up with visual wobbles and audio static bursts, you can have one delivered as soon as we have established suitable measurement coordination for delivering it into a stable orbit, or to a particular set of moon coordinates. That could be done within a handful of hours. On the other hand, if our communications experts can be given a chance to chat with your experts, we should be able to clear up the problems making the video and audio feed imperfect in a matter of days. To install the adjustments to the hardware and get an updated satellite delivered would take approximately fourteen days on top of that."*

"Why should we not move this one?" Empress Hana'ka asked.

"This is not meant as a threat, Empress, but I shall speak bluntly so that you understand that moving it is not an option. Not a safe one. The satellite is designed to explode with enough force to vaporize its entire interior should anything or anyone tamper with it. That means it will cause a great deal of damage to whatever is within close proximity because I can guarantee *the structural integrity of its outer casing will not survive intact. Think of it not as a threat, but as a reassurance that our potential mutual enemy, the Salik, will not be able to gain access to our technology long enough to figure out how it works."*

"It also would prevent our technicians from doing the same, even if it is not meant as a threat to us," Hana'ka stated with a touch of dryness in her voice.

"Your Eternity is wise in the ways of proprietary knowledge," Jackie returned just as dryly. She smiled politely. *"We won't keep it from you forever, but neither will we give it away for free. As I said, ten thousand or so years is enough time for technologies to develop in very different directions. Your ships reportedly take an hour to travel a single light-year in*

relative comfort. Ours take a handful of seconds, but with the trade-off of physical discomfort. Your members of the Alliance lack interstellar communications. Our people have yet to develop artificial gravity. There is much to be discussed, and much of potential trade worth discussing, in the coming days, months, and years."

". . . You have given us much to consider, Ambassador."

"If you are willing to pass this communications channel to the appropriate personnel on board your ship, I can arrange for our scientists to begin finding methods of exchanging and calibrating measurement systems, starting with consistently measurable things such as atomic mass and the speed of light through the vacuum of space as starting points. With those and other basic measurement tools in hand, we should be able to fine-tune things quite a bit better. In the meantime, which quality of probe would you like delivered within reasonable proximity of your homeworld, if any?"

"We will consider that as well." A faint smile curved her thin lips, making the straight lines on her cheek swerve a little. *"In other words, that means you should begin work on a top-quality version. You can always deliver a crude version at our command in the meantime. If and when our potential mutual enemy finds out we can use these things to communicate, they will try to destroy them, so it is best to have several options on hand."*

Jackie smiled back, this time a warmer than merely polite one. *"Thank you, Eternity. I would like to turn control of the channel over to the appropriate specialists at this time. Once they have calibrated the two systems a little more, we will reserve a channel specifically for you, as the head of the V'Dan government to contact us—the Terran government—and a channel for you to contact your son. If there are any personnel on board your ship who are related to or at least personally concerned over Leftenants Superior Shi'ol Nanu'oc, Ba'oul Des'n-yi, V'kol Kos'q, or Dai'a Vres-yat, we will establish channels for that as well. If not they will be established if and when a probe reaches V'Dan nearspace.*

"We Terrans understand how close families and friends can be, and how much it can hurt to miss a loved one. Even if protocol demands it not be displayed, in case an enemy is

watching," Jackie added, in case that was the reason why the Empress of V'Dan was acting so formally toward her own child.

"We will consider your offer. Thank you for communicating with us, Ambassador . . . and thank you for rescuing Captain Ma'an-uq'en and his fellow survivors." The Empress shifted her arm, and her image vanished, replaced by the crisscrossed lines of the Empire.

Admiral Nayak leaned his hands on the edge of the console table. "Please pardon my bluntness, Your Highness, and please understand that it comes strictly from within my *own* culture, and thus has no intended insult meant toward yours . . . but your mother didn't seem very happy to see you. She did acknowledge your rank, but . . ."

"I will not take offense because you do not know our culture, Admiral," Li'eth returned. He dragged in a deep breath and let it out slowly, moving his shoulders subtly to release some of the tension in his back. "Right now, she is the War Queen, and . . . it is not proper to confess this, but she is losing that war. She knows she is losing it. She will throw anything and everything—even her own children—into the path of the oncoming destruction in the hopes that something will stop our enemy. Even if it has to be her own body, to save the Empire. The Salik, unlike yourselves, have had open access to all Alliance technology, including V'Dan communications technology. We know that they can break our best cryptography efforts in a matter of months, sometimes even weeks. It also takes literal days and weeks to deliver the new code systems across the Alliance."

"I wish we could speed things up on our end," Jackie told him, leaning her hip against the table and tucking her arms across her chest. With this jacket, she didn't have to worry about the buttons popping out of their holes. "But we can't. We don't have the ships, yet. We don't have enough relay satellites made. That's part of why we're occupying your time with tours of this and that.

Li'eth opened his mouth. Admiral Nayak beat him to it. "The ships we send out right now are on a twenty-day trip one-way, just to get to your homeworld. Some of that is time spent processing our version of fuel, which while reasonably abundant in the galaxy, is not swiftly refined. We *need* the coming weeks to continue to work on establishing supply points for fuel, food, and more. Be glad you get to attend a bunch of parties in various places while you wait. Everyone else is busy breaking in their boots trying to get the resources in place to get you back home."

". . . Sir, we're getting a message from the V'Dan; they say they have a measurements specialist on the line to help us calibrate between Terran and V'Dan units," one of the nearby techs stated, touching his headset earpiece.

"Get Lieutenant Souk in here—you did give him V'Dan last night, yes?" Nayak asked Jackie.

She nodded. "A full set, sir, along with Master Petty Chun, right after I gave you yours. The master petty's a minor clairsentient, a very disciplined, intuitive mind, and the lieutenant practices meditation, as well as already speaks three languages, so both only took two hours each. Chun's in charge of communications maintenance under the lieutenant," she added to Li'eth, before returning her attention to her military superior. "It all went very quickly, sir, which is why I had time and energy to do two in a row before retiring. Lieutenant Souk recommended Chun when our session ended, and I mentioned I could do one more before exhausting myself."

Nayak glanced from her to Li'eth and back, a speculative look in his dark brown eyes. "Are you sure that's not a result of the Gestalt speeding things up?"

"That's on *top* of the Gestalt speeding things up," Jackie admitted freely. "Captain Ma'an-uq'en sat in on the session and assisted, at Master Sonam's recommendation. It occurred to me very early on that we're going to need a *lot* of people who can speak both Terranglo and V'Dan fluently, particularly in the military, if we're to help these people in their war."

"How do you figure that, Major?" Nayak asked.

"It was in my earliest reports, sir. Cryptography can be cracked, but steganography—using keyworded images instead of coded patterns replacing letters and numbers—requires you to have the key to what those images mean."

"Right. Navajo code-talkers. I'd forgotten about that," the admiral apologized. "I think I'm going to have to go back over *all* of your reports, yours and the others', before we finish getting you and the V'Dan launched in their homeworld's direction. I don't want to miss any other aspect that might be important," he stated. Giving her a nod, he lifted his chin. "Good work, Major. And good work as our Ambassador. I'll write up a report for the Council to let them know you handled this meeting well. That is, I *presume* she did, Captain?"

Li'eth nodded. "She did make a good impression. Mother rarely smiles."

"You call that a smile?" one of the other techs quipped under her breath.

"Hey! Be respectful, Lieutenant," Jackie ordered, noting the single bar on the other woman's shirt collar. "I'd be hard-pressed to smile, too, given what these people are facing. Particularly after finding out not only did my son face it directly, but is now in the hands—and at the mercy—of an almost entirely unknown group of sentients."

"Sir, yes, sir. My apologies, sir," the lieutenant stated promptly.

Nayak flicked a finger around the room. "Get back to work, all of you. Or back to bed in your cases, you two," he stated, ending with Jackie and Li'eth. "Sleep when you can, while you can. There may come a day when you'll need to be fully rested to get through everything."

"Sir, yes, sir," Jackie said, straightening briefly to Attention.

"Understood, sir," Li'eth agreed, straightening and squaring his shoulders as well.

(*You know, you don't have to salute him. So to speak. You're not in his chain of command,*) Jackie reminded him.

He shrugged as they exited together. (*True, but I will give respect where respect is earned. Besides, this is his territory, and it's clear he's earned your respect. You don't suffer disrespect.*)

(*You do realize your quarters are in the opposite direction from mine?*) she pointed out.

(*I want twenty Terran minutes of cuddling time, and there's a lounge where we can hold hands and practice our abilities in public. It's not far from where you're quartered,*) he replied. (*That, and my so-called quarters are so small, I start feeling claustrophobic within a handful of minutes if I'm not busy sleeping.*)

(*It's either a tiny closet of a cabin, or you share quarters with someone else . . . and the only person who won't rub your shields raw is me,*) she reminded him. (*Even if all we'd be doing is sleeping . . .*)

(*. . . It's still a bad choice politically. Let's fall asleep on a couch in public instead,*) he offered.

(*I love the way you sweet-talk me. If I remember that lounge, there is a couch big enough for the both of us if we prop our feet on the coffee table.*) She caught his undercurrent of thought in the next moment. (*Hey, coffee runs the world in this star system. Worlds. Plural.*)

(*Planets. You need to colonize other star systems to start talking worlds, plural. We need to get your people out of this system and settling into new places. This "third-child lottery" idea is abhorrent.*)

(*Well, excuse us for only just developing interstellar travel,*) Jackie quipped. (*We've had insystem tech for a while, but without artificial gravity, it just isn't wise to raise a child anywhere but on Earth right now. Their bodies just don't develop right. Skeletal structure, musculature, stamina, reflexes . . .*)

(*Your subthoughts are borderline cranky. Both of us need more sleep.*) Catching her hand, he tugged her into the lounge in question. Given the early hour, there were a couple of Mars dwellers trying to wake up over mugs of the noxious brew, but they were seated at one of the tables. The couch the pair of psis aimed for was free.

(*Dibs on your shoulder,*) Jackie sent, flopping down in the middle.

Li'eth settled against the armrest and tucked his other limb around her when she slouched against him. (*Sure. Wait, what* is *this word "dibs," exactly? Where did it come from?*)

(*I don't know. Now, hush. Napping time, now,*) she ordered . . . and received a mental smile and a physical hug from one arm in return.

CHAPTER 19

"We should have used the naval base on Ni'ihau," Ayinda muttered as soon as she joined Jackie and Li'eth on the beach. The tide was set to come in for a few more hours, bringing with it what looked to Jackie like perfect, calm, easy surfing weather, with puffy clouds that would do nothing but drift placidly on by, and maybe dump a little rain on the highest peak. The navigator, however, wasn't looking at the surf. She bumped Jackie on the arm with her elbow and lifted her chin at the shoreline. "That, at least, would have been far more private than all this."

Houses lined the grassy gardens marking the end of the high tide zone. And on nearly every single piece of property, though they were respectfully staying back behind the flimsy-looking low barricades, throngs of cheering, hollering, waving Terran Humans were busy trying to get the attention of the V'Dan exiting the hovercars.

"Ni'ihau is a protected reserve for the Hawai'ian culture," Jackie demurred. "Even more so than northside Kaho'olawe. It's far easier to get cooperation from the homeowners here on O'ahu to allow us to rope off a section of their beach than it is the people who live out there."

". . . Is it *always* going to be like this?" Li'eth asked her. "We have been all over this planet, from hot to cold, mountaintop to canyon gorge, and now this beach, and only in the *most* remote locations have there not been . . . crowds . . . of Terrans all trying to get our attention."

"So what's wrong with that?" Ayinda asked him. She dipped her head to the side, dreadlocks swaying. "Aside from being pestered and annoyed and yelled at, so on and so forth."

"It's . . . It's their lack of focus," Li'eth complained, finding the right words. "When they do get our attention, they hardly know what they want from us. Most are not business owners or government employees; *those*, at least, know what they want to discuss. These . . . masses of people have no business, no agenda . . . questions yes, but purpose, no. Back home, people don't usually cross the Tiers without knowing what they want from someone."

Robert had moved up from his own hovercar ride, the one still disgorging Maria and Ba'oul. Like the rest of them, he was wearing knee-length shorts and a tee shirt, the former dyed in colorful flower patterns and the latter sporting some logo for a Texan college. He had on a leather cowboy hat, not one of the woven ones more popular in the Isles, battered and sun-faded and clearly much-loved. Tugging on the brim and tightening the drawstring to make sure the wind wouldn't catch it wrong while the hovercar lifted off again, he addressed Li'eth's question.

"You have to realize, Your Highness, we're *all* celebrities right now. This is their first in-person glimpse of people who were born on another world, and the heroic crew that rescued you from certain death. Heck, even I feel a little giddy about all this from time to time, and I'm in the thick of it.

"But five years from now? If we expand our contact and keep exchanging visitors at a steadily increasing rate? This won't be nearly so exciting for everyone. And *ten* years from now, you V'Dan will be old news. After all, you look like us," the pilot added, flashing Li'eth and V'kol a grin. "You'll be old and *boring* news compared to the *real* aliens that are out there. Assuming any can safely visit."

"Most can visit our world," V'kol told him. His shirt was sleeveless and brightly patterned in shades of yellow and orange and pink, while his shorts were plain beige. They didn't look too bad with his hot-pink marks spiraling around his arms. "I don't see why they cannot visit yours, with the appropriate precautions in the beginning. Now, I believe, Ambassador, you said you were going to give us *surfing* lessons?"

Jackie shaded her eyes, peering at the pop-up tents that had been staked firmly into the sand a short distance away. She pointed. "First, we go greet my family and see how the food is coming along. My brother-in-law said he'd started digging the roasting pits before dawn. One pit for the boar, and another for a pair of roasted turkeys, and a third for pit-roasted fish, for those who are on religious or dietary restrictions. We don't want to go in the water if the food's almost ready. Well, the first course of it, at any rate. This is an all-afternoon *lu'au*. The boar will be served later, since it takes the longest to cook."

By diet, she meant members of the security teams, since the V'Dan didn't seem to have any restrictions. Some of those guards were dressed in tactical gear for combat, while some were dressed for the beach; the plan was to rotate them out on overlapping shifts so that the Space Force security specialists could have some time relaxing at the party as well as spending time guarding their V'Dan guests. When the last of their nonsecurity group came up, being Sonam, Shi'ol, and Brad, Jackie raised her voice a little.

"We're now going to go meet up with my *'ohana*, which is Hawai'ian for *family*, and several of their neighbors, plus some important locals. My mother, if you will recall, is the Lieutenant Governor of Oceania, which is sort of like a junior version of Governor, the executive position of government for the region. But this is a *lu'au*, not a formal meeting, so there will be no formal clothes, no formal speeches, and no formal behavior, save for two things:

"Politeness is, as ever, at the top of the list of how to behave, as is refraining from leaving garbage on the beach. It is all one and the same: It is polite to enter a place, to behave politely within it, and to leave it as pleasant or more so than you first found it. Also, please remember what I told you about the *na lei* which you will be offered, the flower-and-leaf garlands. You need not wear them, but if you do not wish to wear them, or wish to take them off, please leave them on a tree branch near those awnings.

"It is considered rude in Hawai'ian culture to just toss them in the trash. You can fetch them back later, or you can leave them there, as it is proper to either dry them, burn them, or let them return to the environment from which they came. Some will be leaves, some will be flowers, some a mix of both. If your *lei* has a lot of yellow flowers, it is because the flower species, *Sida fallax*, symbolically represents this particular island. There will be flowers representing the other islands, too.

"So remember, hang them on one of the trees within the perimeter if you do not want to wear them, even if it's just for a little while. Or, if you prefer, there will be a table under one of the tents with a box where you can put your lei permanently; Any that are left on the trees at the end of the day and those put in the box will be carefully unmade and the flowers and leaves distributed free to all those people out there, one per person, so that they can have a memento of your visit in exchange for the courtesy of letting us have this section of the beach to ourselves."

(*That's a nice touch,*) Li'eth praised. (*Giving all those people a little keepsake like that.*)

(*It was Grandmother's idea,*) Jackie confessed. She turned and started leading the way toward the others, gesturing with a sweep of her hand for them to follow.

(*Is that the one who will demand I recite a long line of my ancestors?*) he asked.

(*The very one. I think I saw her in a blue-and-white dress in one of the tents. She said she'd save a seat for Master Sonam.*)

He raised his brows. (*Hints of a romance?*)

(*No, just the courtesy of one elder to another. Grandma always gets the best seat on the beach, as the eldest of the family.*) Nearly to the shade tents, she called out, "Aloha, 'ohana! I bring visitors."

Just as the people under the awning looked up to reply in greeting, several shouts and yells erupted from their right, from farther down the beach. Jackie moved out warily. Sure enough, a pair—no, a trio—of yelling teenagers were trying to dodge around the security guards. Teens, or maybe college-aged youths. Sighing, Jackie held up her hand and concentrated.

Six suntanned feet left the sand, kicking and spraying grains in startlement. The trio of boys hollered, this time in fright, not in excitement. She twisted them upside down, making their heads dangle and the blood rush to their face. Two of them stopped yelling, eyes wide with fright, while the third screamed for help. It was difficult to move herself on the uneven surface of the beach while hefting all three in the air, but she closed the distance between them and fixed the youths with a stern look.

"Do I have your attention?" she asked, coming to a stop in both mind and body. The last one ceased yelling and panted, blinking at her. His dark braid dangled and swayed in the breeze. Jackie met his gaze, and those of his companion. ". . . Yes? I have your attention? Good. This is a private party. It is meant to show our visitors the *hospitality* of O'ahu. Yelling and party-crashing is something a child does."

A twist of her hand, a turn of her mind, and the trio righted, two stocky and heavily tanned, one skinny and somewhat sunburned.

"By doing so, by alarming the security team, you are not showing our honored guests respect. A day at the beach is meant to be relaxing. Being yelled at by overexcited children is not relaxing. Apologize, and step back beyond the barriers—and no, you do not get to be introduced, and you do not get to shake their hands," she added, since that thought was very strongly uppermost on the two left youths' minds. One of them might even have a touch of telepathy or empathy, it was that strong.

The skinny teenager wrinkled his nose. "But we—"

She cut him off flatly. "*No.* You did not act in a mature manner. You could have *asked* if we would like to meet you. The answer might have been *yes.* Now, it is no. Apologize, and leave."

A voice spoke up in Hawai'ian from behind her. "*You should be more gentle, Grandchild. They are just children trying to have fun.*"

She glanced at her ancestress. She didn't have time to explain the complexity of the problem, nor were there quite the right words for it in Hawai'ian. "*Grandmother, the V'Dan respect maturity. Anything childish reduces our honor in their eyes. Please do not encourage their immaturity.*"

Leilani Kapule folded her aged arms across her chest, while two of the three youths blushed, understanding Jackie's chiding words. "Hmmph."

Great. My own grandmother hmmphs *at me.*

(*All grandparents do that to the youngest generations,*) Li'eth commiserated, overhearing her thought. He joined her, his shorts red and flowered, his shirt white and loose, thin enough to show some of the stripes through the soft knit. The shorts had a similar pattern to her red sarong dress. "You heard the Ambassador," he stated, hands on his hips. "Apologize, and leave."

"Pupule," the middle-sized tanned male breathed, his brown eyes wide as he stared at Li'eth. He continued in Terranglo, clearly overwhelmed. "The prince *talked* to me . . . !"

"I—I was just trying to get them to stop," the biggest of the trio said, stammering in his anxiety. "I didn't think it'd be respectful to—to crash your *lu'au*. I apologize for myself and my friends."

(*Should I acknowledge him?*) Li'eth asked her, undercurrents of thought pointing out that the young man was trying to take some responsibility, show some maturity.

(*No hand-shaking, but you can ask his name,*) she returned, adding, (*Just don't publicly thwart my authority/decisions.*)

"What's your name?" Li'eth asked the tallest of the three, while the guards stood close behind, watching the moment play out. (*You know I wouldn't.*)

"K-Kapa'a, sir," the tallest stammered. "I'm Kapa'a." He poked his thumb to his left. "These are my friends, Steve, and Lars."

The slightly sunburned Caucasian puffed up his chest. "I share my name with the geophysicist!"

Li'eth turned to him. "You have not apologized, young one. Do so now, or say nothing at all, as the Ambassador instructed you."

Lars swallowed. Steve quickly cleared his throat, bobbing a bow as he spoke up before his friend got to it. "Sorry, sir. Highness, sir. Ma'am."

"Yeah. Sorry," Lars added. "Excitement, and all." He tried peering past them at the other V'Dan on the beach behind them. They were busy being introduced by Master Sonam and receiving the various garlands that had been prepared for them.

"Thank you for apologizing. You may go." Jackie flicked her hand, motioning for the trio to leave. Steve pulled Lars away, while the guards parted to let them pass. Li'eth held up his hand toward Kapa'a, the tallest and most respectful.

"Because of things beyond your people's control, my people will have a problem viewing yours as mature. At least, until we come to know each other better. But your prompt apology is mature. You are young, but you are a man. I believe the Terranglo phrase is 'keep up the good work'?" He smiled, glancing briefly at Jackie. She smiled back, dipping her head in confirmation.

"*Thank* you, Your Highness," Kapa'a said, grinning. "Uh . . . . welcome to O'ahu! I hope you have a great time, here." He backed up a few steps, stumbled a little on the sand, then turned and hurried after his friends.

"*Crisis averted,*" Li'eth muttered in V'Dan, turning back toward the tent. Or rather, toward the short, wrinkled, stout, tanned but unmarked woman with gray hair swept up in a braid-wrapped bun and a periwinkle-and-white-flowered dress rippling in the sea breeze. He dipped his head politely toward Jackie's family matriarch. Her grandmother eyed him in return, then *hmmphed* a second time before giving him a curt nod.

Jackie subtly herded her ancestress and Li'eth back toward the tent. She spoke aloud, addressing the group. "My apologies for the interruption. Since the rest of you have been introduced—and thank you, Master Sonam, for doing so—please allow me to make the final one. Everyone, this is His Highness, Li'eth V'Daania and captain of these fine officers. Li'eth, I give you the matriarch of my mother's family, Leilani Kaimana Kapule, who owns the blue house behind these tents—if you need to use the bathrooms, just go up the path behind this tent, and someone in the house will show you where to go from there; there will be guards inside all day long, if nothing else.

"Behind her is her son-in-law, my father, Jean-Jacques MacKenzie," she added, gesturing at the tallish, graying man in dark shorts and a blue-flowered shirt. "Next is my mother Lily Kapule-MacKenzie in the green dress, and behind her in the brown shorts and no shirt is her boss, the—*hey!*

"*No* surfing until I've made introductions, Your Honor," Jackie added sternly, waggling her finger at the dark-skinned woman who had a surfboard tucked under her arm. Jackie had caught her in the act of trying to sneak past behind the others' backs with the board. "You can play *after* you've been introduced. Li'eth, this is Her Honor, Governor Amara de la Couer.

She has been the Polynesian champion long-distance pipe surfer for her age category for three of the last four years, as well as the Governor of Oceania . . . which is why she wants to go play.

"Next, we have her husband . . ."

It had been a long, surprisingly fun, tiring afternoon. The sun rode low on the horizon to one side, and their moon, Luna, could be seen rising opposite. With the tide well on its way out, the party was winding down. Exhausted from learning how to surf, from playing *frizz-bee* and *volleyball* . . . and introducing them to the concept of guanjiball, which his officers had all helped in explaining, demonstrating, and teaching these enthusiastic Terrans how to play . . . Li'eth was happy just to sit on a sandy, dusty pillow set out on the beach above the tideline, and sip at a fizzy, tangy, fruit-flavored drink, which for some odd, incomprehensible Terran reason was called a *cooler*.

He had been offered *beer* earlier, which was a bitter sort of alcohol—Li'eth had no idea why these Terrans were enamored of bitter drinks—but Sonam had already warned him it would be wiser to keep a clear head by steering away from alcohol. As far as he knew, the *cooler* drink was some sort of fruit-flavored *soda*, flavored liquid filled with compressed carbon-dioxide gas.

The belching was amusingly different, even enjoyable . . . but only because there was no formality in the moment. It would never, ever catch on back home. At least, not in the highest Tiers of society.

Wisps of Ba'oul's voice drifted Li'eth's way, something about how the moon here was so big and solitary, and marked like a face, compared to seeing the much smaller, littlest-fingernail-sized dots back on V'Dan, or the thin but glowing rings of Tai-mat, their most dramatic colonyworld.

He didn't hear V'kol approach, not between the wind, the surf, and the laughter of the group with Ba'oul a little ways away, but he did sense his friend's aura approaching, shades of green and blue with streaks of cream. Dropping onto the sand next to him, V'kol set down a couple extra bottles, twisted off the cap of the one still in his hand, and spoke under his breath. Or as much as the evening wind would allow.

"You do realize that going home will be nothing like this," the gunner stated, gesturing with the bottle once it was open. It smelled of something just as fruity as Li'eth's drink when the wind tossed some of that opening hiss Li'eth's way. V'kol clarified his meaning. "This . . . openness. This warmth, and welcoming, and the casualness, the relaxation of it all. I may be a commoner, but even I know what the Imperial Court is like. You get it in miniature at Second Tier in the military, and in spades around the First Tiers."

"The Terran Ambassador will be able to handle it," Li'eth stated. He had to put it that way because he didn't know, and wouldn't know, until after tomorrow's special meeting of the Council who that Ambassador would be. Jackie had explained that the Council normally met only five days a week, with two days off before five on again, but the special Saturday session was being called specifically to address their Gestalt and its impact on the diplomatic embassy the Terrans wanted to send to his homeworld, so as not to disrupt the normal functioning of their government.

V'kol, in the midst of drinking down his own soda, quickly lowered it, shaking is head. "Oh, no, not her. She's wonderful. Magnificent, if you can get past the lack of marks that keep screaming in my head to not think anything personal about her. She's part of the warmth of these people."

"If not her, then what did you mean?" Li'eth asked . . . and got poked in the shoulder by the gunnery officer's finger.

"You. I got to know Li'eth Ma'an-uq'en on board the *T'un Tunn*. I'm going to mourn your having to go back to being His Imperial Highness, Kah'raman V'Daania. All stuffy, proper, concerned with the Empire—which you properly should be," V'kol allowed. "But I am going to *miss* the man who sat in a tavern on planetside leave with me, using your ability to see auras and read motives to help me rake in enough money at *kaskat* to pay for my mother's new Spring Temple robes as her birthing-day gift."

"I'm beginning to regret that," Li'eth stated dryly. He drank down a good part of his cooler before catching V'kol's suspicious look. "It's that monk, Master Sonam. He told me I can't use my gifts to cheat at gambling. Even if *I* did not benefit from it, it's still cheating."

"He's a sly *ba'chok*," V'kol agreed. "He had me asking where the universe came from, the 'Big Bang' as they call it, if not as an act of miraculous wishing power from some god." He tipped back his own drink. "I was forced in the end to tell him I don't know where the First Spark came from. What triggered it. He asked me if I could prove it wasn't a god. I asked him if he could prove it *was*. He said that we're able to intelligently question our own origin, in polite discussion, and that is a profound set of miracles entirely on their own, given the contentiousness of the Human species. Whether or not we believe in gods."

"And at that point . . . ?" Li'eth asked, curious to know what his atheist friend thought.

"I couldn't come up with anything better than that as a rejoinder, and he made me clean his quarters for losing the bet. This was back in quarantine, before we started traveling all over." Lifting his bottle, he saluted Li'eth with it, drank, and sighed. Everything now had a distinct golden cast to it, one that was tinging toward orange. "Sunset on yet another alien world. Given the fossils we've seen, the many theories proposed by their top scientists after centuries of investigation and pondering . . . welcome to the Motherworld of our species. Welcome— *aloha*, as they say, a *warm* welcome full of love, openness, and honor . . . which is what we will not get nearly enough of, back home. Not from *our* government. So . . . *aloha*, and good-bye."

"She says they say *aloha* when they part, not just when they meet each other," Li'eth said, draining his bottle.

He set it carefully aside, mindful of Jackie's words much earlier in the day, that they had to clean up the beach when they were through. The bottles were some sort of super-recyclable substance called *plexi*, able to be used over and over again. *A planet where the roads are paved in solar panels for cheap daily energy needs,* he acknowledged silently, *where all of their containers are completely recyclable, and their vehicles and power-draining manufactories use* water *plucked from the far edges of their system to get around with or to tackle any huge energy-requiring function . . . and yet they still don't have artificial gravity . . .*

Picking up the next one, Li'eth cracked the lid on it. "Thank you for bringing more, by the way. These *cooler* things taste really good."

"I know. I've had two," V'kol admitted. "I think they're herbal. The husband of the governor said if I had a few, I'd relax. I'm starting to feel relaxed."

"This is my third. No, fourth. Had to use the matriarch's house before opening my third. Jackie's father recommended them, said he'd join me for a chat while drinking them . . . I think it's some sort of unspoken ritual or custom they just haven't explained yet . . . but then his wife's mother called him away to clean up the roasting pits. I think I like this *lu'au* thing. Even if it's named after a bunch of leaves."

"They're a little odd, but they're ni—" V'kol, paused belching midword. "—ice . . . Oh. Oh! *Do* pardon me, Your Highness," he groveled a little. Mock-groveled, replete with an obsequious little bow. "This lowly commoner peon should never have been so crass and vulgar as to *belch* in the Imperial presence . . ."

"Oh, please, my mother farts," Li'eth found himself admitting. "Particularly after eating certain vegetables."

Dropping onto an elbow to support his upper body, V'kol's brows rose. "She does? She admits it?"

"Oh, no. No no no no no," Li'eth denied, waving a hand through the air. "*No* one admits to it. But we all do it. The kitchen staff is simply trained to limit her intake of those specific vegetables . . . but she *likes* them, so every once in a while, she'll order a meal with them. When there aren't any formal evenings scheduled."

Twisting farther onto his side, V'kol adjusted his weight on his elbow, sipping at his bottle. He squinted against the sunset glow. "*Which* vegetables? C'mon, you can tell me . . ."

"Nope." He liked that Terranglo word, so he used it again. "Nope, nope, and nope. State secret. I'd have to kill you if you knew. Or just position you behind her."

Both men started snickering, at that. Li'eth grinned and . . . belched. And laughed. "Sorry, sorry . . . how crass of me, a pillar of highest society, a son of the Imperial Tier, emanating noxious noises and odiferous fumes when they aren't supposed to exist, so high . . ."

"I am very much going to miss this, my friend. You'll have to go back to being a stuffy, repressed prince." V'kol sighed. "As one of your leftenant superiors in the military, *Captain*," he enunciated carefully, using the Terranglo word-equivalents, "I am, and was, free to associate with you. To laugh about farts and belches and other obnoxious but perfectly normal things. Unfortunately . . . Those days are ending. I'm glad I got to be the friend of my captain. I'm sorry I cannot stay the friend of my prince."

". . . Who says you can't?" Li'eth asked, bottle paused halfway to his lips.

"Protocol. I don't have enough clout to wade through all the layers of the Empire that will slide into place between us the moment we get back home," V'kol reminded him. "Unless you get shipped out again, and we get reassigned to the same ship, I'll only ever get to see you again on the vids. As part of the news."

"No . . ." Li'eth shook his head. He didn't like the picture V'kol was painting. His mind ticked over, trying to find a way around it.

"*Yes* . . . So . . . this is good-bye, you . . . uhh . . . what was that phrase the copilot uses . . . You bootless tosser! No, no . . . you *boot*-tosser. That's it. Boot-tosser. You are one, and a complete and total one," V'kol added, pointing vaguely at the prince. "I have *no* idea what that means, but it's my only chance to be rude to a member of the Imperial Blood. Without being actually rude, because I like you." He drained his bottle and set it down, then picked up the remaining spare. "I'll just have to . . . I don't know . . . fart at the vid in fond memory. Except that's a rather markless thing to do, and I'm all grown-up."

"No, I mean no, you don't *have* to go away. I'm not the Heir. I can have whatever friends I like," Li'eth pointed out. "Vi'alla is the Heir . . . and she's a stiff little copy of Mother. She follows the book. Prays to all the Saints. Has the blessings of the High Priesthood."

"She's not very good at military tactics," V'kol stated. That earned him a sharp look from his captain. Looking off across the waves, the gunnery officer shook his head. "I heard about an operation—training exercise, before the war—which she'd tried to pull off as the CO. The official word is that five ships didn't follow through on time, so it was their fault. I looked over the recordings, and there was no way that could have been pulled off on time. She's got big ideas, but not enough . . . *practicality* to see when they won't necessarily work.

"I've seen it in other officers, too. Following the book, praying to the Saints on all the right holy days, but not a speck of imagination in them. Your sister is not going to know what to do with these Terrans . . . and if she's like your mother, your mother isn't, either. No offense to the War Queen."

Li'eth shook his head. The sun was setting off to his right, a rich orange light forcing him to keep his head averted so that it wouldn't give him a headache through the corner of his eye. "They'll have to listen to them."

"Because your precious *Book of the Immortal* and the *Book of Saints* say so?" V'kol scoffed.

"No. Because we're losing, and Mother is aware of just *how* badly the Alliance has been crumbling under each and every assault. We need these people. We take them in under the roof of the Empire. Welcome them. Learn from them. And we need to do it *fast*."

"And how do we do that, with a group of First Tiers who insist on praying to every Saint on his or her day, without deviation?" V'kol asked.

"I don't know," he muttered, shaking his head even as he tried to think of the right thing to say. Tipping up his bottle, he swallowed, then lowered it. A burp welled up, and he let it out. Somehow, it brought an idea up to the surface. Not necessarily the greatest idea, but at least it was an idea. "I don't know. Throw a bunch of Terrans at them. Then throw a bunch more. Fill the whole damned Court with Terrans, all bouncing around, breaking all the rules because they don't *know* all the rules . . . until either the Court has to move and learn how to play, or they just . . . They just become obstacles in a guanjiball game."

A *snerk* sound escaped V'kol. "So . . . what does that make your mother? The goal alcove, or the prime mangora root?"

"I'm more interested in knowing who's the ball, so I know who to kick around the Court to get things done."

Another snort escaped the gunner. "Saints—your sister!

Her Imperial Highness, Heir to the Empire," V'kol snickered in V'Dan. *"Ping-ong, thumplethumple* BONK*!"*

"Bonk?" he asked, curious.

"Bonk! It's a Terran word," V'kol asserted. "It means . . .
um . . . the noise thing, when you bump into something hollow.
I think."

"Ah. Like *boop.* They have the *strangest*-sounding language, don't they?" Li'eth mused, draining his drink dry.

". . . I bet they say the same thing about ours," V'kol
stated after a moment . . . and burped.

Li'eth belched. Both men snickered

Footsteps *chuffed* through the sand, and a hand came down
to snatch up one of the bottles. Waves of anger and a hint of
cream . . . oh! *Cream is intoxication!* Li'eth realized. Just as
his pretty Bright Stone called out in a disgusted voice to the
others within hearing range on that stretch of the beach.

"Alright, who the *hell* thought it was a *good* idea to give
the *high-ranked telepath* alcohol? *Who* did it?"

Li'eth snickered, and flopped onto his back. He reached
up and patted her leg awkwardly. "It's a *soda . . .*"

"It's a *wine* cooler! Which one of you bootless, modo rats
was responsible!" she demanded again in a shout toward the
others, before lowering her voice, free hand going to her
forehead. "Great. I'm getting dizzy off secondhand drunken-
ness . . . made worse now because you're *touching* me.
Amplifying our connection. Great. Just . . . booting *great*!"

The Imperial prince, who would never, ever be caught
dead in knee-length shorts and a sleeveless shirt within the
bounds of his Empire, curled gracelessly over onto his side,
laughing almost too hard to breathe.

MARCH 26, 2287 C.E.
THE LOTUS, ALOHA CITY, KAHO'OLAWE

(*Do you know . . .*) Li'eth broke off with a grunt, unable to continue his question. Lifting a hand to his forehead, he gingerly
pinched the bridge of his nose. He was in his approximation of
a V'Dan dress uniform, and she was in a very nice dress, black
with flowers on the flared sleeves and flowing hem.

"I told you, don't use your telepathy," Jackie muttered under her breath, gesturing for them to turn left to head for the special waiting room that would be their place to relax until they were called to the Council Hall floor.

"I know. I just forgot," he muttered aloud.

"Well, I told you, you'll want to avoid using your gifts while you're still suffering from a hangover." Jackie sighed. "But then, it's not *my* fault you sucked down nearly four whole wine coolers last night."

"Don't your people have a saying that gloating from being right is annoying?" he demanded. "Besides, how should I know what I was drinking?"

"Did you even try reading the label? It's clearly marked by law if and when a drink is alcoholic," Jackie told him. She had little sympathy for his plight this morning, because *his* headache was *her* headache, thanks to their growing Corsican-twins joy of being a Gestalt pair. Not quite as strong as his, but it wasn't leaving her at her best.

"I read enough to know it said Blackberry Blend. It sounded like a harmless fruit drink. Besides, why didn't you stop me earlier, back before I became intoxicated?"

"Because I didn't realize you were getting drunk until I started tripping over things, helping to clean up. Even then, it took me a few minutes and a few bruises before I realized it wasn't because *I* was simply tired." She paused, then added telepathically, deliberately, (*Besides, those who know the effects of alcohol on strong telepaths will have reason to trust that you and I aren't in constant silent contact.*)

"*V'shova v'shakk!*" he hissed. Struggling with his breathing, he controlled the pain. His biokinesis was still a struggle to activate at will for things like this. Specifically, for things he hadn't practiced curing. "Pardon my language, but that *hurt.*"

"Yes, and all the cameras trained on us are now aware that neither of us can use telepathy with the other without *you* showing signs of pain," Jackie stated. Li'eth stopped, which meant she had to stop, too. Raising her brows, she waited for his answer.

He narrowed his gaze at her. "You planned this."

"Definitely not," Jackie denied. "But I *am* going to take

advantage of it to prove we're following the rules every step of the way."

"Fighting for your career?" he muttered, studying her.

"Yes," Jackie admitted bluntly. "What do you think I'm going to do on V'Dan, sit in a corner until I bear your babies? Such things are admirable as ambitions and milestones in one's life, and one day I should like to have a few children, but my *biggest* ambitions are off in an entirely different corner. What do you think *you* would do, here on Earth?"

He frowned at her in puzzlement. "What do you mean, what would *I* do here on Earth?"

"We forgot to discuss that," Jackie told. Realizing they had stopped in the corridor, a corridor with people passing this way and that, she gestured for him to continue onward with her. "We've talked about my going to V'Dan and staying there as if it was some sort of given. But what if it ends up being the other way? What if I returned to Earth, with you in tow? Depending on how things unfold, I could take up a Council seat again, or I could go back to being a translator—I could make a fortune in telepathic language transfers alone, public or private sector. What would *you* do, as my Gestalt partner, if we ended up back on Earth?"

"I . . . don't know. Train my abilities. Maybe try my hand at learning how to transfer languages and work alongside you. But not until the war is won, Jackie," he asserted, cutting his hand through the air between them. "I will not abandon either the Empire or the Alliance. Not easily. Even if all I can do is pick up a weapon and charge at the enemy, if there's a chance a single body more will stop them, then . . . let that body be mine. And yours. Even if I don't want to risk you."

She touched his shoulder with a soft, "I know," before turning him into the waiting room. Only to be gestured forward by the gray-robed aides. Jackie looked at the pair waving her toward the inner door. "What . . . ?"

"Everyone is here; they're just waiting on you, miss," the older of the two women stated. "They want you to take the Oath of Service with everyone else—you can stay here if you like, sir. Someone will come for you when they're ready."

"No, I'm going with her," Li'eth stated. He looked to

Jackie. "Let them watch me as I listen to their oath-swearing. Let them be aware that *I* am aware of those words."

She nodded and held out her hand. He gripped it briefly, squeezing her fingers, and lifted his chin at the door, releasing her.

"You first. It's your government."

CHAPTER 20

". . . Today, I shall do my best to serve well and fully for the entire time I work. I am Jacaranda MacKenzie, and I represent the people of the Terran United Planets."

Only because he was standing next to her could Li'eth hear her exact variation on the incredibly long speech which everyone—save only the Fellowship members—had just recited. More or less in unison, like some sort of mass religious ritual, save it was a secular oath. A few voices fell into the quiet at the end, but the chamber was large and absorbed the sound fairly well when the sound pickups weren't focusing on a specific person.

Still, as they resumed their seats on the edge of the Council Hall floor, he muttered under his breath, switching to V'Dan to be politely discreet in case anyone seated near them overheard. *"Saints above, that things is annoyingly long. Why does it have to be so long?"*

"To groove good habits into our heads. To ensure understanding, which leads to cooperation. And to not be able to claim ignorance of consequences," Jackie returned, lips barely moving. They were parted on a pleasant smile, a neat trick of ventriloquism.

Premiere Callan took the podium, commanding their attention. "Thank you for coming here today, on a Saturday. I know a lot of you undoubtedly had other plans. However, in the light of our ongoing and increasing interstellar communication with the V'Dan Empire—predominantly in the areas of exchanging basic scientific knowledge for the specific need of accuracy in measurement conversion and terminology translation between our two different systems—we will soon be able to reach a point of understanding where the real negotiations can begin."

Hands raised in the Fellowship seats. The Premiere held up his own hand. Jackie and Li'eth were seated with their backs to the Fellowship, but there were screens placed up high around the circular chamber displaying various viewpoints.

"Please, hold your questions for the moment; there will be an opportunity for the Fellowship to join these discussions. I can guess what the main questions are. The points of information we are currently sharing and calibrating are things like . . . how long is a centimeter, a meter, a kilometer, compared to their own units of distance measurement. How many joules of energy does one of their standard-sized engines produce. Do they use base ten mathematics like we do, and do they have conversion programs for binary, trinary, and so forth. We are not giving away our proprietary technological information. We are simply establishing a mutual lexicon of language, where 4.3 centimeters equals one *krogg*, or something. And no, that is *not* an official V'Dan word. It is just a word I made up to illustrate the language and information barriers that still exist between our respective branches of humanity."

A few members of the Fellowship and the Council chuckled at his dry-voiced denial, but for the most part, the crowd seated in the rounded hall remained respectfully attentive.

"Once we have established how to convert basic measurements, terms, and labels, we will be able to begin the real negotiations. We are aware the V'Dan are at war; we ourselves were forewarned by the validated precognitives within the United Planets that conflicts with the same enemy are probable, and are preparing for the day that their war might indeed become our war. We are striving our best to hide our star system's exact location so that this enemy will have to look long and hard to find us.

"But we have reached out to nonhostile life-forms, and have found that some of them, at least, are very much like us," Callan continued, looking at the datapad he had set on the podium, which no doubt contained the points he wanted to make in his speech. "The V'Dan are different in many ways socially and culturally, but they and we are the same species biologically.

"If what our V'Dan guests are saying is true, the Salik—their enemy—sees us as just another source of *lunch*. To put it bluntly, they eat sentient beings for fun and food. This enemy will not differentiate between the others and us and will not respect boundaries, borders, or other differences. As we ourselves have learned through our history, victory comes when allies with a common cause work to overcome the obstacles and problems in their path. Still, we do not yet know all of the particulars of their war, and it would be foolish to join forces with them without knowing what, exactly, we will be up against.

"Among the things we do know, while we have learned that the V'Dan and their Alliance allies are advanced in many ways compared to us, we know that they in turn do not have access to several of our technologies. These are the sorts of negotiations that need to be conducted: Information exchanges, threat assessments, tactical evaluations, and technology discernments. These things require a presence in V'Dan space, an embassy filled with agents who can observe, learn, understand, explain, and make decisions which, like soldiers in the field versus generals back home, have to be made on the spot with immediate knowledge and understanding of the situation at hand.

"Even with our advanced interstellar-communications abilities, we cannot peer over the vast distances into the heart of the V'Dan and Alliance problems nearly as easily as the members of a flexibly designed embassy would be able to do." Callan stated, head held level but gaze flicking between his datapad and the Hall. "To that end, the Office of the Premiere of the Terran United Planets has ordered that the needs of such an embassy be examined, calculated, and enumerated. The lesser positions will be filled with specialists, but the ultimate authority of such an embassy must be entrusted to someone who lives, breathes, and recites every day the same Oath of Civil Service you and I have just recited today. Honor and integrity *must* be maintained within the embodiment of that on-the-spot authority, in order to properly represent our people before the greater galactic community that awaits our admission into its ranks."

Jackie forced herself to take a slow, steady breath, listening to Augustus Callan's words. Beside her, Li'eth debated making a physical show of support, or a telepathic one. The slightest flex of his mind made his head ache. He settled for shifting his knee so that it briefly brushed hers, along with a glance her way. She looked back and nodded faintly, encouraged.

"Up until today, that person has been one of our own, former Councilor for Oceania, Jacaranda MacKenzie, who has acted with honor and integrity in the role of Ambassador of the Terran United Planets to our foreign guests. Under other circumstances, I would simply confirm her appointment one last time and send her on her way when the new fleet is ready to launch, transporting the foundation of that embassy toward our potential new interstellar friends. Unfortunately, her situation—this *entire* diplomatic situation—has been complicated by a confluence of . . . fate, luck, and whatever sense of humor might be held by any Creator that may be out there.

"Ambassador Jackie MacKenzie and the confirmed third-born son of the Empress of the V'Dan Empire have been tested and vetted as a *bona fide* Gestalt pairing. As we have learned over the many decades in which psychics and their abilities have been proved to exist, these two share not only thoughts as telepaths, but gifts as well. Their abilities have been expanded to the point where they can each tap into the other's unique abilities to at least some measurable degree, and their shared abilities have been magnified by verified kinetic inergy testing."

He paused in reading his notes off of his datapad, looking up and around the Hall at his fellow Councilors. A faint rustle of movement, of startled whispers, had gone around the room at his announcement, but it settled quickly. Men and women from around Earth and its meager collection of research bases gave him their undivided attention, save for an occasional glance toward the pair under discussion. When he tried using his holy wabilities to read the crowd, which made his eyes ache, Li'eth could see the mass of their auras, a shifting opalescent display that nonetheless was predominantly lavender in mutual concentration.

"To separate such a pairing is to invoke emotional and

psychological suffering, including depression, anxiety, attention-deficit disorder, and other concerns," Callan recited from his notes. "These sufferings increase over both time and distance, and can only be alleviated by frequent contact and/or close proximity. To keep them together is to strengthen the bond that has already begun to grow, and which to our knowledge cannot be broken without serious consequences. In all experiments and case files, once that bond has set, separation leads to suffering, and the demise of one will lead to the demise of the other. To separate such a pairing has therefore been labeled as cruel and unusual punishment, and is considered to be against both military and civilian law.

"It has also been determined through decades of research that we have *no* idea why this happens," Callan asserted, ignoring the hands being raised among not only those in the white-seated tiers, but those in the other sections as well. "There is no cure; to try to prevent it from happening only leads to suffering . . . and we are bound by our oaths to be compassionate toward those who are suffering. These things are therefore not in dispute, and shall not be in dispute. Jacaranda MacKenzie and Kah'raman Li'eth Ma'an-uq'en V'Daania are a proved Gestalt pairing . . . so in the discussions that are to come, please keep to the actual topic at hand."

"Is he ever going to get to it?" Li'eth asked under his breath in V'Dan.

"Shh," Jackie returned in an equally faint hiss.

"The question, therefore, is not whether or not Jackie MacKenzie will be included in the mission to return the V'Dan to their homeworld. She *will* be going, traveling at the side of her Gestalt-bound partner, the Imperial prince. The problem lies in whether or not she should remain Ambassador, if she should step down and serve merely as a translator or a cultural liaison, or if she should travel with no official capacity save that as a Gestalt partner to His Highness. These things must be considered carefully . . . but while I have the executive authority to appoint Ambassadors, the potential ramifications are too complex in my opinion for the decision to be made by my hand alone.

"Please turn your attentions now to the screens as the Secondaire lists the various pros and cons. We will discuss whether or not Miss MacKenzie has the ability to maintain professional distance without undue influence from her partner while maintaining the office of Ambassador, whether or not she would be unduly influencing the prince, whether or not the *V'Dan* will understand and accept her professionalism if we judge her capable of doing so, and so on and so forth. If you have something new to add to the lists being assembled, please raise your hand.

"If all you have to say is a confirmation or a slight variation, please lower your hands as we go along. All speeches will be capped at one subject per discussion, one minute or less, so compose your thoughts before you raise your arm. If you have more than one point to make, please either state them within the allotted minute, or hold your second and further points while we move on to the others, so that they, too, may have their turn."

"And now we get to watch the pretty words appearing on the pretty screens," Jackie whispered in Terranglo. At Li'eth's questioning look, she lifted her chin. "Graphics artists are compiling information charts on the fly, diagramming pluses, minuses, and caveats or points of insufficient information."

"This feels more like a business meeting than a lawmaking session," he observed. "A single minute to ask a question or make a point?"

She nodded. "That's how it goes. Some days, the Council sessions pretty much are run like a business meeting. Technically, this isn't a matter of law but rather a matter of business: the business of trying to figure out what version of my career is going to be the best for the United Planets."

"I guess you did say you have rules to keep any discussions by committee from descending into chaos." He sighed under his breath.

They sat in silence for a while, though the Hall itself was busy. When it looked like the additions being suggested were trickling down to minor variations, Callan switched to a number-coded risk assessment on each and every point raised: Was Jackie MacKenzie trustworthy enough to separate her personal situation from her professional one? That one was judged a middling risk. Would the V'Dan Empire accept someone as an Ambassador who was, in effect, in a personal relationship with a V'Dan of high rank? That was an unknown factor, and thus judged middling. Would they consider the Gestalt itself to be a positive, or a negative, in building diplomatic relationships? Again, an unknown and therefore middling risk.

Next came a definition of different parameters, to try to move those "middle-of-the-road" risks one way or the other. Did the Council believe Jackie was capable of being a good Ambassador, period? That one was a strong belief. That one even came with five members of the Fellowship who stood up and spoke on behalf of her record of service. Did the Council believe that Li'eth had serious influence within the V'Dan Empire? Another unknown, leaving it in the middle.

Just as Li'eth was about to ask Jackie what the point of all of this was, he found himself called up to speak. She gave him an encouraging nod and gestured for him to rise.

"Thank you, Your Highness, for your patience with our government process," the Premiere stated once Li'eth was on his feet. "As half of the grand equation in these debates rests on a knowledge and understanding of a culture very few of us have even begun to glimpse, let alone grasp, we would like you to answer what questions you can, and to answer them with absolute honesty. I give you my personal reassurance that these questions will not compromise the safety or the sovereignty of your home nation. Are you willing to answer?"

"I am willing to listen. I cannot guarantee any answers," Li'eth replied, clasping his hands lightly in front of him.

"We have debated whether or not you may have a significant level of influence or impact upon the functioning of your government. Setting aside both humility and hubris—pride, if you will—and using a scale of zero to ten, with zero being an absolute lack of influence and ten being absolute control . . . when it comes to negotiating policies between the V'Dan Empire and its allies, what level of influence on your own government would you say that you have?"

"That is not an easy question to answer—since you say I should set aside both pride and humility in favor of honesty," Li'eth clarified. "There are several things to consider. I do not at this time have an official policy-making . . . employment . . . in the Empire. Before the war began, I was designated to train as an officer of the Second Tier—First Tier is generally reserved for those with aptitude and preference for a lifelong profession in the military. It is a requirement that members of the royal family serve in the military in order to uphold our understanding of the rigors and dangers to which our soldiers are exposed and to ensure that we grasp the consequences of tactical and strategic decisions.

"However, as I am a member of the military, I have a working knowledge of what is going on in our unwanted war with the Salik species," he continued. "In that regard, were I a normal soldier, an officer of common or noble birth, my reports could be flagged for attention at the highest levels of both the military and the government, should I encounter something . . . extraordinary. Such as a potentially helpful new ally. As I am a member of the royal family, I can make those reports directly to the Empress and bring to her attention any details that might be overlooked otherwise by those who are not as directly involved or able to observe as I myself might be.

"The way that the Imperial Family conducts its interactions is not quite as . . . It is not Terran," he stated, changing his mind on how much he would reveal to these people. It would take too much time to explain the differences in the various Tiers of social life. "There is a lot of tradition and protocol involved. Where I not a member of the Imperial Family, I would be debriefed upon my return and my report distilled into a summary for the Eternal Empress to study. As it is, I will still be debriefed and my report distilled into a summary. I will, however, have opportunity to expand and explain in person. I have the right to demand audience with the Empress as a member of the bloodline, and I have the right to demand audience with the War Queen as a royal currently active in the military. I can and will be heard if need be.

"As for the other considerations . . . as a member of the Imperial bloodline, I am vetted with the power to give someone I deem worthy an introduction to the Imperial Court, and with it, a temporary amount of high-ranked hospitality. I cannot guarantee any results further than that, however. You will be judged through V'Dan eyes on your own merits after that," he warned them. "As you say, on the bright side of things . . . because of my close familiarity with how our government thinks and works, I am able to make reasonable estimations of how my people will react to your people. I cannot guarantee that these estimations will be completely accurate, but I can attempt to make them in advance if I am informed of what you wish to attempt."

"Does this advanced estimation include assessing whether it would be worthwhile to open an embassy with your people?" Callan asked.

Li'eth nodded firmly. "Yes, Premiere Callan. Even if my people were to lose their wits and decide not to pay much attention to the enormous *tactical* advantages you could bring . . . it is my opinion as an officer as well as a member of the Imperial Court that it is worth both our nations' efforts in opening peaceful discussions and negotiations on many other topics. As an officer, my primary consideration is the tactical and strategic aspects, but I can see the advantages of the cultural and historical exchanges as well. Finally being able to answer where our species evolved will fill in a gap in our sense of self-identity, if nothing else."

"So on that scale, with all these things considered, where do you think your influence in the Imperial Court ranges on a range of zero to ten?" Premiere Callan asked.

"Probably about an eight," Li'eth stated. "I do not make policy. I do not have the final say. But I can pour information into the right ears, including Her Eternity's. And if I am to be absolutely honest . . . I can also *refrain* from getting that information into the right ears. My understanding of how the Imperial Court works in general is probably ranked at an eight, perhaps a nine, but because of my absence for the last few years, my grasp of the most current flow of influences is probably a seven. It would rise to an eight once I have a few weeks to study the Court upon my return.

"As for how loyal I am to my own people . . . my probability of siding with you Terrans over my own people is at most a two . . . and only that high because I know, down to my boots," he emphasized, using their own colloquialism on them, "that we need you. Your technology, your fresh eyes, and your unique strengths will give us an advantage over our enemies. We are the same species, but the Salik do not know *you*. They've had a little over a hundred V'Dan years, which I am told are within a few hours in length of your years, in which to study my people. Plenty of time to learn how we act and react.

"But you?" he said, turning to look at a face here, a body there. "You Terrans are very different in several ways from the V'Dan. If we can keep that knowledge from them while gaining access to your other advantages, we could win the war. What they do not know, they do not understand. What they do not understand, they cannot anticipate. What they cannot anticipate, they cannot hunt down, swarm, and kill.

"Your people and mine do share the trait of wanting peace rather than war. Which would be preferable, because while I am *descended* from War King Kah'el, and while my mother currently wears the regalia of the War Queen out of necessity . . . we V'Dan do prefer to live in times of peace and its corresponding prosperity. We understand and value cooperation as a social system, not just as a hunting strategy." He swung around to face the Premiere again, in his business suit and long, sleeveless white overrobe. "With all of that in mind, I will admit openly that I do plan to emphasize how useful an alliance between our peoples would be, once I return home. I speak honestly because I believe your technology and your differences will help us win our war. All else can be explored at our mutual leisure after peace is attained."

Premiere Callan nodded. "Thank you, Your Highness, for your honesty in your estimation of your influence, your assertion of your loyalties, and your evaluation of your people's needs and policies. In your consideration, keeping all these caveats in mind . . . do you believe that Jacaranda MacKenzie could be a good Ambassador to your people?"

"I have not met a lot of your people," Li'eth reminded them, again looking around the room. "But I believe I have met enough, and I have gauged their actions and their words all this time. Ambassador MacKenzie is refreshingly honest, direct, ethical, honorable—painfully honorable—and at the same time has displayed a level of sophistication in her grasp of situations that is both compassionately understanding yet able to acknowledge and use the ability to view situations with the cynicism inherent in our joint species.

"While she does not grasp the nuances of the Imperial Court—few people ever perfect it when they start from outside the system—I know she is capable of listening to expert advice, and I do believe she is capable of smoothing over differences with a diplomatic touch. Comparing her to others whom I have met, she is at the top of the list of candidates I would recommend for the position. Her military background would enhance an understanding of the current difficult situation my people face—a bonus to our side evoked by her sense of sympathy, to be sure, but this is not to say she is pliable, or reshapable . . . What is the word . . ." Li'eth paused, trying to find the right word. *"Za-der baduuj? Ka'a-stornei za-der baduu-aj, ai?"*

"'Easily swayed,'" Jackie translated.

"Thank you. She is not easily swayed—for her translative abilities alone, I would insist to the Empress that she be introduced to the Imperial Court and the Imperial Army," he added bluntly, pointing at Jackie while looking at the others. "But I tell you, with the sheer honesty which your culture seems to prefer, that Ambassador MacKenzie can be quite stubborn and unmovable, *not* easily swayed, when she believes she is faced with a case of either doing the right thing, regardless of cost, or doing the wrong thing.

"The proof of it lies in this meeting today," he reminded them. "Her career hangs in the balance, a career she clearly cherishes, yet she is willing to let you people decide what to do with her . . . in your rather unique Terran way."

"Thank you for that assessment, Your Highness," Premiere Callan stated. He touched something on his pad, his gaze on the slim device resting on the clear stand, then looked to Li'eth again. "In your opinion as a V'Dan familiar with the workings of your Empire, how well will your people grasp the concept of a Gestalt pairing, how well will they understand its potential consequences, and how much do you think its existence will either lend a positive weight to such a situation, or a negative weight, should Jackie MacKenzie be sent to your people not just as your bonded partner, but as our official Ambassador?"

"Another complex question." Li'eth replied. Clasping his hands behind his back, he paced a little on the central floor, looking up at the markless Humans seated all around. "What you grasp in terms of science, we revere in terms of mysticism. We do understand what holy pairings are, at least to a degree. Each such pairing is revered in life and numbered among the Saints in death . . . even if they turn out to be dangerous. In this particular situation . . . the bonding will need to be evaluated by the priesthood, many of whom are gifted holy ones—psychics, in your language.

"The official religion of the Eternal Throne is the Sh'nai faith, though others are allowed to exist. If it is confirmed by the priesthood, then our pairing would be considered the holiest of holies, and it is likely that over half the nation would look to us as living Saints, beings of reverence. On the negative side, great miracles would be expected of us, particularly as this is a time of war—again, I acknowledge even as I follow the Sh'nai faith"—*this one is for you, V'kol*—"that mysticism often includes a great deal of . . . hyperbole, I believe is the word? Exaggeration?"

A glance Jackie's way showed her nodding, confirming the words.

"So you believe this pairing would be seen as a positive thing, a positive influence for both sides, from the V'Dan point of view?" Callan pressed.

"It would . . . if it weren't for the fact that all of you are markless, including Ambassador MacKenzie. We share a common phrase, your people and mine," Li'eth added. "It will be 'an uphill fight' to get yourselves acknowledged as the powerful nation you are."

From the blank looks being shared around the Hall . . . Li'eth could see what Jackie meant by the V'Dan *jungen* marks—and their absence among the Terrans—being a huge problem for both sides. Not just because his own people would have to struggle hard against viewing her people as juveniles but because he could see now that most of her people did not grasp the significance of it *as* a potentially huge problem. Turning slowly, evaluating the blinks, the soft frowns, the confusion-quirked brows, he made up his mind.

". . . Actually, after giving this some thought just now, I must change my evaluation of the Ambassador's suitability for her job," he said. Turning to face the Premiere, who had raised one of his own brows, Li'eth put as much sincerity into his tone, his posture, as he could manage. "I believe she is quite possibly one of only a very few people on this planet who understand just how *difficult* it will be for your people to establish an effective embassy among my own. Not just for the fact that she will be able to consult with me directly, telepathically assisting her in near instantly navigating the . . . the maze of etiquette and protocol that awaits anyone in the Imperial Court, but because I believe she has the ability to anticipate which problems will be the biggest the Terran nation will face in dealing with the V'Dan Empire. Not in a psychic sense, but rather from her personal experiences and the intuitions she has developed in the course of her career as a Terran politician. I would rank her ability to do that job at a nine, if not a ten."

"We prefer the term 'civil servant,'" Callan stated dryly. "It keeps us humble. Thank you for your re-evaluation, Your Highness. If we were to assign someone else to the position of Ambassador, would you be equally willing to work with them, introduce them to the Imperial Court, help them navigate the unfamiliar protocols you mentioned?"

"Of course." He didn't let himself hesitate. "I do not think they would be the best-suited person for the task, but as I have said, we are engaged in a war we did not start, and you Terrans have things that can greatly aid us in ending it. Provided whoever you assign is capable of learning V'Dan protocols and customs, if they can keep an open mind and be forgiving, not quickly led into anger, nor easily frustrated by what they will experience of the many differences in our cultures, then I would be willing to work with whomever you assign. It is your right to select whomever you wish as your chosen representative. In a similar vein, it is my duty as a prince of the blood and an officer of the Empire to ensure that I work toward the betterment of the Empire. We must both act as we feel is best for our nations."

"Thank you. We are not yet prepared at this time to consider appointing Ambassadors to the other members of your multispecies Alliance, but in your consideration—and setting aside for the moment the considerations of your Gestalt bond—would Jacaranda MacKenzie be better suited as a representative to one of the other species? To the Alliance as a whole, or strictly to your people?"

"I *cannot* speak for the other nations," Li'eth cautioned the Premiere and listening Councilors. "Strictly in my own opinion, Ambassador MacKenzie could do a reasonably good job among most of the other members of the Alliance, given time to study their structure, culture, and needs. I believe she would conduct her efforts among them with the same integrity she has shown toward her position as an envoy toward myself and my junior officers. I would, however, suggest that you begin your diplomatic efforts first with the V'Dan. We will be able to explain to your people the other sentient species from a fellow Human's perspective and can assist you in learning how to communicate and negotiate with them, things that will enhance and strengthen your own attempts at peaceful negotiations when the time comes for all of that."

"We are aware of the potential difficulties that could be found in dealing with non-Human species, Your Highness," Premiere Callan replied. He touched his tablet screen again, but kept his gaze on Li'eth's face. "It is why we chose to bypass direct communication with the Gatsugi race of the first officially recognized systems our scout ships passed through on their way to finding the heart of your Empire. Please be advised—and you may pass this along to your Empress—that while we will accept any kind offers of V'Dan instruction and assistance on understanding these other races, we intend to make up our own minds and form our own alliances and negotiations, under our own terms, once we have grasped enough of these other species to be able to open successful diplomatic negotiations directly. Your people's assistance in understanding will be welcome, but not any attempt at control or oversight."

"I will be so advised," Li'eth stated, accepting the warning, "and I will pass it along to the ears of the Empress herself."

"Thank you for your courtesy and consideration, Your Highness. Councilors, Fellows," Callan stated, "please take a few moments now to access your input panels. You may make any needed readjustments to your risk-assessment scales. Your Highness, you may be seated again. Thank you also for your patience, your honesty, and your cooperation."

"Of course." Returning to his seat along the edge of the railing separating the sections of tier seating from the main floor, he sat down next to Jackie and spoke quietly in his own tongue. *Did that go well?*

Well enough. He's sincere in thanking you, by the way," she added in Terranglo.

"I figured he was. I do appreciate the courtesy," Li'eth said.

"Screaming throngs of excited Terran commoners and all?" she asked. "Royalty is a bit of an archaic thrill for us."

"And here I thought it was because of the handsomeness of my face," he quipped back. She shrugged her shoulders but didn't reply verbally or mentally to his quip. They sat in silence, waiting while the occupants of the Council Hall rustled and murmured in their seats.

". . . Imperial Prince Kah'raman Li'eth V'Daania," Premiere Callan stated after a few more minutes. "This Council has collated another set of questions for you."

Curious, Li'eth pushed to his feet, facing the Premiere. "Yes, Premiere?"

"Please be advised that these questions will involve inquiries of a personal nature. This questioning is undertaken to seek a level of understanding and comprehension, and is not being asked out of mere curiosity."

"I understand," Li'eth allowed, wondering what was about to be asked.

"What, in your evaluation of the situation, would happen to you if we sent you back to your world with Jacaranda MacKenzie at your side?"

That made him hesitate. "If she can be proved my holy partner, the odds of her being accepted as your Ambassador are very high, and this would be—"

"I apologize for interrupting, Your Highness," Callan said, "but allow me to clarify this question. What would happen to *you*? What consequences might there be for *you* to endure, upon your people finding out you are one of a holy pair—confirmed or not confirmed."

". . . As I said, I would be revered as a living Saint, as would she," he repeated. "If confirmed, it would be a deep advantage for both of our peoples."

"And if it is not confirmed? Or rather, not *believed*, though we have confirmed it ourselves?" Callan prompted. "What would the consequences be for you?"

Wary, Li'eth narrowed his gaze in thought. "Why do you ask this line of questioning?"

Secondaire Pong stood and approached the podium. Callan stepped to the side to allow him to speak, consulting his datapad as he did so.

"Fellow Ston Barushkev of Tblisi, Georgia Province, has submitted a very salient point: If there are severe negative consequences awaiting you, even as a mere possibility, these must be addressed by preparations, counterarguments, and whatever else it takes in advance to ensure that your mother, the Empress of V'Dan, is not rendered upset by such an outcome," Pong recited.

"We have recordings of you interacting with your mother in various conversations, and we can only guess what life in the Imperial Court must be like," Callan added, his tone remarkably gentle for all his delivery was steady. "But as you *are* her son, at some tipping point on the scales of what she will or will not tolerate, she will react from her position as your mother as well as her position as your leader."

Pong nodded. "We would all like to head off potential trouble in advance, as the Fellow Barushkev recommends."

"That . . . is a rather wise and well-considered query, then," Li'eth acknowledged. He looked over the sea of faces in the white-edged seats. One of the more swarthy gentlemen seated about midway up, toward the right side of the section, raised his hand in a little wave. Li'eth dipped his head slightly in return acknowledgment. "At worst, Fellow Barushkev, Fellowship members, Councilors . . . there would be public censure because of the Ambassador's appearance. My judgment would be questioned, with people believing I have been swayed by what could be considered inappropriate personal feelings.

"Ironically . . . in order to defeat or avoid such things, I would be forced to be bluntly honest with my people," he added, then quickly held up a hand in caution. "This is not to say that we lie as a daily activity, but it is to say that there are protocols that are expected to be followed. Things that may be held back or rephrased for discretion's sake. There are rituals of courtesy and discretion required in the Imperial Court."

He hesitated a moment, debating whether or not to explain more at that moment, then returned to the original topic of the question.

"However, the consequences you speak of would pale in comparison to the losses my people would continue to suffer in battle without your aid—technically, I could get into *equal* trouble for admitting that much to your people, that the Empire isn't perfectly capable of recovering from our constant losses," Li'eth stated dryly. "But as they have already had a solid taste of your communications abilities, I doubt that any such consequences would be too severe. What you bring in potential, even just by that much, is worth a little bit of pride-denting honesty.

"You have, after all, treated myself and my fellow officers with great honor and courtesy. That will also weigh strongly in my mother's mind, as a mother as well as a sovereign. Whether or not she harbors doubt as to the suitability of Ambassador MacKenzie to stay at my side, she will be grateful for that much and will welcome me home. Our priesthood would certainly benefit from Jacaranda MacKenzie's teachings even if she does not serve as your Ambassador.

"I would, however, advise that a suitable instructor in Terran psychic gifts be included in your embassy efforts," he added, changing the subject slightly. This was something he had considered, watching Jackie bounce back and forth between escorting the V'Dan around the United Planets and spending hours of her free time teaching other telepaths and talented translators how to speak V'Dan. "This should be someone *other* than Ambassador MacKenzie. That would not only ease the Ambassador's workload in establishing diplomatic relations, but it will help to explain to my people that this is a true matter and not something conjured by inaccurate accusations of any undue influences.

"As your own charts would put it," he finished, pointing up at the giant screens overhead, "the probability that the question of undue influence would come up is high, around an eight or nine, but the severity of the risk involved is low, around a three at most, in regard to myself. The severity of the risk to the Ambassador would be higher, probably a five, possibly a seven on your ten-point scale, but then you do have the option to appoint a different Ambassador if that becomes the case."

"It is not necessary to assess a risk to the Ambassador. That was already covered," Premiere Callan dismissed.

Li'eth blinked, mind racing back over what he had heard and seen so far. "You . . . what? When?"

"It was covered earlier in the assessment of whether or not she could do her job," the Premiere clarified.

"No, that was covering whether or not she could do her

job. This is a line of questioning about *personal* risk to Jacaranda MacKenzie, the same as you have just asked about my
own personal risks," he clarified.

"We appreciate your concern for Miss MacKenzie, Your
Highness. We understand that the Gestalt situation prompts you
to consider risks to her as well as risks to yourself. We, too, have
considered these things. Thank you for answering our questions, Your Highness." Callan eyed him a long moment while
Li'eth tried to figure out how to voice his concerns. Finally, the
Premiere lifted his hand slightly. "You may be seated."

Returning to his chair, Li'eth kept his outward expression
neutral but let his thoughts race and tumble. What he wanted
to do was to reach out to her, to ask Jackie a few questions. He
was so deep in thought that he missed the next few bits of the
discussion until the Premiere's words finally registered.

". . . so it is therefore clear we need to move on to a discussion of whether or not Jacaranda MacKenzie would be
suitable in the position of translator, versus having no official
capacity. In the course of her work as—"

"Wait!" Pushing to his feet, Li'eth stood and held up his
hand. "*Wait.* You have forgotten something!"

There was a rustle around the room. Premiere Callan
frowned at him, one among many giving the prince a hard look.
Even Jackie quirked her brows, though she remained silent, letting the Premiere speak for all of them. "Your Highness . . . this
is not your culture, and it is certainly not your government. You
have no grounds for an objection."

"The *outcome* of this meeting *is* my government's concern," Li'eth stated. "Are you trying to dismiss the suitability
of Jacaranda MacKenzie as an Ambassador *without* consulting and questioning the single most important person in this
debate? *That* is my objection if you are."

Callan pulled back a little, blinking. He glanced around the
room, then back at the prince. "I'm sorry, Highness . . . but I
really don't see why *I* should be questioned in this matter. My
confidence and risk assessment have already been tabu-
lated . . ." He broke off when Li'eth slashed his hand between
them, shaking his head. "Then I do not understand your point,
Your Highness. Did you mean *you*? We have already asked
you the most important questions in this matter."

"Not me, not you, and not *them*," Li'eth said, sweeping his arm at the Councilors in their seats. "We are discussing the suitability of a specific person for a specific job. A job that will take that person *away* from this planet by hundreds of light-years, expose them to unknown dangers, expose them to unknown risks, and expose them to unknown potentials. Yet you have not *asked her*, in specific, any questions. You are forgetting that *this* isn't just a job you can shove anyone into interchangeably, like . . . like identical cogs from a supply drawer!"

"Your Highness, your Gestalt—" Callan asserted

"This isn't *about* the *sh'keth* Gestalt!" Li'eth snapped, slashing his hand again, cutting him off.

Jackie blinked, blushed, and bit her bottom lip, flustered and yet amused by his choice of swearword. Dragging in a deep breath, Li'eth straightened his uniform jacket with a tug. Shoulders level, he stared down the Premiere.

"This, *sir*, is about a person. You are treating her like a *thing*, and she is a *person*. Everything you decide here today will affect the rest of her life—does *she* not have a say? I don't know about your Empire, but in mine, *we* did away with slavery many centuries ago!"

Callan's jaw dropped at the implied accusation. He wasn't the only one. A burst of noise spread through the room as dozens, even scores, of Councilors and Fellowship members all tried to voice their opinions. The shared light purples of concentration had shifted to a sort of shocked and somewhat offended lemon brown. Shutting his mouth, the Premiere let the noise surge for a few moments, then pressed a button on his tablet. A loud cracking noise resounded three times through the chamber, then another trio of times, quieting the hubbub.

When the conversations died down, Premiere Callan spoke. ". . . Speak your words more carefully, Prince. You are a *guest* in these Halls."

"Even if I did not like her, sir, I would still advocate for her right to voice her own opinion," Li'eth asserted sternly. "You are asking someone to go so far away from this world and her people, her friends and family, she will be isolated in an alien culture, even if she technically goes with a staff to help her. She will be subjected to heavy social pressures and difficult decisions under foreign circumstances, with all the burden of her position resting solely upon her and no other.

"Even if she served under the most friendly and welcoming of circumstances, I know that *you* know that no situation is ever so perfect all of the time," Li'eth told the head of the Terran government. The others in the Hall stayed silent, listening to his words. "You can talk about trust in her, and risk assessments of her all you like, but the one person who has the strongest ability to assess whether or not she can do the job, and whether or not she *wants* that job, is the woman herself.

"Except, you are not *actually* questioning *her*, are you?" he pointed out. Literally pointing, thrusting his finger in Jackie's direction. "*She* is the one who must carry out the tasks you would assign to her. *She* is the one who must bear the weight of the consequences for all her decisions, all of her responsibilities, whether that's as an Ambassador, as a translator, or as a *chair*-warmer, sitting on the outskirts of her life. Not your life. *Hers*. When are you going to ask *her* what *she* thinks of what she will have to do? *You* do not have to live with the weights, the responsibilities, or the consequences of this decision, but she *does*.

"Jacaranda MacKenzie is not a child to be told by her parents what she has to do, with no say in any of the process. Jacaranda MacKenzie is an adult, and this is about *her* life. Not mine, and not yours. Ask her what she thinks she can do. But ask *her*, not just yourselves." He moved toward his seat, then turned to face the Premiere again. ". . . I apologize for interrupting your decision-making process, but since you all seem to value treating the people around you ethically, the people whose lives *your decisions* will affect . . . I thought it pertinent to remind you that this is Miss MacKenzie's life that *is* being affected, and that *she* should be consulted, too.

"After all, isn't that why you have the Fellowship sitting in on each of these conferences?" He flicked his fingers up behind him, at the white-edged seats of the Fellowship tiers, whose spiritual colors were bleeding back toward lavender again. "Average citizens whose lives *will* be affected by your decisions, whom you have here as guests and witnesses, to be able to give the answers you seek, as well as to ask questions of their own? Or was I misinformed on how your political process works?"

Flicking his gaze around the room, gauging the looks of the faces of not only the Councilors but the Fellowship, Callan dipped his head. Acknowledging Li'eth's point. The general attitude in the Hall was one of intense concentration. Some of the Fellows were nodding, and some of the Councilors. Others had thoughtful looks . . . but none protested his words.

"You are quite right, Your Highness. That is how our system works," the Premiere replied. "I will admit I thought her feelings on the matter were already on record, and so did not need to be discussed in this session."

"Circumstances change, Premiere," Li'eth countered. "Sometimes, so do feelings. I may now be telepathically linked to this woman, but even *I* would not presume to know what she is thinking. It is wise to . . . what is the phrase in Terranglo . . . assess frequently?"

"Touch base?" Callan offered.

"That one will do," Li'eth said. It was some sort of metaphor for a sports game he didn't understand, but it would do. "It is wise to 'touch base' frequently, just in case more than mere circumstance has changed."

Secondaire Pong smoothed down the front of his white overrobe and the deep brown suit underneath. Stepping close to his superior, he murmured in the Premiere's ear. Callan nodded. ". . . Thank you for the reminder, Your Highness. Please be seated. We will, in the interest of expediency, forgo the discussion of simply sending Jacaranda MacKenzie along on the expedition to return you to your people, with no discernible role other than that of being your Gestalt partner. We will not inflict a separation upon the two of you, so her mere inclusion does not matter. It will happen regardless of the outcome of this meeting."

Only somewhat content with that, Li'eth seated himself. He waited impatiently for the Premiere to call Jackie up for questioning.

"We will now discuss this Council's assessment of the risks versus rewards of sending Miss MacKenzie to V'Dan as a linguistics expert, working in an official capacity as the embassy's translator."

Tensing to rise, Li'eth was stopped by a touch from Jackie. When he glanced her way, she shook her head and patted his thigh. Risking the pain of his hangover, he clenched his jaw against the ache in his skull. (*I will ensure that they listen to what* you *want. It's your life, not theirs.*)

(*I know.*)

"I object."

Both of them craned their necks, looking up and behind them. The speaker was a woman with very dark skin, grayish-white hair, and the lines of age seaming her face. Her dress under the short white vest was a mild shade of pale gray, matching the silver cane she leaned upon as she stood.

"Fellow . . . Agnathia Ecklestone," Callan acknowledged, checking his tablet briefly. "It is the right of the Fellowship to lodge an objection. What is your objection?"

"I want to hear what the girl has to say," Ecklestone stated.

"We will get to that after the discussion of our assessment of her ability to be a translator."

"Young man," Ecklestone called out, one of her hands going to her hip, which she cocked somewhat to the side, "I *know* you were born with a brain that functions. *Everyone* here knows that Miss MacKenzie speaks more languages than anyone else outside of a computer. There is *no* need for debate on her record as a translator, a linguistics facilitator, a cultural advisor—the girl lived and breathed it for years! That point is moot because we all know she'd be damn fantastic at it.

"Since we all know all of this, if she isn't gonna be the Ambassador," Ecklestone stated, "then she'll automatically be the chief translator, end of debate. So, rather than wasting our time with mind-numbing nonsense with a foregone, obvious conclusion, *I* want to hear *her* evaluation of which job she wants to do. *That's* the only thing that matters at this point. Am I right, or am I right?"

She turned to either side, looking at the other Fellows. Many of the nearest nodded. A number of Councilors nodded, too. Facing Callan again—who briefly looked like he was trying to swallow something that threatened to stick on the way down—the elderly woman braced both hands on the top of her silver cane, drawing herself up in a more formal posture.

"I therefore call for a vote of the Fellowship on this point of objection," the old woman stated. "As is my right as a member of this session of the Fellowship. The vote, specifically, is to skip the damned translator nonsense because we all know she'd be the best at that job, and to go straight to asking the girl what *she* wants to do, and what *she* thinks she's capable of doing. Because she *could* be even better as our official diplomatic representative, if she feels up to it. The rest of this is all procedural nonsense."

"Very well," Callan stated, recovering some of his poise. "Let the record show that Fellow Agnathia Ecklestone has called for a vote from among the Fellowship on the following points: skipping the risk assessment of Jacaranda MacKenzie as being suitable for employment as an embassy translator; asking Miss MacKenzie directly if she wishes to be an Ambassador to the V'Dan people and their allies; asking Miss MacKenzie if she would rather be a translator in the embassy to the V'Dan people and their allies; and asking Miss MacKenzie her personal risk and evaluation assessments as to whether she thinks she is capable of handling either or both jobs. Are there any objections among the Council?"

The screens overhead were divided; some showed the list of points the Premiere had outlined, and some showed panoramas of the Councilors. None of them raised their hands.

". . . Let the record show that there is no Council objection to the Fellowship's proposal. Fellows of the Terran United Planets, please input your votes on the steps that have been outlined by Fellow Ecklestone's proposal. Councilors, please be patient while the Fellowship votes."

Numbers appeared beside each bullet point as each white-vested Terran typed in what they thought. It was a strange way of conducting a government, but when the numbers finished moving, Li'eth relaxed in his seat. Over 95 percent of the Fellowship voted to skip the discussion of her qualifications as a translator. Over 90 percent wanted to ask Jackie if she wanted to be an Ambassador. Just under 60 percent wanted to ask her if she would rather be a translator. And over 95 percent wanted to hear her own assessment of her situation.

". . . With no objections from the Council, the Fellowship's motions have passed. Jacaranda MacKenzie, the Council and the Fellowship have some questions for you."

Jackie rose obediently. "Of course, sir." Like Li'eth, she clasped her hands in front of her once she stopped in front of

Callan on his little podium stand. "I will not waste the Council's time on any need for long-winded explanatory speeches. I know the questions being asked of me, and would therefore simply answer them, with your permission."

"Permission granted," Callan allowed.

"Thank you. On the point of whether or not I want to be an ambassador . . . I *would* like to be our official Ambassador to the V'Dan. I am beginning to understand them, and believe I can navigate the differences in our cultures in ways that will benefit my constituency," she said, parting her hands briefly to gesture at the Councilors, the Fellowship, the world beyond. Reclasping her hands, she left them lightly laced in front of her. "More than that, I promise I will keep in mind that the decisions I might make will have an impact not only on the United Planets . . . but on the V'Dan, their allies in their Alliance, and their enemies, as people who will also be affected by the decisions I may make on my own constituency's behalf.

"As to whether or not I myself believe I can handle the job of being an Ambassador . . . I believe I can. On a scale of zero to ten . . . an eight. I know it will not be easy bridging the gap between Terran and V'Dan cultural viewpoints and needs, and so I acknowledge the reality that it will not be easy, establishing and holding an embassy. There are also many unknown variables, things none of us will know or grasp until we have opened that embassy. Things which, in my honesty, I cannot claim any higher assessment number for until those potential problems are known." She glanced back at Li'eth for a moment, then lifted her gaze to the Fellowship. Fellow Ecklestone had reseated herself, hands still braced on the top of her cane. "And I will concur with Fellow Ecklestone's assessment of my capabilities as a translator. I *am* good at it. If that is the position I am assigned, I will do my best in that job.

"However, it is my best estimation that I cannot do both jobs at the same time." That caused a stir. She held up her hand, turning to look at the Council. "There will come a point where we can spend days and weeks and months and years teaching the V'Dan how to speak Terranglo and teaching Terrans how to speak V'Dan. At the moment, we do not have that luxury. Each language transfer takes anywhere from two to five hours, depending upon their mental discipline, their willingness to undergo the procedure, and their personal affinity for such things, gifted or otherwise.

"The position of Ambassador will also require many hours each day of getting to know the V'Dan culture first-hand, getting to know various people, making contacts in the government, business, and private sectors, fielding and asking questions, drafting negotiations and treaties, and more. Each will be a full-time job," she pointed out. "I may be one half of a Gestalt pairing, but His Highness will have his own concerns to handle once we reach his homeworld. He is not a member of the Terran United Planets and cannot serve in any capacity as a representative for us. He is also a strong telepath, but he has no training in language transference. He cannot take up any of the burdens of my position from me.

"I must therefore request that I be assigned to one position or the other. Not to both . . . though if I do remain your Ambassador, I will try to schedule some time for more transfers to help speed up the rate at which both sides can begin to understand each other better."

"Thank you. Next question. What is your assessment of your ability to maintain a separation of your personal feelings versus your professional needs?" Secondaire Pong asked her. "You are in a Gestalt with a foreign national, yet you are being asked to represent Terran interests first and foremost."

"I am aware of the potential disparity, Secondaire Pong," Jackie admitted. "If I am to be the Ambassador, I would like a suitable assistant assigned to me so that I can train him or her to question my choices as well as assist me in my office . . . and if needed, to step up to take over the ambassadorship, should I for any reason need to step down. I *am* aware that I must constantly question my motives in this task, particularly as the Gestalt advances.

"However, there are advantages to being the Ambassador while in a Gestalt with a high-ranked V'Dan," she continued. "If there are problems, concerns, questions, even cultural clashes, I know exactly whom to ask for clarification. Whom to go to, in order to smooth over any problems. I don't have to wait for a cultural liaison to be brought in to study the matter before making a recommendation. In turn, His Highness would also have a similar advantage in coming directly and swiftly to me, to the benefit of his own people. Ideally, I would like to recommend to the Empress that he be appointed to the position of cultural liaison and advisor to the Terran embassy. The fact that we are in a Gestalt can become a powerful asset for both sides."

"Duly noted," Premiere Callan stated. "We will take that into consideration as well."

Li'eth noticed something in her replies. Jackie was using several of the points from their own Oath of Service in her speech. *How clever of her, using their own litany of good habits against them. Is this a deliberate ploy? Is it how she truly feels? Or is it simply a pattern of the by-now-ingrained habit of constantly having to swear to do such things?*

"I have a further request to make, predicated on that assessment, that I cannot do both jobs effectively at the same time," Jackie stated, turning to address the Terrans seated around the hall. "I would like to request at least one other polyglot telepath be assigned to the embassy. If not two. Particularly two more, if I am to remain your envoy. Understanding *begins* with communication. If need be—if you have another candidate already in mind for the position of Ambassador—I will be happy to serve as a translator. But . . . I believe my experiences, starting from the very first moment of Terran-V'Dan contact, make me well suited for the role of Ambassador at this point in time."

"Do you have anything beyond your opinion to support this assertion?" Secondaire Pong asked her. Dryly, he added, "As Fellow Ecklestone rightly pointed out, you *are* the best translator we could send."

Jackie nodded, knowing the Secondaire's place was to play devil's advocate at times like this. "Yes, I have additional points to support my post as Ambassador, rather than just a translator. My years of service in the military will help me to better understand the V'Dan war efforts, which in turn will help me and whatever military liaison is appointed to my embassy determine what we can actually supply in the line of what they actually need. My time as a translator and cultural liaison will help the embassy staff to learn how to navigate V'Dan culture. My experiences as a Councilor will allow me to gauge the appropriate needs of each side and the legalities of what is being offered versus what is being asked during treaty, business, and other negotiations.

"There are at least five other telepathic polyglots who can take my place as a psychically assisted translator. And circumstances may change once their current war is over," Jackie allowed, "changing what will be needed. But for right now, in terms of both civilian and military experience, I am the best candidate for the position of Ambassador.

"In short, Councilors, you would be hard-pressed to find someone with the same *useful* variety of skills and experiences that I myself have. My background provides an almost unique, rich, and diverse level of expertise, which I can bring to the job. At least, until I can get an assistant and an embassy staff trained to the point where they can take over, should that ever become a necessity. I know I am not irreplaceable," she allowed with a simple, expressive shrug, "but I am the best option you have at this time . . . and I do not think the V'Dan and their allies can afford to *wait* for a different set of circumstances that are more favorable for sending someone else in my place."

"Thank you, Miss MacKenzie. Are there any other questions for her at this time?" Callan asked. A few hands lifted a little bit, then subsided, but that was all. No one raised a hand strongly. Assessing the Hall, the Premiere nodded. ". . . Very well, then. We will now call for a vote on the final decision as to whether Jacaranda MacKenzie should remain Ambassador of the Terran United Planets to the V'Dan Empire. This is a simple yes/no/abstain vote. To aid you in your considerations, the screens will display a recap of the risk-assessment evaluations, though you are of course free to vote however you determine we should best proceed."

Li'eth turned his attention to the Secondaire, who was apparently controlling what subjects were put up on the big screen. Secondaire Pong had reseated himself at a spot behind the podium and was glancing up intermittently at the screens overhead. The prince realized how odd that was, compared to the V'Dan way. Back home, no one on the Queen's Council—a much smaller body of advisors than the hundreds of adults gathered in this hall—would have lifted a finger to perform such menial tasks. They all had staff for such matters. It was yet another point of cultural difference, one he made a mental note to advise the upcoming Ambassador about.

He hoped that would be Jackie . . . and worried that it would be her at the same time. He firmly believed she *would* be the best choice . . . but that would widen the gulf of protocol between the two of them, unless and until he could get his own people to acknowledge their holy bond.

The final tally appeared a few moments later. When Premiere Callan used the comm system to call for order with another recorded crack of what sounded like wood on hard wood, Secondaire Pong rose, approached the podium, and reported the percentages. "Let the record show that on the subject of appointing Jacaranda Leilani MacKenzie as Ambassador of the Terran United Planets to the V'Dan Empire . . . for the answer of Yes, Appoint Her, the tally is 85.30 percent. For the answer of No, the tally is 13.90 percent. The number of Abstentions is less than 1 percent."

"The motion carries." Premiere Callan touched his tablet, and a single, loud crack resounded through the hall. He turned to face Jackie, who had risen to her feet, her cheeks flushed with the news. "Congratulations, Ambassador MacKenzie. You are hereby confirmed as the ongoing Ambassador to the V'Dan people, with a Council-voted 85% approval rating; may it continue to remain that high in the coming days. We also look forward to your recommendation list for your embassy staff, to be delivered as soon as possible. The Council will put together committees in various categories to evaluate and recommend their own suggestions for the positions of linguistics liaison, military liaison, business liaison, so on and so forth."

"Thank you, sir. Thank you all," Jackie added, raising her voice as she turned nod at a familiar face here, an unfamiliar one there. "I will do my best to serve, as always."

"Thus ends session number 40,656 of the Council of the Terran United Planets," the Premiere stated, and made the cracking noise twice before stepping down from the podium.

The noise level rose as the people, male and female, youngish adult and old, gained their feet and started discussing the session. Three sharp cracks resounded through the hall, surprising Li'eth, who had risen to join Jackie. Conversations died, and everyone faced Secondaire Pong, who had taken the podium once more.

"Gentlemen, Ladies, Council policy is *very* clear on the matter of Saturday emergency sessions. We use the Hall outside of normal hours, we clean up after ourselves," the Secondaire stated firmly. "The carts and cleaning materials are being brought out. Unless you are infirm—and your identity badge will say if you are excused—you are *not* excused from this session until your seat, the floor around it, and so on and so forth are restored and rendered pristine."

Seeing Li'eth's brows raise in amazement, that *high-ranked* government officials had to do menial cleaning chores, Jackie gave him a wry smile. "*I* have to stay and help clean up, too. On the bright side, it doesn't take very long. Not with everyone helping."

Sighing, he shrugged. "Then I might as well help. You have a *very* strange government, Ambassador . . . but I think I am coming to understand it."

"And?" a voice behind him asked. Li'eth turned in time to see Fellow Ecklestone descending the last few steps to the main floor. "Now that you are coming to understand it, what *do* you think of us Terrans and our one-world government, Your Highness?"

"I think I'm beginning to like it, Fellow Ecklestone. I . . . don't think it would succeed in the Empire, but then we have a very different cultural background from yours," he stated diplomatically. "At least, given what I've learned of your history so far."

"Mm-hmm. Well. You go back to that mother of yours, and you let Her Majesty know she's welcome to drop by and see all of this for herself," the elderly woman told him. "And before I leave to go back to Bhisho—that's in Eastern Cape Prefecture, South Africa Province—I am going to make one or two recommendations for that embassy, too," the elderly woman stated. Her aura swirled with aquamarine satisfaction and a mint green overtone of curiosity. "I was never more thrilled in my life when I found out I had not only finally won the Fellowship Lottery, but that the odds were good I'd be on hand here in Aloha City to watch a piece of major history unfold."

"I am glad that you were here, Fellow Ecklestone," Li'eth told her. He offered her his hand, which she clasped firmly with her wrinkled, cool fingers. "Thank you for saying what you did."

"Call me Agnathia, please. I've lived long enough, I don't stand long on ceremony," she told him. Then smiled. "I don't stand long, period. Now, I've been following politics a long time, young man. Sometimes, the will of the people wavers, and sometimes it stands strong. Right now, most everyone is curious about you V'Dan and what'll happen. A bit worried about the possibility of a war. And very curious about all those *real* aliens you have been talking about, as well as you V'Dan."

Li'eth couldn't help smiling at that, as her words unwittingly echoed Robert's own comments. Agnathia squared her shoulders, both hands braced on the top of her cane as she addressed the V'Dan prince. Li'eth found himself impressed by her air of authority, grace, and apparent wisdom when she stood like that; between her expression, her wrinkles, and her nearly white hair, he couldn't imagine any adult looking *more* adult than her, even if she didn't have a single scrap of *jungen* on her dark, weathered face.

"We will trust Miss MacKenzie to get the job done, and get it done right," Agnatia asserted, speaking as if she spoke for everyone in the United Planets, her aura as solid a shade of cerulean blue as the waters around the shores of O'ahu. "You give her your support when you get home, and she'll bring in the rest of us to help watch *your* back, too. Cooperation benefits everyone.

"You remember that, now, when your people start questioning what we intend to do." Reaching out, Agnathia patted his arm, gripped it for a moment, then turned and started heading for one of the nearby pushcarts. "I need to go find a dusting rag, and wipe down a few seats with it. I can manage that much with a cane. Can't let these Councilors do the job all by themselves . . ."

Li'eth turned to watch her go as she moved past him, then looked around for Jackie. The reconfirmed Ambassador, third most powerful person in this entire, unique Human empire, had accepted a spray bottle and a rag from someone, and was spraying down the leather-covered seats on the ground floor.

(*Your people are* decidedly *different from mine,*) he sent, rather than trying to cross the floor to speak to her. A floor that now bustled with activity as people moved to and from the cleaning carts. It hurt to send that much, and it hurt to receive her reply, but not as much as earlier. Proof that the effects of his inadvertent hangover were thankfully fading. *(The others— V'kol and the rest—are still baffled by how you manage to make your government work. It's very different from ours.)*

(There's nothing wrong with being different,) Jackie reminded him. *(So long as those differences don't hurt others, nor infringe upon their own individual, indisputable rights. Different can even be good, sometimes.)*

(No, there's nothing wrong with being different,) he agreed. *(But I don't know what my people will make of yours. So . . . more touring of the planet?)*

(A bit. More for the others than for you, though. The military wants to go over everything you know about the Salik, again. Since the Tower is here on Kaho'olawe next to the Lotus, and I'll be working somewhere here on the island— probably in the Department of Departments while I'm putting together recommendations for an embassy staff—that should keep us in proximity.)

(Jackie, I'm sorry . . . we'll have to discuss this out loud when you're done,) he apologized as the pain started growing unbearable. *(My head still hurts.)*

(Read. The labels. Next time. And that is all I shall say on the matter.)

Her sending was mild, delivered with a touch of humor. If without much in the way of mercy. *Yes, ma'am,* he thought in Terranglo, though he didn't bother to send it telepathically.

CHAPTER 21

The Merrie Monarch Festival was fascinating. There were a lot of varieties of *hula* being displayed in demonstrations and competitions, from slow and sweet, smooth and flowing in each performance, to strong and brisk and energetic. Colorful flowing gowns, painted waist wraps, and bands of flowers and leaves, sea- and nutshells girdling heads, arms, wrists, ankles, and more. Spears, poles, musical instruments . . . and holokinesis were all on display.

At the moment, the group on the stage was conducting a dance wherein the surface of the platform on which they stomped and "rowed" with their poles had been transformed to look like a section of the local sea, dancing on what looked like archaic outrigger canoes. The illusions were transparent, allowing glimpses of the dancers' solid, if bare, feet as they moved across the performance floor. The program given to the attendants said this was an historically based *hula*, a story-dance commemorating the arrival of the Polynesian people to the Hawai'ian island chain, and of all the rich sea and land life they had found upon settling here.

Indeed, as he watched, all twenty-six dancers rose slowly into the air, still dancing as if on a solid, flat surface. The "surface" of the sea rose with them, revealing the sides of the water beneath those rippling waves as if the ocean itself had been trapped in a transparent box. The way they rose caused an upswelling of noise from the crowd, cheering, stomping, whistling, even some shouting before the music rose to overcome and quell their enthusiasm.

Beneath the rippling blue-gray waves, the promised recitation of sea life now swam, some of it splashing up and leaping over the prow and stern of the canoe-shaped illusions, some of it even leaping out of the sides toward the audience before diving back in again. All of it directed in time with the cadence of the gourd drummers and the chanter, and the slow-dancing arms of the woman who sat with them. Looking remarkably tranquil, if a bit red in the face from her efforts, Jackie directed the illusionary aspects of the dancers' approach through the lava-formed rocks and the seaweed beds, the coral sands and wave-kissed beaches. Together, they performed their ancestors' arrival on a shoreline that seemed to rise out of the water even as the dancers slowly descended again.

Someone jostled his arm, settling into the seat next to his. A seat supposedly reserved for Jackie when she wasn't preparing for or actually performing. Li'eth frowned and glanced at the security guards, wondering why they had let the newcomer get so close, then eyed the woman, whom the guards appeared to be smiling at with some actual warmth.

"Madam, this seat is reserved," he stated, keeping his tone polite as he faced the graying blonde woman. "Ambassador MacKenzie plans to return to it when her performance is through."

The woman nodded. "I know, but I thought I'd introduce myself while catching her performance. I almost missed it, too."

"And you are?" Li'eth prompted. She had an accent from . . . somewhere . . . the desert land in the southern hemisphere. Australia, that was it.

The woman turned to him with a warm smile but didn't offer her hand. "I am Rosa McCrary, recent former Premiere of the United Planets . . . and the Ambassador's new chief assistant. I might have replaced her if she hadn't had that confidence vote of 85 percent, save for two things: Jacaranda MacKenzie's face has remained a prominent presence in our precognitives' visions, apparently in a position of some authority, presumably as an Ambassador . . . and the fact that I have never served in the military. I'll be her political liaison more than her understudy for the time being, but I will be her understudy. Now, we should be quiet," McCrary told him, settling back in Jackie's seat. "I'd like to enjoy her performance. The entertainment industry lost a magnificent resource when she decided to go into politics . . . but I think our world has gained immensely by it. Don't you?"

"It's not my world, so it's not mine to say," Li'eth replied diplomatically. "Besides, *my* world will be gaining by it, soon."

"That it will, Your Highness." McCrary agreed.

He nodded and returned his attention to the show. A moment later, he and everyone else gasped as the "volcano" now on display erupted . . . with a gout of real fire sending heat through the open-air stadium, though only for an instant, reassuring everyone that it was just a temporary part of the display. Spontaneous cheers and applause echoed through the arena.

The detail of Jackie's illusions looked amazing; still transparent as colored glass, the volcano's interior had been sketched by Jackie's will—and no doubt authenticated in its inner details with the help of her geophysicist friend, Lars Thorsson—to show the magma chambers, the pulsing and welling of the molten rock inside the volcano's throat, the force of the rocks slung outward, and the goopy gray-and-orange flow of the lava oozing down the sides, which the singer and dancers were now chanting about. A ghostly figure rose from the mountain, some sort of volcano spirit or goddess, he guessed, one with tanned skin, fiery red hair, and a figure as strong as that peak.

McCrary finished applauding, then spoke under her breath to him again. "I'd like to sit down with you to go over the structure of the V'Dan government and a list of protocols and proper behaviors to follow. Today, we have this Festival to enjoy. Tomorrow, we'll have a lot of work to do."

"I'll try to share what I can," Li'eth murmured back. "But I cannot guarantee that I will remember all of it. Some of it . . . It's such an ingrained habit, there is no thought. You just do it."

McCrary smiled wryly. "That is already understood. But I will try my best to evaluate and question everything, so that I can help Jackie be a more effective Ambassador."

"You don't want her job?" Li'eth asked. "Aren't you her . . . understudy?"

"I am, but at the same time, I have also served my time. I was hoping to have more than a few months' vacation. Still . . . we share something in common, she and I," McCrary added, nodding at the oblivious Ambassador on the stage, hands now shaping a new island arising, continuing the narrative.

"And that is . . . ?" he prompted, glancing at the older woman.

"We both live to serve our people. I am here to help explain that to *you*, when she does something that may baffle you. You may be in a Gestalt pairing, but sometimes it's just easier to have a friendly, noninvolved soul to talk to. At least, as a certain red-robed monk explained it to me, since he's too old to go along on this trip as a possible mentor to both of you. I may not be an official psychic-abilities instructor, but I can still be a friend and a private advisor, if you're willing." Patting his hand briefly, she gestured at the stage, returning their attention to it.

Li'eth watched, but his mind mulled over her words. He wondered if there was anyone in or around the Imperial Court he could offer to Jackie as a cross-cultural mentor to help explain what might happen with him and his own actions, once they reached his homeworld.

Possibly, but he just didn't know if there would be anyone *willing* to step into that role.

APRIL 10, 2287 C.E.
MACARTHUR STATION

Jackie looked around the oversized shuttle that would be her home for the next fourteen or so days. Twice as broad and three times as long as the *Aloha 9* had been, the new ship was more of a mobile command center than a research and exploration vessel. According to the specs, the *Embassy 1* would fit within the hyperrift with room to spare and had been safely tested over the last two weeks by an experienced evaluation crew.

Pulling herself into the cockpit, she floated over to her station. This version had two seats, with Li'eth occupying one, and the other awaiting her body. A twist, a tug, and she reached for the restraint straps to bind herself in place.

(*I will be glad to be back on ships and stations that have artificial gravity,*) Li'eth murmured mentally. (*Though I will admit you look very graceful, floating in zero G.*)

(*Thank you.*) As soon as her straps were firmly in place, she reached for the control console, calling up communications information. She now had a number of assistants and staff members of all sorts, but everyone had to pull their own weight, including her. Ambassador on the ground, communications technician in the ship. Out loud, she said, "Okay, people. Everyone in back is strapped in . . . and it looks like *Embassies 2* through *15* are coming online as green for go."

"You really don't have much imagination in naming your ships, do you?" Li'eth stated, sighing. "Some of them, that is. Ones like the *Katherine G* at least have some meaning to their names."

"We have plenty of imagination in naming our ships," Robert called back from his place in the pilot's seat. Brad sat next to him as usual, with Ayinda and a lieutenant named Aksha at the navigator's position behind the copilot. Dr. Du sat with Maria at the life-support console, having won the coin toss on who got to travel to V'Dan as one of the Terrans' top two pathology experts. "We're just saving all the special names for when we *have* special ships."

"He's teasing you," Ayinda told Li'eth while Jackie slipped a headset over her ear, finally strapped into place. "The ships that do patrols and such, they usually have unique names. But sometimes a name is so popular, it's repeated several times, like the *Enterprise VII*. Sometimes, however, it's easiest to refer to a specialized task force of several ships by a single name and a set of numbers, to show the unity of the project."

"Ayinda's right. The *Aloha* ships were designed specifically to explore, greet, and return," Jackie told him. "The *Embassy* line is designed to travel between our two main worlds and to serve as a backup embassy in case there's something wrong on the ground. They can also fight in a pinch, with more armor and armaments than the *Aloha* class."

"As far as I know, nobody is intending to fight you," Li'eth told her. "At least, nobody associated with the Empire."

She smiled. "We know. But you forgot one thing. You yourself told our generals during one of your debriefings that the Salik have been known to attack the heart of your Empire. The very planet that we're headed to. We're not yet ready to enter into any real war effort on our part, but each one of these ships is ready to fight."

"That's not exactly reassuring, making me think about fifteen fully armed ships heading toward my home planet," Li'eth warned her.

"It's not a threat," Jackie reassured him.

"And I don't take it as one. But it is still a possibility," he told her. Silently, he added, (*I may know better, but others may still take it as a threat. This is not going to be easy. Establishing an embassy, gaining the respect your people deserve, and being given the leeway our Gestalt bond requires.*)

(*Some say that those things in life that are easily won are easily forgotten and little valued. Those things that are hard-fought and hard-won are cherished all the more for the pains taken or endured to acquire them.*) She meant, he knew, their own personal relationship as two Human beings, not just prince and envoy or even psychic partners. Pausing to mutter into her headset pickup, Jackie waited for a reply, nodded, and murmured thanks, then addressed the burgundy-striped man at her side. Aloud, so the others could hear. "Sometimes, diplomacy is the art of saying 'nice doggy' while reaching for a big stick. Sometimes it's just walking softly, but still carrying a big stick. And sometimes, it's just carrying a stick to ward off random attackers, should any leap out of the shadows. We're just trying to have the tools on hand to cover a wide range of possibilities, that's all."

"I'll be sure to reassure my mother of that," he muttered. (*And of the fact I cannot stand the thought of having to part company from you once our time in V'Dan quarantine is through. Hopefully I can make it clear to her that parting us permanently is not an option.*)

She grinned and touched a couple of controls. "You do that. Robert?"

"Yo," the pilot called out, not stopping in the task of going down through his preflight checklist.

"The loading shuttle has been redocked with the *Mac-Arthur*'s spindle. We are clear for departure when ready."

"Thirty more seconds . . . and we'll be done with the preflight . . . Give the station an *aloha* from us and a thanks for the sweet ride."

"You got it." One hand touched the controls, switching channels so she could discuss things with Orbital Control.

The other reached over and covered Li'eth's fingers for a moment.

He turned them over, twining them with hers.

"MacArthur *Station, this is the* Al . . . *the* Embassy 1," Jackie asserted, correcting herself at the last moment. *"We are ready for departure."*

A touch of her controls broadcast the reply to the whole cabin. "Embassy 1, *you are cleared for departure. Good luck, and godspeed."*

Peering to her right, she caught a glimpse of the Earth as Robert activated the insystem thrusters, sending them gliding forward, away from the station and its orbit around the planet. It would likely be months, if not years, before she saw her birthworld in person again. If things went well.

"Aloha oe, *Earth."*

"Aloha oe, Embassy 1."

Li'eth squeezed her fingers in comfort, and hoped she would like his world and his people, as much as he had grown to like hers. He hoped they would like her, too. Eventually.

READ ON FOR A SNEAK PEEK AT
THE NEXT BOOK IN JEAN JOHNSON'S
FIRST SALIK WAR SERIES

THE V'DAN

AVAILABLE IN JANUARY 2016
FROM ACE BOOKS!

Getting changed in zero gravity was not easy. Clothing did not "fall naturally into place," but had to be tugged this way and that. Hemlines remained rumpled unless pulled straight and tucked into waistbands and so forth. And a skirt? Forget it. Forget all skirt-like objects in the weightlessness of insystem space. Jacaranda MacKenzie wished to dress in a formal outfit to properly represent the people of the Terran United Planets, but she was not doing so in a skirt in zero G.

They did have an illusion of microgravity on board the *Embassy 1*, but only because the ship was gradually slowing down in its approach to the planet V'Dan. That meant anyone or anything unsecured had a habit of "drifting" forward into bulkheads and doors. Jackie was somewhat used to zero gravity maneuvers and could sort of brace herself telekinetically, but that did nothing for hemlines. Or fellow travelers.

"Ah, sorry!" Ayinda muttered for the third time as she swayed and bumped into Jackie's back. "Sorry, Jackie . . . At least we won't have to deal with this for much longer. Right?"

"They did promise us quarantine facilities with full artificial gravity," Jackie replied, adjusting her cuffs. Today's outfit was light blue shirt, dark blue coat and slacks, light blue socks, and dark blue shoes. Slip-ons, no trying to fuss with fasteners or old-fashioned laces in space.

"*Sí,*" Maria de la Santoya agreed, speaking in Spanish. "*But from what I learned from our guests, the facilities are military-grade at best. No paintings, no cushions, no artworks, no colors . . .*"

"Speak in V'Dan," Jackie reminded her. Everyone on this expedition spoke V'Dan, the language of their forthcoming hosts. She and a handful of other telepathic polyglots had spent hours and days transferring the language over and over just to ensure everyone who came along would be able to speak, read, and write in their host nation's tongue. Perhaps not with complete fluency, which would only come with practice, but Jackie was good at psychic language transference.

They also all spoke Terranglo, obviously, but Jackie had wisely suggested a third language. Maria would have preferred Spanish—Terranglo was predominantly English with some Spanish mixed in—but for security reasons, Mandarin had been selected. Mandarin was not in the least bit related to the European languages underlying Terranglo. The phonetically written form of Mandarin had been transferred in its full, but so had a good chunk of classic ideographic Mandarin as well.

"Sorry," Maria apologized. "I think first in Spanish, not in V'Dan. I'll be very bored in quarantine when I am not working, if the quarters are as dull as we were warned. Unless they exaggerated."

"From what I gathered, they are indeed that dull. We will have the equally dubious joys of learning V'Dan etiquette while stuck in cramped quarters," Jackie added, sorting through her bags of jewelry.

Adding a necklace was also not a good idea in zero G, but Jackie did have a pin formed from the ideogram for Double Happiness crafted from silver and a rich blue cloissonné. Deciding it would suit the neckline of her blouse, Jackie started to pin it on. An inbound blob of brown and black warned her in time to quickly angle pin and hand out of reach even as she flung up her arm to physically cushion the woman drifting her way.

"Sorry!" Lieutenant Jasmine Buraq apologized, quickly twisting and grabbing at the nearest handles. "My toes slipped out of the grips when the ship altered speed."

"No harm done, but everyone hold on just in case while I pin this thing on my shirt," Jackie said. "I don't need to go into this first meeting bleeding."

Jasmine twisted around, orienting herself upside down to the other woman. "Let me get that for you, since we don't have a mirror in here. Centered, right? Got it . . . It goes a little weird with the silver oak leaves," she added as her fingers worked deftly. "But not too badly. There, centered. At least, upside down."

"I have to remind the grunts somehow that I'm still a superior officer," Jackie countered mildly. Her own toes were firmly lodged under a set of hand grips. The ship braked again, though this time to the side, making everything first sway, then feel briefly heavier as their bodies pressed against the ship.

Commander Robert Graves' voice came over the speakers in the crew cabin. *"Sorry for the rough maneuvers, folks. We're getting some last minute changes in our approach vectors from our hosts. ETA to buckle-up time, ten minutes."*

"Lock and Web, ladies," Jasmine reminded the others in the crew. There were five guards on this ship, not including herself, three of whom were women. All of them, Jackie included, started packing away everything that was floating and bumping against the cabin walls. It wasn't as if there was anyone else available to do it; while they were a fairly large expedition compared to the usual skeletal scoutship crews, everyone had to be their own janitor as well as whatever other role they were meant to fill.

For safety's sake, the embassy staff, guard contingent, and their V'Dan guests had been broken up across several ships. Rosa McCrary, former Premiere and Jackie's backup for the post of Ambassador, was on a different ship just in case one of their vessels emerged from hyperspace and smacked into an as-yet untracked asteroid or something. It was a very, very small possibility given the vastness of space and the fact that they had done some previous astronomical surveys along the route, but nobody wanted to take chances by placing all their important people on one ship.

The last time that had happened, it had been on the *Councilor One*. Jackie's own grandfather had died, along with a lot of other Councilors. Several safety laws had been enacted since then, some of them common sense, and some of them perhaps a bit redundant and old-fashioned, but ones that had saved lives.

The only exception to that rule was placing Imperial Prince Kah'raman Li'eth V'Daania on the same ship as the premiere Terran ambassador, Jacaranda MacKenzie. That was a necessity, because Li'eth and Jackie were in the earliest confirmed stages of forming a Gestalt bond, a sort of psychic quantum entanglement of their minds and mental powers.

Separating a Gestalt pair brought on mental, emotional, and even physical distress, something that the Terrans had learned over nearly two centuries of scientific study of verifiable psi phenomena. It could be done for short distances and for short durations, but that was it. Putting the thirdborn child of the Empress of V'Dan through unnecessary torment was not considered diplomatically appropriate, and so onto the *Embassy 1* he went.

He, of course, was changing in one of the other long, rectangular cabins, bumping elbows with some of the men. Just as she turned to pull herself out of the crew quarters, Jackie heard with both her ears and her mind his exclamation of pain.

". . . Ai!" (*Saints take you!*)

(. . . ?) Jackie queried. She got an impression of someone's foot having shoved—accidentally—against his face. At least he knew it was an accident; the soldier's quick, almost babbled apology was sincere.

(*I will be deeply grateful for the day when your people install artificial gravity on all your Saints-be-damned ships,*) Li'eth groused. (*No offense meant; I know you lack our tech, just as we lack yours.*)

Jackie, mindful of the others waiting for her to move, pulled herself through the doorway and hovered in the middle passage out of the way while Ayinda and the rest scattered to find their assigned docking seats. She had to wait for Li'eth, since she had the aisle seat for their place in the cockpit. Waiting patiently, she could sense him putting away a few last items and latching the cupboards. (*None taken, don't worry. Even I could wish for artificial gravity—whup!*)

The ship swayed again, and she had to clutch at the handgrips, steadying herself with her mind. The others yelped, and there was at least one thump of flesh into bulkheads that she could hear. Luckily, no one seemed hurt.

"Again my apologies, folks," their pilot called out over the intercom. *"Apparently, they're having to calibrate the automated defenses to accept us as 'friendlies' on their*

Friend-or-Foe targeting programs. That means a lot of quick responses to course changes, to prove we're willing to go wherever they tell us."

(*I could wish your people weren't at war, so such things wouldn't be necessary,*) Jackie sighed.

(You *wish it?*) he challenged dryly. Pulling himself through the hatchway, he reached out a hand to her. She touched it in brief physical reassurance, then caught his lightly shod foot and helped him angle his way into the cockpit. "Swimming" after him, she pulled herself into the foremost cabin, waited for him to strap himself into his seat, then followed suit.

The intercom activated again after three more minutes and two more course changes. *"Lieutenant Buraq to Commander Graves; all cabins are secure. I repeat, all cabins are secure. I am the last thing Locked and Webbed."*

"Understood, Lieutenant. ETA to docking . . . roughly fifteen minutes at this rate," Robert stated, checking his instrument overlays on the main viewscreen. *"But better slow than sorry."*

"Better secured than sorry," Jasmine returned. *"Buraq out."*

Li'eth, peering through the viewports beyond the transparent piloting screens, pointed. He leaned in close to Jackie, gripping their shared console so that he didn't twist the wrong way in his seat. "There it is! V'Dan, Motherworld of the Empire . . . if not the Motherworld of our race," he allowed. "That's the night side, and . . . from the outlines, that's *Ashuul*, the main continent of what we call the eastern hemisphere. Autumn and Winter Temples are located there. The Winter Palace, too, which is where we'll be headed after quarantine. Winter came early this year, so you'll miss out on the autumn holy days, but by the time we get out of quarantine, it should be in time to see the winter festivals getting started."

Ayinda, strapped into the navigator's seat, pointed slightly to the right of dead ahead. "There it is, people. *Dusk Army* Station. Our home away from . . . embassy, I guess, since we're already away from home."

Jackie settled her headset over her ear and turned it on to the channel Robert was monitoring. She had already announced their presence in the system two hours ago, when they had been about fifteen light-minutes out from the planet, and had confirmed among themselves the safe arrival of all fifteen *Embassy* class ships. Nothing but traffic lane course corrections reached her ears.

The Terran version of quarantine had only needed to deal with just over a dozen people at most: five V'Dan guests, six original Terran crewmembers, and three additional guests, being two pathologists and a psi trainer. Then again, they had primitive wheel-spun space stations that were rather small compared to the bulk of the station that lay almost directly ahead. The V'Dan had more than four hundred years of space exploration and colonization, plus artificial gravity.

Dusk Army looked like a hamburger to Jackie. A giant metal hamburger, nothing more than a cylinder ridged and ringed along the sides in place of meat patty and vegetables, with domes at either end representing the buns. Tiny oblongs of light were windows; even tinier pinpricks were sources of light. "Anyone know where we'll be parking?"

Her quip was taken seriously. Robert lifted his chin at their destination. "They're not used to so many small ships needing to go into quarantine all at once. They have enough space for the *1* and two more of our sized ships in the quarantine section's hangar bay, but the rest will have to stack and rack on three docking gantries."

(*Stack and rack?*) Li'eth asked, glancing at Jackie for enlightenment. (*I didn't even think to ask where all these ships will park.*)

(*These ships have dorsal and ventral airlocks—the ones on the topside and the underbelly normally aren't used save in an emergency, or for stack and rack parking,*) she explained, dredging the details out of her memory. It was from her training days shortly before the *Aloha 9* had encountered the Salik warship holding Li'eth and his crew. (*In the event of an emergency, a line of ships can be linked up airlock to airlock, each one parking at a right-angle to the one below it, belly to back. The tailfin just clears the wings. You can stack them left-right-left-right, or in a left-hand or right-hand spiral, or even nose-to-toes, alternating the opposite way.*)

(*Why do I get the feeling there's a story behind that design?*) Li'eth asked her.

(*Because you're getting better at reading subthoughts?*) Jackie offered. Her eyes were on the station they were approaching, but her inner thoughts were on her training lectures. (*There was a bad case of carbon dioxide scrubbers on three of the earliest* Aloha *models. One of them went to the rescue of the other . . . and then* their *atmo-scrubber broke down, which required calling in a third ship. There was a lot of awkward maneuvering, of coupling and decoupling. None of the hulls were damaged, but all three sets of pilots and copilots complained so much to the design teams that they wrapped up production on the* Aloha *models and immediately modified the next generation to include stackable airlocks.*)

(*Don't worry,*) she added in reassurance, catching his own subthoughts. (All *of those scrubbers were replaced and all of the replacement parts as well, with the new ones triple-checked before being installed. The last of the* Aloha Class *came into use round about the time I was recalled to active duty.*)

(*And your people put together fifteen new ships in just a couple of months?*) Li'eth asked her, impressed.

(*It didn't take* that *much to redesign the hulls,*) she countered. (*The airlocks were already a long-proven design leftover from modular supply depot construction. The exact same type of depots we stopped at for resupply on the way here, in fact. Even the 1, here, was already under construction when the hatchways were added for modification. The body's thicker, the wings a little broader, but it's still modular construction. The hardest part was rerouting the conduits, and even that wasn't all that difficult.*)

(*Duly noted. I suppose I should remind myself that your ships are a fraction of the size of ours. Ours can take anywhere from half a year to two years to build,*) Li'eth admitted. (*But then again, they're a lot bigger, and they don't make you feel sick each time they travel from star system to star system.*)

(*Plus you get an actual private cabin, rather than a shared one,*) she agreed. That in turn conjured up a strong subthought of his, of how cramped the quarters were no doubt going to be.

(*195 people is a lot of people to put into quarantine, even if some of them are going to be manning some of those docked ships,*) he pointed out. Even he knew that much, that the Terrans were going to keep some of their ships fully crewed and prepared for departure at a moment's notice during the quarantine period. As soon as they were cleared to depart quarantine and had ferried their personnel to the surface, several of those ships were going to deliver precious telecommunications gifts to other worlds in the known galaxy, while the embassy staff set up and got ready for a formal introduction to the Alliance.

(*At least we convinced them to put all the psis into their own shared quarters,*) Jackie said. Then wrinkled her nose. (*At least, I* think *we got it through to them.*)

Jackie had brought four other polyglot telepaths with her on this expedition. That had taken away almost half of her people's most powerful psychic translators. It was deemed necessary, though. With their new potential allies embroiled in an interstellar war, the faster both sides could communicate with each other, the better it would be for everyone involved.

Two of them were even xenopaths. Unlike Darian Johnston, whose military commission—like Jackie's—had been reinstated for this mission, Aixa Winkler had never actually touched a fully sentient alien mind before. He had served for ten years and had faced down the Greys seven times. But Winkler did have a lot of experience as an animal rights advocate in communing with a wide variety of sub-sentient minds.

Min Wang-Kurakara was a newly minted junior grade officer. She had expected to be sent on patrol ships to pay for her secondary career in engineering, being a technosentient psi as well as a polyglot telepath. Clees—Heracles Panaklion—had been included in the Embassy because he was not only a polyglot psi, but a Psi League instructor. His official job would be to assess and offer training to any V'Dan psis, being certified for basic instruction in all known branches with two decades of practice at training and teaching.

He had also declared he would be the embassy's chronicler, hauling along a variety of camera equipment, ". . . to capture the behind-the-scenes history in the making!" Jackie had a hard time imagining where the fifty-two-year-old got all his energy and enthusiasm. He hadn't been one of her instructors—a case of her living all around the Pacific Ocean, while he had lived and taught around the Mediterranean Sea on the opposite side of the planet—but she had read the recommendations from many of his students, appended to his personnel file.

The lowest ranked telepaths were Johnston and Winkler, but low was comparative. At Rank 9 each, they were sensitive enough to pick up thoughts at a mere touch. Bunking with non-psis could lead to tensions and troubles whenever roommates might bump into each other, as they invariably would. Fellow psis could shield their own thoughts, true, but even if the mental walls weren't up, they would be far more understanding and forgiving of any accidental touches leading to accidental eavesdropping.

Robert spoke, though not to her. Still, it drew Jackie's attention back to the actual docking as he chatted with the station's traffic managers. Dead ahead, the *Dusk Army* now filled most of the view through the forward windows. Not just the station, but a large, rounded rectangular set of doors that were sliding slowly open, revealing a well-lit interior.

Terran and V'Dan docking technology were not yet compatible, so Commander Graves was having to dock and land manually. Jackie suspected that the "course corrections" on approach were not only for the sake of the insystem defense grid, but to reassure the station's traffic control center that he would heed verbal directions swiftly and accurately.

Her comm station pinged. As the chief pilot, Robert was in constant communication at this point with *Dusk Army* Traffic Control. That meant this was something else. Jackie noted that it was a video link, and opened the channel. The man who appeared on the screen had both mint and forest green stripes along each cheek and a stripe down the center of his scalp, tinting his brown hair. He wore a dark shade of green for his jacket with grass green lapels, cut vaguely along the lines of Li'eth's Imperial Army uniform and decorated with gleaming silver buttons molded in a pattern of some sort of beast, but it was not an actual uniform.

She offered him a smile. "Greetings. You've reached the communications officer for the *Embassy 1*. How may we help you?"

Hazel eyes narrowing, he frowned at her. ". . . Aren't you the ambassador, meioa? You look like her."

"That is correct, but until I have disembarked from our ship, I am also its comm officer. How may I help you?" she repeated. On her left, Li'eth shifted a little closer, peering at the screen.

He gave her a look somewhere between puzzled and dubious. ". . . May I speak with your protocol officer?"

"That would be me as well. How may I help you, meioa . . . ?" she asked, using the Alliance term for addressing someone politely. Without a suffix, it was gender neutral and thus considered very polite.

"That, Ambassador, is Imperial First Lord Mi-en Ksa'an," Li'eth stated, leaning in even closer to Jackie. (*I know him by sight,*) he added quickly, telepathically, (*but we rarely moved in the same social circles, for all that he's a First Tier relative by four generations, if I remember correctly.*) Out loud, he added, "Greetings, Ksa'an. Are you still working for the Protocol Ministry?"

"Yes . . . Your Highness. It is good to see that you are well. We will need to speak with these Terrans about the proper protocols for welcoming them into the *Dusk Army*'s containment quarters," the green-striped man stated.

Jackie eyed him. "I am confused as to the need for protocol, Imperial First Lord."

He gave her a skeptical look in turn. "How so, Ambassador?

A sudden shift of the nose of their ship made everything sway forward and down. Robert cursed under his breath and corrected, compensating for the transfer from weightlessness to artificial gravity. It felt like Mars, lighter than it should be. Jackie swayed and clutched at her console, then breathed deep to adjust to the sudden need for supporting her own weight after fourteen days in space.

"Please remember that I am not V'Dan and do not understand nor grasp your customs . . . but I would think at this point we are medical patients. Where we come from, all patients are treated equally, save that their needs are based on a triage of whose is in the need of the most immediate attention. Since we are all healthy as we enter quarantine confinement, the only protocol that should then be followed is a security matter."

". . . Security?" the V'Dan on the other end of the linked screens asked.

"Yes. My head of security wishes for one of our doctors and some of his troops to tour and assess the quarantine facilities before I disembark," Jackie told him. "This was outlined in the notes we sent through the hyperrelay node at your system's edge—speaking of which, we have a satellite node ready to deploy. Your people have not yet indicated where you want it."

"That is not my department, meioa," the protocol lord demurred.

"Well, it will give me something to discuss with someone else while we wait for the team to make its assessment sweep. You can arrange that, yes?" she asked him.

". . . Yes." He didn't look entirely pleased about that.

Jackie chose to address that skepticism with a dose of pragmatism. "My people have a saying: 'Trust is earned, respect is given, and loyalty is demonstrated. Betrayal of any one of those is to lose all three.' I believe the speaker was a fellow named Abdelnour from around three hundred years ago . . . This is the 'trust is earned' stage, meioa," she clarified, using the Alliance's preferred form of address, since she was still a bit unclear on what an Imperial First this or that Lord meant. "My people would like to trust yours, that your facilities are adequate for containing pathogens, and safe for us to live in for the duration of our quarantine stay. However, as this is an incredibly important meeting, my people need direct reassurance that everything is indeed safe.

"We would have extended the same courtesy to our guests, save that there were so few of them that it was simply easier to view and demonstrate everything in person, with no security chiefs demanding that their checklists of procedures and requirements be met," she finished lightly. "There are 195 of us, and Captain al-Fulan takes his responsibility as our chief guardian seriously."

Indeed, Captain al-Fulan had literal checklists of everything security- and safety-wise that he intended to mark as acceptable or inadequate. She had rolled her eyes when he had first showed them to her, but the captain had explained patiently that *he* had twelve years of working high-profile security details, including in areas that were dangerous. The Terran United Planets worked hard at representing everyone they could, but there were still pockets of humanity who insisted on rioting, rebelling, and committing acts of violence against each other.

Doctor Du would be accompanying him. The pathologist was now familiar with space station quarantine containment procedures, and intended to study the V'Dan version to make sure they were adequate for her own checklists. Jackie had a few checklists of her own, but all of them were in languages other than Terranglo. It wouldn't be diplomatic to let the V'Dan know what she really thought of the things she observed, right now.

As it was, she observed the Imperial First Lord sighing. ". . . Very well. What is the proper protocol among your people for welcoming aboard a military security team?"

That, she could handle easily. "As is our military custom, he will ask permission for himself and his team to come aboard, and when it is given, he will expect an introduction to the officer on deck, meaning the person in charge of the hangar bay. He will offer a salute in the Terran fashion, since he is a visiting officer. Your people may use the V'Dan version in return, as His Highness has agreed with me that both are meant as a similar symbol of respect. After that, he will introduce Doctor Jai Du, who will accompany his team as they investigate.

"He and the others will then expect to be shown all over, have all the basic procedures for safety drills demonstrated, their questions answered, and then when the captain says it is safe, the rest of us will begin disembarking and offloading supplies. At that point, the only thing you need do is have whoever is in charge of the quarantine procedures welcome me aboard as an ambassador—literally, just say 'Welcome aboard, Ambassador,' or however you wish to phrase it—and welcome the others aboard, and then run our people through the safety drills and explanations. Show us where to stow our equipment. That sort of thing. Simple and efficient. This is quarantine, after all," she finished, "not a grand introduction to your Empress. That comes later, and can be conducted with full ceremony at that time."

Ksa'an hesitated, then dipped his head to the side a little. "I will admit I have not done any formal greeting ceremonies under quarantine situations before. It has not been needed in decades. But if you will find no offense in such an . . . abbreviated greeting as you outline," he allowed, "then that could be acceptable."

"We Terrans will take no offense, so long as we are all polite to each other," she reassured him.

"Ambassador, if you are done speaking with their protocol officer," Robert called out in the pause in their conversation, "we are now safely parked, and *Embassy 2* is coming in for a landing behind us."

"Thank you, Commander. Meioa, if we have satisfied the preliminary needs of protocol, I shall contact Captain al-Fulan to let him know he will be free to board the station upon his arrival."

"Of course, meioa—welcome aboard, Grand High Ambassador Maq'Enzi," he added politely, giving her name a V'Dan twist to its pronunciation . . . and not quite the same one Li'eth had used. The transmission ended.

Sighing, Jackie shook her head to clear it and typed in the link to the *2*. "Time to let al-Fulan know he can start checking off the items on his lists."

(*It's only going to get worse from here on out,*) Li'eth comforted her, in a backwards jesting way. (*Our military's protocols aren't that much different from your own, because so many even of our officers are commoners by birth and etiquette . . . but the civilian sector . . .*)

She reached over and squeezed his hand gently, letting their intertwined fingers rest on the edge of the console. The gravity was still less than Earth Standard by about two thirds, but that was understandable, as it no doubt allowed the incoming ships to maneuver with less wasted fuel. On one of her tertiary screens at the bottom of the main trio, she could see an analysis of the molecules on board, more of the same sort of highly complex, potentially toxic petrochemicals the Salik had used. Not exactly an abundant fuel source when compared to clean, pure water, let alone a safe one. She knew that Maria, their chief doctor, was worried about their exposure to those long-abandoned chemicals.

Aside from certain basic needs, everything was different here. Everything was going to be different in how those needs were met. Some of them were needs the V'Dan simply hadn't considered, but might be able to supply once they were addressed. Some were going to be things they hadn't even dreamt of, yet . . . or might even balk at providing.

(*We'll try to be ready for it,*) she reassured him. (*And try to be understanding whenever a conflict comes up.*)

M1160G0712